ARIFURETA:

ARIFURETA SHOKUGYOU DE SEKAISAIKYOU

FROM COMMONPLACE TO WORLD'S STRONGEST

ARIFURETA: FROM COMMONPLACE TO WORLD'S
STRONGEST, VOLUME 2

© 2015 Ryo Shirakome
Illustrations by Takayaki

First published in Japan in 2015 by
OVERLAP Inc., Ltd., Tokyo.
English translation rights arranged with
OVERLAP Inc., Ltd., Tokyo.

Seven Seas books may be purchased in bulk for promotional,
educational, or business use. Please contact your local
bookseller or the Macmillan Corporate and Premium Sales
Department at 1-800-221-7945, extension 5442, or by
e-mail at MacmillanSpecialMarkets@macmillan.com.

Follow Seven Seas Entertainment online at
sevenseasentertainment.com.
Experience J-Novel Club books online at j-novel.club.

TRANSLATION: Ningen
J-NOVEL EDITOR: DxS
COVER DESIGN: Nicky Lim
INTERIOR LAYOUT & DESIGN: Clay Gardner
COPY EDITOR: J.P. Sullivan
PROOFREADER: Jade Gardner, Maggie Cooper
LIGHT NOVEL EDITOR: Jenn Grunigen
PRODUCTION ASSISTANT: CK Russell
PRODUCTION MANAGER: Lissa Pattillo
EDITOR-IN-CHIEF: Adam Arnold
PUBLISHER: Jason DeAngelis

ISBN: 978-1-626927-80-3
Printed in Canada
First Printing: May 2018
10 9 8 7 6 5 4 3 2 1

ARIFURETA:
ARIFURETA SHOKUGYOU DE SEKAISAIKYOU

FROM COMMONPLACE
TO WORLD'S STRONGEST

#2

Presented by
RYO SHIRAKOME

Illustrated by
TAKAYAKI

CONTENTS

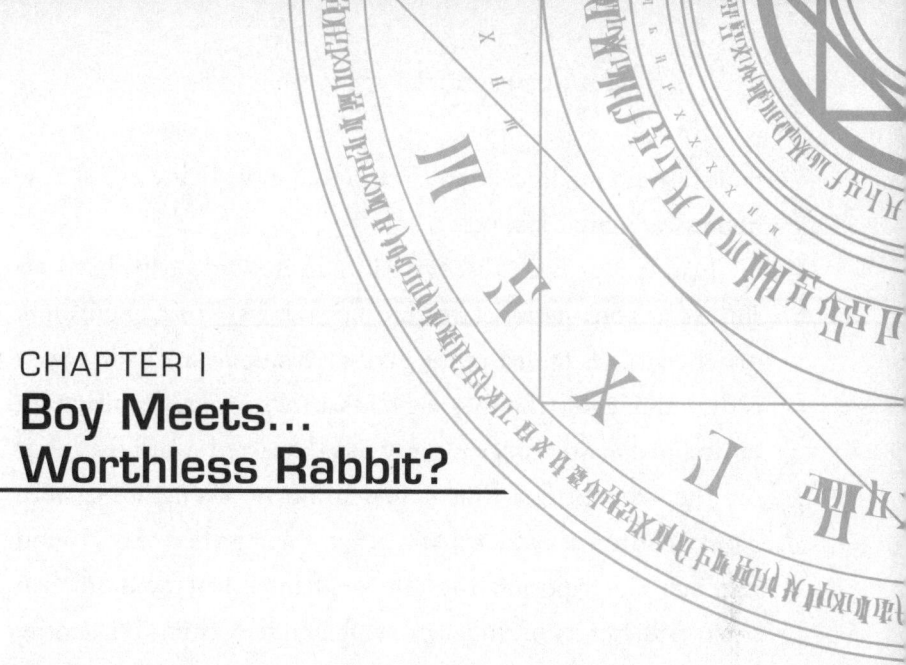

CHAPTER I
Boy Meets...
Worthless Rabbit?

IN A CERTAIN LOCATION, there existed a dark cave where the rays of the sun never reached. The inside of the cave was so silent that one could not even hear the rustling of insects. There was no sign that human hands had ever shaped the rock, and the walls, floors, and ceiling all seemed naturally formed. Still, despite the exceedingly natural appearance of the cavern, it had not a single entrance or exit—one unnatural aspect of this otherwise naturally shaped cave.

It was, of course, possible that an air pocket had given rise to this enclosed space in the ground. However, there was just one other irregularity sitting in the cave's center that made it quite obvious that this cavern was man-made: a complex and detailed circular geometric pattern carved into the ground. In other words, a magic circle. Were anyone of this era to lay eyes on such a sophisticated circle, their jaw would surely drop. Some of the more faint-hearted might even collapse on the spot. That was just how impressive a circle it was.

Had it ever been discovered, then it would have been enshrined as a rare national treasure, but as it was, it sat languishing under centuries of dirt in the dark cavern. It clearly hadn't been activated in ages. The magic circle sat there quietly, waiting for its destined master to appear, just like the sacred sword Excalibur.

Then, for the first time in god knows how long, it began to glow. Tendrils of scarlet mana began tracing their way around the circle's inscriptions. The light was faint at first, no more than a pinprick, but it continued growing in intensity until the entire room was set ablaze with scarlet light.

Finally, there was a blinding flash. The brilliant red light drove away the last vestiges of darkness huddling in the corners of the cavern. It was a truly awe-inspiring sight. Anyone present would have been convinced that whatever was coming from the other side of the circle couldn't possibly have been human.

However, the light eventually began to fade, and two figures that at least appeared human materialized in the center of the circle.

"What in tarnation?" One of the figures spoke, his ridiculous outburst destroying the aura of solemnity.

As the light faded and darkness reigned once more in the cavern, the boy who had spoken looked around in disappointment. He was, of course, none other than the earthling who had been consigned to the depths of hell by one of his classmates during an excursion in the Great Orcus Labyrinth—Hajime Nagumo.

Hajime had delved a further hundred floors past the hundredth floor that was thought to be the end of the labyrinth and had discovered Tortus' secret from the creator of the labyrinth. In the house of the man the gods had labeled a maverick, Hajime had discovered a magic circle that would take him back to the surface.

The mere thought of being able to return to the surface had left him elated after having spent months in the harsh environs of the labyrinth, where he had to risk life and limb every day just to survive. He had unconditionally believed that what awaited him on the other side of the magic circle was warm sunshine and a gentle breeze. Instead, all he found when he opened his eyes were the same rock walls he'd been gazing at for the past few months. But yelling about it in a strange accent wasn't going to achieve anything either.

As Hajime was wallowing in his despair, he felt someone tug on his sleeve. He turned to look down at the girl standing next to him, a quizzical expression on his face. The girl was so short that she barely came up to his chest.

She had wavy golden-blonde hair and crimson eyes reminiscent of the red moon. Her lips were a light pink, and her skin was as white as porcelain. At the moment, her eyelids were drooping sleepily. But despite that, she still looked like an exquisitely crafted bisque doll. She was, of course, Yue—the girl Hajime had rescued from imprisonment deep in the pits of hell, and the girl with whom he had first begun to climb the stairs of adulthood.

In order to comfort him, Yue gently started explaining the situation.

"It's a secret passage...so he probably had to hide it."

"...Oh yeah. You've got a point there. This leads straight to one of the Liberators' hideouts, so it makes sense that he'd need to keep it hidden."

Hajime scratched his head awkwardly. *Can't believe I got so excited that I didn't even realize something that simple.*

Then he poured a little mana into his Treasure Trove, an artifact that opened a gate to an interdimensional room where he could store and withdraw things, and pulled out a green glowstone flashlight. Both Hajime and Yue could use their innate abilities or magic, respectively, to deal with the darkness, but doing something routine like this helped calm Hajime down.

Yue chuckled, realizing exactly why he was doing this. Not because she was making fun of him, but because she thought it was kind of cute. For the sake of his own pride, Hajime pretended not to hear her and instead swept his flashlight across the cave.

"Hm? What's that?" He stopped his pale green flashlight at a part of the wall that looked distinctly different. There was a perfectly straight vertical line running up the wall, and it stopped at a palm-sized heptagon carved into it. A different symbol adorned each of the vertices, and one of them was something the pair had seen quite often over the past few weeks. It was Oscar Orcus' personal crest.

Hajime pulled the proof of them having conquered the labyrinth, Orcus' ring, out of the Treasure Trove and held it up to the heptagon. With a grandiose boom, the stone wall parted, revealing a secret passage.

Hajime and Yue nodded to each other and stepped forward into the passage. They didn't find any forks in the road, so they just kept going. There were a few more sealed doors and traps along the way, but Orcus' ring opened or disabled them all automatically. Both of them were on their guard, but that proved unnecessary as they continued without incident...until finally, they spotted a faint light in the distance.

It was the light of the outside world. Sunlight. The light Hajime had spent the last few months, and Yue had spent the last few centuries, craving.

When they realized they were but a few steps from basking in it again, they came to a halt and looked at each other. Unable to contain their joy, they grinned and started running toward the light at the same time.

The light grew bigger as they got closer. Soon, they could feel wind blowing in from outside. It was nothing like the stagnant air they'd been forced to breath for ages. It was fresh and full of life. For the first time ever, Hajime realized what people meant when they said the air tasted delicious. Both of them burst out into the light at the same time. Onto the sweet, sweet surface.

More specifically, the part of the surface that was known to most as an execution ground. It was nigh impossible to use magic beneath these odd cliffs, and deadly monsters inhabited the bottom of the gorge. The gorge ran anywhere from one kilometer deep at its shallower ends to two kilometers deep in places. It could span anywhere from nine hundred meters wide to eight kilometers wide, depending on the area, and it ran all the way from the Gruen Desert in the west to the Haltina Woods in the east. People called it a great gash in the earth dividing the north and the south.

Its formal name was Reisen Gorge. And the cave Hajime and Yue had just exited was located at the bottom of it. But even if they were deep in the bottom of a ravine, they could still at least see the sun shining high overhead, and the wind rushing through carried with it the familiar scent of soil and life. No matter how harsh a place they had found themselves in, it was at least still the surface.

Hajime and Yue's smiles slowly grew wider as they gazed up at the sun with awe. And, despite how expressionless she usually was, Yue's smile was—if anything—even wider than Hajime's.

"We...really made it back..." Hajime quietly muttered, his voice thick with emotion.

"...Yeah." Yue's response was just as expressive. The reality of their escape finally washed over them, and they tore their gazes away from the sun to look back at each other. They stood that way for a second before hugging each other tight and screaming at the top of their lungs.

"Yeaaaaaaaaaaaaaaaaah!!! We did iiiiiiiiiiiiiiiiiiiit!"

"Yeah!"

Hajime lifted Yue up and started twirling her around. Their smiles were completely out of place in the location that had been dubbed hell by the rest of the world. At some point Hajime tripped on a rock, sending them tumbling to the ground. But they found even that funny and started laughing hysterically while lying spread-eagled on the floor.

By the time their laughter had finally run out...they were surrounded by monsters.

Hajime stood up amidst the howling monsters surrounding him on all sides and grumbled to himself.

"Sheesh, how rude can you get? You could have let us enjoy ourselves a bit longer." He pulled out Donner and Schlag before pausing for a second and tilting his head.

"Wait, I think I remember reading something about magic not working down here." Back when he had just been summoned, he had been paying close attention to his classes during training, and now he remembered the inability to use magic being one of the gorge's main features.

"...It'll get dispersed. But that shouldn't be a problem," Yue replied. The reason people couldn't use magic in Reisen Gorge was because the mana that went into the formation of a spell was dispersed before the spell could activate. Yue's magic was no exception, either.

However, Yue was still an ancient vampire princess that had once been feared as one of the strongest creatures in the world. She possessed a massive amount of mana, and now she had the magic stone accessory series at her disposal. All she had to do was cast a spell so large and powerful that the gorge wouldn't be able to disperse all the mana in time. Hajime smiled wryly when he heard how confident she sounded.

"How much more mana will it take?"

"Hmmm... About ten times as much."

So I'll need enough mana for an advanced class spell just for something simple, huh? *That would affect his range greatly.*

"Ah, in that case, I'll handle these guys. Yue, you just focus on keeping yourself safe."

"Aww... But—"

"This is like the worst possible place for a mage like you. You're at a huge disadvantage here, so just leave it to me."

"Okay...if you say so." Yue reluctantly backed off. She was having a hard time accepting being left out of their first battle on the surface. It probably hurt her pride a little, too. She was clearly pouting, after all.

Though it hurt him to say it, Hajime nonetheless put Yue out of his mind for the moment and fired Donner. He hadn't even looked as he smoothly brought Donner up and took perfect aim at his target. His movements were so fluid that the monsters didn't even realize they were under attack. By the time they finally did, one of their comrades had already had its head blown clean off. The rest of them all froze stiff, unable to grasp what had just happened. Only the gunshot's echoes broke the silence.

As long as he used ten times as much mana, Hajime could still activate Lightning Field, the spell essential to using his railguns. He smiled fearlessly as he surveyed his opponents.

"Well, I wonder if you're any tougher than the enemies I faced down below... Let's find out, shall we?" He brought his right foot back and slowly lowered his waist while crossing his guns in front of his chest. His artificial left arm was thrust slightly forward, and Schlag was held just a little lower than Donner. With his two guns, he would now be able to cover his back and front simultaneously. Hajime placed his prosthetic limb a bit further out than the rest of his body in order to deal with any unexpected situations. This stance was the fundamental aspect of the gun-fu he'd pounded into his body after long hours spent training in the abyss.

There was a murderous gleam in Hajime's eyes once he finished settling into his stance. His pupils were cold, emotionless pools, hardened by the harsh conditions he had lived through.

That chilling gaze alone was enough to cause all the monsters present to take an involuntary step back. They could all feel it instinctively. The person they'd picked a fight with was a ruthless "beast." The pressure was so great that a normal person would have fainted from the intensity of his glare alone. Eventually one of the monsters was unable to stand it and let out a wild roar before leaping forward.

"Graaaaaaaah!" However, not even a second later, there was another loud bang, and the second monster had its head blown off before it even had a chance to react. The headless monster slid to a halt, crumpling lifelessly on the ground, where it stopped. A faint wisp of smoke rose from Donner's muzzle. Hajime didn't even spare the pitiful husk on the ground a single glance. His swirling torrent of bloodlust was already directed at the remaining herd. What followed was more of a massacre than a battle.

Hajime didn't let a single one of them escape. Yes—each and every one of them had its head blown cleanly off. As the gunshots echoed louder and louder, the monsters' desperate cries grew fainter and fainter. In a mere five minutes, the ground was littered with corpses of monsters.

He spun Donner and Schlag's cylinders, reloading them both before returning them to the holsters strapped to his legs. After that, he tilted his head slightly as he surveyed the mountain of bodies.

Yue trotted briskly up to him.

"...What's wrong?"

"Nothing. It just feels like that was too easy... I'd heard the monsters in Reisen Gorge were ferocious and brutal, so maybe we came out somewhere else?"

"...You're just too much of a monster, Hajime."

"That's a pretty harsh way of putting it. Well, I guess that just means the monsters in the abyss were way stronger."

Hajime shrugged his shoulders indifferently and shifted his gaze from the monsters to the canyon walls.

"Now then, we could probably scale these walls easily enough, but...what do you think? They say one of the seven great labyrinths is in Reisen Gorge. Since we're already here, wanna look around a bit while we head to the forest?"

"...Why the forest?"

"I mean, who wants to go to a desert after all that time surrounded by rock? Besides, I bet there's more towns on the forest side."

"...Okay. You have a point there." Yue nodded in approval. Judging by how weak the monsters were, it was clear the gorge wasn't the labyrinth itself. Which meant there must have been a proper entrance somewhere. Hajime's Aerodynamic and Yue's wind magic would be more than sufficient for scaling the walls, but they'd have to search the gorge eventually, so there was no reason not to do it now.

Hajime poured a trickle of mana into the Treasure Trove that he was wearing on his middle finger and pulled out Steiff. It was a large, American-style vehicle with a black body. Unlike motorcycles back on earth, it didn't use gasoline as fuel; it was powered purely by mana. Thanks to that, it ran quieter than an electric car.

He had actually been hoping for a louder engine, since to him that was way cooler, but he only knew how to make simple engines, so he wasn't able to make a more complicated combustion one. He could control Steiff's speed by adjusting his mana output. Due to Reisen Gorge's mana-scattering properties, he wouldn't be able to keep it running for long.

Hajime stylishly mounted his motorcycle. Yue hopped on behind him, sitting sidesaddle. She wrapped her arms tightly around Hajime's waist. Once she was situated, she patted his stomach lightly with her arms, and he quickly started pouring mana into Steiff.

Reisen Gorge ran from east to west with almost no north-south variation. There were almost no side routes either, so it was quite difficult to get lost.

Since there was no worry of losing their way, Hajime drove Steiff forward at a leisurely pace as they looked for anything resembling a labyrinth entrance. He had transmuted a machine to the bottom of the motorcycle that smoothed out any ground before the wheels hit it. Normally, an American-style bike would have a hard time dealing with such rough terrain, but thanks to his transmutation they were able to drive across the valley floor smoothly.

"Feels nice to ride like this, right, Yue?"

"...Yeah. It really does."

They were riding through the wind, basking in the light of the sun, and inhaling the smells of the surface world. For them, that was more than enough to make their drive pleasant. Yue happily leaned her head against Hajime's back. Throughout their leisurely drive, Hajime's hands alone kept moving. He didn't miss a single shot as he continually dispatched the groups of monsters that came to attack them.

After a while, he heard a ferocious roar off in the distance. It was more intimidating than the others. At the very least, it was stronger than the monsters they'd faced in the gorge so far. With their current pace, they'd run into it in about thirty seconds.

Hajime poured more mana into Steiff, rounded a large curve, and found a massive monster waiting for him at the end of the bend. It looked similar to the dinosaurs Hajime had faced in the labyrinth, but this one had two heads. It was a two-headed T. rex. But what was even more surprising was the rabbit-eared girl hopping to and fro beneath it, desperately trying to escape its clutches.

Startled, Hajime stopped Steiff and gazed at the girl curiously.

"What on earth is that?"

"...A bunny girl?"

"I get that, but why is she here? Are bunny people the type that live in gorges?"

"...Not as far as I know."

"Then is she one of those criminals that gets thrown down here as punishment? I read that Reisen Gorge is a famous execution ground."

"...Hmm. Maybe she's an evil rabbit?"

Hajime and Yue had a casual conversation while they watched the bunny girl run for her life. Neither of them seemed interested in saving her. It wasn't because they were seriously worried that she might be some kind of dangerous criminal that was thrown down here. Hajime simply didn't have any interest in strangers. He just thought saving her would have been more trouble than it was worth.

Truly, this was a far cry from the old Hajime. Even if he hadn't been the least bit capable, the old Hajime would have still tried to save her.

The situation was different from when he'd saved Yue. He didn't sympathize with this bunny girl's plight one bit, and since he could see no benefits to saving her, he felt no desire to. If he helped everyone that begged for it, he'd be old and wrinkled before he could focus on his own goals. Besides, this world was nothing more than a prison to Hajime. With a few exceptions, he had no interest in helping any inhabitants of this world.

However, it was then that the bunny girl spotted Yue and Hajime. She got blown back by the two-headed T. rex and crashed into a nearby boulder, but she recovered quickly and scuttled behind it, staring at Hajime all the while.

The T. rex brought its claws down again, this time blowing the entire boulder away along with her. She tumbled backward, using that momentum to run as fast as possible...right toward Hajime and Yue.

There was quite a bit of distance between them still, but the amplified echo of the gorge let the bunny girl's words reach him.

"Finally! I finally found youuuuuuuu! Pleashe shabe meee! Eek, it's gonna kill me! I'm gonna die! Shabe me, pleashe! I'm begging you!" Tears streamed down her face as she ran with all her might. The two-headed T. rex chased after her, intent on devouring its prey. At the rate things were going, she was destined to be dinosaur food before she ever got to Hajime and Yue.

As she pounded toward them, Hajime thought, *She 'finally' found us? That's an odd choice of words. Also, she's got a train of monsters chasing after her. Seems best not to get involved. Yeah. Seems like a pain.*

And so, despite being pleaded with so earnestly, he still had no intention of helping her. Even her heartfelt cries couldn't reach him. In fact, they just made things worse.

When she saw them turn away from her, the bunny girl realized they had no intention of helping, so even more tears started rolling down her cheeks. It was amazing how her eyes never seemed to run out of liquid to pour.

"Waiiiit! Pleashe don't abandon meeeee! I'm begging youuuuu!" she yelled, even louder this time. If Hajime did nothing, she really would get eaten. Or she would have, if it weren't for the fact that the monster had bared its fangs at Hajime too. Once the T. rex noticed Hajime's existence, it rested its hungry gaze on him and roared angrily.

"Graaaaaaaaaaah!"

Hajime wasn't about to let that one go.

"What was that?" The monster had threatened his life. It wanted to eat him. Hajime's body instinctively reacted to its bloodlust. *This enemy bars your path! And enemies that get in your way are to be killed!* Those were the only words his mind screamed at him.

As it continued chasing down the bunny girl, the T. rex opened one of its jaws wide. Despair filled her eyes as she turned and saw countless rows of teeth bearing down on her.

"Ah, so this is where it all ends..."

But an instant before she became dinosaur chow—*bang!* A sound completely alien to her reverberated throughout the gorge. A red streak passed right between her two twitching bunny ears. The speeding bullet flew right into the T. rex's open maw and mercilessly pulverized its skull as it passed out the other end of one of its heads.

The destroyed skull sank to the floor of the gorge, sliding a little before coming to a stop. Unable to maintain its balance, the T. rex fell to the ground with a resounding thud.

The shockwave of the impact sent the bunny girl flying again... directly toward Hajime.

"Kyaaaaaaaa! H-help meeee!" She reached her arms out to Hajime as she hurtled toward him. Her face was a mess of tears, and her lady bits were shamelessly exposed for all to see. But even then, any normal guy wouldn't have hesitated to save her.

"Hell no! Get away from me!" Our esteemed hero simply wheeled Steiff back a bit to avoid colliding with the bunny girl.

"Eeeeeeh?!" Still screaming in surprise, she fell to the ground a few inches in front of Hajime with a sickening thud. She lay spread-eagle on the ground, her body occasionally twitching. It appeared she was still conscious but couldn't move due to the pain.

"...What a pathetic rabbit." Yue said such harsh words nonchalantly, her head peeking out from behind Hajime's shoulder to watch. Meanwhile, the two-headed T. rex had successfully ripped its deceased head off, leaving just a normal T. rex with an extra neck sticking out at an odd angle.

With its balance thus restored, the one-headed T. rex roared ferociously. That roar was enough to shock the bunny girl to her feet. She was unexpectedly tough. Her face still a mask of tears, she moved surprisingly swiftly and hid behind Hajime.

It seemed she was determined to rely on him until the end. While it did make sense, since she'd die for sure on her own, and Hajime had clearly dealt with its other head, even if she didn't know how...her ironclad faith in him still felt a little unnatural.

Not only was this their first meeting, Hajime was a human, a member of a race that despised her people. Normally someone in her situation would have just used Hajime as bait and run off. The fact that she hadn't implied that she had some unknown reason to trust him. Hajime suddenly remembered the words she'd said when she first saw him. That she'd "found" him. He had definitely found that odd. But the way she kept clinging to him had started to get annoying, so instead of questions, what came out of his mouth were insults.

"Hey, you—you walking joke of a bunny girl. I never said you could use me as a shield. Come on, don't you have the courage to at least try a suicide rush before forcing your problems onto other people?" Hajime said, clearly annoyed by the bunny girl clinging on to his coat for dear life. He really didn't mince words anymore. Behind him, Yue's hands were pressed up against the bunny girl's cheeks as she tried to push the girl off him.

"I-I don't have that kind of courage. And besides, if I let go, you'll just try to abandon me again, won't you?"

"Obviously. I have no reason to save some annoying bunny girl I don't even know."

"A-an instant rejection?! How can you say that...? Isn't there a shred of goodness left in your heart? You wouldn't really leave an innocent beauty like me to die, would you?"

"I left my humanity behind in hell. And what kind of person has the gall to call themselves a beauty?"

"Th-then if you save me...I-I'll do a-a-any one thing you ask!" She blushed as she said that. The whole thing was very, very cleverly played. Had the image not been ruined by the tears and snot running down her face, it would have actually been perfect. She hadn't been lying when she called herself a beauty, either. Beneath all the grime and tears, one could tell she really was quite pretty. Any normal guy would have fallen for it, even if they knew it was a trick. Unfortunately for her, Hajime was no normal guy.

"No thanks, I'm good. And get your filthy face away from me; you're getting my shirt dirty." His savagery knew no bounds. It was enough to make one doubt he had any human compassion left at all.

"F-filthy...! You didn't have to put it like that... I can't believe you! I am not—"

"Graagaaaaaah!"

"Eek. P-pleashe sha—"

Angry at being ignored, the T. rex let out a bestial roar, interrupting the bunny girl's protests. It then bent low, preparing to charge.

The bunny girl screamed hysterically and tried to wedge herself between Hajime and Yue. Thoroughly annoyed by that point, Yue tried to kick the bunny girl off of Steiff, but even after her face was covered in shoe prints, she refused to let go. Her tenacity was truly commendable.

The T. rex grew steadily more enraged as they continued to ignore it, until finally, unable to stand it any longer, it charged forward.

Hajime reflexively brought his arm up and took aim at the T. rex's forehead. A gunshot followed not even a second later, and a red streak of light flashed by as the bullet pierced the T. rex's skull.

Its charge was abruptly cut short, and it fell on its side with a thunderous crash.

"Eh?" The bunny girl unconsciously let out a confused gasp. She peeked out from behind Hajime's back to make sure the T. rex was dead.

"I-It's really dead... You killed that Dihedwa in a single shot..." Her eyes were as round as dinner plates. Apparently that two-headed T. rex was called a Dihedwa.

Even as the bunny girl looked down at the Dihedwa's corpse in shock, Yue relentlessly continued to try and kick her off. However, her firm grip on Hajime wouldn't budge. Tired of having her ears whack his eyes every few seconds, Hajime brought his elbow down on the back of her head.

"Hawugh?!" She screamed incoherently and started writhing on the ground while moaning, "My head. My heaaaad." Hajime gave her one last cold look before nonchalantly pouring mana into Steiff.

She must have sensed the flow of mana, because the bunny girl instantly hopped back up and ran to Hajime before he could leave.

"You're not getting away from me!" For a bunny girl, she was surprisingly hardy.

"Thank you very much for saving me earlier! My name is Shea. I'm a member of the rabbitmen tribe of Haulia! I know this is presumptuous of me, but could you please save my family, too?! Please, I'm begging you!" And quite pushy as well.

Hajime gave the desperate bunny girl a sidelong glance, then sighed heavily. Of course the first thing he'd run into after escaping hell would be this nuisance.

Seeing his exasperated expression, the bunny girl, Shea, fretfully repeated her plea even louder.

"Please, you *have* to! I'm begging you, you have to save my family!" By the end, she was practically shouting. It seemed her family was in dire straits as well. Hajime finally realized why she was so persistent. Her plea was so heartfelt that even Yue stopped trying to kick her off for a moment.

When he saw just how desperate she was, Hajime reluctantly shrugged his shoulders. Thinking he'd finally agreed, Shea breathed a sigh of relief. In reality...Hajime simply activated his Lightning Field.

"Ababababababababaa?!" He had controlled the voltage so it wouldn't kill her, but it would at least leave her paralyzed for a while. The shock made her rabbit ears and fur all stand on end like a cartoon character. After he released the spell, Shea fell to the ground, twitching all the while.

"You never know. Give it your all, and maybe you'll be able to save them yourself. Good luck, I guess. All right, Yue, let's go."

"Okay..." He left behind some generic words of encouragement, if they could even be called that, and began pouring mana into Steiff once more. However...

"I-I'll never let you get away!" Like a zombie, Shea dragged herself to Hajime's foot and clung to it for dear life. Surprised, Hajime accidentally stopped sending mana to Steiff.

"What are you, some kind of zombie? I made that shock pretty strong...so how are you still able to move? You're seriously starting to creep me out."

"...Yeah. She's creepy."

"Hic—why do you two have to be so mean...? First you elbow me, then you kick me, and now you shocked me! Don't you think you're being a little cruel?! I'm against violence! If you want my forgiveness, then please save my family!" Even in her anger she didn't forget to throw in her request once more. It actually was a little scary how she seemed completely unharmed. The word "hardy" no longer did her abnormally sturdy body justice. That wasn't the only thing weird about her, either: she also kept muttering odd things to herself, like "If I mess up here, the future'll change."

Hajime had considered just starting Steiff up and shaking her off, but her absurdly strong body and those prophetic mutterings of hers had finally sparked his curiosity a little. Besides, he had a sinking feeling that even if he tried to shake her off, she'd somehow cling on anyway...and even he wasn't so heartless that he'd drag her around until she was a horrific, bloody mess.

So, reluctantly, he finally decided to hear her out.

"Fine, fine. What is it? I'll at least hear you out, so let me go. And quit wiping your face with my coat." Shea broke out into a beaming smile the moment those words left his mouth, though she continued surreptitiously wiping her face with his coat. She really had no restraint. Hajime elbowed again to get her to stop, eliciting another strange squeal from her.

"Hagyuun! Y-you hit me again... Even my father never hit me. I can't believe you'd keep hitting such a beautiful girl over and over... Don't tell me you prefer men? Is that why my feminine wiles didn't work on you earlier? That has—" Hajime brought his boot down on Shea's head before she could slander him any further. A vein stood out on his forehead.

"Who the hell are you calling gay, you damn rabbit?! And how do you know all these words?! You and Yue both—who taught you these things? Anyway, I can't tell if your feminine wiles were supposed to be an actual attempt at seduction or a joke, but the only reason they don't work is because I've already got a girl far prettier than you by my side. I honestly don't get what gave you the idea you could beat her in the first place." Hajime turned back to look at Yue as he said all that to the bunny girl. She was blushing bright red, her hands cupping her cheeks as she squirmed shyly.

Her golden-blonde hair sparkled dazzlingly in the sunlight, and her slightly flushed porcelain skin was flawless enough to charm any man that saw it.

She was no longer emaciated and weak from her long imprisonment either, as she had been when he first met her. On top of that, her clothes were far more fitted as well. She had on a frilly white dress shirt and a black miniskirt, also with frills. Covering it all was a white coat with blue lining. Adorning her feet was a short pair of boots and knee-high socks. Each article of clothing was one Yue had sewn using the old clothes they'd found in Oscar's room combined with materials harvested from monsters. They were enchanted to grant her heightened stamina, and functioned very well as defensive gear.

By the way, Hajime was decked out in a black coat with crimson lining, and the rest of his outfit was also a combination of red and black. His left sleeve was joined to the shoulder by a kind of special adhesive he'd crafted from monster parts, and it could be easily detached. He usually stowed it away in the Treasure Trove during fights, to leave his prosthetic arm completely unencumbered.

That sleeve was Yue's masterpiece.

Shea faltered slightly after looking up at Yue.

Admittedly, they were both extremely beautiful women, but which one was more beautiful was a subjective decision that came down more to one's preferences than anything else. Objectively speaking, they were both about equal.

Shea had long blue-white hair and azure eyes that sparkled like sapphires. Her eyebrows and eyelashes were both blue-white as well. They complemented her pale skin quite nicely, and as long as she stayed quiet, most people would find her quite alluring. Her limbs were slender, and her glossy rabbit ears and round tail only added to her charm. Any fan of bunny girls would break down in tears of joy at the mere sight of her.

Most conspicuous was...the one thing Yue lacked. Namely, boobs. Shea's in particular were huge. The torn-off scraps of cloth barely covering them did more to emphasize their presence than hide them. Without anything to hold them in place, they jiggled suggestively every time she moved. Veeery suggestively. Just to remind everyone they were there.

Basically, she had every right to call herself beautiful. Hajime was the weird one for being so put off by her. The old Hajime would have done a Lupin Dive straight into those soft valleys of hers, while screaming "Rabbit ears!" Anyway, his current indifference had definitely hurt Shea's pride a little. And thus, she said the one thing that was absolutely taboo...

"Y-yeah, well...I beat her in boobs at least! That girl's as flat as a board!"

...Flat as a board...
...Flat as a board...
...Flat as a board...

Her accusatory shout echoed over and over throughout the gorge. Yue suddenly went silent, her earlier blush vanishing in an instant. Her bangs hid her expression as she slowly dismounted Steiff.

Hajime simply looked up at the sky and brought his hands together, offering a small prayer for the poor bunny. *May your rabbit ears rest in peace...* In all fairness, Yue wasn't quite *that* flat, but her boobs certainly were on the small side. They weren't like the sheer cliffs that currently surrounded the party.

Shea cowered before Yue like a mouse in front of a cat. Yue's next words were barely whispers, but everyone heard them surprisingly clearly.

"Any last words?"

"If I apologize, will you forgive me?"

"......"

"I'm sorry, I don't want to die! I really don't want to die!"

"Storm Gust."

"Aaaaaaaaaaaaaaaaaaaaaah!!"

Shea was swept up in a whirlwind and flung high up into the sky. Precisely ten seconds after her screams faded away, she fell to the ground with a wet plop.

Her head was buried in the ground, and her limbs flailed wildly as she struggled to free herself. She resembled a certain cartoon character, looking like that. It really was a shame that a beauty like her carried herself so pathetically. Her tattered clothes had been ripped up even further—they could barely be called clothes at that point. Upside down as she was, her private parts were exposed for all to see. Even a hundred-year-long love would fade if someone saw their loved one in such a state.

Yue wiped an imaginary bead of sweat off her brow, as if to congratulate herself on a job well done, before trotting back to Steiff and remounting it.

"...Do you like big boobs?"

Now that was a loaded question if Hajime ever heard one. He was about to answer yes but thought better of it when he saw the bunny girl still doing her best impression of a dog with its head stuck in the ground. He didn't want to end up like that.

"...Yue, the size isn't what's important. It's about whose boobs they are."

"......"

He decided to dodge the question entirely, so he gave an answer that was neither yes nor no. What a coward. Yue closed her eyes and pondered that for a minute, before apparently accepting his answer and situating herself in the back seat.

Hajime could feel cold sweat running down his back. He cast about for a topic to break the awkward silence, but nothing came to mind. Even MasterCard couldn't buy what he needed here.

As he was looking around, trying to find something to talk about, he noticed Shea had finally gotten her hands on the ground and was now earnestly trying to get her head unstuck. Fortunately, that made for a great topic.

"She's still going... That girl has to be some kind of zombie. No matter how strong your body is, no normal person would be fine taking that attack..."

"...Yeah."

Though it did take her longer than usual to reply, she still at least gave him one. Hajime breathed a sigh of relief as Shea popped out of the ground, her face and hair matted with dirt.

"Ugh, that was terrible. This scene wasn't in my predictions, either..." Shea tearfully patted down her tattered clothes before crawling back to where Hajime and Yue were waiting. She still looked unhurt.

"What the hell is wrong with you? Being unhurt after all that isn't normal... Just what are you?" Seeing that they were finally ready to listen, Shea settled herself down comfortably under Hajime's puzzled gaze. Her expression grew serious once she'd sat herself in front of Steiff. Though it was a bit too late for anyone to take her seriously...

"Allow me to reintroduce myself. I'm Shea Haulia, the daughter of the Haulia tribe chieftain. The truth is..."

In essence, this was what Shea's story boiled down to:

Shea's tribe, the Haulia, was populated by the rabbitmen subspecies of beastmen. There were a few hundred of them, and they lived in a village hidden deep within the Haltina Woods.

Though they possessed excellent hearing and were skilled at hiding themselves, their stats were a lot lower than most other beastmen. Plus, they had no other special traits to speak of. Because of that, they were considered weak by many others of their kind. In general, they were a kind, peace-loving race that treated the whole of their village like family and cared deeply for each other. Most of them were also very good-looking, but unlike elves, who were renowned for their beauty, the rabbitmen were more known for their cuteness. Many collectors in the Hoelscher Empire coveted them for that very trait, so they were a popular target for slave traders.

Among those rabbitmen, one of the tribes, the Haulia, had given birth to a strange girl. Rabbitmen generally had dark blue hair, but this girl was born with very light blue hair. Furthermore, she was an anomaly among beastmen as she had mana running through her body. What was even more shocking was that she could directly manipulate that mana, and even use a certain special magic like most monsters.

This, of course, caused a huge uproar within the village. This was unheard of in the entire history of rabbitmen—no, in the history of beastmen as a whole. Under normal circumstances, anyone with the same power as monsters would have been persecuted and ostracized. But this girl had been born to the one race that valued family above all else. The one race that treated an entire village of hundreds as one big family. Which was why the thought of abandoning her never even crossed any of the Haulia's minds.

However, the forest was home to its own country, Verbergen, which was located deep within the sea of trees. If any of their ruling class learned of the girl's existence, she would surely be executed. Such harshness was indicative of just how badly the beastmen hated monsters.

And so, the Haulia decided to raise the girl in secret. Sixteen years passed. However, a few days ago, someone from the outside learned of the girl's existence. In order to escape Verbergen's retribution, the entire village decided to flee the forest.

With no set destination in mind, they headed first for the mountains in the north, their reasoning being that they would be able to live off the land there. The mountains were harsh, but it was still better than being sold off as slaves in the Hoelscher Empire or executed by Verbergen.

However, the very empire they were afraid of destroyed all of their plans. By an extreme stroke of misfortune, they ran into imperial soldiers right outside the forest. There was no way to know if they were on patrol or just on a routine training exercise, but in the face of a battalion-sized army, the Haulia had no choice but to flee to the south.

The men stayed behind to give the women and children more time to escape, but the gentle rabbitmen couldn't hold a candle to the battle-hardened soldiers of the Hoelscher Empire, and in no time at all over half of them had been captured.

As a last-ditch measure, the group ran toward Reisen Gorge in order to avoid complete annihilation. They hoped that the inability to use magic around the gorge would give the soldiers pause, and their caution would overrule their desire to capture more slaves. It was a complete gamble. There was no telling if the soldiers would tire before the remaining rabbitmen were eaten by stray monsters.

However, contrary to all expectations, the imperial troops continued to give chase. At the eastern and western ends of the gorge were stairs cut directly into the cliffs, allowing one to descend safely. Most of the troops went back, but they left a battalion to guard the stairs. Once the rabbitmen came under attack by monsters, they would have no choice but to run right back into the waiting soldiers' arms.

As expected, monsters eventually came to attack the rabbitmen. Deciding they would rather surrender to the Hoelscher Empire than be eaten, the Haulia readied themselves to run back—even if it meant slavery. However, the monsters would not allow the rabbitmen such a luxury and instead chased them deeper into the ravine. And so, the rabbitmen were trapped within the gorge, forced to constantly run around to survive.

"...Before we knew it, our group of sixty had been whittled down to forty. At this rate we'll all be killed. Please, please, you have to save us! I'm begging you!" The grief on Shea's face was nothing like the comedic expressions she'd had before when she was crying.

Once she finished her story, Hajime nodded.

"I see." That simple, short statement was all he said in response. It seemed that, just like Yue and Hajime, Shea was another one of the misfits of this world. The reason she was so resilient was most likely because she was unconsciously strengthening her body with mana manipulation. Maybe it was a form of atavism, like Yue's ability.

Satisfied that the mystery had now been cleared up, Hajime

looked squarely at Shea and, after careful deliberation, gave his reply.

"No." Time itself came to a halt. Or at least, that was what it felt like.

Shea's mouth opened and closed wordlessly, her mind unable to comprehend what had just come out of Hajime's mouth. It was only when Hajime started getting ready to power up Steiff again that she finally came back to her senses and started protesting.

"W-w-wait a second! Why?! Isn't the normal reaction to smile reassuringly and say, 'Oh, you poor thing, don't worry. I'll save your tribe!' or something?! Even I'm starting to get fed up with this! What kind of heartless monster abandons a beautiful girl alone in this dangerous gorge?! Hey, quit ignoring me. I won't let you get away, no matter how hard you try!" Hajime ignored Shea's complaints and tried to start Steiff again but was stopped when the bunny girl threw herself at him once more. The solemn rabbit that had been sitting there moments ago vanished, and the worthless one returned to take her place.

No matter how hard he tried, Hajime couldn't shake her off his leg, so he finally sighed exasperatedly and glared at the rabbit.

"So what do I get out of saving your family?"

"Y-y-you want a reward?"

"You've been exiled from your old kingdom, are on the run from the Hoelscher Empire, and are considered dangerous elements by every other member of your species. So far, it seems like all I get for saving you is a heap of trouble. Besides, even if I do get you out of this gorge, where are you going to go? From the sound of it, you're all doomed to get captured anyway. So are you going to ask for my help with that, too? Protect you from the Hoelscher Empire until you make it all the way to the mountains?"

"Umm, I-I...b-but!"

"We have our own goals too, you know? Carrying someone as troublesome as you around would make our job harder."

"But...but I *saw* you protecting us!"

"...You mentioned something like that before too. What do you mean, you saw? Does it have something to do with your special magic?"

"This isn't the future I saw!" Shea wailed tearfully at how stubborn Hajime was being. Hajime guessed that her strange utterances had something to do with the reason she was acting independently from her tribe.

He wasn't exactly dying to know what it was, but since he'd heard her out thus far, he figured he might as well ask. Shea was dumbfounded by Hajime's question for a moment, before realizing this might be her last chance to convince him. Gesturing wildly, she began explaining.

"Huh? Oh, uh, yes! My special magic is called Future Sight, and it lets me see into possible futures. As in, if I choose x, y will happen, kind of... It also just activates by itself when I'm in danger. Though, the futures I see aren't absolute... Still, I promise I'll come in handy! You'll see danger coming thanks to my Future Sight... I used it back there too! It showed me a vision of you guys saving me! I'm so glad the future I saw of meeting you two actually came true!"

As she had explained, Shea's Future Sight was a special magic ability that let her see what future outcomes would result from certain choices. However, it consumed a great deal of mana, enough to usually leave her exhausted after use. It also activated automatically whenever Shea was in danger. Whether or not this danger was a direct threat to her, or something that would indirectly harm her didn't matter. This took up a great deal of mana too, but not nearly as much as activating it voluntarily did. Specifically, it only took up a third as much.

From the sound of it, Shea had seen a future where Hajime was protecting her and her family. Which was why she set out to find him.

"If you've got an ability like that, how did those Verbergen guys find you? Shouldn't you have been able to avoid them because you can see the future?" The smile Shea gave Hajime was one he couldn't read. He couldn't tell if it was self-deprecating, sad, or simply her trying to act tough. It might have even been all three. Even her voice was inscrutable.

"...The future is something we always have the power to change. At least, that's what I believe. But there are some things you can't change no matter how hard you try... I realize that again every time I fail to change something. I couldn't change the one future I really wanted to. Maybe if I'd just tried a little harder, I could have..."

"You..." Hajime couldn't fathom what it must feel like to know the future. If it were a future you desired, of course you'd happily be counting down the days until it came. But what if the future you saw were full of tragedy? Could you really just sit there and accept it as inevitable? He couldn't tell earlier because of her energetically annoying personality, but maybe Shea had been lashing out against it all this time. And up until now, there must have been countless other visions she couldn't prevent either. That was the burden this bunny girl had to bear.

Even right now, her precious family was being captured and killed before her eyes because she couldn't do anything about the future she saw. That explained why she had tried so hard to enlist their help, no matter how much they abused her. She was trying to achieve that "little harder" she couldn't before.

Shea Haulia was literally betting the fate of her entire tribe on being able to enlist Hajime's help. For the first time, Hajime's expression clouded over. He certainly could understand the feelings of someone crawling desperately forward for the sake of their desired future, trying to survive the only way they knew how. However, when he thought of his own goals, he began to feel a little conflicted. That was how much Hajime had changed.

Finally, he decided that no matter how hard she begged, he'd just forcibly leave her behind... But before he could start Steiff, Shea found herself an unexpected ally.

"...Hajime, let's help her."

"Yue?"

"Oh! I knew you were a good person when I first saw you! I'm sorry for calling you flat earlier!"

Shea's eyes sparkled excitedly, while Hajime's were filled with feelings of bewilderment, as they both looked at Yue. But before anything else could happen, Shea's unnecessary comments earned her a slap from Yue. The serious atmosphere from earlier had all but vanished. It was only natural, though. Despairing one second and jumping for joy the next was just how Shea was.

Yue turned away from Shea, who was rubbing her stinging cheek, and explained her reasons to Hajime.

"...She can guide us through the sea of trees."

"Ahhh, you've got a point." There was a dense fog that permeated the Haltina Woods, and only the beastmen could navigate their way properly through it. Having a bunny girl guide would certainly be a great help. They did have a makeshift plan for navigating the forest themselves, but it was pretty rough, and there was no guarantee it'd work. Worst case, they could have captured a beastman and asked them to be their guide, but having someone who would willingly guide them would be easier on their conscience.

Considering how troublesome Shea's request was, though, Hajime still hesitated to say yes. But Yue's next words blew away all of his hesitation.

"...Don't worry. Together, we're stronger than anyone." Those were the same words he'd said back in Orcus' room. They'd hold nothing back against anything that stood against them, even if it were the whole world. As long as they had each other's backs, they'd be stronger than anyone. Hajime smiled wryly; he never thought he'd have his own words thrown back at him in such a manner.

Having the rabbitmen's help would definitely make navigating the woods a lot easier. Of course, that came with the caveat that they would become embroiled in the Hoelscher Empire and rabbitmen's little war. Hajime had no intention of purposely sticking his nose into trouble, but avoiding the simplest option because it came with some obstacles went against his personal creed. Enemies that stood in his way were to be killed.

"You're right. You're absolutely right, Yue. We'll use everything we can. And kill everyone that gets in our way. That's all there is to it."

"Yeah." Yue replied with her trademark as Hajime gently patted her head.

"Did they forget I'm still here?" Shea muttered to herself as she watched the two of them flirt. Finally, Hajime turned around to look at Shea.

"Rejoice, you stupid rabbit. We're hiring you as our forest guide. In return, we'll guarantee your family's safety. You better not have any complaints." He was agreeing to her request, but the way he phrased it made him sound completely like a mafia boss. Though, perhaps it was fitting as Shea had just gotten the cooperation of the kind of demon that took down hordes of monsters without batting an eye. For her part, she was overjoyed that she'd safely managed to bring about her desired future.

"O-of course not! Thank you so much! Hic, really, dank you shoo mush!!" This time she was crying tears of happiness. But for the sake of her comrades, she couldn't afford to celebrate for too long. She quickly regained her composure and stood up.

"U-umm, really, thank you so much for agreeing to help! M-may I ask what your names..."

"Huh? Oh, I guess we didn't introduce ourselves yet, did we...? I'm Hajime. Hajime Nagumo."

"...Yue."

"So Hajime-san and Yue-chan, then."

Shea repeated them to herself a few times to make sure she didn't forget. However, Yue didn't seem satisfied with the way she was being addressed.

"...Call me Yue-san, you stupid rabbit."

"Fweh?" It was rare for Yue to order anyone around, and Shea clearly hadn't been expecting it, either. It appeared Shea had thought Yue was younger than her, which was why she'd called her Yue-chan. But once Yue explained that she was an ancient vampire princess, Shea got on her knees and started begging for forgiveness. It appeared that Shea had managed to get on Yue's bad side. Though Hajime couldn't exactly tell why Yue held such resentment against Shea... Just because she was always staring hatefully at a certain part of Shea's body didn't mean that had to be the reason!

"Hey, get on already, you stupid rabbit." In the end, Hajime decided to ignore Yue's complex entirely. Shea looked at Hajime blankly. That was hardly surprising. Motorcycles didn't exist in this world. All Shea could tell was that this was some kind of vehicle. Timidly, she edged herself onto the bike behind Yue.

The back seat was made of monster leather, and because of how small Yue was, there was more than enough space for Shea, too. Shea wrapped her arms around Yue, surprised by how soft the seat beneath her was. As she did so, her two deadly weapons pressed against Yue's back.

Yue jumped a little as Shea's soft mounds made contact with her back, and she suddenly stood up and crawled over Hajime so she was sitting in the front. She was small enough that Hajime had no problem reaching over her to drive. It looked like having Shea's boobs press up against her made Yue uncomfortable. She sullenly leaned back against Hajime, and all he could do in response was smile awkwardly.

"Huh? What's going on?" Shea asked, clearly confused. But then she cheerfully sidled forward and hugged Hajime's waist instead. Unlike Yue, Hajime didn't even notice and nonchalantly started up Steiff. He definitely didn't even notice Shea's boobs pressing up against him. That was an undeniable fact.

Unaware of the turmoil in her rescuers' hearts, Shea inquisitively peeked her head out from behind Hajime's shoulder and asked a question.

"U-umm... I was so caught up in getting you to help that I forgot to ask, but... what is this thing? Is it some kind of carriage? Also, Hajime-san and Yue-san, both of you used magic back there, right? I thought you couldn't use magic inside the gorge..."

"I'll fill you in on the way."

That was all Hajime said before gunning Steiff's accelerator, sending them speeding through the gorge. Shea let out a terrified scream as she watched the bike effortlessly tear its way through the rough terrain. The canyon walls sped by as they raced through the ravine.

Shea had her eyes firmly shut for the first segment of the ride, but her fear slowly began to give way to excitement as she got used to Steiff's speed. Every time Hajime rounded a curve or dodged a boulder she'd let out an excited squeal, since she'd finally plucked up the courage to open her eyes and all.

On the way, Hajime briefly explained what Steiff was, how Yue could use magic inside the gorge, and that his weapons were something akin to artifacts. By the time he'd finished his explanation, Shea's jaw was hanging wide open in surprise.

"W-wait…does that mean you two can also directly control mana and use specialized magic?"

"Yep, we can."

"…Yeah."

Shea stared at them in astonishment for a few seconds before suddenly burying her face into Hajime's shoulder and then subsequently bursting into tears.

"…Now what? First you get all excited, then you get depressed, and now you're crying… You're just one big bundle of emotions, aren't you?" Hajime said.

"…Is it too late to save her?" Yue added.

"What do you mean too late to save me? Save me from what? I'll have you know that I'm a perfectly normal girl… I was just so glad to find out…to find out that I'm not alone…"

"……"

She must have felt terribly alone thinking she was the only person in the world with the same power as a monster.

Obviously, her family must have showered her with a lot of love if they were willing to hide her for sixteen years and then even abandon their home for her sake. However, despite all that, or perhaps precisely because of it, Shea must have always been tormented by the fact that she was different from everyone else, which led to her loneliness.

Shea's words must have resonated with Yue as she suddenly lapsed deep into thought. And while the change was slight, her expressionless face grew even paler than usual. Somehow, Hajime could just tell what she was thinking about. Chances were Yue saw a lot of herself in Shea. They both had the ability to use specialized magic and control mana directly, and neither of them had anyone they could have truly called a "comrade" in their own time.

However, there was one definitive difference in their circumstances. Yue hadn't even had a family that loved her. She wasn't exactly jealous of Shea per se, but there still were a lot of complicated feelings swirling about inside her. And besides, Shea had been able to find her comrades far sooner than Yue ever did. From Yue's perspective, Shea must have been quite blessed.

Hajime gently patted the top of Yue's head. For Hajime, who had been born in the peaceful country of Japan and raised with love by both of his parents, it was impossible to truly understand the despair Yue must have felt at not only being the only one of her kind, but also being forced to bear the solitary title of queen. Which was why he didn't know what to say to her. All he could do for her was remind her that she wasn't alone anymore.

He may have been transformed in that labyrinth, but he still had enough of his old self left to remember to be kind to those close to him. And the one who had preserved that humanity of his was none other than Yue. Had he not met Yue when he had, there would certainly have been nothing human about him left. Hence, Yue was currently Hajime's only remaining pillar of support. As proof, the only reason Hajime planned on keeping his promise with Shea was because of her. He was even ready to fight back against the empire if they started targeting the Haulia clan.

While Hajime's attempts at comforting Yue were pretty clumsy, his heartfelt feelings got across to her, and she relaxed the tension she hadn't realized she'd been holding in and leaned back into Hajime's lap. She was just like a cat looking to be stroked by her owner.

"Umm, did you forget about me again? Shouldn't you be saying something like 'You must have had it tough, being all alone this whole time. But it's okay now, because I'm by your side,' or something? I'm clearly depressed right now, so shouldn't you be cheering me up? This is like the easiest opportunity to get on a girl's good side. But no, you just go and ignore this perfect chance and start flirting with someone else. You guys are starting to make me feel lonely! Let me in, too! Besides, you two..."

"Shut up, you worthless rabbit!"

"...Okay... Hic..."

Shea suddenly started yelling in Hajime's ear in a tearful voice, but she was quickly silenced by Yue and Hajime. Though, to be fair, it was pretty cruel of the two of them to keep flirting when there was a crying girl sitting right behind them. Worse, they got mad at her when she was well within her rights to get mad at them. However, Shea's one redeeming feature was her hardiness.

She had already mentally switched over to a new goal. That was how fast she rebounded from failure. *All right, first I'm gonna get them to call me by name. I finally found the comrades I've been looking for, so there's no way I'm letting them get away that easy!*

They continued like that for a while, alternating between Shea growing noisy and Yue and Hajime yelling at her to pipe down, until finally they heard the roars of monsters in the distance. Quite a few of them, too.

"Ah! Hajime-san, we're almost to where everyone else is waiting! Those monsters' howls must mean that...th-they're close! Father and the others are very close!"

"Quit yelling in my ears! I can hear you just fine. I'm gonna speed up now, so hold on tight."

Hajime poured more of his mana into Steiff, accelerating it even further. The canyon walls merged into a gray blur as they sped by at an incredible pace.

There was so much mana going into Steiff that the entire bike was glowing crimson. It took only thirty seconds to get to the source of the howling. Hajime rounded one final curve, drifted around a boulder, and saw a number of rabbitmen under attack by a group of monsters.

Screams of terror echoed throughout Reisen Gorge. The rabbit ears were all scurrying to hide behind boulders or squeeze into crevices. A number of rabbit ears could be seen sprouting behind various boulders. From what Hajime could tell, there were around twenty pairs. All told, it seemed like there were about forty people running around.

Terrorizing them from above was a group of flying monsters, a breed that had been rare even in the depths of the abyss. They resembled the wyverns common in fantasy games. Their bodies were around three to five meters long, and sharp claws studded their legs like the spikes on a morning star. Their tails too, were spiked.

"H-Hyverias..." Shea said in a trembling voice. It seemed those wyvern-like raptors were called Hyverias. There were six of them in total. Currently, they were circling high above the rabbitmen, as if appraising their prey.

Finally, one of them decided to make a move. It dove toward one of the boulders some rabbitmen were hiding behind, did a flip in midair, and sent its tail crashing down onto the boulder with all the force of gravity behind it. With a thunderous impact, the boulder was shattered to pieces, and screams echoed from the exposed individuals as they scurried away as fast as possible.

Tired of waiting, the Hyveria opened its jaw wide, attempting to eat the slowest of the rabbits. Specifically, two of them. One of the youngest children's legs had given out on him, and one of the men had stayed behind to try and protect him.

Despair flickered in everyone's eyes. They all figured that the both of them were doomed to be Hyveria fodder in another few seconds. However, someone had arrived who wouldn't allow that.

The monster of the abyss had given his word that he would protect them, so protect them he would. *Bang! Bang!* Two gunshots reverberated throughout the gorge. At the same time, two crimson streaks shot through the sky. The first passed cleanly between the brows of the Hyveria that was trying to eat the pair of rabbitmen. Its head exploded into a thousand flesh chunks, and its body veered to the side of the cowering group as it fell to the ground, raising a dust cloud in its wake as it slid across the canyon.

There was a terrifying howl behind them at the same time. Without even the time to process what had just happened, the rabbitmen all turned to the source of this new noise to see that another one of the Hyverias had gotten a claw blown clean off. It had somehow managed to sneak right behind the cowering pair of rabbitmen.

It had probably hoped to launch a sneak attack on the pair while their attention was focused on the Hyveria coming at them from the front. The second bullet was what had blown its arm off. With its balance destroyed, the second Hyveria crumbled to the ground, writhing in pain.

"Wh-what..." The adult rabbitman's gaze flitted from the dead Hyveria in front to the one screaming in pain behind him, his jaw open wide in absolute amazement.

A few more gunshots followed right after, and the Hyveria that was writhing on the ground was turned into a pincushion. It gave one last pitiful high-pitched scream before it died, its torso more or less blown to bits by that point. There was another re-sounding thud as it collapsed.

Enraged at the deaths of their comrades, the remaining Hyverias all attacked at once. The rabbitmen, frozen stiff with fear, suddenly heard a noise completely alien to them.

Their sensitive rabbit ears picked up on a strange high-pitched keening, like the sound of something letting off steam. As they all turned as one to see what was the source of the sound, they saw a strange black vehicle of some sort rushing toward them at high speed. There seemed to be three people riding atop it.

One of which was a girl they all recognized. She had disappeared earlier that morning, and the entire clan had been out looking for her. Worried about her family as she had been, there was none of the usual cheer in her expression that morning. She must have felt responsible for her clan's plight, as her expression had been filled with guilt. Everyone had assumed the reason she'd vanished was because she was worried about them and had headed out to try something rash. Because of that, they had foregone caution in their haste to find her and had been caught by the Hyverias. They had expected to be wiped out there without ever finding her, but... There she was, standing at the back of the weird black vehicle, waving happily. Her usual innocent smile was plastered on her face again. Everyone stared at her in disbelief.

"Everyone...I've found help!" Her familiar voice brought them all back to reality, and the fact that they really were saved finally hit them. And as it did, they all yelled out her name.

"Shea?!" Hajime clicked his tongue irritably as he watched Shea happily wave to her family. He, of course, didn't let Steiff's speed drop at the distraction.

It wasn't her happiness that bothered him, but the fact that she was leaning all her weight against him in order not to fall off, which of course meant that every time she happily jumped up and down, her dreadnought-class boobs whacked into the top of Hajime's head. In fact, the reason he had missed his second shot earlier was because her boobs had distracted him.

Annoyed by her continued jumping, Hajime grabbed Shea by what remained of her clothes. She looked down at him questioningly. Because he was still facing forward, she couldn't tell what kind of expression he had, but for some reason she had a bad feeling about this. She questioned him in a timid tone.

"U-umm, Hajime-san? What's wrong? Why are you grabbing my clothes like that?"

"If you're just going to get in my way, I'd rather put your energy to good use in helping me out."

"Wh-what do you mean... P-put it to good use how?"

"Oh, nothing much, just throw you to the pack of starving monsters."

"W-wait, what...? Ah, please don't lift me up like that. Please stop looking like you're about to throw meeee." Shea struggled helplessly against Hajime's iron grip, but his strength stat was over nine thousand! She never had a chance.

Hajime drifted Steiff with just one hand and then used the centrifugal force of his turn to lob Shea at the group of Hyverias flying overhead.

"Have at them, you worthless rabbit!"

"Noooooooooooooooooooooooooooooo!"

Shea flew through the sky with a surprising amount of speed. Her screams could be heard throughout the gorge. Her family all yelled out in alarm, their eyes open wide. In fact, this turn of events was so surprising that even the Hyverias were taken aback. Even when she was right in front of them, they did nothing more than stare at her, their bodies stiff with surprise.

That moment of hesitation was what Hajime had been waiting for. The stilled Hyverias made for great target practice. Four gunshots rang out, and four Hyveria heads were blown into oblivion.

It was all so sudden that they didn't even have time to cry out in pain before they were dead. And so, four headless corpses fell to the ground. Hyverias were considered even more dangerous than the Dihedwa that Shea had encountered earlier, but Hajime dropped the entire flock like it was nothing. Having seen such an overwhelming display of power, the rabbitmen were at a complete loss for words.

But the screams of a familiar girl brought them back to their senses.

"Aaaaaaaaaaaaaaaaaaah! Save me pleaseeee! Hajime-saaaaaaan!" They all quickly started running to where Shea was landing, but Hajime easily outstripped them all with Steiff and drifted to a halt underneath her landing point before suavely plucking her out of the air. He then unceremoniously dropped her onto the ground.

"Owie! Ugh, you don't have to be so rough with me, you know? I demand better treatment. I want you to treat me nice like you do Yue-san." Teary-eyed, Shea began protesting her rough treatment.

It wasn't like Shea had any particular romantic feelings for Hajime. She had just met him a few hours ago, after all. However, the fact that he was the "hope" she had seen in the depths of despair led her to have a great deal of unwarranted trust in him. Regardless of how brusquely he treated her, she seemed certain he wouldn't break his promise. Besides, Hajime was the same kind of anomaly that Shea was. That alone was enough to make her feel a sort of kinship with him.

Furthermore, he treated Yue, who was also an anomaly like her, very tenderly. Despite the short time they'd known each other, that much was obvious to Shea. Frankly speaking, Shea was jealous of their intimacy. So it wasn't love but just a desire to be pampered.

Her short stint as a flying bunny girl had left her clothes even more tattered than they already were. She really did look pitiful, sobbing on the ground dressed in nothing but rags. *Maybe I did go a little too far...* Hajime thought. Reluctantly, he reached into his Treasure Trove and pulled out a spare coat that he then dumped on Shea's head. He was tired of her bursting into tears at every little thing.

However, Shea was surprisingly pleased by the gift. She stared at him blankly for a moment before realizing that he'd given her a coat and beamed happily as she wrapped it around herself. It was a white coat, and looked identical to the one Yue was wearing. Yue had sewed the extra in hopes of getting Hajime to match outfits with her.

"O-oh my! Hajime-san, you should be more honest with yourself! Giving me a coat that matches with Yue's... Are you trying to make a move on me? Well, unfortunately, I'm not that easy.

There's an order to these things, you know?" Shea fidgeted shyly as she played with the hem of her coat. Feeling his annoyance rise up again, Hajime silently pulled out Donner and fired it at Shea's forehead.

"Hakyun!" The bullet he had fired was coated with a rubbery leather farmed from monsters and was packed with far less blastrock. It was meant for non-lethal shots. However, it still hurt, and Shea arched back from the impact of the blow before she collapsed to the ground and rolled around in pain, screaming "My head... My heaaaad!"

Of course, being as sturdy as she was, Shea quickly recovered and started hotly protesting her treatment once more. Hajime shut her up in the usual fashion, and the rabbitmen all started crowding around Shea before the cycle could continue further.

"Shea! You were safe!"

"Father!"

The first one to reach Shea was a rabbit-eared man with cropped navy blue hair, in his mid-forties (though as far as Hajime was concerned, there was no value in putting bunny ears on an old dude). He watched as Shea spoke with her father, appreciating how strange this looked from his earthling perspective. Once they were done reaffirming each other's safety, they both turned to face Hajime.

"You would be Hajime-dono, correct? My name is Cam Haulia. I'm Shea's father, and the chieftain of the Haulia tribe. You have my deepest gratitude for saving both my daughter and the rest of my tribe. And I've heard that you're even going to assist us in our escape... As both a father and a chieftain, I simply cannot thank you enough." The rabbitman named Cam bowed his head deeply as he finished. Behind him, the rest of his tribe followed suit.

"Well, thanks are all well and good, but don't forget, you're going to be guiding us through the sea of trees after this. Also, I'm surprised you all trust me so easily. I thought humans and beastmen didn't get along too well..." He had almost forgotten because of how eclectic Shea was, but the beastmen were supposedly being persecuted by the other races. In fact, the reason they were stuck in this gorge in the first place was because of humans. Yet despite that, they were all bowing their head to Hajime, another human, and truly seemed to believe he would save them. While it may have been true that he was their only hope at this point, he still found it suspicious that they seemed to harbor no resentment toward him at all, and that they were so easily willing to accept him.

Cam smiled awkwardly as he replied.

"You're someone Shea trusts. That's why we're also putting our faith in you. We're all one big family, so..." Hajime was half amazed, half completely dumbfounded. No matter how kind a people they might be, trusting a complete stranger simply on the word of one of their own showed an utter lack of wariness.

"Ehehe, don't worry, Father. Hajime-san might be cruel towards women, demand compensation for everything he does, and mercilessly use people as bait, but he'd never break a promise or trample on the hopes of someone else! I'm sure he'll protect us!"

"Ha ha ha, I see, I see. So what you're saying is he's just shy. In that case, we're in good hands."

At Cam's words, the surrounding rabbitmen all started murmuring at once. Sentences such as "I see, he's just shy," and the like. They all nodded to themselves while gazing kindly down at Hajime.

Hajime angrily pulled out Donner, but before he could do anything, he got blindsided by a surprise attack.

"...Yeah, Hajime's really shy—in bed."

"Yue..."

His face cramped up at that, but he figured if he kept arguing for too long they'd just have more monsters to deal with, so he instead focused on getting everyone ready to leave. Once all forty-two rabbitmen were ready, he started leading them to the gorge exit.

They ran into many monsters along the way, as a caravan of defenseless rabbitmen made for an easy target, but not a single monster got past Hajime. Any time something that threatened them showed up, Hajime would promptly shoot it down without mercy.

With every gunshot, another of Reisen Gorge's ferocious monsters met its end, unable to put up even a modicum of resistance. The rabbitmen were all astonished at how easily he dispatched monsters that others would struggle to even escape from. Before long, they all respected him for his overwhelming strength. The little bunny children all stared at Hajime with glowing eyes, like he was their hero.

"Eeheehee, Hajime-san, look! All the kids are staring at you! Why not give them a little wave at least?" Seeing how uncomfortable Hajime was at being adored by the children, Shea started poking fun at him. An angry vein pulsed on his forehead, and he wordlessly fired Donner at her.

Bang! Bang! Bang!

"Awawawawah?!" The rubber bullets headed straight for her feet, and Shea had to do an impromptu tap dance to avoid them. Having gotten used to this spectacle, Cam only smiled wryly while Yue just looked tired of the ongoing skit.

"Shea seems to have taken quite a liking to you, Hajime-dono. To the point that one would suspect she might... Well, I suppose she is getting to that age now. As her father, I do feel a little sad about it. But I'd be relieved if it was you I entrusted her to, Hajime-dono..." Cam seemed to be completely unconcerned about the fact that his daughter was still being shot at, and tears pooled in the corners of his eyes as he spoke about her growth.

"Someone save meee," Shea screamed, but the other rabbit-men also just watched with warm expressions as she danced around a storm of bullets.

"There's something wrong with you guys. You look at this and *that's* what goes through your heads?

"...They're weird."

As Yue had said, there was definitely something odd about these people's idea of common sense. Or perhaps they were naturally inclined to be airheads. Though there was no way to tell if that was something specific to the Haulia clan in particular, or applicable to all rabbitmen.

Soon enough, the party arrived at the staircase that would lead them out of Reisen Gorge. Hajime used his Far Sight skill to scout out the area, and his first impression of the stairs was that they were quite an impressive feat of engineering. The staircase was actually a series of switchbacks cut directly into the cliff face. Each switchback went about fifty meters before turning. Past the staircase was the sea of trees, of which only a glimpse could be seen from down in the gorge. It would take an average person about half a day to go from the exit of the gorge to the entrance of the Haltina Woods.

Shea realized Hajime must be doing something to magnify his sight, so she timidly asked him, "Do you see any imperial soldiers?"

"Not sure. It's possible they gave up and went home, but..."

"U-umm, if we do run into them...Hajime-san...what will you do?"

"What do you mean?" He tilted his head in confusion, and Shea took a moment to steel herself before continuing. The other Haulia members all perked up their ears in order to listen in.

"Our opponents this time wouldn't be monsters, but soldiers... Other humans like you, I mean. Will you really be able to fight them?"

"Worthless rabbit, didn't you say you saw me helping in the future you got a glimpse of?"

"Yes, I did. I definitely saw you fighting imperial troops, Hajime-san, but..."

"Then what's there to be worried about?"

"I'm not exactly worried; I just wanted to make sure. Protecting us from the empire might make you into humanity's enemy. I was just wondering how you felt about fighting your own people..."

All of the Haulia silently gazed at Hajime. The smaller children obviously didn't fully grasp what was going on, but they could tell the atmosphere was tense and that all the adults were looking at him, so they did too.

However, Hajime was completely unfazed by the serious atmosphere and answered frankly.

"I don't really see a problem with it."

"Huh?"

Despite Shea's serious tone, Hajime replied casually, without a hint of doubt.

"I mean, what's wrong with turning all of humanity into my enemy?"

"B-but I mean, they're your people, aren't they?"

"Aren't you guys being chased by 'your people' right now, too?"

"I mean, I guess that's true, but..."

"Besides, I think you guys are misunderstanding something."

"What do you mean?" This time it was Shea who tilted her head in confusion. The other Haulia were all puzzled as well.

"Okay, listen up. I've hired you guys to help me navigate through the sea of trees, which is why I'm protecting you right now. I can't exactly let my guides die. I'm not doing this because of some sense of justice or because I sympathize with you guys or anything. Can't say I plan on babysitting you guys forever, either. You haven't forgotten that, have you?"

"Umm, no...I haven't forgotten..."

"I'll protect you as long as it takes to get you guys to guide me through, for my own sake. And it doesn't matter who we're up against. Anyone who gets in my way, whether they be monsters or humans, is an enemy. And the only thing that awaits my enemies is death. That's all."

"I-I see..."

Shea smiled bitterly at how Hajime-esque his reasoning was. Even if she had seen them protecting her tribe from imperial soldiers, the future wasn't set in stone. While her visions had a high chance of coming to pass, on the off chance that the empire did get their paws on the Haulia, a fate worse than death awaited them. They would be sold off as slaves. Though she never let it show, Shea felt a lot of guilt about getting her family wrapped up in this situation, which was why she needed to be one hundred percent sure that Hajime would save them.

"Ha ha ha, I like a man who can keep things simple. Don't worry. Just leave guiding you through the sea of trees to us." Cam laughed cheerfully. It was easier to trust a person who was doing this as part of a contract rather than someone who said they just wanted to be a hero of justice or something. His laugh wasn't one bit forced. That was just what he truly thought.

The rabbit party slowly approached the foot of the staircase. With Hajime in the lead, they began climbing the multitude of stone steps. Despite the fact that they probably hadn't had a chance to eat since fleeing into the gorge, the Haulia's footsteps were full of energy. In return for not having any magical ability, most beastmen were quite sturdy.

Finally, they cleared the last switchback and escaped from Reisen Gorge.

What waited for them as they crested the last set of steps was...

"Holy shit, you serious? They're actually still alive! And here I thought the commander was nuts for leaving us here. Well, this'll make a nice present to send back home." There were around thirty or so imperial soldiers waiting around the exit. They had created a makeshift camp near the staircase, and there were a few large carriages dotting the campsite. Each of the soldiers was wearing an identical khaki uniform, and most of them had swords or spears or shields slung across their backs. They were clearly surprised to see Hajime and the rabbitmen. But they quickly recovered from their initial shock. Smiles erupted on their faces as they began appraising the stock they would soon sell.

"Boss, the light-haired girl's with them, too! You were eyeing her before, right?"

"Oooh, today really is my lucky day. I don't care what you do with the old farts, but you better not harm a hair on her head, you hear?"

"There's plenty of women to go around, so it's fine if we examine a few of the goods before shipping them off first, right? They made us wait here in the middle of nowhere for three whole days, so it's only fair, right, boss? We definitely deserve a little bonus, don't you think?"

"Sheesh. Fine, but you better not do them all. Behave your-selves and keep it to just two or three."

"Hell yeah! I knew you were a nice guy, boss!"

The soldiers clearly didn't even see the Haulia as a threat, as they weren't even bothering to get into formation. Their atten-tion was completely focused on the female Haulia, and vulgar smiles were on each of their faces. The rabbitmen were all shiver-ing with fear.

Finally, the grinning man the others had called "boss" noticed Hajime's presence.

"Huh? Who the hell are you? You're...not a rabbitman, are you?"

Judging from their tone, it didn't seem likely they would just let Hajime and the others pass through, so he decided to humor them by answering.

"Yeah, I'm a human."

"Huuuh? And what's a human like you doing with the likes of them? Coming from Reisen Gorge no less. Wait, are you a slave trader? Did you come here because someone tipped you off about the rabbits? Well, you're quite the dedicated merchant, you know. Sucks for you, though. Unfortunately, those cuties over there are property of the empire, so I'm gonna have to ask you to leave."

The soldiers' commander made his own assumptions and barked out orders with the clear belief that they would be fol-lowed unquestioningly.

Obviously, Hajime had no intention of obeying.

"No."

"What'd you just say?"

"I said no. These people are with me. I'm not handing a single one of them over to you. I suggest packing up and going home."

Thinking he surely must have misheard, the leader asked again. However, he was just met with an even more arrogant refusal. A vein pulsed on the soldier's forehead.

"Kid, you better watch your mouth. Do you not realize who we are, or are you just that damn stupid?"

"Oh, I know exactly who you are. But you of all people really don't have the right to be calling anyone stupid."

The smile vanished off the commander's face at that. The rest of the soldiers all started glaring angrily at Hajime, too.

Suddenly, Yue stepped out from behind Hajime, grabbing everyone's attention. Despite her childlike appearance, there was an aura of maturity surrounding her, captivating all the men present.

For a moment, the commander was stunned too, but then he noticed how tightly she was clinging to Hajime's sleeve and realized she must be with him. Suddenly, he was wearing the same vulgar smile from before.

"Aaah, now I get it. I see how it is now. You're just a little brat that doesn't know how the world works. Well, allow me to give you a free lesson about just how harsh it can be. Kuku, that girl over there looks mighty fine. Think I'll rape her in front of your eyes after I chop all your limbs off. After that, I'll sell her off to slavers." Hajime's eyebrow twitched, and despite her unchanging expression, Yue's gaze clearly dripped with hatred. She raised her arm regally, as if rejecting that this man even had any right to exist.

However, Hajime held her back before she could do anything. She glanced at him dubiously, but he cleared up her confusion with his next words.

"So you're our enemy, is that it?"

"Huuuh?! You still don't get it, kid? You can get down on your knees and beg if you want, but it's—" Before he could even finish his sentence, he was interrupted by a gunshot. As Hajime had expected, the commander had been too proud to even talk things through, and as a result he was now missing his head. He wouldn't be badmouthing anyone again. His headless corpse fell limply to the ground a few seconds later.

The remaining soldiers stared dumbly at the corpse of their dead boss, and before they could even gather their wits, they were hit by a follow-up attack.

Booom! There was another gunshot, but this one decapitated five soldiers at once. Actually, there had been five gunshots, but Hajime fired so fast that their sounds melded together.

Panicking now at the sudden death of their comrades, the soldiers scrambled to point their weapons at Hajime. Even if they couldn't tell how it was happening, it was clear who was responsible. All told, their reaction was pretty quick. They might have had rotten personalities, but they were still professional soldiers. Their training was the real deal.

"Get him!"

"Everyone, start chanting!"

The troop quickly organized themselves into a backline and frontline. However, as if mocking the frailty of their formation, a small object suddenly rolled up to one of the backline members. It was a black cylinder of some sort. The backline members all stared at it, but they didn't stop chanting. In the next second, that ceased to matter, however, as they were all turned into corpses.

With a thunderous roar, the cylinder exploded, the shock wave sending lethal shards of metal tearing through every single one of the backline members.

Said cylinder had, of course, been one of Hajime's grenades. This one was a frag grenade packed to the brim with metal scraps. It was far more powerful than frag grenades made on Earth.

The initial explosion alone was enough to instantly kill the ten or so soldiers closest to it and fatally maim another seven.

Furthermore, the remaining seven soldiers that made up the front line were blown forward by the force of the blast. Six of them turned to look back and instantly lost their heads as bullets rocketed through their skulls. The resulting spray of blood drenched the lone survivor, who lost all will to fight and slumped to the ground. It was only natural. In only an instant, his entire platoon had been annihilated. It hadn't been an especially weak one or anything, either. In fact, they had been one of the more elite units in the army, which was precisely why his eyes were currently darting about, his mind unable to accept what was happening as reality.

Meanwhile, the monster who had caused such a tragedy spoke with such casualness that one might think he were commenting on the weather.

"Yeah, like I thought, I don't even need Lightning Field

against humans. Plain bullets are more than enough."

The soldier jumped with a start and gazed fearfully at Hajime. Hajime tapped Donner's barrel against his shoulder while he slowly walked up to the soldier. His fluttering black coat and the ease with which he delivered death made him seem like the grim reaper. Or well, at least he did to the sole surviving soldier.

"Ah... G-get away from me! N-nooo! I don't want to die! S-someone! Anyone! Save me!"

The soldier crawled backward on all fours as he begged for his life. His face was twisted in fear, and the dark stain near his crotch indicated that he'd wet himself. Hajime looked down at him, ice in his eyes, before suddenly aiming Donner at the soldier's back and firing multiple times in quick succession.

"Ack!" The soldier desperately shrunk back, but there was no impact to his body. That was because Hajime had only finished off all the soldiers who had been mortally wounded by his grenade. Terrified, the soldier turned around, only to see his entire platoon well and truly annihilated.

His entire body stiffened at the sight, and he couldn't even move as Hajime pressed Donner's barrel against his head. Trembling in terror, the soldier desperately attempted to plead for his life.

"P-please, I'm begging you! Please don't kill me! I'll do anything! Anything!"

"Anything? In that case, tell me what you did with all the other rabbitmen you captured. I've heard you took quite a few... Have you already shipped them back to the empire?"

The reason he'd asked was because Hajime was sure it would take a decent amount of time to transport over a hundred people, which meant it was possible they were still nearby. If they were, he didn't see any problem with saving them on the way to the sea of trees. Though if they'd already been sent to the empire, he wasn't going to go that far out of his way to mount a rescue.

"I-If I tell you, will you let me go?"

"I don't think you're in any position to be making demands here. Can't say it's information I need that badly, anyway. If you don't wanna talk, I'll just kill you now."

"W-wait, please! I'll talk! I'll talk, so please don't kill me! I think they transported them all. After whittling down the numbers a little..."

By "whittling down the numbers," he probably meant the soldiers had killed all the elderly and anyone else that wasn't likely to sell. The Haulia all despaired at the soldier's words. Hajime spared them a quick glance before returning his attention to the soldier. Murder dwelled in his eyes now that he no longer had a use for him.

"Wait! Please! I'll tell you anything else you ask! I'll spill whatever you want, so please!"

The soldier began pleading for his life again when he realized Hajime planned to kill him. However, the only reply he got...was a single bullet to the head.

There was a collective intake of breath as the Haulia all gasped. It appeared they were taken aback by how utterly merciless Hajime was. For once, there was some fear in their eyes. Even

Shea was looking at him a little timidly. "U-umm, couldn't you have just let that last one go...?"

He gave her a withering glare, and she shrank back fearfully. *These are the people who killed and enslaved her comrades, and she still wants to show them mercy? These rabbitmen are way too nice. Or wait, maybe they're all just pacifists?* Hajime was about to open his mouth to protest, but Yue beat him to the punch.

"...Don't you think it's rather selfish for an enemy to throw down their sword and beg for their life only after they know they're outmatched?"

"B-but..."

"Besides, Hajime's the one who protected you, so don't you think you're scared of the wrong person?"

"......"

Though her tone was quiet, Yue was clearly angry. She couldn't forgive the rabbitmen for being afraid of him when he'd been the one who protected them. Put that way, it did seem terribly ungrateful, and the Haulia all awkwardly looked away.

"Hmm, I apologize for my rudeness, Hajime-dono. We never meant to criticize your actions. However, we are not used to such brutal conflict... Your methods simply shocked a few of us."

"I'm sorry too, Hajime-san." Shea and Cam apologized on behalf of their tribe, but Hajime waved their apology off, indicating that he hadn't been offended in the slightest.

He sauntered over to the untouched horses and carriages and beckoned the others over. It would take them half a day to make it to the sea of trees on foot, but there was no real reason not to use the perfectly good set of carriages they'd found.

He pulled Steiff out of his Treasure Trove, then hitched it up to the carriage. He split them up between a horse-riding group and a carriage-riding group before leading them toward the sea of trees.

Before they left, Yue used her wind magic to hurl the imperial soldiers' corpses into the ravine. All that remained of the carnage that had ensued were a few pools of blood.

The Haltina Woods could be seen in the distance. Deep within its recesses was the beastmen country of Verbergen, and somewhere within that was one of the Seven Great Labyrinths. They rode forward at a good pace, and the woods quickly grew larger on the horizon.

As usual, Yue was sitting snugly in Hajime's lap as he drove Steiff, with Shea clinging on to him from behind. Hajime had tried to convince Shea to ride in the carriages, but she had insisted on riding Steiff with him. Yue had tried to kick her off over and over, but she would just rise back up like a zombie, so Yue eventually gave up.

The reason Shea was so persistent was because she wanted to better get to know the two comrades she'd finally found—hence why she looked so happy clinging to Hajime. It seemed Shea had taken a liking to Steiff's backseat; or rather, she just enjoyed being behind Hajime in general... Mentally, Yue made a note to tie her down if things started getting out of hand.

Sandwiched between a somewhat annoyed Yue and an overjoyed Shea, Hajime continued driving Steiff on muscle memory as he gazed off into the distance, slightly spaced out.

Suddenly, Yue spoke up.

"...Hajime, why did you fight them alone?"

"Hm?"

She was, of course, referring to the earlier fight with those imperial troops. Back then, Hajime had held Yue back and taken care of them all on his own. Whether she had helped or not, the soldiers would have been annihilated instantly regardless. However, after the fight Hajime had seemed lost in thought, which was what had piqued Yue's interest.

"Hmm. Well, there was something I wanted to confirm, so..."

"...What did you want to confirm?" Yue asked. Shea peeked out from behind Hajime's shoulder, also very interested in hearing the answer.

"Well, you see..." His explanation ran on for quite a long time, but the gist of it was more or less as follows:

The first reason he'd held Yue back was because he wanted to conduct a little experiment. He'd aimed at everyone's heads just in case, but he'd also fired a few experimental shots into their armor. The reason he wanted to make sure his normal bullets could pierce armor was because his railgun would be overkill against most human opponents, and in enclosed spaces like towns, he might accidentally incur casualties.

While he had no compunction about slaughtering anyone who opposed him, even he balked at the thought of accidentally killing a perfectly innocent bystander or accidentally shooting through someone's house and killing a family. Just because he no longer had any reservations about killing didn't mean that he had any desire to kill people indiscriminately. And so, he had wanted to test how much blastrock was needed to kill armored soldiers. Fortunately for him, he'd gotten a lot of good data. Thanks to the results, he had a decent idea of how much he'd need to regulate the firepower.

The second reason was that he wanted to see if he would hesitate when his opponents were fellow humans. No matter how much he'd changed, that had still been his first time fighting an actual person. So, he wanted to make sure he could mentally handle killing someone, both in the act itself, and after the deed was done.

In the end, he concluded that "I didn't really feel much over it." At that point, his philosophy of killing anything that opposed him had firmly sunk in.

"The reason I was spacing out was because I was thinking about how much I must have changed to not even bat an eye after killing someone..."

"I see... Is that okay with you?"

"Yeah, I don't really mind. This is who I am now, and this mindset will definitely help in the battles to come."

Shea was surprised to hear this had been his first time killing someone, considering how mercilessly he'd slaughtered the soliders. At the same time, she was amazed that Yue's sharp senses, at least when it came to Hajime anyway, had noticed this slight change he was going through. Underlying all of that was a faint sense of loneliness at not knowing anything about Hajime or Yue.

"Umm! Hajime-san, Yue-san, could you two please tell me more about yourselves?"

"Hm? I thought I already told you about myself."

"No, I don't mean like your abilities and stuff. I mean, how did you end up in that abyss or whatever, or why you guys are on a journey, or what you have been doing until now. I want to know more about you both."

"...Why?"

"There's no real reason. I just want to know... Because of the way I am, I've caused a lot of trouble for my family. I always hated myself for that... Of course, everyone always told me I wasn't a burden, and I'm sure they all meant it, but...I always felt like I didn't belong in this world. That's why I was happy when I first met you two. For the first time ever, I'd finally found people like me. For the first time ever, I didn't feel like the odd one out... I know it's presumptuous of me, but I was glad to have finally found people that felt like c-comrades... That's why I want to know more about you two... I'm not exactly sure how to put it, but..."

The more she talked, the more embarrassed she got, and by the end she was just whispering into Hajime's back. Hajime and Yue didn't know what to say to that. Thinking back on it, Shea had been surprisingly happy to meet them.

At the time, they'd been busy rescuing the Haulia tribe, so Yue hadn't had time to sort through her vague feelings. As a result, all she'd told Shea was simple things like why she could use magic. Shea must have been wondering about her two new companions this whole time.

It was a fact that in this world, people with a physical disposition similar to that of monsters weren't very accepted, so it was only natural that Shea would feel a sense of camaraderie. That being said, Hajime and Yue couldn't see her as a comrade quite so easily.

However, it would still be a while before they reached the sea of trees. Since they had no real reason to hide it, Hajime and Yue decided to talk about their past in order to kill some time. When they finished their tale...

"Uweeeeh... Hic...! That's terrible. You poor things. Hajime-san, and you too, Yue-san...compared to what you suffered, I've practically been blessed... Uweeeh, I can't believe I was so pathetic." Shea was a mess of tears. She kept muttering things like "I can't believe I was so spoiled," and "I'll never complain again," in between sobs. At the same time, she surreptitiously wiped her face with the hem of Hajime's coat. After having learned just how much the two of them had suffered, Shea felt pathetic for thinking her own situation had been harsh.

She continued crying for a while, but then she suddenly made a fist and looked up resolutely.

"Hajime-san! Yue-san! I've decided! Allow me to accompany you on your journey! I'll be the shining ray of light that illuminates the darkness in your lives! There's no need to be shy; the three of us are all comrades linked by a shared bond. Let's overcome the trials ahead together and achieve your dream!" Both Yue and Hajime gave Shea a cold look as she worked herself up on her own delusions.

"And what gives you the right to say that, you weakling of a rabbit? Need I remind you that we're still protecting you right now? You'd just get in the way."

"...And we've already gone from people that 'felt like comrades' to actual comrades... What a shameless bunny."

"Y-you don't have to look at me so coldly... You're going to break my heart... Also, could you please call me by my name already?" She was a bit shaken at how coldly they'd refused her heartfelt proposal. However, they weren't done yet.

"...You just want comrades to travel with, don't you?"

"Wha—?!"

It looked like Hajime was right on the mark, as Shea suddenly jumped.

"Once you're done making sure your family's safe, you were planning on leaving them behind, weren't you? And since two 'comrades' just happened to show up around the same time you decided to leave, you thought you'd travel together with them, right? I doubt such a pretty little rabbit would last long on her own."

"...Umm, that's true, but...I also really want to help you two..." Flustered, Shea tried to cover up the fact that Hajime had been right. In truth, Shea had already decided. Come hell or high water, she was going to get Hajime to save her family, after which she was going to leave the tribe. As long as she was with them, they'd always be in danger. In this incident, she'd also lost many of her precious family members. The next time she got them into trouble, they really might all die. And that was the one thing she wanted to avoid at all costs.

Of course, this went against the express wishes of her clan, and in a sense it could even be called betraying them. However, her mind was made up.

Worst case, she would have struck out on her own, but she was sure that if she did that, her family would get worried and chase after her. But if she told them she was going to help the invincible Hajime in his travels as thanks for saving her family, they'd surely let her go. Despite all appearances, Shea was earnest and quite desperate about the things she wanted to do.

That wasn't to say she wasn't also deeply interested in Yue and Hajime, because she was. As Hajime had said, she was happy to have finally found comrades, which was why she felt inexplicably close to them. All things considered, her meeting with Hajime honestly felt like destiny.

"I'm not trying to blame you or anything. But I recommend throwing away those misguided hopes of yours. Our goal is to conquer the Seven Great Labyrinths. Just like the abyss we crawled out of, they'll probably be teeming with monsters that are just as strong as us. You'd be killed in an instant. That's why we can't take you along."

"……"

Shea fell silent at Hajime's mercilessly blunt explanation. However, the nonchalant way Yue and Hajime seemed to deliver that reasoning depressed her even further. For a while she was quiet, sinking deep into thought, a complicated expression plastered on her face.

A few hours later, the group arrived at the entrance to the Haltina Woods. From the outside, it looked like nothing more than a normal forest, but once anyone stepped inside, they were instantly surrounded by a dense fog.

"Now then, Hajime-dono, Yue-dono. Please stick very close to us once we're inside. You'll be traveling in the center of our group, but it's still possible you might get separated, so be careful. Also, you just want us to guide you to the center, where the Grand Tree is, right?"

"Yeah. As far as I can tell, that's probably the labyrinth entrance."

Cam reminded Hajime of the dangers while also confirming their destination.

The Grand Tree that Cam had referred to was a massive tree that sat in the deepest reaches of the forest. The beastmen called it the Sacred Tree, Uralt, and the area around it was considered holy. Rarely did any of them ever approach it. Hajime had heard all of that from Cam after they'd escaped the gorge.

At first, Hajime had thought the entirety of the Haltina Woods itself was the labyrinth, but on second thought he'd realized that would mean abyss-level monsters would be crawling around the entire forest, making it completely uninhabitable for the beastmen. So just like the Great Orcus Labyrinth, it stood to reason that the entrance to the true labyrinth lay elsewhere. And from what Cam had told him, the Grand Tree seemed like a good place to start. Cam nodded and gave a signal to the rest of his clan, at which they all began crowding around Hajime and Yue.

"Hajime-dono, could you please erase your presence as much as possible? The Grand Tree is considered holy ground, so people usually don't approach, but it's not exactly forbidden land or anything. It's possible we might run into people from Verbergen or other outlying settlements there. Since we're all wanted, we'd rather avoid being found by anyone."

"All right, I understand. Both Yue and I are pretty good at taking covert action, so you can count on us."

As he said that, Hajime activated Hide Presence. Yue used her innate talents that she'd cultivated in the abyss to hide.

"Ah?! This is quite...Hajime-dono, would it be possible for you to hide yourself to Yue-dono's level?"

"Is this good?"

"Yes, that's perfect. If you completely erase your presence like you did earlier, we might lose sight of you ourselves. In fact, I'm certain we would. You're quite something."

Though the rabbitmen's stats were average, their extremely sensitive hearing made it very easy for them to pick up on almost all nearby presences, and they were also skilled at hiding. The fact that they could pick up on even Yue's presence, despite the skills she'd honed in the abyss, attested to their abilities. They were master trackers.

However, Hajime's Hide Presence was of an even greater level than Yue's power. Normally the rabbitmen would never lose sight of someone they'd marked, even in this vast sea of trees, but Hajime's skill was so absolute that even they couldn't sense him.

Cam smiled bitterly as he realized this human had surpassed

him in the one field that he thought his race couldn't be beaten in. For some reason, Yue was puffing her chest out proudly. Shea, on the other hand, had an oddly pained expression on her face. She was finally realizing the difference in ability Hajime had hinted at earlier.

"Very well, let us depart."

With their preparations thus complete, the party headed into the forest, with Cam and Shea leading the group. They continued down a winding trail that could hardly be called a path. The dense fog appeared almost instantly, limiting everyone's visibility. However, Cam walked forward confidently. He knew exactly where they were and precisely what their bearing was. Hajime didn't understand the underlying reason behind it, but it seemed that every beastman was born with the innate ability to traverse this dense sea of trees.

After a period of smooth progress, Cam suddenly came to a halt, warily surveying his surroundings. He'd sensed the presence of monsters. Hajime and Yue had sensed them, too. It seemed that they were surrounded by a good number of them.

The Haulia all pulled out knives Hajime had furnished when they'd entered the forest. Normally, they would have just used their superior stealth skills to escape, but it seemed that wasn't going to work. Everyone had equally nervous expressions on their faces.

Suddenly, Hajime thrust out his left arm. There was a faint hiss, and the sound of multiple somethings being ejected could be heard. A second later, *Thud. Thud. Thud.* "Kiiiiiiiiiii?!"

Three monsters of unknown appearance could be heard falling to the ground, screaming in pain. A moment later, three four-armed monkeys suddenly burst out of the fog, each of them about sixty centimeters tall.

Yue brought her hand up against one of them and whispered her spell's name.

"Wind Blade." A sharp blade of wind flew through the air, cutting one of the monkeys in half. The two halves fell to the ground, the monkey dead before it even had time to scream.

The remaining two split up and tried to pincer the group. One of them headed for a nearby kid, while the other bared its claws at Shea. Both the kid and Shea stiffened in fear, making them easy targets for the monkeys. The nearby adults tried to cover them both...but their worry was needless.

Hajime swung his left arm at them, and with another pneumatic hiss, both monkeys died, their heads punctured by ten-centimeter-long needles.

He was using the needle gun he'd installed into his prosthetic arm.

He'd stolen the idea from the scorpion he'd fought, and he could fire either single bolts or a shotgun-style spray. He ejected them using his Lightning Field, and while it didn't match the strength of Donner or Schlag, it was still quite powerful in its own right.

It only had an effective range of ten meters, but it was very quiet, and the needles were coated in poison, making for a very effective assassination tool. He hadn't used Donner specifically because he didn't want to attract attention with the gunshots.

"Th-thank you very much, Hajime-san."

"Thanks, oniichan!"

Shea and the boy he'd saved both thanked him for his timely intervention. He waved his hand casually, indicating that it was nothing. The boy's eyes were shining as he looked up at Hajime. Shea, however, slumped her shoulders, disappointed at herself for freezing up at the first sign of danger.

Cam smiled awkwardly, and he started leading them again at Hajime's urging.

They were assaulted by monsters a few more times during their trek, but Hajime and Yue quietly repulsed each wave easily. The monsters inhabiting the forest were considered strong by the locals, but they posed no problem at all for Hajime and Yue.

However, a few hours after they'd entered the forest, they found themselves so thoroughly surrounded that they had to stop. These monsters' numbers, bloodlust, and even coordination were levels above any of the monsters they'd faced so far.

The rabbitmen's ears all twitched nervously as they tried to figure out how many there were. When they discovered the identity of their opponents, the rabbitmen all grimaced. Shea took it a step further, and her face was completely pale. As Hajime and Yue realized who surrounded them, they too frowned in annoyance. After all, the ones surrounding them were none other than...

"You there... Why are there humans in your midst?! State your race and clan!"

A burly beastman with a striped tail and a pair of tiger ears barred their path.

It was definitely not normal to see beastmen and humans together in the sea of trees. The tiger beastman was looking incredulously at Cam, as if he were some kind of race traitor. There was a dangerous-looking two-handed sword in his hands. The couple dozen beastmen surrounding them were all glaring at the rabbitmen, clearly outraged.

"U-umm, we're..." Cold sweat poured down Cam's forehead as he tried to think up some kind of excuse. However, the tigerman caught sight of Shea before he could get very far.

"A white-haired...rabbit girl? You must be the Haulia tribe in the reports. You're a disgrace to all beastmen. You tricked your fellow beastmen for years, hiding that despicable demon girl, and now you're even bringing humans into our midst?! Traitors! I won't listen to any of your excuses! You're all going to be executed here! Everyone, cha—"

Bang! Just before he could finish giving the order to charge, Hajime's gun went off. A red streak scraped past the tigerman's cheek, carving a hole right through the tree behind him, vanishing deep into the sea of trees.

A trail of blood ran down the tigerman's cheek as he stood frozen in place. Had his ears been on the side of his head like a human's, one of them would have been blown off completely. Everyone stiffened suddenly at this new attack that had come so fast that no one even had time to react.

Despite his casual tone, Hajime's words carried a surprising amount of weight. That was due to the Intimidation skill that he was using, which made his opponents feel a physical pressure from his words.

"I can fire off attacks like that multiple times a second. I know *exactly* where each and every one of you are. And hell, if I wanted to, I could kill you all in under a minute."

"Wh-wha—? There wasn't even a chant."

The tigerman faltered. Not only was this human capable of firing off an unknown attack of immense power, he could apparently fire it off multiple times a second without even chanting. Plus, to top it off, he supposedly knew where they all were. As if to prove his point, Hajime unsheathed Schlag and pointed it into the distance—right where the tigerman's right-hand man was waiting in ambush. Hajime could tell he was trembling behind the fog.

"If you order your men to attack, I won't show any mercy. Until our contract is complete, these guys' lives are under my protection... Don't think even a single one of your men will go home alive if you try and hurt them."

Hajime poured bloodlust into his words on top of his Intimidation. The threatening aura oozing from his every pore caused the tigerman to break out in a cold sweat. He desperately fought down the instinctive urge to howl in fear.

You've gotta be kidding me! N-no human can do something like this! That guy's some kinda monster! In order to avoid being engulfed by the fear, the tigerman tried to psych himself up, but Hajime leveled both Donner and Schlag at him before continuing.

"But if you're willing to leave quietly, I won't chase you. If you're not my enemy, then I don't need to kill you. Now make your choice. Are you going to quietly go home or die for the sake of your foolish pride?"

The tigerman was certain. If he gave the order to attack, that skill from earlier would wipe out his entire troop. There wasn't even the slightest chance any of them would make it out alive.

He was the captain of Verbergen's second guard squad. It was his job to patrol Verbergen and its outlying settlements, and to keep them safe from monsters or invaders. He was gladly willing to die in the line of duty, which was why he couldn't back down so easily, even knowing it might invite the death of his entire squad.

"...Can I ask you something first?" The tigerman hoarsely managed to croak out those words. Hajime flicked his head, indicating that it was okay for him to continue.

"...What are you after?" A simple question. However, whether or not he ordered his men to rush to their deaths depended entirely on the answer. His glare showed that if Hajime intended to bring harm to the citizens of Verbergen, he wouldn't back down no matter how hopeless the fight.

"We just want to visit the Sacred Tree, Uralt."

"You want to go to the Grand Tree... But why? What for?"

The tigerman had been certain this human had come to enslave the beastmen or the like, so he hadn't expected that response. While they did hold the area as sacred, it wasn't of much practical importance, which was why he was so confused. It was actually more of a tourist attraction than an idol to be worshipped.

"Because the true entrance to one of the labyrinths might be there. We're on a journey to conquer all of the Seven Great Labyrinths. And we've employed the Haulia tribe to guide us there."

"True entrance? What do you mean? This forest itself is considered one of the Seven Great Labyrinths. A natural labyrinth where anyone other than a beastman will get lost forever once they step foot inside."

"Yeah, but there's a problem with that logic."

"What?" the tigerman asked suspiciously, unsure of where Hajime's confidence came from.

"The monsters here are way too weak for this to be the true labyrinth."

"...Way too weak?"

"Yeah. The monsters I encountered in the last labyrinth were all on a whole different level. At least, the ones in the depths of the Great Orcus Labyrinth were all like that. And besides..."

"Besides?"

"The labyrinths are trials that the Liberators left behind. If any old beastman can make it all the way through the forest, then it doesn't really make for much of a trial. That's why I don't think the forest itself is the labyrinth."

"......" The tigerman was utterly bewildered by Hajime's explanation; what he was saying made absolutely no sense to him. Whether it was that the monsters were too weak, or the talk about the depths of the Great Orcus Labyrinth, or the Liberators, or trials and whatnot...none of it was anything he'd ever heard of.

Under normal circumstances he would have dismissed it all as nonsense. However, there was no reason for Hajime to lie. He was the one with all the advantages, so there was no need for him to make up any excuses.

Besides, it somehow just didn't sound like a lie. And if his goal really didn't rest with Verbergen, then it made a lot more sense to just let him go to the Grand Tree and finish his business so he'd bother them no longer. The tigerman wouldn't have to waste his subordinates' lives that way either.

The tigerman reached that conclusion in an instant. However, because of how overwhelmingly powerful Hajime was, he couldn't just let him go like that. On the other hand, he was also aware that someone of Hajime's abilities was completely beyond his power to handle. And so, he offered a compromise.

"If you don't mean any harm to my country or its people, then I don't mind letting you visit the Grand Tree. I have no interest in wasting my men's lives, either." The others surrounding Hajime all seemed shaken. It was completely unprecedented to allow an interloping human even further into their territory.

"However, a mere captain of the guard like me doesn't have the authority to allow that. Allow me to contact my superiors. It's possible our elders might have some information on that true entrance you seek. If you really mean no harm to those that aren't your enemy, then surely you'll be willing to wait here while we send a messenger."

Despite the cold sweat pouring in waves down his back, his eyes were resolute. At his proposal, Hajime lapsed into thought.

Chances were this was the biggest compromise the tigerman could make. Hajime had heard intruders in the sea of trees were usually executed without question. He was sure that deep down the tigerman still wanted them eliminated, too. However, if he gave the order to attack, his men would all die. And so, he had come up with a compromise that kept his men alive and hopefully reined in the dangerous element that was Hajime.

He was actually rather impressed with the tigerman for coming up with such a rational solution. So he weighed the benefits of just killing them all and pushing his way through versus the benefits of letting Verbergen monitor his movements but still at least getting their permission to pass...and decided the latter would be less of a hassle.

On the off chance that the Grand Tree wasn't the labyrinth entrance, he'd need to do some more scouting anyway. Having Verbergen's official approval was certainly for the better. Of course, it was entirely possible he'd just make an enemy out of an entire nation instead, but if things could be resolved peacefully, then that was best. It was less a decision made out of compassion than it was a simple cost-benefit analysis.

"All right. But make sure you relay my message properly, you hear?"

"Of course. Zam, you heard us! Head to the elders as fast as you can!"

"Roger!" One of the presences surrounding them vanished. Hajime holstered both of his guns and stopped using his Intimidation skill.

The tension relaxed a little. While he was relieved, the tiger-man was still a little suspicious at how easily Hajime had lowered his guard. A few of his men were even ready to launch a surprise attack on him. But Hajime, who had guessed their intentions already, simply smiled fearlessly.

"Which do you think is faster, your charge or my quick draw...? Can't say I mind testing it, if you wanna push your luck."

"...No, I'd rather not. However, please don't do anything rash. If you do, we'll be forced to attack."

"Fine by me."

Though they were still surrounded, Cam and the others breathed a sigh of relief upon learning that there wasn't about to be an immediate bloodbath, and everyone settled down a little. That being said, the glares the tigermen directed at the rabbitmen were anything but pleasant, so it couldn't really be called a peaceful situation.

After a while, Yue got tired of the pointless staring contest, and, heedless of the heavy atmosphere, started teasing Hajime to pass the time. Tired of the oppressive air, or perhaps just hoping to lighten the mood, Shea joined in as well. Hajime begrudgingly put up with her too, and the tension relaxed a little. The rabbit-men were all dumbfounded when Hajime started "flirting" in the middle of enemy territory.

Around an hour later. Shea had gotten a bit too cheeky, and Yue now had her in an arm lock. The bunny girl was desperately screaming "Uncle! Uncle!" while the rest of her family looked on in disbelief. Finally, they sensed a number of figures rapidly approaching them.

The tense atmosphere returned in an instant, though Shea was still screaming in pain.

From the fog appeared a retinue of unfamiliar beastmen. The elderly man in their center stood out among them. He had long, flowing blond hair and a pair of striking blue eyes that spoke of long-accumulated wisdom. His body was so frail that it seemed a strong gust would blow him away. Though his majestic face was creased with wrinkles, they only served to highlight his noble appearance. The most distinctive part of his appearance, however, was his long, tapered ears. He was one of the fey folk of the forest, an elf.

Hajime guessed that he must be one of the elders. And his hunch turned out to be correct.

"Hmm, so you're the human that's been causing a ruckus in our forest. What's your name?"

"Hajime. Hajime Nagumo. Who're you, old man?"

The surrounding beastmen were shocked by his arrogant attitude. However, the old elf held out a hand to calm them before their anger boiled over.

"I am Ulfric Heipyst. I have the honor of representing Verbergen as one of its elders. Now then, I have been informed of your request, but before I give my reply, I would like to ask you something. Where did you come to learn of the Liberators?"

"Oh, we just heard about them from the man himself, in Oscar's house at the bottom of the abyss."

Hajime was surprised Ulfric was more interested in the Liberators than their objective in the forest. And while Ulfric didn't let it show on his face, he was astonished Hajime knew of the Liberators—the reason being that only people very close to the Liberators had known their true name, or that Oscar Orcus had been one of them.

"I see. So you claim to have discovered it at the bottom of the abyss. I can't say I've ever heard of such a place, though... Can you prove your claim?" Ulfric was worried there might be someone among the beastmen leadership that had leaked classified information, which was why he asked.

Hajime's expression clouded over. The only thing he could think of would be to display his strength, but that still wouldn't prove it. As he was puzzling over the issue, Yue came up with a suggestion.

"...Hajime, how about the mana crystals or some of Oscar's things?"

"Oh yeah, good point. Let me just find them..."

Hajime clapped his hands together before opening up the Treasure Trove and pulling out mana crystals so large that no monster on the surface could have produced them. He handed one over to Ulfric for inspection.

"I-I don't believe it... I've never seen a mana crystal of such purity..." The tigerman's jaw dropped open in shock. Likewise, Ulfric raised his eyebrows in mild astonishment.

"Oh, there's this, too. Apparently it's the ring Oscar wore or something." Hajime also pulled out the ring with the Orcus crest on it. This time Ulfric was unable to contain his shock and opened his eyes wide in surprise when he gazed upon the crest.

He started taking slow, deep breaths in order to calm himself down.

"I see... So you youngsters really did reach Oscar Orcus' resting place. There are still some things I'm very curious to learn, but...very well. I shall grant you passage through Verbergen. By my right as elder, you are free to travel as you please. Of course, the Haulia are welcome as well."

The beastmen around him weren't the only ones surprised. In fact, Cam and the others were shocked as well. All at once, the tigermen started hotly protesting the elder's decision. It was only natural. Not once had humans ever been allowed passage through Verbergen.

"We must treat them as honored guests. They've earned that right. This is one of the ancient laws that only those who sit on the elder's council are told of." Ulfric's stern tone left no room for disagreement, so the beastmen quieted down. However, surprisingly, Hajime was the one who raised an objection.

"Wait. Don't go deciding our plans for us. The only place I have business with is the Grand Tree; I'm not planning on going to Verbergen or anything. If we're free to go, then we'll be heading straight to the Grand Tree, thank you very much."

"I'm afraid you can't."

"What?"

So they really are going to try and get in our way, then? Hajime instantly put up his guard, but Ulfric simply replied bemusedly.

"The fog around the Grand Tree is so thick that even beastmen lose their bearings near it. It waxes and wanes in cycles, and only when the fog is thinnest can we safely approach. I'm afraid the next cycle isn't for ten days... I had thought all of the beastmen were aware of that fact, but..." Ulfric gave Hajime a puzzled stare before turning to look at Cam. After a moment spent absorbing this new piece of information, Hajime too turned to look at Cam. Faced with two expectant stares, Cam replied with...

"Ah," as if he'd only just now remembered it. A vein pulsed on Hajime's forehead.

"Cam?"

"Oh, uh, I'm not quite sure what to say... Well, there was an awful lot going on, so it's only natural that I'd forget... Yeah, I've only been there once, myself, when I was a small child, and I didn't really pay attention to the cycles or anything back then..." He kept trying to make excuses, but Hajime and Yue's relentless gazes wouldn't let him escape. Finally, he snapped and turned on his brethren.

"Hey, Shea! The rest of you, too! Why didn't you say something? You all knew about the fog cycles too, didn't you?!"

"What?! Why're you blaming us all of a sudden, Dad? You looked so confident that I was sure you knew that this was the right time in the cycle... This is all your fault!"

"Exactly! We all thought it was a little strange too, but you were so confident about getting us there that we thought maybe we were the ones who'd gotten the dates wrong..."

"Yeah, you sounded so sure, Chief..."

Cam's misguided anger made Shea lash back at him in turn, and his tribe started averting their eyes, shifting all the blame onto him.

"Y-you guys! I thought we were family! Doesn't that mean we share both the good times and the bad?! Hajime-dono, if you must punish me, please punish us collectively!"

"Coward! Dad, I can't believe you'd try and pull something like that! Just because you're scared of getting punished doesn't mean you should drag us down with you!"

"Leave us out of this, Chief!"

"Fools! Didn't you see how merciless Hajime-dono was to his enemies? I'll die if I have to face that punishment alone!"

"I can't believe you still have the gall to call yourself our chief!"

Those were the people that were renowned for being the kindest among the beastmen, but at that moment they were busy trying to shift the blame onto each other. *Where'd all that supposed kindness go...? Well, I guess they* are *Shea's family.* The whole lot of them were worthless rabbits.

Hajime muttered just a single word.

"Yue."

"Okay." Yue stepped forward, then raised one of her hands. The Haulias' expressions all stiffened simultaneously.

"P-please wait, Yue-san! If you have to punish someone, punish Dad!"

"Ha ha ha, we'll be together forever!"

"Get the hell away from me!"

"Yue-dono, please leave us out of this and just discipline the chief!"

"I didn't do it! I didn't do it! The chief's the one who's at fault!"

Yue only smiled thinly in response, then muttered a single phrase.

"Storm Gust."

"Aaaaaaaaaaaaaaaaaaah!!!" The sky suddenly started raining bunny ears. Their screams could be heard throughout the entire forest. Though it was their own people who were being tortured, Ulfric and the others didn't seem the slightest bit angry. In fact, they were looking up at the sky in awe. Judging by their expressions, they too knew how pathetic the Haulia were.

The forest floor looked like the remnants of a battlefield. Scattered among the leaves were heaps of twitching bunny ears. Hajime mercilessly followed up with a barrage of rubber bullets, prompting the Haulia to their feet, tears streaming from their eyes.

Still somewhat nonplussed, Ulfric signaled to one of the tigermen, Gil. Gil sighed tiredly, then started guiding the group through the fog.

They walked in formation, with Hajime, Yue, Ulfric and the Haulias in the center, and the tigermen surrounding them in a defensive perimeter. An hour later, they still hadn't arrived at the city, and Hajime realized for the first time that Zam must have sent quite a fast runner for the elder to have arrived so quickly.

After another hour or so of walking, the fog started to grow thin. But only in a line directly in front of them, like a tunnel. The rest of their surroundings remained shrouded in dense mist. Upon closer inspection, Hajime realized that both sides of the path were marked by luminous blue crystals that had been embedded in the ground. It was almost as if those crystals were warding off the fog.

Ulfric noticed Hajime was eyeing the crystals, so he volunteered an explanation.

"Those are called verdren crystals. For some reason, they drive away both the fog and monsters. Both Verbergen and the surrounding villages are protected by these crystals. They work perfectly for the fog, but they're only somewhat effective at driving off monsters."

"I see. Makes sense. I mean, you'd probably all go crazy having to live in the fog all the time. Even if you know where you're going, you probably don't want to stay there."

While the forest may have been covered in fog, it seemed at least the villages within were spared such a fate. Considering they'd be spending the next ten days here, that was good news. Yue's eyes lit up happily, too. She clearly hadn't been thrilled by the idea of spending ten days in the fog either.

Finally, the group found themselves standing before a massive gate. Thick trunks interlocked together to form an arch, and the double doors enshrined within were also made of wood. In place of walls was a towering barrier of living trees, each one at least thirty meters tall. A very fitting marker for the border of the beastmen's country.

Gil gave a signal to the gate guard, and the massive doors slowly creaked open. A great number of people were staring down at Hajime's party from atop the branches of the trees. Everyone had been terrified to hear that a human would be allowed into their land. Had Ulfric not been there, a fight probably would have broken out. Perhaps the reason he'd come in person was precisely because he'd expected that kind of reaction.

Past the wall of trees, a new world spread out before Hajime.

Numerous massive trees dotted the landscape, a dwelling carved into each one. Warm lamplight poured out of the windows that had been cut into the trunks. Thick branches, wide enough for dozens of people to walk across abreast, linked the treetops together into one big aerial highway. Vines served as pulleys, allowing for huge elevators big enough to pull up carts. There were even wooden aqueducts, carrying water from tree to tree. And each of the trees was at least as tall as a twenty-story building, too.

Hajime and Yue stared in awe, their mouths hanging open at the fantastical scenery. After a few seconds, Ulfric cleared his throat to grab their attention. It seemed they had been so enraptured by the city that they'd forgotten to keep walking.

"Hoho! It seems our fair city of Verbergen is to your liking." Ulfric smiled warmly. All of the surrounding beastmen, even the Haulia, were all puffing their chests out proudly. Seeing how happy they were, Hajime gave his honest impression of the city.

"Yeah, this is the first time I've ever seen such an amazing city. Even the air smells wonderful. It really feels like you guys are one with nature."

"Yeah...it's really pretty."

The beastmen were all surprised at such honest praise. Happy and embarrassed at the same time, they averted their gaze, their ears and tails wagging happily. Hajime and Yue were unperturbed by the gazes of curiosity, fear, confusion, and hatred the residents sent their way, and continued enjoying the scenery as they walked through the city, led onward by Ulfric.

"...I see. So the reward for clearing the trials is ancient magic, and the gods have actually been deceiving us all along..."

Once they'd arrived at the hall Ulfric had prepared for them, Hajime and Yue had explained what they'd learned. Hajime had gone over the speech Oscar Orcus had made about the Liberators, the magic he'd inherited from the Age of the Gods, the fact that he was a human from another world, and that he was looking to conquer the labyrinths in the hopes of finding a spell that could take him home.

Ulfric hadn't seemed terribly surprised when he'd heard about the gods' true intentions. When Hajime had asked him why he seemed so calm, he had said, "This world isn't very kind to us beastmen, so what reason would we have to believe the gods are benevolent?" Whether the gods were raving lunatics or benign overlords didn't matter to the beastmen. After all, they'd be oppressed either way. As the Holy Church had no influence here, most beastmen weren't very religious either. If anything, they worshiped nature.

Once Hajime had finished his tale, Ulfric told him about the ancient law that had been passed down among the elders of Verbergen.

It was a very vague law that simply stated if anyone bearing a crest belonging to one of the Seven Great Labyrinths were to appear in the sea of trees, the beastmen were not to oppose that person regardless of who they were, and were to guide them wherever they wished to go, if they seemed nice.

The creator of the Haltina Woods labyrinth, Lyutilis Haltina, had told the first elder she'd found that she was a Liberator—though she hadn't explained what the Liberators were—and what her comrades' names were. This had been long before Verbergen came into existence, and so the knowledge was passed down through the ages. The reason she'd probably stressed not to oppose them was that she must have known the beastmen would be no match for anyone strong enough to clear a labyrinth. And the reason Ulfric had seemed so surprised when he'd seen Orcus's crest was because there was a stone tablet near the Grand Tree that had the seven Liberators' crests carved into it.

"So that's why you let me in..." After Ulfric's explanation, Hajime finally understood why he'd been invited to Verbergen. However, not all beastmen were privy to the knowledge Ulfric had, so there would probably be a need to explain his presence later.

Sometime during Hajime and Ulfric's conversation, a commotion began on the floors below. The two of them were on the highest floor of this particular tree, while Shea and the other Haulia were waiting down below. From the sounds of it, they'd gotten into an argument with someone. Hajime and Ulfric exchanged glances before standing up at the same time.

Downstairs, a bearman, tigerman, foxman, some kind of winged beastman, and some small dwarfish fur-covered beastman were all glaring angrily at the Haulia tribe. The Haulia were all huddled in a corner, with Cam desperately trying to protect Shea. Both of their cheeks were red and swollen, meaning they'd already been hit at least once.

As Hajime and Yue descended the last few steps, everyone turned to glare at them. The bearman was the first to speak.

"Damn you, Ulfric... What were you thinking, bringing a human here?! And these damn rabbits, too! You even allowed the cursed girl to step foot in our land... Depending on your answer, I might have to call for your execution at our next elders' meeting." The bearman was just barely restraining himself from rushing at them. Both his hands were balled into fists, and his arms were shivering with barely suppressed rage. *So most beastmen really do see humans as mortal enemies, then.* The situation was only exacerbated by the fact that Ulfric had invited the detested Haulia tribe as well. All of the other beastmen were glaring angrily at Ulfric, not just the bearman. However, Ulfric seemed completely unfazed by their display of anger.

"I simply abided by our ancient traditions. You all are elders of your various clans, so surely you must realize my reasons."

"What ancient traditions?! All that's nothing but bull! We've never once had any use for that ancient law since Verbergen's founding!"

"Then that'll make this a first. Calm yourselves. You all are elders here; you know you must abide by the laws. If we don't set an example as leaders of our people, then what use are any of our rules or traditions?"

"Are you trying to say that little brat really did get through a labyrinth?! That he's too strong for us to fight?!"

"That is correct." Ulfric spoke nonchalantly the entire time, as if he were simply commenting on the weather. The bearman's incredulous gaze shifted from Ulfric to Hajime.

Within Verbergen, all of the prominent powerful races elected one of their own to be their elder, and that individual represented the entire race in the elder council. The elder council met regularly to discuss the affairs of state, and laws and taxes were decided by a vote among them. They were, in effect, the rulers of the country. They also acted as the country's judges. Apparently, the members gathered here were all of the country's elders. However, not all of them were in agreement about the ancient laws.

Though Ulfric may have held the tradition in high regard, the other elders seemingly did not. Elves like Ulfric were known to live longer than most beastmen. From what Hajime remembered of the books he'd read, they usually lived to be around 200 on average. That would mean that Ulfric and the other elders' views were probably different because of the huge age gap between them. Most other beastmen only lived to be around 100.

All of the other elders couldn't stand the thought of a human and a pack of wandering criminals being allowed into their sanctuary.

"...Fine, why don't we test if he's really qualified, here and now?"

The bearman finally snapped and charged at Hajime. It was so sudden that no one else had any time to react. Even Ulfric hadn't expected him to charge, so his eyes went wide in surprise.

In an instant, the massive 2.5 meter lump of fat and muscle was bearing down on Hajime, one arm heading straight for his face.

The bearmen were known for their impressive stamina and overwhelming arm strength. And this particular bearman was the head of his clan. One swing of his arm was enough to fell a tree. Everyone but Yue and the Haulia thought Hajime was a goner for sure.

However, they all froze stiff in fear as they saw what happened next. Hajime lazily caught the bearman's paw with his prosthetic left arm.

"Pathetic. You call that a punch? But, well, you still came at me with the intent to kill. I hope you're prepared for what that means." Hajime strengthened his grip. There was a sharp cracking noise from the bearman's arm. Panic quickly overcame his shock, and the bearman desperately tried to free himself from Hajime's grasp.

"Gaaah! Let go!" He pulled with all his might, but Hajime, who barely came up to his chest, didn't budge an inch. In truth, Hajime had simply transmuted the metallic plates he'd put in his boots into spikes to keep him rooted, but the bearman didn't know that. To him, Hajime was as immovable as a boulder.

Hajime poured more mana into his left arm, strengthening his grip further.

"Ah?!" With another sharp crack, the bearman's arm snapped. However, he didn't cry out. He still had his pride as an elder to preserve. That didn't stop him from stiffening up in pain and surprise, though. Taking advantage of his immobility, Hajime drew his hand back. While the bearman was still off balance, Hajime ducked into his guard and threw a punch.

"Out of my sight." He activated his Steel Arms skill as he did so, and for good measure burned a blastrock cartridge embedded in his elbow to further add force to his blow. His fists were deadly as is, but at that point they were backed by the force of a gunpowder explosion.

His doubly empowered fist sunk mercilessly into the bearman's abdomen, sending him flying backward. The bearman wasn't even given enough time to scream as he crashed right through the tree wall and fell to the ground. Only when he hit the ground did the screaming finally start.

What Hajime had actually activated was the shotgun installed on his arm. However, the shotgun shells fired behind him. The reasoning was that he could use the recoil to empower his punches, and if he was fighting with Donner and Schlag, he could fire at enemies behind him without having to turn around. He'd used it for the punch empowering effect this time. Combined with Steel Arms, it made for quite a formidable weapon.

Everyone was at a complete loss for words. There was a clicking noise as Hajime expended the used cartridge. By default, there didn't have to be one, but he'd added it in as a fun gimmick. After that, he swept his murderous gaze over the rest of the elders.

"So? Are you all still my enemy?"

No one nodded. Hajime's actions had prevented the situation from becoming a bloodbath, and Ulfric managed to calm things down after that. The bearman had taken serious damage to his internal organs and fractured almost every bone in his body, but was still miraculously alive. They had to use copious amounts of rare and expensive healing medicine to keep him from succumbing to his wounds, though. And while he was going to recover, his fighting days were over. Once his condition was stabilized, the tigerman elder Zel; the winged beastman elder Mao; the foxman elder Lua; the moleman, or dwarven, elder Guze; and lastly, the elf elder Ulfric all sat down together with Hajime. Yue, Shea, and Cam were all sitting next to him, with the rest of the Haulia tribe cowering behind his back.

Aside from Ulfric, the elders were all clearly nervous. The bearman, Jin, had been one of their strongest fighters, but Hajime had dealt with him in an instant.

"So? What do you guys want with me? I just want to go to the Grand Tree. If you don't plan on getting in my way, I have no reason to fight you, but...if the beastmen aren't unified in their decision, I won't know who to kill and who to spare if it comes down to it. And that's just bad for you guys. I'm not so softhearted that I'll care about who I'm killing if someone comes at me."

The elders stiffened at Hajime's casual tone. They realized he was willing to go to war against the entire beastman race if he had to.

"You nearly kill one of our comrades, take that tone with us... and expect us to call you a friend?" Guze half-whispered, half-shouted those few words, his expression twisted in anguish.

"Hey now, that bear guy was the one who attacked first. I

was just defending myself. If he can't fight anymore because of it, that's hardly my fault."

"Y-you bastard! Jin... Jin was only thinking of what was best for his country!"

"And that makes it okay to try and kill a guy you just met?"

"Th-that's—but—"

"If anything, I'm the victim here. That bear dude started it. Aren't you elders supposed to be judges, too? Don't you think you should be a bit more impartial?"

Guze was probably a good friend of Jin's, which was why even if Hajime was correct, Guze still couldn't accept it. However, Hajime had no interest in the feelings of strangers.

"Guze, I understand how you feel, but just leave it at that. He is right, you know." Ulfric's rebuke hit Guze hard, and he sat back down, his face twisted with conflicting emotions. He sat there in sullen silence, still simmering with anger.

"It's certainly true the boy has one of the seven crests and the strength needed to clear a labyrinth. I'm willing to believe he fulfills the conditions."

The one who spoke was the foxman, Lua. His slit-like eyes regarded Hajime for a moment before he swept his gaze over to the other elders. Mao and Zel both voiced their agreement, though it was clear they each had their reservations. Representing all the elders, Ulfric handed down the final decision.

"Hajime Nagumo. We elders of Verbergen have decreed that you do indeed possess the qualifications spoken of in the ancient covenant. We will not oppose you...and we will implore everyone within our domain not to do so either. However..."

"No guarantees?"

"Indeed. As you are aware, most beastmen do not think too kindly of humans. If I may be frank, most of us hate you. I cannot guarantee that some of the more hot-blooded ones among us won't ignore our decision. Especially those belonging to Jin's clan. I highly doubt the bearmen will be willing to let go of their anger. Jin was a very popular leader, after all..."

"And?" Hajime's expression didn't change at all throughout Ulfric's explanation. It was clear from his gaze that he only did what he thought was necessary and would continue doing so moving forward. While Ulfric understood all of this, he too had a responsibility as the beastmen's elder and an unwavering will to match it.

"I would like to request that you do not kill those who attack you."

"...You want me to hold back against someone who's trying to kill me?"

"Precisely. With your strength, it should be an easy task, no?"

"If that bear guy was your strongest fighter, I'd say it's definitely possible. But honestly, I have no intention of holding back if my opponent's determined to turn it into a death match. I understand your feelings on the matter, but they have nothing to do with me. If you don't want your countrymen to die, I suggest you make sure they understand not to mess with me."

The fact that all enemies needed to be thoroughly eliminated was a value that the abyss had instilled in him quite effectively.

After all, there was no telling what consequences letting up on your opponent might have. A cornered rat will bare its fangs. There was always the possibility that holding back could get Hajime killed eventually. That was why he was unwilling to agree to Ulfric's request.

However, the tigerman, Zel, wasn't going to let Hajime refuse.

"Then I'm afraid we won't be able to guide you to the Grand Tree. Even the tradition says we have no obligation to help you if we don't like you." Hajime looked at him dubiously. From the start, he had been planning on letting the Haulia guide him. He didn't need to borrow help from Verbergen. Surely the elders realized that as well. However, Zel's next words revealed his true intentions.

"Don't think the Haulia will be able to help you. They're wanted criminals. They'll be judged according to the laws of Verbergen. I don't know what your agreement with them was, but you'll be parting ways with them here. That cursed demon child and the criminals who protected her have put all of Verbergen in danger. The council has already decided to execute them."

At Zel's words, Shea started trembling, tears welling up in her eyes. Cam and the others already looked like they were resigned to their fate. The fact that none of them were blaming her even now showed just how kindhearted they really were.

"Esteemed elders! I beg of you, please show mercy to my family at least! Please!"

"Shea, don't! We've already made our decision. None of this is your fault. We're not so heartless that we'd throw away our family to live. Every single one of us talked this over, and we're all prepared. There's no need for you to feel guilty about this."

"But...!"

Shea prostrated herself before the elders in her plea for mercy, but it seemed Zel had none to spare.

"The judgment has already been passed down. The Haulia will all be executed. Had you not deceived Verbergen, we would have settled for simply banishing the demon child, but it's too late, now."

Tears were streaming down Shea's face. Cam and the others tried to comfort her. *So their execution really was already set in stone.* None of the other elders spoke. It seemed they cared more about the threat Shea had posed to Verbergen than Shea's fate itself, which was why their sentence was so grave. In other words, the Haulia's kindness had only exacerbated the situation. How ironic.

"So there you have it. Your only other means of reaching the Grand Tree is gone. What do you plan on doing now? Test your luck and see if you can make it on your own?"

If you don't like it, then you'd better listen to our demands, or so the unsaid implication went. The other elders were all in agreement. However, Hajime didn't seem terribly perturbed by their ultimatum.

"Are you all stupid or what?"

"Wh-what did you just say?!" Zel's eyes nearly popped out of their sockets at Hajime's casual insult. Even Shea looked up at him in surprise. Yue already knew what he was thinking, so her expression didn't change.

"I already told you I don't give a damn about your circumstances. Trying to take these guys away from me is the same as getting in my way." Hajime glared down at the elders while placing a protective hand on Shea's head. Her body trembled at his touch, and she looked up at him with a tear-stained face.

"And I believe I've already shown you...what happens to people who get in my way."

"Hajime-san..."

Hajime was just trying to get a return on his investment and eliminate anything that got in the way of that. That was all, really. However, the fact that he was willing to declare war against all beastmen in the heart of Verbergen resonated with Shea, who was in the depths of despair.

"Are you truly serious?" Ulfric's sharp glare and stern expression made it clear that a lie would be met with harsh consequences.

"Of course." Still, Hajime didn't waver. His will was unshakeable. In this world, anyone who meant him harm or intended to get in his way would be slaughtered without mercy. That was what he had sworn back in the depths of the abyss.

"Even if we were to offer you guidance in their stead?" The decision to execute the Haulia was something that had been decided by the council of elders, which meant that if they caved into Hajime's threats and repealed it, it would ruin their reputation as a nation. Even if they'd lose the bargaining chip they'd been hoping to use to entice a promise of clemency for those who attacked Hajime, they couldn't afford to lose face by taking back their decision. That was why Ulfric had offered that compromise. However, Hajime made it clear that there was no room for negotiation.

"Don't make me repeat myself. The Haulia will be my guides."

"Why are you so insistent on having them do it? Anyone could take you to the Grand Tree." Annoyed at Ulfric, Hajime glanced back at Shea. He'd noticed her gaze a while back, so when he turned around their eyes met. Shea could feel her heartbeat quicken. She averted her gaze instantly, but the pounding of her heart didn't slow.

"Because I made a promise. I promised to protect them in return for guiding me."

"A promise? In that case, couldn't you consider it already fulfilled? You protected them not only from the monsters in the gorge, but also the imperial soldiers, correct? All that remains is to receive your reward, no? What difference does it make if we provide that reward or they do?"

"There's a difference. I promised I'd guarantee their safety until they took me where I wanted to go. Just because a better-looking deal showed up halfway doesn't mean I can just throw that promise away..." Hajime stopped halfway and looked over at Yue. She too was gazing at him and smiled slightly when their eyes met. He returned her smile and shrugged his shoulders before turning back to Ulfric and continuing coolly.

"It just wouldn't be cool to break my promise, you know?" Surprise attacks, bluffs, traps, cowardly tricks, the whole gamut. Hajime had no problem using any of them in battle. He was willing to use any means at his disposal in order to survive.

However, outside of a fight to the death, he still had principles he wanted to stick to. If he threw away even those, he'd have no humanity left. And he was still a man. He didn't want to cross that line in front of the very girl who'd saved him from falling that far in the first place. He wanted to stay someone she could be proud of. In short, he wanted to look cool in front of the girl he loved.

Seeing that he had no intention of backing down, Ulfric breathed a long sigh. The other elders all looked at each other, hoping someone might have a solution. Silence filled the room for a few moments before Ulfric brought out one last suggestion with an exhausted look on his face.

"Then let's just say they're your slaves. According to the laws of Verbergen, any who leave the sea of trees and do not return, or those who are captured as slaves, are considered dead. While we may stand a chance against humans in this fog-enshrouded forest, outside of it, their magic would tear us apart. Hence why those who get captured are considered dead and chasing after them is prohibited to prevent there from being more victims... If they're already dead, we can hardly execute them."

"Ulfric! You can't!" Sophistry was all it was, nothing more. The other elders, of course, weren't happy about that proposal. Zel had even gone so far as to protest.

"Zel. Surely you see that this boy isn't willing to back down, nor do we have the strength to force him to. If we try to execute the Haulia, he will fight us. As an elder...I cannot risk the sacrifices that decision would bring."

"But then how are we meant to set an example for the rest of our people?! If people discovered we caved to force and let this monster of a girl run free along with her demonic companions, what will they think of us? Our dignity will forever be stained!"

"But..."

Zel and Ulfric's argument continued, and the other elders began voicing their opinions as well. Before long it had turned into a shouting match. As expected, letting a potential threat run free and ignoring a verdict that had already been decided were not things they could easily swallow. It would set a dangerous precedent and forever taint the name of the council. Growing tired of their bickering, Hajime decided to butt in despite knowing he might make things worse.

"Umm, sorry to interrupt such a lively conversation, but don't you think worrying about this worthless rabbit now, after all this time, is kind of pointless?" Everyone fell silent at once. The elders all looked at Hajime in confusion. He rolled up his right sleeve, then started directly controlling his mana. Crimson veins rose to the surface of his exposed arm. He then activated Lightning Field to further illustrate his point, and sparks started running down his arm.

The elders all gazed in astonishment. When they saw him use magic without a circle or incantation, their jaws all dropped. They had thought Hajime's left arm had been some sort of artifact, and that was how he had defeated Jin.

"Just like her, I can control my mana directly and use

specialized magic only monsters are supposed to have. Oh, Yue can too, by the way. We're all basically monsters here. If having the same abilities as actual monsters is grounds for execution, then shouldn't you be trying to execute us as well? But wait, didn't your law say not to oppose anyone who possessed the right qualifications, no matter who they were? No matter what you do, you're going to have to break one of your laws. So being so hung up over her seems kind of pointless to me." It took a few moments for the elders to recover from their shock, but when they finally did, they started whispering furiously to each other. Eventually they reached a decision, and Ulfric, their representative, delivered it with an increasingly tired sigh.

"Haaah... By the rule of the council, the cursed child Shea Haulia will be considered a relative of the cursed child Hajime Nagumo. As Hajime has shown he possesses the qualifications spoken of in our ancient laws, we shall not oppose his passage. However, he will be barred from Verbergen and its surrounding settlements. Henceforth, anyone who takes any action against Hajime or his kin does so at their own risk, without the blessing or protection of Verbergen... That is all. Is this good enough?"

"Yeah, that's fine. Like I said, all I care about is getting to the Grand Tree and having these guys guide me, so no problems here."

"...I see. Very well. Could I kindly ask you to leave, then? It's a shame we cannot give a more proper welcome to the first person to ever fulfill the ancient pact, but..."

"Don't worry about it. I'm aware I've caused you guys a great deal of trouble because of my own selfishness. I'm just glad you didn't choose to do anything stupid, honestly."

Ulfric smiled bitterly. The other elders all looked equally unhappy and exhausted. It wasn't so much that they bore a grudge, or even hated Hajime—they just wanted him gone and out of their hair. He shrugged his shoulders helplessly and signaled Yue and the others to get up.

Yue slowly rose to her feet. He couldn't tell if she hadn't had any interest in their conversation from the beginning or if she simply hadn't felt like voicing her opinion. However, Shea and the rest of the Haulia were still seated. It seemed the shock of what had happened had been so great that they still hadn't registered the fact that they'd been saved. They had come ready to die, and now they'd just been exiled. Most of them still weren't really sure it was okay for them to just leave.

"Hey, how long are you going to sit there daydreaming? Get up, we're going." The rabbitmen all hurriedly got to their feet and tottered after Hajime at those words. Ulfric and the others tagged along as well, saying they would escort him to the gate.

As they were walking back, Shea timidly walked up to Hajime and asked him a question.

"U-umm, are we...really not going to be executed?"

"Did you not listen to a word we said?"

"N-no, I was listening, but...we got out of it so easily that it still doesn't feel real... I feel like I'm going to wake up at any minute now and find out this was all just a dream..." The other Haulia all had the same bewildered expression on their faces. Hajime supposed that was just how absolute the elder's judgment usually was for the beastmen. Yue suddenly chimed in, seeing that Shea still didn't know what to do with her feelings.

"...Just be happy."

"Yue-san?"

"Hajime saved you guys. That's the simple truth. Why not just be happy about it?"

"......" Mulling over Yue's words, Shea glanced up at Hajime. He just shrugged his shoulders without turning back.

"I mean, that was part of the promise."

"Ah..."

Shea's shoulders trembled. In return for guiding him through the sea of trees, Hajime promised to protect her and her family. She had ground herself to the bone, almost literally, in order to wring that promise out of him.

Though she had seen a future where he was protecting them, there was no guarantee that future would come to pass. Shea's choices constantly affected the futures she saw. That was why she had been so desperate to get his cooperation—even though she had nothing to offer in return, and her potential savior was a human, a member of the race that discriminated against beastmen. All she had to negotiate with was her body and her special magic. When he had ignored both of those things, she had really wanted to cry, but she still desperately tried to squeeze a promise out of him. And so, on their way to save her family, she realized that he wasn't the kind of person that would go back on his word. Part of her conviction came from the fact that he never discriminated against her, a rabbit girl.

However, all of that had been based on her feelings; she had never had a concrete reason to believe Hajime would stick to his promise. That was why she had still been a little worried deep inside. It was why she tried to say things like "He's not a guy who'll go back on his word!" with confidence, and extract promises that he'd be willing to fight against fellow humans. Despite her initial fear, she had actually been relieved when he'd killed those imperial soldiers without hesitation.

Still, when they'd been negotiating with the elders, Shea's fears that he would abandon them had returned. The circumstances were completely different. What he had done was the same as threatening war to the Emperor of Hoelscher's face. And yet, he had kept his promise without backing down at all. Regardless of whether he'd done it for his own sake or not, Yue was right. He'd saved her and her family.

Just thinking about it made her heartbeat quicken once more. She could feel her face flush, and an indescribable feeling welled up within her. She wasn't sure if it was happiness because her family had been saved, or...

Thinking about it any harder would have made her brain overheat, so she decided to stop worrying about it and just be happy like Yue told her to. Her newfound emotions were clamoring to be expressed, so Shea did so the only way she knew how. By hugging Hajime as hard as she could, of course.

"Hajime-saaan! Thank you so muuuuuch!"

"Oof. Where'd that come from?"

"Grr..."

With tears in her eyes again, Shea buried her face into Hajime's shoulder, clinging to him with inhuman strength. There was a beaming smile on her face, and her cheeks were a bright red.

Yue growled unhappily, but then she thought better of kicking Shea off. Instead, she simply took Hajime's hand in hers.

As they watched Shea explode with joy, the reality that they'd been saved finally hit the other Haulia, and they all began embracing each other, reveling in everyone's delight. The elders looked on awkwardly, unsure how to feel. There were plenty of hateful and angry gazes that watched them go, though.

Hajime smiled bitterly as he realized his troubles in the Haltina Woods were just beginning.

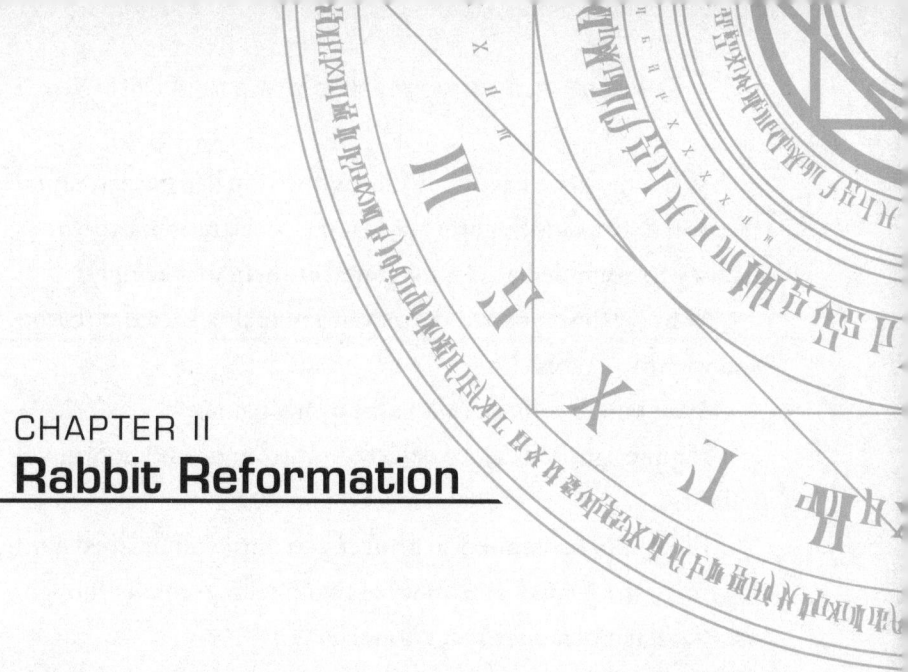

CHAPTER II
Rabbit Reformation

"**N**OW THEN, I'm thinking I need to teach you guys how to fight." After leaving Verbergen, Hajime and the others had set up a temporary base near the outskirts of the Grand Tree. Though perhaps "base" was giving them too much credit. All Hajime had done was steal... no, *take* some verdren crystals from the path and scatter them around their encampment. Most of the rabbitmen stared blankly at Hajime. They were sitting down on stumps and boulders, taking a short break.

"U-umm, Hajime-san. By teaching us how to fight, do you mean..." Shea asked hesitantly, voicing the question her entire tribe had.

"I mean exactly that. We're stuck here for the next ten days anyway, right? Might as well do something useful in that time, don't you think? It's high time you spineless, gutless, cowardly rabbits learned how to hold your own in a fight."

"Wh-why do we have to...?" Shea's question had been a natural reaction to the sudden nature of Hajime's declaration. Everyone's rabbit ears trembled as Hajime glared at them menacingly.

"Why? Why'd you think to even ask such a stupid question, you worthless rabbit?"

"Aww, you're still not calling me by my name..."

Hajime ignored Shea's dejected mutterings and continued talking.

"Listen up, I promised to protect you until you finished guiding me to the Grand Tree. But have you guys given any thought to what'll happen once that's done?"

The Haulia all exchanged glances and shook their heads hesitantly. Cam even had a worried expression on his face. Though they'd had this nagging worry at the back of their minds, the sequence of insane events they'd been thrown into one after another had forced that worry away. Or maybe they just hadn't considered it at all; who really knew?

"Just as I thought, you haven't thought about it at all. Though even if you had, it's not like you'd have an answer for me. You guys are weak. First sign of danger and your only thought is to run. And now you don't even have the sanctuary of Verbergen to protect you. So basically, you guys are screwed as soon as I'm gone."

"......"

Glum expressions settled on the Haulia's faces when they realized Hajime's words hit the mark. They'd been rocked by his stunning statement.

"You have nowhere to run to, nowhere to hide, and soon you'll have no one to protect you. But monsters and humans won't stop attacking you out of pity, you know? At this rate, you're all doomed to die eventually. Are you all really okay with that? Being killed off just because you're weak, I mean. You guys were lucky to survive this long, and now you're going to throw those lives away? Well?"

No one said a word as a grim atmosphere fell over the clearing. Finally, someone muttered quietly.

"Of course we're not okay with it." Those words broke the rest of them out of their stupor, and everyone looked up at Hajime. Even Shea's gaze was filled with determination. Hajime nodded approvingly, and memories of his old powerless self flashed through his mind as he spoke.

"That's right. You're not okay with it. But what can you do? The answer's simple. Get stronger. Tear down anything that gets in your way and fight for your right to survive."

"...But we're rabbitmen. We're not like tigermen or bearmen who have strong bodies, or like the winged races or dwarves that have special traits they can use to escape trouble. We're just..."

The fact that rabbitmen were weak only made them despair even more at Hajime's words. They were weak, so how could they possibly ever hope to fight? No matter how much they struggled, they'd never become strong like Hajime. But Hajime just scoffed at them.

"You know, in the past, my comrades called me worthless too."

"Huh?"

"Worthless. Weak. Useless. Both my stats and my skills were painfully mediocre. I was the weakest person in my group.

Nothing more than dead weight. That's why my comrades all looked down on me. And it was all true, too."

Everyone's jaw dropped open in shock at Hajime's confession. They couldn't believe that Hajime, the boy who'd beaten a bearman elder like it was nothing and taken down scores of ferocious monsters in the Reisen Gorge, had ever been called worthless or weak.

"But when I fell into the depths of hell, I did everything in my power to get stronger. It wasn't about whether I could or couldn't do it. If I didn't, I'd die. I fought like my life depended on it, because it did. And then, before I knew it, I was like this." He spoke casually, but the unbelievable contents of his tale sent a shiver down the Haulia's spines.

If he'd had average stats for a human, then he had to have been even weaker than the rabbitmen. But despite that, he'd fought against monsters far stronger than the enemies they'd been overwhelmed by in Reisen Gorge. Still, it wasn't his strength or the fact that he'd survived that awed them the most. It was his strength of mind that had let him face such monstrous foes without flinching. When they'd been driven to a corner, the Haulia had meekly accepted their demise. Just as they'd meekly accepted the elders' decision.

"You guys are like how I was in the past. But don't worry. So long as I'm bound by this promise, I'll do what I can to save you from despair. If you tell me there's no way you can do it, then that's fine, too. You'll just die when your time's up. I won't come save you once our contract is finished. You can spend the rest of your short lives bemoaning your weakness for all I care."

So what'll it be? Hajime's eyes seemed to say. The Haulia didn't answer immediately. Or rather, they weren't able to.

They'd realized their only path to survival was to get stronger. And that Hajime wasn't protecting them out of some noble sense of justice. He'd leave them without a second thought once their end of the bargain was complete. However, the very idea of fighting was foreign to the peace-loving, gentle rabbitmen. Accepting Hajime's suggestion would mean stepping into uncharted territory. It would probably take an event as radical as what happened to Hajime to fundamentally change their nature.

And so, they simply all looked at each other silently. However, Shea alone stood up resolutely. It seemed she'd made her decision long ago.

"I'll do it. Please, teach me how to fight! I'm tired of being weak!" She shouted so loudly that her voice echoed throughout the entire forest. Everyone present could see that she was filled with determination. Of course, even Shea hated fighting. It was scary, it hurt, but more than anything, she hated hurting others.

Still, it was undeniably her fault that her family was in this mess, and she hated the thought of causing even more of her family's deaths. On top of that, there was one other reason Shea wanted so desperately to fight against her nature and grow stronger.

Shea gazed unwaveringly at Hajime. Cam and the others watched her in amazement, but after a while, their awe gave way to determination, and they too began standing up. Not just the men, either. The women and children as well. When Cam saw that everyone was standing up, he stepped forward as his tribe's representative and addressed Hajime.

"Hajime-dono...please teach us all you can." A concise request. But each word was backed by an ironclad will. The will to resist the unfairness of this world.

"All right. You guys better prepare yourselves. How strong you'll become is all up to you. I'm just here to enable you guys. If you want to give up halfway, then I won't try and coddle you to keep you here. We've only got ten days, so I'm going to be working you to the bone. Whether you live or die will depend on how strong you get." Everyone nodded grimly. No one was going to back down now.

Before their training began, Hajime first pulled out equipment he'd made to practice his transmutation from his Treasure Trove and passed it out to them. In addition to the knives he'd passed out earlier, everyone got their own curved shortsword, similar to a Japanese kodachi. Those swords were all spares Hajime had made to practice his precision transmuting, which meant their edges were all wickedly sharp. And because they were made of taur stone, they were also quite sturdy. Despite how slender the blades were, they wouldn't break easily.

Once everyone had been armed, Hajime began teaching them the fundamentals of combat. Of course, Hajime was no martial artist. What little he knew of swordfighting came from games and manga, and it certainly wasn't nearly enough to teach anyone else. So what he taught them were not techniques, but the movements he'd learned in the depths of hell that helped him counter monsters. He passed down all the knowledge he'd picked up and found suitable monsters for them to use as live practice. The Haulia excelled in stealth and scouting. In order to capitalize on that, Hajime taught them how to use surprise attacks and pack tactics.

Yue had taken a special liking to Shea and was teaching her more about how to use magic. Though she was a beastman, Shea had mana and could control it directly, so with the right knowledge, she'd be able to use magic. She wouldn't need to chant thanks to her ability, but she'd still need a magic circle, since she didn't innately possess the skills for it. Occasional screams could be heard from beyond the fog, meaning Shea's training was going well.

However, around two days after they'd begun their training, Hajime was angrily watching the Haulia's practice. As they'd promised, they were trying to fight their pacifistic nature and learn how to fight properly. They'd even managed to beat some monsters, though they'd sustained injuries. But... *Snnnrk.* There was a wet noise as one of Hajime's special short swords sunk into a monster's flank.

"Aaah, please forgive such a sinful act." The rabbitman who'd killed the monster gently embraced its dead form. In fact, he looked like a father who'd been forced to kill his son.

Thud! Another monster fell to the ground.

"I'm so sorry! I'm so sorry! I had no choice!" A Haulia girl trembled uncontrollably as she cut the head off her quarry. It looked like she'd just accidentally killed her lover.

Snap! On the verge of death, one of the remaining monsters used the last of its strength to fire a projectile at Cam. It flung him backward, but instead of cursing he just lay on the ground and muttered his last will.

"Heh, so this is my punishment for baring my fangs at someone. It's no more than I deserve..." Tears welled up in the other Haulia's eyes, and they all looked at him pitifully.

"Chief, please don't say that! We all share the same sin!"

"Exactly! Even if we have to be judged for our crimes one day, that day isn't now! Get back up, Chief!"

"We can no longer turn back, so let's at least see how far this road can take us, Chief."

"Y-you guys... You're right. We can't stop here. We must overcome the death of this tiny rat monster and continue onward!"

"Chief!"

They were having a rather heartwarming moment. Unable to take it any longer, Hajime finally butt in. "Gaaah! You guys are so annoying! Quit getting so emotional after every monster you kill! Seriously, what the hell?! Are you guys just pulling my leg?! This looks like it came out of a crappy soap opera! You don't have to make a scene every goddamn time—just kill it silently! And quickly, too! Also, stop humanizing the things you kill—it's creepy!"

Hajime knew they were trying their best, but he hated how they had to make such a big deal out of every monster they killed. This had happened multiple times over the past two days, and Hajime had calmly tried to point it out every time. However, they showed no sign of fixing their habits, so Hajime finally snapped.

They all flinched in the face of Hajime's wrath, but they still mumbled excuses like "Easy for you to say..." or "But even if it is a monster, I still feel bad for it..." over and over again.

Veins bulged on Hajime's forehead. One of the Haulia boys stepped forward to try and calm Hajime down. He was the one Hajime had saved from being eaten back in Reisen Gorge, and he'd taken quite a liking to Hajime. However, just as he was about to take another step forward, he suddenly jumped back. Confused, Hajime asked him a question.

"Huh? What happened?"

The boy gently patted down the soles of his feet before replying.

"Oh, you see... I was about to step on that flower there... Phew, good thing I noticed in time. Might've crushed it if I didn't. It's so pretty. Man, it'd have been such a waste to kill it." Hajime's expression stiffened.

"A-a flower?"

"Yep! You know, I love flowers. And there's so many around here that it was pretty hard to not step on any while we were training." He grinned happily at Hajime. The other Haulia all gazed proudly at him, too. Slowly, Hajime lowered his head. His white hair covered his face.

"...Are you telling me the reason you all jumped around randomly sometimes...was just because you were worried about the flowers?" He spoke softly, his voice barely a whisper. As Hajime had mentioned, the Haulia had oftentimes jumped in strange directions at odd intervals during their training. It had been bothering him for a while, but he'd thought it was just something they did to make their next action smoother, to better finish off their enemies.

"Oh no, of course not. We would never..."

"Ha ha, yeah, who would do that?" Hajime said, clearly relieved.

Cam smiled awkwardly, and Hajime's expression finally began to relax a little. However...

"Naturally we wouldn't only be wary of flowers. We have to be careful not to crush the bugs, either. They're the ones that come out of nowhere, so they're much harder to watch out for. Though we've managed to avoid stepping on them so far."

Hajime's jaw dropped at that. He began swaying back and forth, like a ghost. Worried that they might have said something wrong, the Haulia all glanced uneasily at each other. Still swaying slightly, Hajime walked up to the boy, then burst out into a beaming smile. The boy smiled back.

Then, still smiling...Hajime crushed the flower underfoot. He didn't just step on it, he ground his heels deep into it.

The boy watched on blankly. Finally, Hajime raised his foot. All that remained of what had once been a pretty flower was a few scattered petals and a stem that'd been stamped into the ground.

"Th-the flower!" The boy's despairing wail echoed throughout the sea of trees. Shocked, the Haulia all gazed at Hajime. He turned to face them, both the beaming smile and popping vein still present on his face.

"All right, I get it. I finally get just how soft you all are. This is my fault. I misjudged your race. Ha ha, I can't believe you'd actually worry about flowers and bugs when you're in a life-and-death struggle... Your problem is far more fundamental than a lack of combat ability or practice fighting actual enemies. I should have realized this sooner. I can't believe I was so naive... Ha ha ha."

"Hajime-dono?"

Hajime's smile had taken on a ghastly appearance, and Cam and the others slowly began backing away. Instead of a reply... *Bang!* He fired Donner. Cam was flung a short distance through the air before he crashed to the ground with a resounding thud. The rubber bullet that had slammed into his forehead fell off him seconds later with a soft plop. Only the wind stirred in the silence that followed. Hajime slowly walked up to Cam, who had been knocked unconscious, and fired another bullet at his stomach.

"Hauugh!" Cam let out something that was a cross between a cough and a scream as he woke up and blinked back tears as he looked at Hajime. There was something absurdly surreal about an old man with rabbit ears sitting up in a pose Hajime had often seen girls do in anime, but he put that aside for the moment.

"All right, you worthless little shits. If you don't want your heads blown off, you better start fighting these monsters like your lives depend on it! Don't you dare worry about the flowers or the bugs or any of that crap! I'll make you regret it if you do! Now hurry up and get to killing, you maggots!" The Haulia all stiffened in fear at his exceptionally abusive language. But as exasperated as he was, he didn't even wait for their reply before firing Donner again.

Bang! Bang! Bang! Bang! Bang! Bang! They scattered like the four winds, tripping over themselves to escape Hajime's wrath. All except for the little boy, who clung desperately to Hajime's leg.

"Hajime nii-chan! Why are you doing this?! What happened to you?!"

A dangerous light glinted in his eyes as he glared down at the boy. Hajime looked around, trying to spot all of the nearby flowers. Silently, he began shooting at all of them. One after another they died. The boy screamed.

"Why?! Why are you doing this?! Stop it, Hajime nii-chan!"

"Shut it, brat. Get it yet? The longer you sit here crying, the more flowers die. Your tender love and care won't save them. They'll all be killed, and you'll just be sitting here with tears in your eyes. If you don't like it, then get out there and kill some monsters!"

To emphasize his point, Hajime shot a few more flowers. Still crying, the boy ran off into the fog.

For a while after, screams intermingled with the howls of monsters as the Haulia endeavored to avoid Hajime's wrath. He had to be this hard on them, or else he'd never change the rabbitmen's overly pacifistic nature. Right now, it was more important for them to learn the right mindset than actual combat techniques. Though his Spartan-style techniques were starting to resemble Sgt. Hartman from *Full Metal Jacket*... And thus, ten days passed under Hajime's near-brainwashing as he rewired their brains for combat. As their training continued into the final day, somewhere beyond the fog, there was one other member of the Haulia who was finishing up as well.

Boom! Bang! Snap! Crackle! Pop! Bam! Thunderous sounds echoed throughout the trees. The area looked like a war zone. Massive trees with thick trunks lay strewn about like reed stalks, some charred, others frozen, others just twisted horrifically, and huge craters dotted the ground as if a meteor shower had struck the earth.

Two girls had been responsible for all of this destruction. And said destruction was still continuing.

"Teyaaaaaah!" There was a spirited yell, and suddenly a tree at least one meter in diameter flew through the air. It soared toward its target at tremendous speed, fast enough that a casual observer might miss that it was bent at the middle. Velocity and mass granted a deadly amount of force to the tree, and it obliterated any obstacles in its path forward.

"Crimson Javelin." This nigh unstoppable force was met with a flaming spear that burned all it touched to ash. Despite the significant mass it possessed, the tree was burned to ash almost instantly. For a moment, it was converted into a blazing fireball— before the last of the wood finally burned away and the flames vanished.

"It's not over yet!" The impact of the Crimson Javelin and the huge tree created shock waves large enough to blow away the fog for a few seconds. In that brief window of time, a faint silhouette could be seen dashing through the woods. An instant later, another log hurtled down from the heavens like a meteor. However, its intended target backstepped in time to avoid the thunderous impact while preparing another flaming spear.

But before she could unleash it, the silhouette ran up to the tree trunk impaled into the ground and gave it an earth-shattering kick. The force of it blew the tree apart, and splinters of wood shot toward the girl with unimaginable speed.

"Ah! Blazing Barrier." The barrage of splinters was cut short by a flaming wall that suddenly appeared in midair. Not a single sliver of wood made it through to her. However...

"Now I've got you!"

"Ah!"

The time it had taken her to cast that spell had been enough for the shadow to get behind her. The girl who'd kicked the tree had hidden her presence right after, and then she had used the fog to slip behind her quarry. She held in her hands a massive hammer that must have weighed more than the girl herself, but she swung it down with the ease one might swing a flyswatter.

"Wind Wall." The hammer hit the ground with tremendous force. Stone pellets flew in every direction as the rock below was pulverized. However, this barrage of stone was deflected by the barrier of wind the other girl had erected. Additionally, she used the swirling eddies to whisk herself to a safe distance. The girl with the hammer stiffened momentarily—the consequence of using such a huge skill—and her opponent took advantage of that opening.

"Crystal Coffin."

"Fweh?! W-wait—" Realizing her folly, she quickly tried to call for a ceasefire, but naturally her opponent wasn't going to listen. Thinking quickly, she dropped her hammer and tried to jump back, but the ice magic had already frozen her feet and was crawling up her legs... Before long, everything but her head was encased in a tomb of ice.

"I-It's so cold! Please let me out... Yue-saaan."

"...I win."

Of course, the two girls that had been fighting so ferociously were Yue and Shea. After their ten harsh days of training, Shea's final challenge had been to fight a mock battle against Yue. Her conditions for passing had been to land even a single scratch on Yue. The end result being...

"Waaah... I didn't—wait, right there! There on your cheek! There's a scratch, Yue-san! My attack hit you! Aha ha, I really did it! I won!"

There was indeed a small scratch on Yue's cheek. One of the pieces of gravel must have gotten past Yue's defenses and grazed her. It was barely even noticeable, but a win was a win. Shea had cleared her trial.

She smiled triumphantly as she pointed at Yue's cheek. Snot was dribbling out of her nose from how cold she felt, but her smug smile stayed plastered to her face. Her rabbit ears were twitching happily, too. It was only natural. Not only did this signify her graduation from training, but a very important promise she'd made with Yue had been riding on her victory.

Though Yue was not very keen on seeing it fulfilled. Thus—

"...I don't know what you're talking about." Thanks to the fact that her automatic regeneration healed the scratch almost instantly, Yue was able to play dumb. Pouting, Yue turned away as she spoke.

"Wha—?! You cheater! I saw it... I mean, it's gone now, but still! I know it was there! Quit playing dumb, you meanie! And hurry up and get me out of this! It keeps getting colder and colder... Huh, I'm starting to feel a little sleepy, too..." Shea's head started drooping and more snot dribbled out of her nose. She might've died from the cold if that kept up. Reluctantly, with a big sigh, Yue dispelled the magic she had cast.

"Achoo! Achoo! Waah, that was cold. Think I nearly crossed over to the other side there." Shea sneezed cutely a few times before blowing her nose on some nearby leaves. Once she was done, she looked back at Yue with a serious expression. Noticing her gaze, Yue's own expression turned steadily more sour. Enough that her poker face actually crumbled, in fact.

"Yue-san, I won."

"...Yeah."

"You promised, remember?"

"...Yeah."

"That if I hit you even once in these ten days...you'd let me join you guys on your journey. That was the promise, right?"

"...Yeah."

"Or at the very least that you'd try and help me convince Hajime-san."

"...I wonder what's for dinner today."

"Hey! Don't try and change the subject! And if you're going to do it, you could at least be a little less obvious about it! Besides, you only ever drink Hajime-san's blood for food, don't you?! Why do you suddenly care about dinner?! You better help me, okay?! Because if you say we should do something, Hajime-san almost always says yes!"

Yue was starting to get annoyed by Shea's incessant badgering. But as Shea had said, Yue had made a promise. If Shea managed to land a single blow on her, no matter how glancing it was, it would count. And Yue would allow Shea to accompany them on their travels. On top of that, she'd help try and convince Hajime together with Shea to get him to consent.

Currently, Shea's greatest wish was to travel together with those two. Half of it was because she didn't want to burden her family any longer, but the other half was just because she wanted to spend more time with Hajime and Yue.

However, she knew that no matter how she asked she'd just be coldly turned down. That much was clear from their attitude. That was why she'd come up with the idea of having Yue make that promise.

Shea had realized how soft Hajime was on Yue and had decided to weasel past his defenses using her as a weapon. More than anything, Shea was also a girl. She knew exactly how Yue felt about Hajime. After all, she felt the exact same way. Naturally, that meant the reverse had to be true, too. Yue must have realized how Shea felt about Hajime, and chances were she probably wasn't happy about it. Hence why Shea needed Yue to accept her first, before anything else could happen.

She had no intention of stealing Hajime away from Yue. The thought hadn't even crossed her mind, honestly. Even leaving Hajime's feelings aside, Shea really did respect Yue, and wanted to get closer to her. Her feelings were most likely influenced by the fact that Yue and Hajime were the only "comrades" she had ever found. Put simply, Shea just wanted to be friends with them. That way she could be close to the man she loved, and the girl who also loved the man she loved. That was the future she dreamed of.

The real question was why Yue consented to making such a promise. There was nothing in it for her. Something like twenty percent of it was just because she felt some sympathy for Shea. When she had first heard Shea's story at the bottom of Reisen Gorge, she had initially thought that Shea had been far more blessed than she had been. But even then, she couldn't help but feel like Shea really was a "comrade." And that faint feeling of camaraderie had led Yue to spoil Shea just a bit.

The remaining eighty percent was...simply because she was stubborn. Shea had taken advantage of that to lure Yue into making the promise. She had framed it like this: "If you really think I'm just in the way, then force me out. If you can't, then that just proves I deserve to be with Hajime-san." Shea had hoped to goad Yue into agreeing by using her feelings for Hajime. Had it been any girl other than Shea, Yue wouldn't have cared. But, however slightly, Yue had still accepted Shea as a comrade. And when she'd seen how zealous Shea had been in her training, showing just how strong her feelings were, Yue couldn't back down. As a result, the promise had been made, and Shea had won.

"...Haaah. Fine. I'll keep my promise."

"Really?! No taking it back now! You're going to have to help me!"

"...Okay."

"You still don't sound all that convincing, but...you'll really help me, right?"

"...So annoying." Grudgingly, ever so grudgingly, Yue conceded the win to Shea. Shea was still a little worried about Yue's reply, but from the looks of it, Yue was just like Hajime in that she would never go back on her word.

It was nearly time for Hajime to finish training the other Haulia as well. Shea, who was smiling happily, and Yue, who was frowning unhappily, both made their way over to where Hajime was.

They found Hajime leaning against a nearby tree, his arms folded and his eyes closed. When he sensed their presence, he opened his eyes and turned to look at them. He found it curious that they were wearing completely opposite expressions, and he raised a hand to them in greeting.

"Yo. How'd it go? Did you two finish your duel or whatever?" Hajime knew they had some kind of bet riding on a match of some sort. It would be odd if he didn't, as he was the one who had crafted Shea's hammer. He still remembered the night Shea had come up to him, begging him to make her a weapon that could help her defeat Yue. Yue herself had no objections to it, and all they would tell Hajime when he asked was that there was a bet of some kind they'd made. He'd figured even with a strong weapon

Yue would have no problem winning, so he'd made the hammer for Shea.

After all, nine times out of ten, Yue would've won. Hajime had seen just how strong Yue was back down in the abyss. Even if she had the same ability to manipulate her mana freely, Shea had lived a peaceful life thus far.

However, judging from their expressions, it seemed to Hajime that his guess had been off the mark. He internally marveled at the fact that Shea had been able to win. Still beaming, Shea started talking to Hajime.

"Hajime-san, Hajime-san! Listen to this! I finally beat Yue-san! It was amazing! Man, I wish I could have shown you how cool I was! When Yue-san found out she'd lost, she—gwaah?!" With sweeping gestures, she started excitedly recounting the details of her fight. Annoyed by how Shea was getting carried away, Yue jumped up and delivered a slap so powerful that it sent Shea flying through the air. She fell to the ground with a thud and lay there twitching awkwardly. Yue harrumphed unhappily and turned her back to Shea, while Hajime grinned knowingly before turning back to Yue.

"So? How'd it go?" He was more interested in the contents of the match than its outcome. Frankly speaking, he found it hard to believe Shea could ever have beaten Yue. That was why he wanted to hear Yue's appraisal of her. Yue's expression clearly implied that she didn't want to talk about it, but she answered reluctantly nonetheless.

"...Her aptitude for magic is the same as yours."

"Now that's a surprise. What a waste, considering her abilities... So? That can't be all, can it? After all, she's able to use that massive hammer."

"Yeah. She's really good at body strengthening. Insanely good, even. She's a monster in her own right."

"...Wow. How strong compared to us?"

Hajime narrowed his eyes in curiosity. Yue's assessment of Shea was a lot higher than he'd expected. And her sour expression answered Hajime's question far better than any words could have. After a moment of thinking about it, Yue met Hajime's gaze and gave him a more concrete answer.

"Maybe close to sixty percent of your strength, Hajime... When you're not using Limit Break, anyway."

"Seriously? Is that the strongest she can make herself?"

"Yeah... For now, anyway. She could get stronger with more training."

"Wow. That is pretty crazy."

Though he didn't show it, Hajime was shocked at how monstrous Shea's strength was. He looked down at the monster in question.

Sixty percent of his strength without Limit Break still meant that all of Shea's stats could easily clear 6,000. That was more than 1.5 times the stats of an average hero using Limit Break. Calling her strength monstrous was no understatement. No wonder she'd been able to land a hit on Yue. *You'd never be able to guess it with how she looks now, though.* Hajime thought, as he watched tears well up in Shea's eyes as she cradled her cheek.

Half-dumbfounded, half-amazed, he watched as she finally noticed his gaze, stood up, and walked over while struggling to keep her emotions in check.

A few feet away from him, she straightened her back and squared her shoulders. Her blue-white hair was fluttering in the wind, and her rabbit ears were standing straight up. This was going to be the most important request of her life. Or perhaps...*confession* would be the better word for it. Trembling, her expression stiff, she nevertheless took a few more determined steps forward. Finally, she looked him straight in the eyes, and Hajime saw the resolve burning within her own.

"Hajime-san. Please let me accompany you on your journey. Please!"

"No."

"Just like that?!"

Considering the atmosphere, Shea had expected him to at least ponder her request a bit before replying. She opened her eyes wide in surprise at his sudden response. Hajime just looked down at her with an expression that all but screamed "where the hell did that come from?"

Shock gave way to anger. *You could at least take my request a little more seriously!*

"Y-you're so cruel, Hajime-san. I was being so serious, and you said no just like that..."

"Didn't look all that serious to me. Besides, what are you going to do about Cam and the others? You can't expect me to take them all with me."

"N-no, that's not it! I meant just me! I asked you before too, remember? Back then you said me not wanting to burden my family wasn't a good enough reason to take me, but now..."

"But now what?"

Shea fidgeted awkwardly. Her fingers trembled and a faint blush crept up her cheeks. How sly. She truly was a master of her craft. Unfortunately for her, Hajime just looked at her suspiciously. Next to him, Yue was glaring angrily at her.

"But now...I'm asking to go with you because I want to, so..."

"Huh? Why do you want to come with us? You won't even be a burden to your family anymore with how strong you've gotten. Hell, you could probably take on any kind of enemy that shows up on the surface."

"I-I know, but..."

"......" She fidgeted silently for a few minutes before Hajime finally grew impatient and drew Donner. Realizing she had to say something soon, Shea quickly gathered her courage and opened her mouth, deciding to let her feelings do the talking for her.

"I want to stay with you, Hajime-san! Becaushe I like you!"

"You what?"

Crap, I bit my tongue! Flustered, Shea tried to compose herself, while Hajime just looked on in complete shock. It was almost as if he couldn't believe what he'd just heard. Eventually, the gears in his brain started turning again and he parsed her words.

"Wait, wait... wait. This doesn't make any sense. Where'd I even trigger any of your flags? I mean, even I know I've been pretty mean to you this whole time... Hold on, don't tell me you're into that?"

Though he thought his conjecture couldn't possibly be true, he still took a step back just in case. Naturally, Shea denied his accusations.

"How dare you call me a pervert! I'm nothing like that! And if even you've realized you're being mean, don't you think you could stand to be a little nicer to me?"

"I don't see why I have to be nice to you in the first place... Do you even really like me? Are you sure it's not just some heat of the moment thing?"

Hajime still couldn't believe she really liked him, hence his assumption that the suspension bridge effect had come into play. And considering how he'd treated her until now, it was hardly surprising. However, it looked like Shea was pretty unhappy that he was doubting her feelings.

"I can't say I was completely unaffected by the situation. After all, you saved us from so many terrible predicaments, and you're an outcast just like me...and I was definitely happy when you told the elders you'd keep your promise no matter what... But whether it was because of all that or not, the fact that I like you now hasn't changed. Even I think it's kind of strange. Why you, of all people? You don't even call me by my name, any time you get mad you instantly start shooting people, you're mean, you don't care about other people's feelings, you just throw people into hordes of monsters, you have no mercy, you're mean, you never do anything nice, you're only kind to Yue-san, you're mean... Huh? Really, why do I like you? Huh?"

Partway through her tirade, Shea began questioning her own feelings. She tilted her head in confusion, and while Hajime desperately wanted to whip out Donner, he held himself back. Nothing she'd said had been wrong, after all.

"Either way, no matter what your feelings are, I don't plan on taking you with us."

"No way! Look, all that was just a joke, okay? I really like you, so please take me with you!"

"Look here, even if... Even if your feelings are real, I already have Yue. Actually, I'm surprised you confessed all that when she's standing here in front of you... Come to think of it, the really scary thing about you isn't that body strengthening ability, but how shamelessly bold you are. Is your heart made of azantium or something?"

"Excuse me, my heart isn't that hard! Aww, I knew this would happen...but that's okay. I already knew I couldn't deal with you through normal means, Hajime-san." Shea snickered triumphantly, which made Hajime look at her suspiciously.

"I already planned for all this! That's why I put my life on the line! Now, Yue-sensei, if you would be so kind!"

"Huh? Yue?" Hajime blinked at this sudden turn in the conversation. Annoyed, Yue nevertheless faithfully turned to look at Hajime. Her expression made it look like she'd just swallowed a hundred cockroaches, and she very reluctantly opened her mouth.

"...Hajime, let's take her with us."

"Wait, uh... What? What's going on here? You obviously don't like the idea, but... Wait, is this what the bet was about?"

"...I was careless."

Yue shrugged her shoulders despondently, and Hajime, who'd finally guessed what happened between them, couldn't help but be amazed.

Shea must have known asking him directly would only get her a prompt refusal, so she'd done everything in her power to get her request across to him. She'd even understood Hajime well enough to realize that he would listen to Yue, even if he didn't listen to her.

That was why she'd tried to enlist Yue to help her cause. In a very real sense, she had risked her life to obtain such a powerful ally. Half-baked feelings would never have gotten through to Yue, after all. Hajime had barely seen Shea these past ten days, but he was certain she must have trained like her life depended on it in order to beat Yue. And that meant her feelings were undeniably real.

Hajime scratched his head awkwardly. Even if Yue had approved of her, albeit unwillingly, there still wasn't any good reason to take Shea along with them. So, in the end, it still boiled down to Hajime's feelings.

Though Yue had agreed to help only reluctantly, it looked like she'd already given up. She'd seen her up close these past ten days, and knew just how hard Shea had trained to get past the obstacles Yue had thrown her way. That was why she was willing to take her along. Besides, leaving aside Shea's feelings for Hajime, Yue had very little reason to hate her.

Shea had smiled triumphantly when she'd asked Yue for help, but now worry lined her face once more, and she gazed uneasily at Hajime. She'd done everything she could, and now all that was left was to wait for his decision.

Finally, Hajime took a deep breath and locked eyes with Shea. Each of his words was picked very carefully. At each turn, Shea replied with conviction.

"Even if I let you come, that doesn't mean I'll respond to your feelings, you know?"

"Don't you know? The future's not set in stone."

Since she was someone who could see the future, she knew that for sure. Depending on one's actions, the future could be changed.

"It'll be nothing but danger."

"Good thing I'm a monster, then. I won't get in your way during fights."

The elders had scorned her with that name once before, but now she wore it with pride. And it was all because she'd learned there were some things that couldn't be done unless you were a monster.

"My goal is to return to my own world. You might never see your family again if you come with me."

"I've already talked to them about that, but I still want to go. Dad understands, too." Shea felt nothing but gratitude for the family that had protected her for so long. She'd probably never be able to describe what she'd felt when the family she'd lived with all her life had sent her off with a smile after she'd told them her intentions.

"You might not have it easy living in my world."

"I'll say it as many times as I have to... I still want to go."

Shea's mind was made up. Mere words wouldn't deter her anymore... No, they *couldn't* deter her. That was just how strong her feelings were.

"......"

"Hee hee, is that all you have to say? Does that mean I win?"

"What is there to even 'win' here...?"

"There is something. It means my feelings won you over... Hajime-san."

"...The hell does that mean?"

She decided to reiterate her, Shea Haulia's, intentions.

"Please take me with you."

Hajime and Shea stared at each other for a while. Reflected in Shea's sapphire eyes were Hajime's own pupils. Finally...

"...Fine, do whatever you want. Damned weirdo."

Whatever he'd seen in her eyes must have been enough to convince him, as Hajime finally gave in with a sigh.

A single shout of joy (followed by the unceremonious noise of someone blowing their nose) echoed throughout the forest. Hajime could only smile wryly as he lamented the future that awaited him.

Shea cupped her cheeks and let out a strange series of laughs that sounded like "Ehehe! Uheheheh! Oohoohoo!" as she happily jumped with joy. Her serious expression from earlier had vanished without a trace.

"...Disgusting." Yue muttered, unable to watch any longer. Shea's sensitive rabbit ears didn't miss the whispered insult, though.

"Hey, just what's disgusting here, huh? I can't believe you... I'm just so happy that I can't help it, okay? This is like the first time Hajime's been nice to me. Did you see him? How he looked at the end there? I felt my heart skip a beat when I saw that. At this rate, I'll be head over heels for him pretty soon."

Shea was over the moon. In fact, she was probably over the stars even. Tired of her excited giggling, both Yue and Hajime simultaneously opened their mouths.

"...Stupid rabbit."

"Wha—?! What was that?! Why can't you just say my name already! Pleaaase, we're even traveling companions now. Don't tell me you're going to keep using those terrible nicknames forever. You won't, right?"

"......"

"Wh-why are you suddenly going quiet...? Wait, please don't avert your eyes like that. Come on, it's not a hard name to say. Shea. She-ah. Repeat after me. She-ah."

They ignored Shea, who kept trying to get them to say her name, and began discussing their future plans. At which point, Shea started clinging to them, crying, "Please don't ignore meeee... I'm one of you guys now, toooo!" Just because they'd become companions didn't meant they'd treat her any better.

And so, the trio noisily—mostly due to Shea—made their way through the fog to where the rest of the Haulia were waiting. They had cleared Hajime's harsh trials, the proof of which was resting in their hands. Upon closer inspection, it was apparent that Cam was with them.

Shea smiled happily as she saw her family for the first time in a while. The last time she'd spoken with them was before the training had begun, when she'd told them her intentions. It had only been ten days, but with how harsh their training had been, that time felt like an eternity. To Shea, it felt like it had been months since she'd last seen them.

She made a beeline for her father the moment she spotted him. There was a mountain of things she wanted to tell him. But as she drew closer, her mouth reflexively snapped shut. Cam and the others had a strange aura surrounding them.

He gave Shea only a quick smile before turning back to look at Hajime. Then...

"Boss. We slaughtered the monsters you requested."

"B-Boss? D-Dad? What's with that way of talking...and why do you look so..."

Cam ignored his daughter's confusion, then presented the fangs and claws of some of the forest's more powerful monsters to Hajime.

"I thought I told you one was enough..."

Hajime's final task for his students had been to take down one of the stronger inhabitants of the sea of trees as a team. But judging from the quantity of monster parts the rabbits had harvested, they'd easily killed more than ten. Cam grinned wolfishly as he replied.

"That you did, Boss. But as we were hunting our target, the damned thing's friends showed up... Those bastards dared to bare their fangs at us, so we simply did what was natural. Isn't that right, guys?"

"That's right, Boss. Those damned monsters need to learn their place."

"We made sure none of them escaped. They all got what they deserved."

"They were a bit of a pain to deal with, but...hearing their screams was all worth it. Heh heh..."

"Maybe we should have hung them from the trees as an example to the others..."

"Well, we chopped them up into pieces, so that's probably good enough."

Each of their words was very unsettling. Their usual gentle expressions were nowhere to be seen. With a dangerous glint in their eyes, they reported the results of their mission to Hajime. Shea watched them all in amazement.

"...Who are you guys?" Suddenly, she returned to her senses and rounded on Hajime, as he was most likely responsible for the radical change in her family.

"Wh-what on earth is this?! Hajime-san, what did you do to them?!"

"C-calm down... I didn't do anything... This is just a result of their training..."

"No way! What kind of training would turn them into this?! They're all totally different people! Hey, don't you avert your gaze! Look at me!"

"...They haven't changed *that* much."

"Is that eye of yours just for show?! Look at them! They're all staring at their knives with murder in their eyes! Look, one of them even named theirs Julia! They're totally in love with their weapons! This is *not* normal!" Shea's hysterical screams rang out through the sea of trees. Cam watched the exchange with a puzzled expression on his face. While Shea was yelling at Hajime, even more of the Haulia returned to the clearing. Each and every one of them had a somewhat...*wild* look to them. Even the women and children and elderly.

Hajime awkwardly averted his eyes from Shea's glowering glare and tried to make excuses to explain away the situation. Realizing she wouldn't get anywhere questioning Hajime, Shea turned to Cam instead.

"Dad! Guys! What happened to you all?! It's like you've become completely different people! Even the way you guys talk has gotten scary... Come back to your senses, everyone!" Shea desperately pleaded with her father, and the dangerous glint in his eyes slowly faded away as his normal gentle expression returned. She let out a sigh of relief. However...

"What are you talking about, Shea? We're perfectly sane. We've just come to learn something about the truth of this world. Thanks to our boss here."

"Th-the truth of this world? What does that even mean?" Shea suddenly had a bad premonition, and Cam proudly puffed out his chest.

"Ninety percent of the world's problems can be solved through violence."

"You really are insane after all! My kind, gentle dad is gone for good! Waaaaaah!" Unable to bear the shock of what she'd come back to, Shea ran crying into the sea of trees. But before she could vanish into the fog, she ran into a small silhouette. She let out a cry of surprise and fell on her butt. The figure she'd bumped into managed to retain their balance, and they held out a hand to Shea.

"S-sorry. Thanks."

"Don't worry about it, Lady Shea. It's only natural for a guy to help a girl."

"L-Lady Shea?"

From the depths of the fog emerged the Haulia boy who had once loved flowers. Slung across his shoulders was a massive crossbow, and two knives and a slingshot dangled from a belt strapped to his waist. His smile was surprisingly nihilistic. Never in her life had Shea ever been addressed so formally. It was doubly shocking because she distinctly remembered the boy calling her "Shea-oneechan" in the past. He walked past Shea and gave Hajime a crisp, respectful salute.

"Boss! I apologize for returning empty-handed! However, I have a report to make! Permission to speak?"

"G-go ahead. What is it?" When he saw the boy acting like a seasoned veteran, Hajime did have to admit that he might have taken his Spartan training techniques a little too far. The boy nonchalantly continued his report.

"Sir! As I was pursuing the target, I discovered a battalion of armed bearmen. I located them on the route to the Grand Tree. I suspect they foolishly believe they can ambush us!"

"Ah, so they really came. I figured they'd try and track us down right away, but... I see. So, they actually have the gall to try and stop us right before our destination, huh? They've got guts... And?"

"With your permission, sir, we Haulia shall take care of them!"

"Hmm... What do you think, Cam? You heard the kid."

Cam grinned that same wolfish grin, then nodded his head in agreement.

"With your permission, we'll gladly destroy them. This is a good opportunity...to see how well we fare against opponents of their caliber. Don't worry, we won't bring shame to your name." At Cam's words, the other Haulia all began sporting bloodthirsty grins. Suddenly, it felt like even more of the rabbitmen were giving names to their weapons. Shea watched on in utter despair.

"...Are you sure you can do it?"

"We are, sir!"

The one who'd replied was the boy who delivered the initial report. Hajime closed his eyes, took a deep breath, and opened them again.

"Listen up, men of the Haulia! Proud and courageous warriors! Today is the day you finally graduate from being worthless maggots! You used to be pieces of trash that were worth less than the spit on my boot! But that's true no longer! With force, you crush the irrationality of this world, and with cunning, you run circles around any who would dare oppose you! You have been reborn as great *warriors* of the Haulia tribe! Now go, and teach those bear bastards that can't think of anything but their misguided revenge who's boss! They're nothing but stepping stones in your path! Worthless bastards that don't even deserve consideration! Build a mountain with their corpses and plant your flag atop its summit! That flag is proof that you're alive! That the Haulia are meek little rabbits no longer! Let all of Haltina Woods know of your existence!"

"Sir, yes sir!"

"Tell me, men! You are the most powerful warriors in all of Haltina! What is your wish?!"

"Slaughter! Slaughter! Slaughter!"

"What is your specialty?!"

"Slaughter! Slaughter! Slaughter!"

"And what do you do to your enemies?!"

"Slaughter! Slaughter! Slaughter!"

"That's right. Slaughter them! That is what you achieved strength for! Fight for your right to live!"

"Aye aye, sir!"

"That's the spirit! Proud members of the Haulia tribe, here are my orders! Search and destroy! Now go!"

"Yahaaaaaaaaaaaaaaaaaaaaaaaaaa!"

"Waaaaaah, my family's all goooone. They're all deaaaad."

At Hajime's command, the Haulia all turned as one and ventured forth into the fog.

There was no trace of the old peace-loving race they used to be. Shea crumpled to her knees and wailed wordlessly. Her cries echoed throughout the forest. Even Yue couldn't help but be moved by such a display of emotion, and she comfortingly patted Shea's head.

Aiming to join his companions, the little boy ran out from behind Shea, but she called out to him to hold him back.

"Par-kun! Please wait! L-Look, there's a pretty little flower right here! You don't have to go with them... You can just wait here with me. What do you say? Don't you want to stay?" If nothing else, she wanted to at least save this one little boy from going down the wrong path. She was desperately trying to entice him back with the promise of flowers. Why flowers? That was because he was none other than the same boy who had been so enamored with them before.

At Shea's words, the young boy, Par, stopped. He breathed out an exasperated sigh and shrugged his shoulders. It was a bit of an exaggerated reaction considering the question.

"Lady Shea, please don't dig up bad memories. I've already thrown away my past. That weak, flower-loving boy's no more."

For reference, Par was still ten years old.

"B-bad memories? Thrown away your past? Umm, I don't really get it, but does that mean you don't like flowers anymore?"

"That's right, I threw that love away along with my past."

"But you used to love them so much..."

"Hmph. That was nothing more than the folly of youth."

To reiterate, Par was only ten years old.

"Anyway, Lady Shea."

"Wh-what?" Seeing how drastically the boy that had used to run around going "Shea-oneechan, Shea-oneechan" had changed left Shea nearly speechless. It had taken every ounce of her remaining consciousness to just reply to him. But those words she'd worked so hard to squeeze out only made things worse.

"Along with my past, I've thrown away that old, weak name of mine. I'm called Baltfeld now. Baltfeld the Executioner. Please use my new name from now on."

"What?! Where'd a name like Baltfeld come from?! And what the heck is 'The Executioner' even supposed to mean?!"

"Whoops, sorry. My comrades are waiting, so I gotta go. See ya!"

"Hey, wait! Get back here! I'm not done—holy crap, you're fast! Wait! I said waiiiiiit!" Shea helplessly stretched her hand out to the fog, looking like she'd just been abandoned by her lover. But there was no reply; her macho-ified family had all marched off to war. And so, she simply hung her head and resumed her sobbing. The family she had known was gone. One couldn't help but pity her plight.

Unsure of what to say to cheer her up, Yue could only smile awkwardly. Even Hajime uncomfortably averted his gaze. His wandering eyes caught sight of Yue, and she quietly muttered.

"...You're amazing, Hajime. You keep doing things normal humans could never even dream of like it's nothing."

"Not really, it's not like..."

"You brainwashed all of them without using dark magic... Unbelievable."

"To be honest, even I think I went a bit too far. But I don't regret it."

For some time after that, the only thing that could be heard in that part of the forest were the sounds of Shea's sobbing. Meanwhile...

•/• •/• •/• •/• •/• •/• •/• •/• •/• •/• •/• •/• •/•

Regin Vanton was next in line to be the chief of the Vanton clan, the strongest among the bearmen. Rumor had it that he was one of the strongest bearmen in Haltina. He was the right-hand man of the chief, Jin Vanton, who he practically idolized.

It wasn't just Regin either. All the members of the Vanton clan, especially the younger ones, adored him. Jin's broadmindedness and zealous patriotism, combined with his considerable strength, were the main reasons for his overwhelming popularity.

When they'd first learned of Jin's fate, most of his clan had laughed it off as a bad joke. There was no way a mere human could have defeated Jin so easily, or hurt him so badly that he'd never be able to fight again. But when the proof was thrust before their eyes, they could no longer ignore reality. Jin's weakened body lying in a hospital bed was irrefutable evidence of those claims.

Regin's stunned disbelief upon first seeing Jin's emaciated frame had quickly given way to seething rage. Swept away by his anger, he had stormed off to the Elders' Hall and pressed them for details on the incident. Once he'd learned the truth, Regin ignored the elders' warnings and told the rest of his tribe what he'd heard, urging them to follow him in getting revenge.

Thanks to the elders' words, some of the bearmen chose to stay behind, but all of the hot-blooded youths of the Vanton clan, along with a few others who'd been especially close to Jin, swore to join Regin's revenge party. All told, about fifty people chose to follow Regin. As they knew the hateful human's destination was the Sacred Tree, Uralt, they decided to lay in wait along the path leading there—their reasoning being that getting cut down right in front of his goal would be that much more painful for him.

Their foes were nothing more than a ragtag group of rabbitmen led by a human. And even if that human had beat Jin, it must have been by way of some kind of underhanded sneak attack. In this deep fog, he'd be even more handicapped with his senses in disarray, and those weak rabbitmen weren't even worth counting as a fighting force.

Regin was a very skilled bearman. Under normal circumstances, he wouldn't have underestimated his enemies so. But his rage had blinded him, overcoming such prudence.

However, even if he was willing to admit his anger had made him act in haste...

"This is still too much!" Regin screamed, his voice filled with despair. The reason for his anguish stemmed from the fact that the rabbitmen, one of the weakest beastmen tribes in existence, had completely destroyed his army of bearmen, one of the strongest beastmen tribes in existence.

"Come on! That all you got?! Pathetic!"

"Aha ha ha ha! That's right, scream like the worthless pigs you are!"

"You guys are trash! Hya ha ha ha!"

The Haulia's raucous laughter echoed through the clearing, and countless knives glinted in the dim sunlight. Their original gentle, peaceful expressions were nowhere to be found. The bearmen were clearly shaken at the unexpected ferocity the rabbitmen displayed.

"Dammit! The hell's going on?! What kind of monsters are these guys?!"

"There's no way these guys are rabbitmen!"

"Eyaaaaah! Get away from me! Get away from meeeee!"

The ambushers had suddenly found themselves on the receiving end of an ambush. Worse, the supposedly weak rabbitmen had displayed a strength beyond what anyone had thought possible for them. Arrows and rocks rained down on the bearmen, who had no way to retaliate. Not only did the rabbitmen skillfully hide their presence in the fog, their coordination was perfect. But worst of all were those bloodthirsty howls of laughter. All of those factors combined were what led the bearmen, who possessed superior stats, to be pushed back.

Had the bearmen actually fought the rabbitmen one by one, they would have won easily. However, thanks to the beyond hellish training they had received, the Haulia had the advantage when it came to combat experience and group tactics.

Normally, the rabbitmen were far weaker than the other beastmen races. But because of that innate weakness, they had perfected their ability to sense danger and hide themselves. Those were the tools they had polished to survive.

Used as a weapon, those same skills were perfect for ambushing foes. One could even say that they were the race most suited to be assassins. But because of their pacifist nature, those skills had never been used as such.

Until Hajime had stripped away their aversion to fighting during their training, that is. He'd driven them into a corner, pushing them so hard that they had needed to overcome their distaste for fighting just to survive. As a result of his Spartan training, their hearts had been reforged into something hard and unforgiving in just ten days. Still, Hajime might have overdone it just a little bit... After all, not only did they not have any hesitation to fight, they eagerly sought out conflict. And their bonds had already been strong to begin with, so they had no problem coordinating their attacks perfectly, which multiplied their strength. Combine that with their ability to swiftly analyze a foe's strengths and weaknesses, and they became a force to be reckoned with.

Of course, another one of the big reasons they'd grown so powerful so fast was the specialized weapons Hajime had crafted for them.

Each of them had two shortswords, crafted by Hajime to be ultra-thin, ultra-light, and ultra-sharp. And because they were made of taur, they were ultra-durable as well. They also had a brace of throwing knives made in the same fashion.

Long-range weapons were part of their arsenal, too. Using thread he'd harvested from a spider-like monster down in the abyss, Hajime had crafted them slingshots and crossbows stronger than anything one could find on the surface. Many of the Haulia children weren't suited to close combat at all, but thanks to their excellent senses they made great snipers even in the thick fog.

Par—or rather, Baltfeld the Executioner—along with the other children, had taken to the crossbows instantly.

"One shot, one kill! I'll blow all these bastards' heads off! I swear it on my title of Executioner!"

Par—Baltfeld the Executioner—had gotten pretty foul-mouthed over the past few days. By the way, his "title" was something self-proclaimed. Originally he'd been fond of saying "Bang!" every time he shot down an enemy, but Hajime had put a stop to that. Mostly because it creeped him out. Regardless, it was thanks to the hellish training that the bearmen were being pushed back by the Haulia. Unable to mount any resistance, they'd already lost half of their forces.

"Regin-dono! We won't last much longer!"

"Please order a retreat!"

"Allow me to take up the reargua—gwaah?!"

"Tonto?!"

Though his men all urged him to retreat, Regin hesitated. Logic warred with rage, as not only had Jin been crippled, but now Regin had lost his precious subordinates as well. But that hesitation only led him to lose more men. The bearman who had volunteered to take up the rearguard now had an arrow sprouting through his forehead.

Shaken by the rabbitmen's unerring accuracy, the bearmen's formation was thrown into disarray. Sensing their opportunity, Cam and the others decided to finish it in one final push.

Arrows and rocks struck with pinpoint accuracy at the ankles, wrists, and other vital areas of the bearmen. While their attention was occupied by the rain of projectiles, the other Haulia snuck up on the beastmen, slicing and thrusting with their wickedly sharp swords.

Finally, when the bearmen had their hands full fending off attacks from various directions, a Haulia would sneak behind each one and deal the finishing blow. Using the advantage of numbers, the Haulia ran circles around the bearmen. Soon enough, Regin and the others were trembling in fear. *Are those guys seriously the same stupid, gutless rabbitmen we saw before?!*

Though they held out for an impressive amount of time, before long even Regin was covered from head to toe in wounds, and he had to use his axe as a crutch just to keep himself standing. The Haulia had switched off attacking in waves, leaving the bearmen no time to rest. Currently, Regin and the others were all panting heavily, with their backs to a large tree as the rabbitmen surrounded them.

"Come on, you worthless bastards! This can't be all you've got! Or are you all just a bunch of spineless losers?!"

"You're bringing shame to your name as the strongest race, you know that, you screw-ups?! Where'd your balls go, you cowards?!"

"Come on, pick up your weapons! You bunch of pussies!"

Their insults were so crude that no one expected any race, least of all the rabbitmen, to be hurling them. *Something crazy must have happened to these guys to make them like this!* The bearmen had lost the will to fight. Burly, macho bearmen were all crying as they begged for mercy... It was an odd sight, to be sure.

"Hoohoo, any last words? Mr. 'I'm part of the strongest race'?" Sarcasm dripped from Cam's voice. Now that he'd awoken to his battle instincts, it seemed he wanted to get back at the world for being looked down on all his life. The old Cam would never have been so cruel.

"Ngh..." Regin only grunted in frustration. After they'd regrouped from their initial confusion, Regin had finally returned to his senses. Witnessing the overwhelming might of the Haulia had been like having a bucket of cold water splashed onto his face. The flames of resentment at what had happened to Jin still smoldered within Regin's breast, but he knew that his current responsibility was to save as many of his men's lives as he could. He was well aware that it was his fault so many of his comrades were caught in this predicament.

"I don't care what you do with me. Torture me, kill me, do whatever you want. But everyone else is only here because I forced them to come. So please, let them go."

"Wha—Regin-dono?!"

"Regin-dono! You can't..."

His subordinates all started talking at once. They couldn't stand the fact that he was trying to sacrifice himself for their sake. But he simply silenced them all with a booming voice.

"Shut up! I'm the one who got blinded by anger and led you guys into a death trap! The rabbitmen's... I mean the Haulia's chief—I understand I'm asking a lot of you. But please, spare their lives! I'm begging you!"

Regin tossed aside his weapon and knelt before Cam. His men all knew just how much pride he took in his abilities, so they also knew just how much it took out of him to prostrate himself before the enemy. When they saw how deep his resolve ran, they couldn't bring themselves to fight back.

Cam, too, saw the determination in Regin's eyes. Thus, his reply was...

"I refuse." He threw one of his knives as he said that.

"Whaaah?!" Regin just barely managed to twist out of the way. But Cam's knife was nothing more than a signal. Seconds later, a storm of rocks and arrows rained down on the helpless bearmen. The Haulia roared with laughter as they watched Regin and the others desperately defend themselves with their broadaxes.

"Why?!" Regin barely managed to groan that one word out.

"Why? Isn't it obvious? You guys are our enemies. What other reason do we need?"

The logic in Cam's answer was simple.

"Guh, but—!"

"And besides...it's fun seeing you arrogant bastards brought low, crawling through the dirt like the scum you are! Ha ha ha!"

"What?! You monsters! How could you?!"

The glee in Cam's voice was unmistakable. His tribesmen were all firing their slingshots and crossbows from a safe distance as they tormented the bearmen. They were all exhibiting the tell-tale signs of people who've gone mad due to their first taste of power. The rush of victory against one of the strongest subspecies of their race had caused them to take leave of their senses. They were completely out of control.

The ferocity of their attacks increased until Regin and the others were all huddled together in a pitiful heap, barely holding on. But even that wouldn't last for much longer. Though none of them had been fatally injured yet, they were all covered in wounds both minor and major. The next barrage would finish them.

Cam grinned cruelly and raised an arm into the air. Gleefully, the rest of the Haulia nocked their crossbows and loaded their slingshots. Realizing nothing he could do would prevent this from being his grave, Regin dropped his weapon in surrender. Inwardly, he apologized to his men for foolishly leading them to their deaths.

Cam's arm swung down like the scythe of the grim reaper itself as he gave the signal to fire. Everyone loosed at once. Regin stared defiantly at the barrage that was to be his death, determined to at least not give them the satisfaction of looking away. But then...

"Cut it ouuuuuuuut!" A white silhouette darted in front of the bearmen and blew away the projectiles with a massive metal hammer.

"Huh?" Regin's jaw dropped open in surprise. It was only natural. Right as he was about to die, a pale-haired bunny girl had dropped from the sky along with a massive hammer. And the shock wave as it had hit the ground had blown away all the arrows and rocks heading toward him and his comrades. His shocked face was almost comical to look at. The other bearmen all had similar expressions.

The enraged bunny girl was, of course, none other than Shea. Thanks to Hajime's compression transmutation, the hammer was unimaginably dense. Still, Shea swung the ridiculously heavy hammer up like it was nothing, then pointed it at Cam. Even a simple motion like that caused a powerful gale.

"I can't believe you guys! Dad, and the rest of you too, come back to your senses already!" They were taken aback by Shea's sudden entrance, but they quickly composed themselves and glared angrily at her.

"Shea, I don't know what you're playing at, but get out of our way. We can't kill them if you don't."

"Oh no, I'm not moving. You're the ones who need to stop!"

Cam's eyes narrowed angrily.

"Stop? Don't tell me you plan on siding with the enemy, Shea. Depending on your answer, I may have to..."

"No, I don't really care if these guys die or not."

"You don't?!" The bearmen had all been convinced that she'd come here to stop her tribe's murderous rampage, so they were positively stunned by her reply.

"Of course not. I wouldn't have survived Yue-san's training if I was still soft enough to go easy on people trying to kill me. Even I know that's just going to get you killed."

"Hmph, then why exactly are you stopping us?" Even though he was talking to his daughter, Cam's tone was rough. The rest of his tribe all glared suspiciously at her as well.

"Isn't it obvious?! Because if I don't stop you guys, you'll break! You'll sink into depravity!"

"Break? Sink into depravity?" It was obvious he hadn't understood a single word Shea had said.

"That's right! Don't you see?! Hajime-san might not show any mercy to his enemies, or listen to their pleas, or ever have pity, but he never *enjoys* killing! He taught you how to kill your enemies, not how to torment them!"

"W-we weren't..."

"Do you even know what kind of expression you were making just now, Dad?"

"Expression? I mean, I can't look at my own face..." At Shea's words, the Haulia all turned to look at each other. Shea paused to take a deep breath and then quietly, but firmly, continued.

"...You guys looked just like the imperial soldiers that attacked us."

"Wha—?!"

That was a shock. A big enough one to blow away the veil of bloodlust that had clouded their thoughts thus far. They were no better than the monsters who had laughed mockingly at them while enslaving most of their tribe... It was precisely because the Haulia had seen such ugliness up close that they knew how disgusting it was. Worse than the scum who had taken their families... That was a bitter truth to swallow.

"Sh-Shea...I..."

"Hmph, looks like you've finally calmed down a little. Good. I was worried I'd have to kick all your asses first before you came to your senses."

Shea casually swung her hammer around a few times. Her stern expression relaxed a little as she saw the bloodthirsty smiles fade from her family's faces.

"Well, this was your first battle, so it's all good as long as you realized your mistake in time. Besides, this is all really Hajime-san's fault. I know he needed to toughen you up mentally too, but he went too far! He turned you into berserkers, not warriors!" This time her anger was directed at Hajime. She quietly added, "How on earth did I fall for a guy like that anyway?" to her monologue.

Suddenly, a gunshot rang out throughout the clearing. One of the bearmen behind Shea let out a strangled groan and crumpled to the ground. Realizing they'd completely ignored their opponents for the past few minutes, Shea and Cam scrambled to see what they were up to. When they looked back, they saw Regin cradling his forehead and moaning in pain.

"Don't you even think about trying to escape while they're not looking. You better sit quietly until their conversation's over." Hajime and Yue materialized from within the fog. Apparently, Regin and the others had tried to sneak off while Shea and Cam had been arguing. For some reason, Hajime had decided to use one of his non-lethal rubber bullets.

Despite Hajime's words, the bearmen were still carefully observing their surroundings, looking for any chance to escape. Hajime activated his Intimidation in order to keep them docile. With the pressure of his magic keeping them shivering in place, Hajime was free to walk leisurely over to Shea and the others. Hajime looked around awkwardly for a few seconds before steeling his resolve and staring apologetically at Cam.

"Uh, well, you know, my bad. I was fine with it, but I forgot about what the shock of killing a person can do to someone. Really, I'm sorry."

Cam and Shea's were stunned. No one had ever expected Hajime, of all people, to ever apologize.

"B-Boss?! Are you all right?! Did you hit your head somewhere?!"

"Medic! Medic! We need urgent assistance!"

"Boss, keep it together!"

Hence the overblown reaction. There was a familiar vein bulging on Hajime's forehead.

Hajime had honestly thought he was at fault, and he was sincerely apologizing. Because he'd been fine with killing people, he'd failed to take into account what the shock of it might have done to someone else. Strong as he was, Hajime had no experience teaching others. And that inexperience had nearly caused him to break the Haulia's minds. That was why he'd given a heartfelt apology. But rather than accepting it, those stupid bunnies had questioned his sanity. Though, in a way, he wasn't sure if he should get angry or reflect on the way he'd been acting. He decided to shelve the issue for later, and instead walked up to Regin. Then, he slowly pressed Donner against the bearman's head.

"Now then, would you prefer to die a manly death or live on in disgrace?" It was the Haulia who were even more surprised by his ultimatum than the bearmen. It was unthinkable that Hajime would actually offer to spare an enemy's life. This was the same person who had mercilessly slaughtered anyone that had bared their fangs at him for as long as they'd known him.

"He really did hit his head somewhere, didn't he...?" Cam muttered softly. Another vein joined the first, but if he let everything the rabbitmen said get to him, they'd have gotten nowhere.

Regin looked up at Hajime in confusion. As he was undoubtedly the one who'd turned the Haulia into bloodthirsty monsters, Regin had not expected him to show any mercy.

"What do you mean? You're willing to let us live?"

"Yeah, if that's what you want. But I have a condition."

"A condition?" The other bearmen all began clamoring noisily at the prospect of salvation.

"If I hit him again, maybe it'll fix it..." Shea muttered surprisingly seriously as she looked from the back of Hajime's head down to her hammer and back again. Cam and the others all nodded vigorously.

I think they'll need some very strict discipline when we get back. But for now, Hajime ignored them.

"Yep, a condition. When you get back to Verbergen, I want you to deliver a message to the elders."

"A message?" Regin had been worried he'd ask something outrageous of them, so he was a little relieved to hear they'd just be messengers. However, the contents of that message made his blood run cold.

"You owe me."

"...Ah?! You don't mean—"

"Well? What'll it be? Yes or no?"

Regin couldn't suppress his voice when he realized what Hajime intended. Hajime waited patiently for Regin's answer.

If this message were delivered, it would mean that Verbergen would one day have to repay their debt to him. The elders had lost one of their own, and even overturned a decision of their council to keep Hajime away from their city, but if Regin delivered that message, then they'd be forced to unconditionally accept any request of his. Looking at it objectively, both Regin and Jin had been the ones to attack first, so letting Regin live would mean

Verbergen would be honor bound to agree. Ignoring that debt would make them look disgraceful. Besides, if they didn't accept, Hajime might really attack them. In other words, if Regin chose to live, he would be exposing his country to danger. Not only had they ignored the elders' warning, they'd lost, with half of their men dead. After all that boasting they'd done about being the strongest, too... As Hajime had said, it really would mean living on in disgrace. While Regin despaired at his choices, Hajime delivered the final blow.

"Oh, and you'd better tell everyone the death of your subordinates was entirely your fault. And that you were defeated at the Haulia's hands, no less."

"Ugh."

There was a reason Hajime was willing to let this opponent go. Mercy didn't factor into his decision at all. Verbergen had cut him off completely, but it was possible he'd have to return there at some point if his search for the other labyrinths ever pointed in that direction. After all, one of the Liberators had personally left an edict behind for the people of the country. He'd felt like the situation with the elders could have been handled a little more diplomatically, and had regretted being chased out just a little. So now that an unexpected windfall of good luck had dropped in his lap, he intended to make the most of it. Regin seemed unsure of what to do, but Hajime didn't have the patience for him to think it through.

"You have five seconds. If you don't answer by then, I'll start killing your men one by one. Your kind values prompt decisions, right?" Hajime slowly started counting down, and Regin gave his answer in a panic.

"F-fine. We choose to live!"

"I see. Then get out of my sight. And you better relay my message, you hear? If I ever come back and find out you haven't, well..." Bloodlust so thick it was palpable pressed down onto Regin. He gulped fearfully.

"Let's just say Verbergen might not exist anymore." The way Hajime phrased his threats made him look like a yakuza loan shark, or rather, a terrorist. Relieved sighs could be heard behind him.

"Aah, thank goodness we have the old Hajime back," "Boss is back to normal," and the like could be heard from the group of rabbitmen. Hajime pointedly ignored their remarks; however, they still served to ruin the tense atmosphere he'd built up. *Oh yeah, they need some very harsh discipline when we get back.*

None of the bearmen disputed Regin's decision to beg for their lives, and he dejectedly led what remained of his troop back home. The fact that so many of his soldiers were young had probably played a part in Regin's despair. He'd never again be able to swagger around Verbergen like he owned the place. In fact, it was likely he'd be ostracized by everyone. He supposed he'd been let off lightly, though, considering he was the one who'd initiated hostilities. Within minutes, the bearmen had all been swallowed up by the fog.

Once they were out of sight, Hajime rounded on Shea and Cam. His head was downcast, so nobody could see his expression, and there was a strange aura surrounding him. All of the rabbit-men were still getting over their shame at having nearly fallen into madness, so they walked up to him like nothing was wrong. Only Shea broke out in a cold sweat as she realized there was a danger-ous aura emanating from him.

Trembling slightly, he raised his head to look up at them. There was a content smile on his face, but it never reached his eyes. Finally, Cam and the others realized there was something wrong with Hajime too.

"B-Boss?" Cam questioned timidly.

"Yeah? You know, I really did feel bad about what I did to you guys. Even if it was to train you as quickly as possible in the short time we had, I should have put a stop to it after a while."

"N-no, Boss, it was...all because we were too immature..."

"Now now, I'm perfectly willing to admit my own mistakes. But... but you know, even though I apologized so sincerely...the way you guys reacted was just too much. I mean, I get it. It's partly my fault for being so mean every day...I know. I know that, but I still have to do something about all this rage building up inside me... You understand, right?"

"N-no, sir. I can't say I do..." Cold sweat started pouring down Cam's back. *Oh crap, he's pissed.* Cam slowly started backing up. Hajime's attitude brought back memories of their hellish training, and more than a few of the Haulia broke down crying.

"Now's my chance!" Shea yelled, then tried to take advantage of Hajime's momentary hesitation to flee. She even used the other Haulia as meat shields as she ran. However... *Bang!* Hajime's bullet flew between a Haulia's legs, ricocheted off a nearby root, and hit Shea right in the butt.

"Hakyun!" This was just one of Hajime's many sniping skills. By ricocheting bullets off of various surfaces, he could attack from any angle. And so, he could accurately aim for Shea's butt no matter where she hid. It was a completely pointless gun skill that had no wasted movements to it.

Shea hopped around in pain as she held her butt cheeks. She then tripped over a root, exposing her ass for all to see. A faint tendril of smoke rose from where the bullet had hit her. She showed no signs of getting up and simply twitched helplessly on the ground.

Cam and the others all watched on in horror as Shea spasmed on the ground. The man whose legs the bullet had passed between was holding his crotch protectively and sobbing uncontrollably. The shock wave that Hajime's bullet had left behind had touched his balls slightly.

Hajime casually holstered Donner and smiled demonically. His loud voice carried to every one of the Haulia.

"You're all eating one bullet before I'm through!"

"Waaaaaaaaaaaaaaaaaaaaaaaaaaaaah!" The Haulia all skittered away like spiders, but Hajime didn't let even a single one of them escape unscathed. For a long time, the terrified screams of bunnies echoed throughout the forest. Until only Shea remained, smoke still rising from her buttocks.

"...So when can we go to the Grand Tree?" Yue, who'd been quiet this whole time, finally spoke up.

A few hours later, after Hajime had thoroughly vented all of his frustration, Cam and the others led them through the fog to the Sacred Tree, Uralt.

Cam was in the lead, while the other Haulia, much wiser now thanks to their training, spread out to scout the surrounding area. The idea that carelessness led to death had been thoroughly ingrained into each of their minds, so they all took their jobs seriously. The lumps rising on various parts of their bodies broke the tension a bit, though...

"Gaah, it still stings." Shea complained bitterly as she rubbed her butt. She glared angrily at Hajime.

"Quit looking at me like that, it's annoying."

"That's what you have to say for yourself? Unbelievable. I can't believe you'd shoot a girl in the butt. With such a pointlessly advanced skill, too."

"Says the girl that was seriously contemplating whacking me on the head. And you even tried to use the guy next to you as a shield when you ran... I don't think you have any right to talk."

The guy she'd hid behind nodded vigorously. He was walking a few steps back from them.

"That's just because of Yue-san's training."

"I raised Shea well."

"That wasn't a compliment."

Yue puffed out her chest proudly as she looked at Shea. Hajime made use of the Ignore skill that he'd recently had a lot of time to hone.

Fifteen minutes passed while Yue and Shea bantered

cheerfully. The party had finally reached the Grand Tree, and Hajime was the first to speak.

"The hell is this?" His voice was tinged with both disbelief and amazement. Yue also gazed up in confusion. The two of them had been expecting a super-sized version of the trees they'd seen in Verbergen. A kind of majestic, awe-inspiring spectacle. Instead, what they got was...a very withered tree.

Its size was still what they'd expected. Actually, it was larger than either of them had imagined. It was hard to measure its girth with just a glance, but it must have been at least 50 meters in diameter. Far bigger than any tree they'd seen thus far. And yet, despite the fact that all the trees surrounding it were lush and healthy, the Grand Tree looked as if it was already half-dead.

"The Grand Tree has supposedly been like this since before Verbergen's founding. Yet it's never rotted away. It's stayed withered like that for as long as we've known. Because of the way the fog acts around it, and the fact that it never dies despite being so withered, the people of this forest consider it sacred. Well, I say sacred, but it's more just like a fancy tourist attraction..." Seeing their confused faces, Cam offered an explanation. Hajime slowly walked up to the tree's base. Just as Ulfric had said, there was a stone marker with a lithograph carved into it.

"This is...just like Oscar's..."

"...Yeah. It's the same."

Engraved into the stone was a heptagon, with a different crest at each vertex. The same one they'd seen in Oscar's house, or in the hidden cave the magic circle had teleported them to.

Just to make sure, Hajime pulled out Orcus' ring. The crest matched one of the ones on the stone.

"So this really is one of the labyrinth entrances. But... how are we supposed to get in?" Hajime rapped the trunk with his knuckles, but naturally that did nothing. Cam and the others didn't know anything more than this either, it seemed. Nothing in the legend Ulfric had told him said anything about how to enter this labyrinth. Though it was always possible Ulfric hadn't told Hajime everything he knew. *Should I call in my favor right away?*

Suddenly, Yue called out to him.

"Hajime...look at this."

"Hm? What's up?"

Yue was pointing to the back of the stone tablet. There were seven indents carved into the back, in the same spot the crests were on the front.

"So then..."

Hajime fit the ring into the hole corresponding with Orcus' crest. A few seconds later, the stone tablet began to glow.

The other Haulia all crowded around it as well, eager to see what was happening. After a while the glow began to fade, and floating letters appeared in the air above the stone. This is what they said:

> *—Four markers of strength.*
> *—The power of restoration.*
> *—A beacon woven from bonds.*
> *—Only with those three ingredients in hand*
>   *will the path to a new trial be opened.*

"What does that mean?" Hajime questioned.

"Four markers of strength...probably refers to getting four crests from other labyrinths?"

"Yeah, that makes sense. Then what about the power of restoration and a beacon woven from bonds?" Hajime tilted his head in confusion as he asked that, but surprisingly, Shea had an answer.

"Hmmm, well a beacon woven from bonds probably refers to whether or not you can get the beastmen to guide you here, right? Most beastmen never leave the sea of trees, and getting one to guide you here like you did is something that's never happened before."

"I see. It does sound like you could be right."

"All that's left is the power of restoration... Does that mean me?" Yue points to herself, no doubt referring to her automatic regeneration. As an experiment, she cut her own finger and pushed it against the tree's bark as her magic activated...but nothing happened.

"Hmm... I guess not."

"Well, maybe we have to...restore the tree...and bring at least four crests from other labyrinths...? So not only do we have to clear over half of them, we need to get ancient restoration magic from one of them?"

Such was Hajime's conjecture. Yue nodded in agreement.

"Haaah, damn. So we can't start on this one just yet... What a pain in the ass. Guess we'll just have to do the others first..."

"Yeah..."

Hajime was frustrated that they'd have to turn back after expending so much effort to get here. Yue didn't look too happy either. But unless they could find some alternate entrance, there was no point in sitting there complaining about it. Hajime quickly got over his frustration and decided to change his immediate goal to clearing three other labyrinths.

He stood up and called all the Haulia over.

"As you saw, we'll have to clear three other labyrinths before we get back to this one. My promise to protect you guys until you led us here has now been fulfilled. As you are now, even without Verbergen's protection, you should have no trouble living safely in this forest. And so, this is where we part."

He then turned back to Shea. His gaze made it clear that if she had any parting words she wanted to say to them, now was the only time to do it. Even though they were guaranteed to return here eventually, conquering three labyrinths would take take a good deal of time. She wouldn't be able to see her family for quite a while. Shea nodded resolutely and walked up to Cam and the others.

"I—"

"Hey, Boss! There's something I want to say!"

"...Wait, Dad? It's my turn to talk right now..." Cam ignored her and walked up to Hajime. He gave him a crisp salute and stood at attention.

"Dad? Hey, Dad?" Shea kept pestering him from behind, but like the royal guardsmen of England, he ignored her completely and looked only at Hajime.

"Yeah, what is it?" Like Cam, Hajime decided this would go faster if he just ignored Shea. Cam took a deep breath before voicing the will of his tribe.

"Boss, please let us accompany you in your travels!"

"Huh?! Dad, you wanna go with him, too?!" Shea cried out in surprise. When they'd had this discussion ten days ago it had sounded like Shea was going to be the only one leaving, so this caught her completely off guard.

"We are at once both Haulia and your subordinates, Boss! Please allow us to journey with you! This is the will of the entire tribe!"

"Wait, Dad! That's not the problem here! And wait, if Hajime-san says yes, then what was the point of all my hard work..."

"Honestly speaking, we're jealous of Shea!"

"Wow, you confessed that easily! I can't believe it! What happened to you guys over these past ten days?!"

Cam's loud voice drowned out Shea's protests. Somewhat confused, Hajime still gave an immediate reply.

"Not happening."

"Why?!" Like Shea had been before, Cam was taken aback by his immediate reply. The other Haulia began pestering him too.

"Because you'd be dead weight."

"But—"

"Don't get ahead of yourselves now. You might have improved a little, but it's 180 days too early for you guys to be anywhere near my level."

"What an oddly specific number!"

Despite Hajime's curt rejection, Cam refused to give up. He even went as far as to say "Even if you don't give us permission, we'll just follow you anyway!" in response. Hajime's Spartan training had built an odd sense of camaraderie between him and the rabbitmen, so they all respected him immensely now. He was convinced they really would follow him no matter where he went, so he decided to let them join on a condition.

"Fine, we'll do it this way. You guys focus twice as hard on your training. If you've grown strong enough by the time I come here again, I might consider letting you join."

"...You're not just lying to get rid of us, are you?"

"I'm not."

"If you are, then we'll go to every human town we can find and yell out your name like some kind of crazy cult, okay?"

"Y-you guys just don't give up, do you?"

"We're proud to call ourselves your men, Boss."

Hajime cringed a little when he saw how "manly" his so-called subordinates had become. Yue patted his arm comfortingly. He'd really overdone it this time, in more ways than one.

This was his own fault though, so all he could do was sigh. The next time he came back here he was going to have a huge headache to deal with.

"Waaa...! No one's paying any attention to me...even though I'm about to set off..." Shea was drawing circles in the ground as she wailed, but that didn't get her any attention either.

They parted ways at the edge of the forest. Once the goodbyes were finished, Hajime pulled out Steiff, and soon they were racing across the plains. Their riding formation was as before, with Yue in front, Hajime in the middle, and Shea in the back. It seemed to Hajime that Shea was clinging to him even more tightly than before, but he did his best to ignore it. If he reacted to it even slightly, he was sure Yue would notice. Shea's bunny ears flapped in the wind, and she closed her eyes happily as she enjoyed the sensation of riding freely under the open sky.

"Hajime-san. I forgot to ask this earlier, but where exactly are we headed? The Grand Gruen Volcano?"

"Oh? I didn't tell you?"

"Nope!"

"...He told me." Yue puffed out her chest proudly.

"I-I'm one of you guys now, okay?! Quit keeping secrets from me! Communication is important between allies, isn't it?!"

"Sorry, sorry. We're heading back to the Reisen Gorge."

"The Reisen Gorge?" Shea repeated, clearly not following. Aside from the Haltina Woods, the only other known labyrinths were the Grand Gruen Volcano and the Great Orcus Labyrinth. Hajime had already cleared Orcus' labyrinth, so Shea had naturally assumed their next destination was the volcano. Sensing her confusion, Hajime elaborated on his decision.

"There's rumors that Reisen's one of the Seven Great Labyrinths too. Since it runs from here all the way to the western continent where the desert is, we might as well ride through it and check on our way."

"S-so we're just going to pass through it like a landmark..." Shea's face stiffened. Not only was it considered the world's execution grounds, it was also where she'd just recently lost a lot of her family. Even knowing their strength, she was a bit shocked that they could just treat it like a highway. Because of how tightly she was clinging to him, her reaction was conveyed perfectly to Hajime, who let out a sigh.

"You know, you should have a little more faith in your own strength. As you are now, the monsters at the bottom of the gorge are barely any more of a threat than the monsters you fought in the forest. The reason everyone fears Reisen so much is because mana disperses quickly right after it's emitted from the body, but that won't even affect you since you use body strengthening. In fact, down there, you're way stronger than everyone else."

"...As your master, I'm ashamed you didn't realize something so simple."

"Ohhh...I'm sorry." Tears welled up in Shea's eyes at Yue's rebuke. Awkwardly, she tried to change the subject.

"S-so then, are we going to camp in the valley? Or are we going to find a town to rest at?"

"I think a town. I want to stock up on food and convert some of the stuff I have lying around into cash. If the map I saw earlier is accurate, there should be a town around here somewhere."

Hajime was more than ready to have a proper meal for once. Neither Hajime nor Yue had ever learned to cook, so all the food they'd made in the abyss had tasted bland. Then, in the sea of trees, they'd been too focused on training the rabbitmen to worry about cooking, so they'd just eaten whatever preserved food they had left. He was craving something that was cooked by someone with actual skill. And if he was going to be spending nights at inns and buying supplies, he'd need money. He had more rare monster materials than he could shake a stick at, so he wanted to convert some of them into cash. He also just wanted to relax a bit before they went back down into the gorge and started fighting again.

"Haaah... I see... Thank goodness." Shea sighed with relief. Hajime gave her a puzzled look and asked why.

"Oh, I was just worried you'd head straight to Reisen Gorge and say something like 'I can just live off monster meat.' And Yue's fine with your blood, so...I was worried I'd have to convince you to buy food. Thank god you still have some common sense. I didn't know you still ate normal food, Hajime-san!"

"Of course I do... No way I'd eat monster meat if I had a choice. And what kind of monster do you see me as, anyway?"

"Some kind of new, super carnivorous one?"

"Sounds to me like you want me to tie you to the back of the motorcycle and drag you to town."

"Hey, wait, stop! Where'd you get that collar from?! Please don't... I don't want to die! Yue-san, help meeeeee!"

"You reap what you sow." The merry trio's banter was all that could be heard for miles along this vast empty plain.

They caught sight of the town a few hours later, around the time the sun was starting to set. A smile split Hajime's face. Just like when he'd first seen the sun, the sight of that town really drove home the fact that he was finally free of the abyss. Yue was bouncing up and down in his lap too. Like him, she was excited to see civilization again. They exchanged glances and their smiles grew even wider.

"Um, sorry to disturb you two, but could you please take this collar off me now? I can't seem to take it off on my own... Um, are you listening? Hajime-san? Yue-san? Please don't ignore meee! You're going to make me cry, okay? Do you really want to see me cry that bad?!" Both of their smiles only grew wider. When they were like that, no one could interrupt them. Not even the loud wailing of the poor little rabbit sitting behind them.

A few more minutes of driving brought them closer to the town, and the two finally returned to reality. Now that they were much closer they could see that it was a small village surrounded only by a makeshift fence and moat. There was a wooden gate where the village met the road, with tiny huts lining either side of it. That was probably where the gate guards were stationed. This meant it was at least big enough to warrant a guard, which signaled that Hajime would definitely be able to stock up on supplies. He smiled happily.

"If you're in a good mood, could you please take this collar off me?" Shea grumbled unhappily as Hajime surveyed the town. There was a small inconspicuous jewel set inside the black collar attached to Shea's neck. Though it had been her punishment for mouthing off to Hajime, it was actually a very stylish piece. But for some reason she couldn't take it off, which was why she kept asking Hajime to do it for her.

They were close enough that the guardsmen would be able to spot them soon, so Hajime put away Steiff and they kept going on foot. There would've been a huge commotion if he rode into a town on a jet-black motorcycle, after all.

Shea complained during the entire trek, but Hajime and Yue simply ignored her all the while, as they swiftly journeyed towards their next destination.

Eventually, when they reached the town, two armored men came out of the huts on either side of the gate. They were covered in simple leather breastplates, and the longswords strapped to their waists were the only arms they carried. Rather than soldiers, they looked more like adventurers. They called for Hajime to stop.

"Halt. Show us your status plates, and tell us what you're here for." Standard procedure. The guards knew it too and didn't seem all that alert. Hajime dutifully took out his status plate and offered it to one of the guards.

"I'm mostly here to stock up on supplies. We're on a journey." The soldier-adventurer hmm'd disinterestedly and took a look at Hajime's status plate. His eyes went wide. He quickly held it up to the light, then rubbed his eyes to make sure he wasn't just seeing things. Realizing what must have happened, Hajime knew he must have forgotten to disguise his stats.

There actually was a skill that let one alter the numbers on one's status plate. Adventurers and soldiers made use of it extensively, as having their information get out to the wrong people could be fatal. A dozen different lies flashed through the back of Hajime's mind, so he just picked one at random.

"I was attacked by monsters a while back. It's been broken ever since."

"B-broken? But..." One of the gate guards sputtered. It was only natural. Not only was level listed as unknown, but his stats and skills were utterly ridiculous. Status plates could break, but usually only in the physical sense, never something like this where it looked like it was glitching out. Normally, the guard would have laughed at him for telling an obvious lie, but with Hajime's numbers being so stupidly high meant he wasn't sure what to believe anymore. Hajime just shrugged his shoulders helplessly, then followed up on his previous statement.

"How else do you explain those numbers? If it was real, then I'd be some kind of monster. Do I look like the kind of person who could blow this whole town away just by lifting my finger?" He spread his arms wide like he was joking, and the guard smiled with him. If the status plate really was telling the truth, then Hajime was a monster far more powerful than any hero or demon lord. Even if it was unheard of, it still made more sense for his plate to be broken.

If the soldier-adventurer had known the truth, he would have fainted on the spot. Yue and Shea watched on in amazement as Hajime spun his lies without batting an eyelid.

"Ha ha, yeah, you certainly don't look anything like a monster. I've never heard of a status plate breaking like this, but I guess there's a first time for everything... Anyway, moving on to you two..." The guard switched his gaze to the two girls standing behind Hajime. They'd been partially hidden by Hajime's frame before, so he hadn't gotten a good look at them earlier, but he froze when he saw who Hajime was traveling with.

A crimson blush slowly spread up his face as he stared at Yue and Shea. Yue was, of course, a stunning beauty who resembled a masterfully crafted bisque doll. And Shea was just as alluring, as long as she kept her mouth shut. Basically, the two gate guards were completely smitten.

Hajime cleared his throat loudly. Returning to their senses, the two quickly looked back at Hajime.

"These two lost their plates when we were attacked by the monsters I was telling you about earlier. And this bunny girl here is, well...you understand, right?" The two of them nodded knowingly and returned Hajime's status plate to him.

"But man, you sure got your hands on a cutie. I hear light-haired rabbitmen are pretty rare. You must be pretty rich, huh?"

The two of them kept stealing glances at the girls as the man spoke, his voice clearly filled with envy. Hajime merely shrugged his shoulders in reply, saying nothing.

"Well, whatever. You're free to pass."

"Thanks. Oh, yeah. Is there anywhere I can sell some of the materials I harvested?"

"Hm? There's an adventurer's guild down the central road. They'd be the people to ask about that. They've got maps of the town there too, if you need one."

"Cool, thanks for the heads up." This information in hand, Hajime and the others headed into town.

According to the sign hanging from the main gate, the town's name was Brooke. The town was bustling with activity. Horaud, the town Hajime had been to when they'd first gone to train in the Orcus Labyrinth, had been bigger, but a number of stalls could still be seen lining the main road, with merchants hawking their wares and customers heatedly haggling.

For some reason, seeing all this activity around him made Hajime giddy with excitement. Yue, too, was grinning happily. Only Shea was trembling uncontrollably, glaring at Hajime with teary eyes. She didn't yell, but simply glared angrily at him. Unable to ignore her any longer, Hajime let out a tired sigh. Grumbling to himself, he turned to face Shea.

"What is it? I finally get to enjoy being around other people again, so what are you glaring at me for? You look like some kind of terrible gorilla monster that I have to keep myself from dropping a boulder on."

"Excuse me! I don't look like a gorilla! And what's with that description? I'm starting to feel bad for this poor gorilla you probably killed!"

"...But aren't you all teary-eyed because you smelled your armpit?"

"Not you, too?! How mean—I did not!"

Shea was as boisterous as always. She frantically flapped her arms, protesting his words hotly. As an aside, that gorilla monster Hajime was referring to was the one he'd ended up using as a test subject for his Compression Synthesis. It had been purely for research, not enjoyment. Though it *had* tried to sniff Yue. Hajime's Steel Arms skill had come from it, actually.

"Do something about this collar! Everyone thinks I'm your slave... Hajime-san, you put this on me on purpose, didn't you?

How cruel. I thought we were comrades!" Even when she was angry, Shea didn't really sound like it. Though she'd still found it quite a shock that her supposed companions were trying to make her look like a slave. Of course, the collar Hajime had put on her wasn't an actual slave collar, nor did it really have any ability to bind her. Shea knew that as well. Still, it was a shock.

Seeing her in honest distress, Hajime scratched his head awkwardly.

"Look, do you really think a beastman could walk around town in the open if they weren't someone's slave? Especially a little bunny girl like you, since you're so popular. Plus, you have light blue hair and a nice figure. I can guarantee you that if you weren't wearing that collar, someone would try and capture you the moment we entered town. And then it'd all become one huge mess of kidnappers. And that would be a pain... Wait, what are you blushing like that for?" Over the course of his explanation, Shea's angry glare had been replaced by a shy blush. By the end, she was cupping her cheeks in her hands and squirming in embarrassment. Yue just glared at her coldly.

"O-oh you—Hajime-san. I can't believe you'd be so bold out in public. Saying things like I've got a nice figure, or a great personality, or that I'm the cutest, sexiest girl in the world. My, how embarra—bugaah?!" Yue's fist interrupted Shea's exaggerated delusions. Her subsequent scream had not an iota of cuteness to it. Also, since she hadn't defended herself with body strengthening, her cheek had a big red welt on it.

"...Don't get ahead of yourself."

"I'b shorry, Yue-san."

Shea trembled at the coldness in Yue's voice. Tired of their little skit, Hajime cut them off by continuing his explanation.

"Anyway, pretending you're a slave when we're in human territory is for your sake. I'd rather not end up having to save you from trouble every time we go to a town."

"I...get that, but..." She understood logically why Hajime was doing it. But she still found it hard to swallow. She'd placed great importance on the idea that they were comrades, and she was loath to throw it away, even if it were just a pretense. This time, it was Yue who tried to convince her.

"...It doesn't matter what everyone else thinks you are."

"Yue-san?"

"All that matters is that the people important to you know the truth... Right?"

"...Yeah, you're right. You're absolutely right."

"...Good. Though it kind of irks me. You're someone I've recognized, Shea...so stop getting worked up over every little thing."

"Yue-san... Eh heh heh... Thanks."

In the past, Yue had wielded her power for the sake of her people. Though she spoke little, the answers she'd found after her dramatic betrayal carried a great deal of weight. Hence why they resounded within Shea's heart. Hajime, Yue, and the other Haulia all knew she was their comrade, which was all that mattered. There was no need to shout it to the rest of the world if that would bring unnecessary trouble. Of course, that still wouldn't stop her from wishing she could... Shea smiled shyly at Yue before turning to look back at Hajime. There was a hopeful look in her eyes. *Guess I've gotta say something too.* Hajime shrugged his shoulders.

"Well, if word gets out and slavers come after you, we won't abandon you, at least."

"Even if you have to turn everyone in town into your enemy?"

"You know I've already killed a bunch of imperial troops, right?"

"So you'd help me even if it meant making the entire kingdom your enemy? Oohoo..."

"Don't be ridiculous. Even if I have to go up against the entire world, or the gods themselves, if they make themselves my enemy, I'll fight them."

"Oohoohoo, Yue-san, did you hear that? Hajime-san sure says some pretty embarrassing things. He must really care about us!"

"...The only one he cares about is me."

"Hey, come on, read the mood! You were just supposed to say '...Yeah,' like you always do there." Though she was complaining, Shea still had a smile on her face. Hearing Hajime say that he'd fight the entire world for her sake had made her feel extremely happy. Especially since she'd fallen in love with him.

Hajime ignored their antics and continued explaining his decision to put a collar on her.

"Also, that collar has a telepathy stone and a sight stone packed into it, so you can use them in an emergency. Just pour some mana into it and they'll activate."

"A telepathy stone and a...sight stone?"

As its name suggested, the telepathy stone allowed its wielder to telepathically communicate with others. Hajime had created it using the creation magic he'd learned in the labyrinth. The distance from which one could reach another with it was dependent on the amount of mana put into the stone. However, any transmissions made with the telepathy stone would be broadcast to anyone in range who also possessed one, so they weren't suited for secret conversations.

The sight stone was also something he'd crafted with creation magic. He had added Sense Presence [+Precision Sensing] into a regular stone. This skill allowed a previously marked target to be pinpointed among a group of other presences. Thus, the collar also served as a kind of beacon for Hajime to find Shea at any time. The strength of that beacon, much like the range of the telepathy stone's transmissions, was dependent on how much mana Shea poured into it.

The longer she listened to the explanation, the more grateful to Hajime she grew.

"Oh, also, you can remove it by putting a set amount of mana into it, okay?"

"I see. So in other words...you gave this to me so you could hear my voice whenever you wanted and so that you'd always know where I am, right? Are you really that obsessed with me? That's a little weird, but, well, it's not like I hate it or anyth—bragahgwa?!"

"Don't get ahead of yourself."

"Ugh... I'm sorry."

Yue's hand carved a perfect arc before connecting squarely

with the back of Shea's head and sending her sprawling to the ground. Her voice was as cold as ice. Hajime was beginning to wonder if Yue really was as bad at close combat as she claimed. And just because Yue had allowed Shea to accompany them, that didn't mean she appreciated her making passes at Hajime. Though it was in doubt whether or not Shea's actions could even be considered "making a pass."

After a few more minutes of walking, the merry band found themselves staring at a building with a big longsword drawn onto its signboard. It was the same sign Hajime had seen in Horaud: the mark of the adventurer's guild. Though this building seemed to be only roughly half the size of the one in Horaud.

Hajime pushed open the heavy wood doors and stepped inside. Since the words "Adventurer's Guild" brought to mind images of rough and tumble types, Hajime had expected the inside to be dingy, but it was surprisingly clean. There was a counter directly ahead, while the entire left-hand side seemed to be a restaurant. A number of adventurers were sitting around chatting or eating meals. Judging by the fact that not a single one of them was drinking alcohol, Hajime assumed the establishment didn't serve any. *Guess they don't want drunks messing up the place.*

The moment Hajime stepped through the door, everyone's attention shifted to him. Normally, an unknown group of three wouldn't attract attention for too long, but their curiosity was piqued once people's gazes shifted from Hajime to the two girls standing behind him. There was more than one appreciative murmur, and a few of the adventurers were smacked by their female companions. That there were more punches than slaps seemed fitting for a group of adventurers.

Judging by how things went in fantasy novels, Hajime anticipated a few catcalls too, but contrary to expectations, most people remained silent. It was a bit anticlimactic, but Hajime was still glad no one decided to get in his way.

As he walked up to the counter, he found himself face to face with a charmingly smiling...middle-aged woman. A very well-built one at that. Her torso was twice as wide as Yue's. The stereotype that all guild receptionists were beautiful woman seemed to be a false one. Just like how in reality most of the maids were actually older women. No matter which world one was in, truth was harsher than fiction.

Not that Hajime had been hoping the receptionist would be a beauty. Nope, not one bit. That was why he was hoping Shea and Yue would stop glaring at him soon. It was starting to get uncomfortable. Whether she guessed what was going through Hajime's head or not, the receptionist simply continued smiling at him.

"You've got two gorgeous girls with you already and you're still not satisfied? Well, unfortunately for you, this receptionist's no beauty."

...*Can this lady use mind-reading magic or something?* Hajime's expression stiffened and he tried to casually reply.

"Oh, I wasn't thinking anything like that at all."

"Aha ha, don't underestimate a woman's intuition, boy. We can read you men like an open book. Your two friends over there won't like it if you keep looking to ogle every girl you meet, you know?"

"...I'll keep that in mind."

When she heard his despondent reply, though, she apologized immediately.

"Oh, look at what age does to you. I'm sorry for lecturing you when we've only just met."

It was hard to hate someone like her. When Hajime glanced back at the other adventurers, he saw they were all giving him looks of pity, as if to say, "Poor kid, so she got you too, huh?" It appeared the reason the adventurers here were all so mature was because of her.

"Anyway, welcome to the Brooke branch of the adventurer's guild. What business do you have with us?"

"Oh, yeah, right... I'm looking to sell some materials."

"I see. May I ask to see your status plate?"

"Huh? I need to show you my status plate just to sell things?"

The older lady gave Hajime a puzzled look.

"Are you not an adventurer? You don't need your status plate just to sell things, but if you're a registered adventurer you get a ten percent bonus to your sales."

"I didn't know that."

According to the lady's explanation, there were a lot of other benefits to being a registered adventurer. As they were the ones who went out to gather the mana crystals and medicinal plants most towns needed, they were treated well. Since the areas outside of cities were always crawling with monsters, regular people would have a hard time harvesting anything. It was only natural for those that took up the more dangerous jobs to have special privileges.

"A lot of inns and shops that do business with the guild will give adventurers ten to twenty percent off for their services, and if your rank is high enough, you can charter carriages for free. What do you think? Would you like to register with us? The registry fee is only a thousand Luta." Luta was the standard currency used throughout the northern part of Tortus. By combining zagalta ore with various metals, one could create alloys of varying colors. Luta was made from those alloys, and marked with a special seal. The denominations came in blue, red, yellow, purple, green, white, black, silver, and gold. They were worth 1, 5, 10, 50, 100, 500, 1,000, 5,000, and 10,000 Luta respectively. Interestingly enough, these were the same values Japanese bills and coins came in.

"Hmm, I see. In that case, I guess I might as well register. Unfortunately, I don't have any money on me right now. Could you just deduct it from the value of all the stuff I'm selling? I don't mind taking the base rate for however much I need to register."

"What are you doing, walking around penniless with two cute girls like that? I'll give you the bonus for everything, so just make sure you treat them right, okay?" *This old lady's actually kind of cool.* Hajime graciously accepted her offer, then handed over his status plate.

He'd remembered to properly conceal his stats, so only his name, age, gender, and job should've been listed. She asked if Yue and Shea wanted to register too, but they refused. They didn't even have status plates, so they'd have to get some from the old lady. But then she'd see all of their ridiculous stats and skills before they had a chance to hide them.

Hajime was curious to see what their stats were like, but it would've caused a huge uproar. Dealing with that would've been a pain, so he decided to keep laying low instead.

When she returned his plate to him, there was something new written on it. Next to the job column was an occupation column, which currently read "Adventurer." There was a little blue mark next to it.

That mark denoted his rank. As it rose it would change to red, then yellow, then purple, then green, then white, then black, then silver, and finally gold... *Ah, I get it.* The adventurer ranks were the same as the Luta coin colors. In other words, a blue rank adventurer was basically as worthless as a penny. How depressing. The first guild master who had designed this system must have had a pretty twisted personality.

Also, it seemed that anyone without a combat job couldn't rise above black rank. Though they could just barely manage it, even non-combat jobs could at least rise up to the quadruple digits. Those who made it that far were even more admired than combat-focused adventurers who made it to gold, so one could see just how much importance they placed on these colors.

"If you're a man you better aim for black, you hear? You don't want to look uncool in front of your lady friends, right?"

"Yeah, I'll work hard. All right, so I can sell my stuff now, right?"

"Feel free. I'm a qualified appraiser, so I can take care of it for you." So not only was she a receptionist, but she was also an appraiser. What a talented woman.

Hajime had put some of the materials in his Treasure Trove into his bag beforehand, which he now pulled out. It was an odd assortment of monster pelts, claws, fangs, and mana crystals. He put them all in the little container on the counter designed for this purpose, and the old lady stared at them in awe.

"Th-these are—!" She timidly picked up each item, examining them thoroughly. After a nerve-wracking examination, the old lady sighed and looked up at Hajime.

"You've brought me some crazy things here, boy. These...are from monsters found in the sea of trees, right?"

"Yep, that's right." This too, deviated from Hajime's expectations. Hajime had purposely avoided trying to sell anything he'd harvested in the abyss, since he'd assumed such monsters didn't roam the surface. If he brought those out, there would've been a huge commotion. He had expected materials from monsters in the forest to still be somewhat rare, but he hadn't had anything else on hand to sell. And based off the old lady's reaction, they were indeed rare.

Of course, Hajime definitely hadn't been hoping for the guild receptionist to panic at the sight of what he'd brought, call over the branch head, and instantly have him upgraded to the max rank for adventurers. Nor had he been hoping she'd instantly fall for him after seeing how amazing he was... Nope, not one bit. *So could you two please stop looking at me like that? You're starting to scare me.*

"You just don't learn, do you?" The old lady glared at Hajime.

"I have no idea what you're talking about." The abyss could shave away every other part of his personality, but the heart of an otaku was not so easily wiped away... Not that it was something to be proud of. Hajime averted his gaze and tried playing dumb.

"Most things from the sea of trees are pretty high quality, so I'd be happy to take these off your hands." She continued nonchalantly. *Looks like she knows how to take a hint, too. What a nice old lady.* Hajime doubted there was any old woman out there more amazing than her.

"So they *are* rare?"

"Well you see, humans get lost easy in the sea of trees, and a lot of people who wander inside never come out again. That's why most people avoid it like the plague. There's a few with beastmen slaves who go in there hoping to strike it rich, but if they don't treat them right, it's not hard for the slaves to lead their masters astray. And the few lucky enough to come back with anything usually go closer to the capital to sell the things they picked up. They'll be able to get a higher price there, and their fame will rise more quickly."

The old lady glanced at Shea. *She probably thinks we got her to guide us through.* Thanks to Shea's presence, it didn't seem too odd for Hajime to have materials from the sea of trees. Instead, the lady had a worried look on her face and mumbled something like, "Doing something so dangerous even though you're so young..."

I wonder what she'd think...if I told her I went all the way to Verbergen and transformed an entire tribe of rabbitmen into bloodthirsty monsters? Though considering how she's been acting so far, she might not even be all that surprised. Hajime smiled wryly to himself.

After appraising all of the goods, the old woman offered a price of 487,000 Luta for the entire stash. Quite a large sum.

"Are you really all right with that? You could get more near the capital."

"Nah, that's fine. This is enough."

Hajime gratefully received his 51 Luta coins. Perhaps it had something to do with the ore they were made of, but the coins were extremely light. They were also thin enough that even 51 of them could be carried around easily. Though even if they had been bulky, Hajime could have just stored them in his Treasure Trove.

"By the way, the gate guard mentioned something about you guys having maps of the town..."

"Oh, yes, we do. Excuse me for just a moment... Here, found it. The inns and shops I recommend are all marked on it." The map she'd handed over was minutely detailed, and all of the most important information was easy to find. It resembled tourist pamphlets Hajime was used to. He couldn't believe the guild gave away something this nice for free.

"Hey, is it really okay to just take this for free? This is a really good map. Hell, I'd totally be willing to pay for something like this..."

"I don't mind. I just draw them for fun in my spare time. Actually, my job is Scribe, so something like this is easy for me."

Is this lady Wonder Woman or something? What's someone so

skilled doing in a backwater town like this? Hajime was certain the story of how she ended up here would make for an interesting tale.

"You sure? Well, thanks then."

"It's fine. Anyway, since you've got a decent amount of money now, I'd recommend staying somewhere nice. This town's pretty safe, but I'm sure there's at least a few guys that'll try and do something stupid since you have those two by your side."

Helpful until the very end. Hajime smiled appreciatively, thanked her, and headed for the door. Yue and Shea bowed to her too before following after him. The adventurers were all whispering furiously to each other as they watched the girls leave the building.

"Heh, what an interesting bunch..." the old lady muttered to herself.

٭ ٭ ٭ ٭ ٭ ٭ ٭ ٭ ٭ ٭ ٭ ٭ ٭ ٭

Hajime and the others looked over their map, which was more of a guidebook really, and decided to spend the night at the "Masaka Inn." Though he wasn't a huge fan of the name, according to the blurb on the map, it had very good food, was in a safe neighborhood, and—most importantly—had a bath. That last one was what decided it for Hajime. It was a bit on the pricey side, but since they were rich, that wasn't a problem. The entire first floor of the inn was its restaurant, and when they arrived they found a few people eating dinner there. And just like with the adventurer's guild, everyone's attention was drawn to Yue and Shea. They ignored the stares and walked up to the counter, where a lively girl of maybe fifteen came out to greet them.

"Welcome to the Masaka Inn! Are you here for a room or for a meal?"

"I'd like to rent a room. We came here following this guidebook. Is the price still the same as what's on here?" Hajime showed her the map, and the girl nodded in understanding.

"Oh, you came here on Catherine's recommendation. Yep, our prices are still the same. How many nights will you be staying?" She continued briskly. However, Hajime's mind was elsewhere. It had come as quite a shock to him that the old lady's name was Catherine.

"Umm, excuse me? Sir?" The girl's words brought Hajime back to his senses.

"O-oh, sorry. Just one night. Also, we'd like dinner and a bath, too."

"Okay. It costs 100 Luta for every 15 minutes in the bath. Right now, we have these time slots free." She held up a little board with time slots written on it. Hajime wanted to take his time in the bath, and they'd have to split up the guys and girls, so he'd need 2 hours at least. The girl cried out in surprise when he mentioned as much, but as a born-and-bred Japanese, Hajime would settle for no less.

"A-also, umm, how many rooms would you like? We have both two-person and three-person rooms available, so..." There was a hint of curiosity in her eyes as she asked that. She was around that age where she was interested in things like romance. Though Hajime wished the other guests would stop trying to eavesdrop on the conversation, too. He'd known Yue and Shea were both very good-looking, but this exceeded even his expectations.

Considering how they'd met, it wasn't that surprising that Hajime was a little ignorant of how others would see them.

"A three-person room should be fine." There wasn't even a hint of hesitation in his voice. The surroundings guests all stared in awe. The girl too, blushed slightly. However, there was someone who objected to Hajime's choice.

"No. Two two-person rooms." Yue. The other guests, especially the men, all grinned smugly. They were, of course, thinking Yue wanted to split the guys and girls. However, Yue's next words shattered their hopes.

"...One for me and Hajime. You can have the other, Shea."

"Hey, why?! I don't want to be all on my own! Come on, let's just all share a room!" Shea protested hotly.

"...Because you'll get in the way."

"Get in the way of what... Wait, what are you planning on doing in there?"

"...Isn't it obvious? Sex."

"Bwah?! H-how can you just say that with so many people around?! Don't you have any class?!"

Yue's words thrust all the men present into the depths of despair. Eyes burning with jealousy, they glared at Hajime. The girl from the inn had gone red as a tomato as she glanced between Yue and Hajime. Hajime tried to step in before the two girls could embarrass him any further, but he was a hair too late.

"F-fine, then you go in the other room, Yue-san! I'm the one who'll share a room with Hajime-san!"

"...Oh, and why is that?" Yue's gaze was as cold as a winter blizzard. That cold gaze brought back traumatic memories of her training, so Shea started trembling in fear, but she steeled her resolve and glared right back.

"S-so that I can give Hajime-san my virginity!"

Silence descended upon the room. No one said a word, or even made a sound. Everyone's attention was firmly fixed on Hajime and the others. Even the girl's parents had come out from inside the kitchen and were watching their exchange with a "must be nice to be young" kind of expression on their faces. At this point Yue could have frozen hell over with her glare alone.

"...Any last words?"

"Ugh. I-I won't lose to you! Today's the day I beat you and take over the role of main heroine!"

"Allow me to teach you that there is no disciple who's stronger than their master."

"Well, it's time for this disciple to surpass her master!"

An intimidating aura began wrapping itself around Yue, and Shea drew the hammer strapped to her back with trembling fingers. Everyone gulped nervously, too scared to make a move. It was in this tense atmosphere that... *Clang! Clang!*

"Huh?!"

"Hakyuu?!"

A metal fist came down on both of the girls. They both crouched on the ground, tears streaming from their eyes. The one who had struck them was Hajime.

"Sheesh, stop bothering the other guests. And more importantly, stop embarrassing me."

"Ooof, your love hurts, Hajime..."

"Y-you could have held back at least a little... I was even using body strengthening, and it still hurts..."

"That's your own fault, moron."

Hajime gave them both a stern glare before turning back to the girl at the counter. She straightened up with a start.

"Sorry for the commotion. A three-person room will be fine."

"...I-If you're getting a three-person room...d-does that mean you're going to do them both at once? A-amazing... Wait, is that why you wanted two hours in the bath? Are you going to be washing each other's backs and stuff?! And then...do something a little more... How scandalous!"

The poor girl had lost it. Unable to keep watching any longer, her mom, who was presumably the owner, dragged her away from the counter. Her father took her place and finished completing the paperwork.

"Sorry about my daughter," he said apologetically, as he handed over the room key. But just like the other guys, his eyes were full of jealousy too. *He's definitely the kind of guy that'll be all sarcastic and go "Well, did you enjoy yourself last night?" in the morning.*

Anything Hajime said would just make the misunderstanding worse, so he just silently took his key, picked up Yue and Shea, slung them over his shoulders, and escaped to his room on the third floor. It took a long time before noises could be heard from downstairs again. The whole ordeal had tired Hajime out, so he just tried not to think about it.

Finally, Hajime went into his room. Ignoring their protests, he threw Shea and Yue onto their respective beds before diving into his own and letting sleep overcome him.

A few hours later, Yue woke him up to tell him it was time for dinner. Refreshed, Hajime headed downstairs together with Shea and Yue. For whatever reason, all of the people that had been sitting when he'd come to check in were still there. Not a single one of them had left.

Hajime's face stiffened a little, but he feigned composure and took a seat. The same girl from earlier came to take his order, blushing furiously.

"I'm sorry about what happened earlier," she apologized. But there was more curiosity than remorse in her eyes.

The food they'd ordered was indeed delicious, but Hajime had a hard time enjoying his first decent meal in ages because of all the curious and jealous gazes directed his way. He sighed as he finished his food, wishing he could have eaten under less draining circumstances.

And even though he'd gotten separate times for the guys and girls, both Yue and Shea had come to intrude on his bath time. Before another scene of carnage could begin, he'd had to calm them down with his fist and forced them to make up with tears still streaming down their faces. Of course, the girl had come to peek at them too, and when her mom discovered her it turned into another big affair, with the girl getting spanked...

Then, when he'd tried to sleep, Yue had sneaked into his bed to sleep with him. Naturally, Shea had to follow suit, so Hajime had ended up with Yue clinging to his right arm and Shea crying softly as she clung to his cold, metallic left one. However, the artificial nerves in his arm still let him feel things like it were a normal one, so Hajime was acutely aware of Shea's twin torpedoes pressing up against it. And that, of course, led Yue to then glare angrily at him, making it difficult for him to get any rest at all... The next morning, Hajime made an oath. Next time, he'd just share a room with Yue. Shea's sulking was nothing compared to her wrath. That cold glare of hers had probably shaved a few years off his life.

Once they'd eaten breakfast, Hajime paid for the food, then asked the two girls to get the supplies they'd need. Checkout wasn't until noon, so he could still use their room for a while longer. There was something he wanted to finish up while Yue and Shea were out buying supplies.

"What is it you need to finish?" Shea asked, curious. Hajime's reply was snide.

"There's something I want to try making. I have the basic idea down, so it should only take a couple hours. I was actually going to make it last night, but... well, I was really tired for some reason." He glared pointedly at them as he said that.

"I-I see. Yue-san, I want to go look at some clothes, is that all right?"

"Yeah, that's fine. I want to see the stalls too."

"Oh, that sounds like fun! We only got to look at them yesterday, so it'll be nice to get something to eat and spend more time shopping around."

They both turned away and began talking about shopping. Both of them knew Hajime's fatigue was their fault, but neither of them wanted to admit it, so they had simultaneously decided to change the topic.

"You two really do get along pretty well." Hajime's comment was conveniently ignored, also.

❖ ❖ ❖ ❖ ❖ ❖ ❖ ❖ ❖ ❖ ❖ ❖ ❖

The two girls fled into town, hurrying to escape Hajime's admonishing gaze. Though they had a few hours until noon, they'd still have to plan their trip out if they wanted to get everything in time. The main things on the list were food, new clothes for Shea, and medicine.

Shea was still wearing the same tattered clothes she had been in the sea of trees. The revealing outfit—which looked more like a swimsuit than anything else—was the rabbitmen's traditional costume, and all she had to put over it was the white and blue coat Hajime had given her in the gorge. But that outfit still left her stomach and legs dangerously exposed. More importantly though, such clothing wouldn't be fit for the kind of rough conditions they were bound to encounter during their journey. That was why Shea wanted sturdier, less revealing clothing. Thanks to Hajime, they didn't need to restock on weapons or equipment.

Even though it was morning, the town was already bustling. Merchants were already trying to lure in customers, and housewives and adventurers alike haggled fiercely. Though breakfast had just passed, the food stalls were crowded with people, and the smell of grilled meat and sweet sauces wafted through the street.

The item and food stores were all packed, so the two decided to get Shea's clothes first. Their map had neatly marked which stores were good for casual clothing, which were good for formal wear, and which were good for adventurers and travelers looking for something more durable. The old woman...Catherine really was something else. She was thorough to the extreme.

The two girls headed straight for the store dealing in adventurer's clothing. The fact that it also sold casual wear was what convinced them to try it first. Both the variety and quality of the clothes in the store was impressive, showing the true depths of Catherine's knowledge. Not only that, but all of the outfits were very practical and very fashionable. It did not disappoint. However...

"Oh my! Welcome. What a pair of cuties we have today. Oneesan's so glad you came! I'll get you two fitted up juuust right." The store was run by a monster. More specifically, a two-meter-tall muscled hulk that could barely be called human. Its face was so chiseled that it looked like it came out of a comic strip, and though the top of its head was bald, the long hair growing from its sides was tied up in a complex weave. It rose up past its bald head like a dragon ascending to the heavens, and at the coif's summit was a cute pink ribbon.

Its muscles rippled with every movement, which destroyed the effect it was trying to go for by cupping its cheeks bashfully. Its clothes were... No, some things are better left unmentioned. Needless to say, its arms, legs, and stomach were all exposed for the world to see.

Yue and Shea both stared in shock. Shea had already fainted where she stood, while Yue looked as if she were preparing to face down a monster worse than any she'd faced in the abyss.

"Oh my! What's wrong, my two little cuties? Such grim expressions don't suit your lovely faces! Come on, smile!"

You're the reason we can't smile right now, both Yue and Shea thought, but refrained from saying so aloud. Those two were among the strongest people on Tortus, and even they didn't think they stood a chance against this monster.

As it continued to approach them with the same beaming smile on its face, Yue finally snapped and muttered something.

"...Are you human?" That single question sent the monster into a fit of rage.

"And just who are you calling a terrifying demon that even legendary monsters flee from?! A creature so horrifying it turns anyone who sees it insaaaaaane?!"

"I-I'm sorry..." Yue took a trembling step back, tears in her eyes. Shea just slumped to the ground, an odd chill spreading through the lower half of her body. The moment Yue apologized, the monster's smile, if it could even be called that, returned. After that, it once again began treating them like customers. The instant transformation was frightful.

"Apology accepted. So, what kind of clothes are you girls looking for todaaay?" Shea was still out of commission, so Yue steeled herself and explained what they were looking for. Shea tugged on Yue's sleeve and shook her head, her eyes pleading with Yue to leave, but before she could reply the monster said, "Just leave it to meee!" and carried Shea over to the back of the store. She looked like a lamb that knew it was about to be slaughtered.

In the end, the two discovered the monstrous shopkeeper, Crystabel, had a wonderful fashion sense. And that she was far gentler than she looked. She'd only carried Shea to the back because of how shoddy her clothes were.

Once they finished buying Shea's clothes, the two thanked Crystabel and left her shop. They'd even come to see her smile—though they weren't one-hundred percent sure she was actually a girl—as one of her charms.

"Man, I wasn't sure what was going to happen to me, but it turns out she's a surprisingly nice person."

"Yeah... I guess you can't judge a book by its cover."

"Yep!"

They made their way over to the item shop as they chatted. Unfortunately, the two stood out a great deal. Before they'd gotten very far, they found themselves surrounded by dozens of men. Most of them were adventurers, but a few of them were sporting aprons and were clearly store clerks.

One of them even stepped forward. Though Yue didn't recognize him, he was one of the guys that had been in the adventurer's guild when they'd visited the night before.

"You two were called Yue-chan and Shea-chan, right?"

"Hm...? Yeah. That's right." Yue narrowed her eyes suspiciously. Shea was surprised anyone else was acting so friendly, since she was a beastman.

The man turned back and nodded to his companions. Then,

with a determined expression, he turned back to Yue. Many others also stepped forward as well. And then...

"Yue-chan, please go out with me!"

"Shea-chan, please become my slave!"

Well, this was hardly unexpected. The reason everyone's request toward Shea sounded so different was because she was still a beastman. Technically, a slave could only be transferred to another owner with their master's permission, but the guys at the inn had seen yesterday that Shea and Hajime were extremely close. That was why they were certain that if they could get Shea's approval, they'd be able to persuade Hajime somehow... Or something along those lines.

As an aside, the conversation last night had been so shocking that it had slipped their minds that a slave normally would never have been able to go against the orders of her master. Had they been paying more attention, they would have realized Shea couldn't possibly have been a slave. It *was* possible to give a slave less restrictions in their contract, but no one ever did. Upon hearing these heartfelt confessions, Yue and Shea...

"...Shea, the item shop's this way."

"Oh, okay. It'd be nice if we could get everything in one place."

...ignored them completely and continued walking.

"P-please wait! Won't you at least give us a reply?! Please, at least just—"

"No."

"Nope."

"Guh... Shot down... so fast." Some of the men crumbled

to their knees after being nonchalantly discarded by the girls. Others were unwilling to give up so easily. Frankly speaking, Yue and Shea were unmatched when it came to looks. It was understandable why some of the guys might want to resort to violence.

"Fine, then I'll just make you mine by force!" At this spirited yell, a glimmer of hope began to glow in the eyes of those that had given up. Everyone began surrounding the two girls.

When the encirclement was complete, the man who had yelled earlier charged at Yue. Had any Japanese person been present, they would have commented on how his lunge looked just like the Lupin Dive. Yue, however, merely gazed coldly up at him and muttered two words.

"Crystal Coffin." An instant later, the man was buried up to his neck in ice. This added weight sent him careening to the ground. He let out a very unmanly grunt as he crashed into the floor.

The others all looked on in amazement. Yue had cast one of the highest level water spells, Crystal Coffin, without a chant. They began whispering furiously to each other. "She must have chanted it ahead of time," or "I bet she's hiding a magic circle under her clothes" could be heard among the many voices.

Yue walked briskly up to the frozen man. Though they were awed by her power, the men all prepared to charge anyway, ready to become the next Lupin for a shot at becoming her lover. In order to save herself time, Yue decided to make an example of the first man.

She waved her hand, and the ice covering him slowly started to melt. Thinking she was freeing him, the man smiled in relief.

Assuming this meant he still had a chance, he gazed passionately at Yue.

"Y-Yue-chan. I'm sorry for running at you so suddenly! Look, I just want you to know that I'm serious—" Still mostly covered in ice, the man suddenly stopped mid-confession. Because he'd realized Yue was only melting the ice around one part of his body. Namely...

"U-umm, Yue-chan? Why are you only melting... the ice down there?" Indeed, Yue was only melting the ice that surrounded his crotch. The rest of him was still firmly stuck in place. A terrible premonition ran through his mind, and he gazed fearfully at Yue. *No way, she wouldn't. She wouldn't, right?*

Yue simply grinned.

"Shoot him down." Spheres of wind started slamming into the man's balls, one after another.

"Aaaaaaaaaaaaaaaaaaaaaah!!! Please stop! Mommyyyyyyy!" The man's screams echoed throughout the streets. Each sphere that slammed into him made a noise similar to the one heard when Mario collects a coin. No, honestly, the real sound was nothing like that, but because it was too gruesome to describe, it's just better to pretend it was something so soothing. His testicles jostled around like a punching bag being hammered by a boxer.

All of the men in the area, even the curious onlookers and the stall owners who had nothing to do with the situation, instinctively clutched their balls.

The continuous barrage finally came to an end around the same time the man lost consciousness. She had purposely made each individual wind sphere weak enough that he wouldn't pass out right away, but still strong enough to hurt. It was truly a god-like feat. Yue blew on the top of her finger like it was a gun barrel and hammered the final nail in the coffin.

"...You might as well be a girl now." That day, one man died, and a second Crystabel—or rather, Mariabel—was born. In fact, he would go on to train under Crystabel, and open up a branch store in her (his?) name. It actually became quite popular...but that is a tale for another time.

From that day on, rumors began to spread about "The Ball Crusher." The rumors eventually reached as far as the capital, and Yue's new alias became a symbol of fear for male adventurers worldwide...but that too is best left for another time.

Yue and Shea ignored the fearful gazes of the other men and walked off to the item shop. A couple of women who had been watching the exchange muttered "Yue Oneesama..." as she walked past, but she ignored them, too.

They completed the rest of their shopping, and when they returned they found Hajime just about done with his work. He was about to welcome them back, but the words died on his lips when he saw how Shea looked.

"Ehehe. What do you think, Hajime-san? Do I look more like an adventurer, now?" Shea did a little twirl as she said that. Her short skirt fluttered up to a dangerous height, and her boobs jiggled wildly underneath a shirt—if one could even call it that—which emphasized her cleavage. Like before, her midriff was completely exposed.

Honestly speaking, her new clothes were about as revealing as her old outfit. The only real difference was that her threadbare sandals had been replaced with sturdy boots. That being said, they laced up only to her ankles, so nothing much had changed even there.

"...What did you guys even go to buy? Looks to me like this worthless rabbit's still wearing the same revealing outfit as before..."

"Come now, what are you saying, Hajime-san? Look closely. Even if my skirt gets flipped up, these hot pants will keep anyone from seeing my panties. See?" Somewhat bashfully, Shea lifted up her skirt to show Hajime. Indeed, there was a pair of white hot pants underneath, which looked surprisingly durable. Apparently the upper part of her outfit, which resembled a swimsuit more than anything, was also a kind of bikini armor, so it actually protected her vitals effectively. *But even so, how's this supposed to protect her stomach, or her thighs, or any other part of her body?* Hajime gazed questioningly at Shea.

"...It's fine. Shea said all the other clothes were too tight and made it hard to move." Yue answered for her. It seemed Shea emphasized flexibility of motion over any amount of protection clothes might offer. Thus, the bunny girl was outfitted in a new ensemble that was practically no different from her old one, with the exception that it was a bit more stylish, and offered marginally more protection. The getup was topped off with one of Yue's handmade coats. *Well, whatever. If she's fine with it, then I guess it's fine.*

"Anyway, as long as we got everything done, that's all that matters. Thanks for doing the shopping. Oh yeah, it was pretty noisy outside a while ago. Did something happen?" Hajime ignored Shea, who was still twirling about in her new clothes, and changed the topic. Even he'd noticed the earlier commotion. Shea deflated a little when she saw Hajime ignoring her attempts to show off her charm, while Yue answered his question.

"...Sort of. It wasn't a big deal."

"Ah, I see. That's good, then."

The monstrous shopkeeper and the man Yue had nearly sent to heaven were all waved off as "no big deal." Hajime gazed suspiciously at the two of them for a few seconds before shrugging his shoulders.

"Do we have everything we need?"

"Yeah. We got it all."

"Yep. We got a ton of food too, so we won't go hungry anytime soon. That Treasure Trove of yours sure is useful!"

Hajime had let them borrow his Treasure Trove while they were out shopping. Shea stared enviously at the ring, at which Hajime only smiled awkwardly. At his current level of skill, he wasn't able to create something like the Treasure Trove. But because of how convenient it was, he wanted to be able to make some for Yue and Shea too.

"Now then, Shea. This is for you." Hajime held out a cylindrical, mechanical object that was about fifty centimeters long and forty centimeters in diameter. The whole thing was a glossy silver, and there was a little grip-like thing attached to the side.

Shea reflexively took it in her hands, and the unexpected weight of it caused her to stumble backward. Hurriedly, she used her body strengthening to steady herself and lift it up.

"Wh-what is this thing? It's super heavy..."

"It's the new warhammer I made for you. Heavier's better, right?"

"Huh? This is...a hammer?" Shea's question was to be expected. The cylindrical handle part did kind of resemble a hammer, but the grip was too short to swing properly. It was far too unbalanced.

"Yep. That's what it looks like when it's in standby, or in bombardment mode. Now, go on, try pouring some mana into it."

"Umm, like this? Ah?!"

When she poured her mana into it, the oddly shaped hammer made a bunch of mechanical clinks as the grip extended backward until it was in the perfect place to hold a hammer.

This was a battle artifact Hajime had created that he'd named Drucken. He'd added a lot of extra features to it that a normal hammer didn't have. In its base bombardment mode, the grip was kept close to the end because it was used as a trigger to fire massive shells at enemies. Pouring mana into a certain section of it made it transform into the more familiar hammer shape Shea was used to. Shooting bullets wasn't the only gimmick this hammer had, either.

This was what Hajime had wanted to stay behind and complete. He'd spent the morning perfecting it while Yue and Shea had gone shopping.

"This is the best I can do for now, but once I polish my skills some more I plan to improve it. There's no telling what we'll run into where we're going. I know Yue trained you, but it was still only for ten days. It's dangerous for you to come with us, so I made this weapon to bring out the most of your power. Make sure you get used to it, all right? You're our comrade now. You better not die, or I'll kill you myself."

"Hajime-san...Fufu, that doesn't even make any sense... Well, don't worry. I'll get even stronger, so I can follow you no matter where you go!"

Shea happily held Drucken close to her chest. Even when she was happy, it was pointlessly over-exaggerated. Yue just shrugged her shoulders helplessly, while Hajime smiled wryly. *I know I'm the one who made it, but it's weird seeing a girl get so happy over receiving a warhammer.*

Hajime and Yue went to go check out of the inn, with Shea following ecstatically behind them. The innkeeper's daughter still blushed when she saw Hajime, but he decided to ignore that.

It was high noon when they stepped outside, and the sun's warm rays blazed down on them. Hajime raised a hand to cover his eyes and took a deep breath. When he turned around, he saw Yue and Shea smiling at him.

He nodded to both of them, then started walking forward. They followed.

And thus, their journey resumed.

CHAPTER III
The Reisen Labyrinth

AROUND THE TIME Hajime was turning the peaceful rabbit-men into ruthless killers, Kouki's party was taking a short break on their journey through the Great Orcus Labyrinth to rest in Horaud.

Their training had taken them all the way to the seventieth floor of the labyrinth, and both the strength and numbers of the monsters they now faced had gone up considerably. In order to regroup, the party had decided to temporarily head back to town and rest up.

They also needed time to mentally prepare themselves, as they'd finally reached a point where Captain Meld and the other knights would no longer be able to follow them. The reason they'd chosen the seventieth floor specifically was because they'd found a magic circle there that could teleport them back to the thirtieth floor. Since they had found a way back, Meld had taken the opportunity to recommend they all head back for a break.

And so, they'd decided to take a few days to relax in Horaud. Everyone was spending their break however they saw fit.

On the outskirts of town was one such student. She was panting heavily from exertion.

"Haaah...Haah... Sacred stigmata of light, descend from the heavens and seal mine foes— Binding Blades of Light!" She braced her knees to keep herself from toppling over, then swung down her pure white staff. This girl was the healer of the hero's party, the Priestess, Kaori Shirasaki.

What sprung forth from the healer's staff was not restoration magic, but a flurry of crosses that resembled swords composed of light. Such was the nature of her spell, Binding Blades of Light.

A pack of wolf-shaped monsters, Deloses, howled, as the barrage of light crosses bore down on them. But the nimble beasts swiftly dodged out of the way and began rushing at Kaori.

"Divine Shackles!" She instantly let loose a follow-up spell. Normally, a spell cast without an incantation would be quite weak, but Kaori had packed the incantation for Divine Shackles into the chant she'd said for Binding Blades of Light. This was an original multicasting technique that she had developed on her own. Thus, this second spell was just as strong as the first.

Chains of light erupted from the ground, entwining themselves around the legs of the Deloses. The strength of the Deloses' charge was nowhere near enough to break the fetters, so they got stuck in place rather quickly.

Two of them had just narrowly avoided being bound, however,

and they now moved to pincer Kaori. Despite the fact that she should have been a backline fighter, and a healer at that, Kaori didn't seem fazed at all by them managing to close in.

"Perish!" At her shout, a deluge of light crosses rained from the sky, skewering the two Deloses mid-leap. However, Binding Blades of Light was fundamentally a restraining skill, and while the crosses succeeded in pinning the Deloses to the ground, they delivered no fatal wounds. Like their counterparts that had been bound by Divine Shackles, they were pinned in place but otherwise unharmed. After ascertaining the effectiveness of these spells, Kaori moved on to another incantation.

"Holy light of judgment, bring retribution upon the wicked and crush those restrained by justice." Suddenly, the light spells that should have possessed no destructive power made the Deloses start howling in pain. The Divine Shackles began tightening around their prisoners, while the Binding Blades of Light pushed deeper into the ground.

Though they could not directly pierce skin, Kaori's spells could still harm her foes indirectly. However, as this was not the intended usage for the spell, it required an enormous amount of concentration, and a re-imaging of the spell's nature, along with a skillfully arranged magic circle.

That was why Kaori had come here. The monsters around the town were far weaker than those they had encountered in the labyrinth, so even someone unsuited for combat like her could stand up to them. She had wanted to practice turning her restraining skills into offensive ones, so weak enemies like these were perfect.

She'd been here practicing alone for hours now, and both her body and mind were nearing their limits. Her supply of mana had been nearly exhausted, and her vision was blurry. She couldn't keep going much longer. And yet, the blazing will shining in Kaori's eyes had never once faltered. It had been burning ever since the day she'd learned the boy she loved had vanished, the day she'd resolved to find the truth herself—a desire so strong that it had melted the ice around her despairing heart, which would not burn out so easily. There was no time to waste on rest. Her resolve would not allow it.

And so—

"Press down, O voluminous light, for as long as my resolve stays true—Heaven Crusher!" Even if more enemies showed up, she would never back down. Even if it were reckless, even if it were pure folly, she would never stop. If she even thought of giving up, something deep inside would whisper "Is that all? You're going to break another promise?" and that stubborn side would force her another step forward.

From the sky came a new wave of monsters. Bahals, raven-shaped creatures with wings as black as the dead of night. They weren't especially powerful, but most adventurers hated them. Namely because of their feathers, a barrage of which was headed right toward Kaori.

They attacked in flocks, never neared the ground, and assaulted hapless adventurers by raining razor-sharp feathers down on them.

Kaori blocked their assault by creating a number of small, palm-sized barriers around her. *I need to make the image clearer, and get them out faster. I can't make huge barriers like Suzu-chan, but I can make up for that with numbers and skill!* Pale-faced, Kaori successfully managed to fend off the Bahals' first wave. Still, despite her accomplishment, she wasn't satisfied. Next, even though creating barriers was outside of her job's abilities, she created dozens of shields, angling them to redirect blows rather than stop them directly.

Had the class's Barrier Master, Suzu Taniguchi, seen Kaori's makeshift shield, she would have been amazed. Even she wouldn't be able to make such a perfect defense without considerable effort. Though both barriers and healing fell under the domain of light magic, it was nigh impossible for a Priestess, who specialized in healing, to match the defensive powers of a Barrier Master, who specialized in defense.

"Haah, haaah..." But even after accomplishing such a herculean feat, Kaori didn't smile. While she had fended off the Bahals' attack, she'd expended too much of her mana and had to bite her lips hard just to keep herself conscious. She leaned on her artifact to keep herself upright, stubbornly refusing to fall.

As the Bahals used part of their bodies to attack, they couldn't attack consecutively; they had to wait for their feathers to regrow. Taking advantage of that, Kaori quickly fired off another Binding Blades of Light up at the flock, then deployed her Heaven Crusher to keep them held down. Like the Deloses, the Bahals were brought to the verge of death by her spells' crushing power alone. But then, as she was about to start her next incantation—

"Ah..." Her body finally gave out, and she slumped to the ground. Unable to keep her magic up any longer, the Deloses were released from their bindings. Most of them had already lost consciousness, but a few of them had managed to stay awake. They coughed violently as they got up, their scarlet eyes glaring at Kaori.

Her mind was screaming at her to run, but Kaori's body would no longer listen. The few Deloses that remained charged at her. Drool dripped from their maws as they howled triumphantly. Kaori got to one knee, using her staff for support. Panting, she started the chant for a binding spell, but...there was no way for her to make it in time.

An instant before their monstrous fangs devoured Kaori, someone intervened.

"Kaori!" It was a voice Kaori knew all too well. Within seconds, the Deloses had been chopped to pieces.

"Shizuku-chan?"

"That's right. It's me, your best friend. Your best friend who's currently furious at you. Your best friend who wants to slap you silly for being so stupid."

"U-umm... Aha ha... Sorry."

Kaori let herself slide down to the ground as she apologized, meeting the angry glare of her best friend, Shizuku Yaegashi. She knew if she said anything foolish like "Why are you so angry?" Shizuku really would slap her silly. Besides, she had already guessed why Shizuku was so mad.

"Unbelievable. I won't tell you not to push yourself too hard. But at the very least, promise you'll take me with you! Even these weak monsters could kill you if you slip up, you know?! I thought you wanted to find Nagumo-kun?! How are you going to find him if you're dead?! You're a moron! A stubborn, stupid moron!"

"I-I'm sorry, Shizuku-chan..."

"Oh no, I'm not forgiving you that easy. I know you'll just run off again if I take my eyes off you. Quit trying to take Ryutarou's place, you thick-skulled idiot! I know you've been trying out a bunch of things, but you're still part of the rearguard. You're at your strongest when you've got someone to protect you while you charge your spells. You'll be able to train more efficiently if I'm around to back you up, and that way you won't have to worry about getting killed! All you had to do was ask me to come along and I would've joined! Why can't you even trust me with that?! Hey, are you listening to me, Kaori?!"

"I-I'm listening... Really, I'm sorry."

"Nope, I don't believe you! Sit up straight! You're going to listen to me this time whether you like it or not!" Shizuku plopped herself down in front of Kaori. What followed was a long and very spirited lecture by Shizuku.

Umm, Shizuku-chan. I think I'm losing consciousness, so I really can't tell what you're saying, sorry. Though the specific words didn't get through to Kaori, she could tell just how worried Shizuku must have been about her, as well as just how desperately she wanted Kaori to rely on her. And so, despite being inches away from passing out, she dutifully sat there and listened to Shizuku's lecture.

Halfway through her lecture the other Deloses woke up, and the Bahals came back with a new coat of feathers, but Shizuku annihilated them all without batting an eye and returned to her lecture. Finally, around the time the whites of Kaori's eyes were beginning to show, Shizuku was interrupted.

"Oh no, it looks like Kaorin's in really bad shape!"

"Sh-Shizuku...I know you want to lecture her, but don't you think you should let Kaori-chan recover some of her mana first?"

Suzu and Eri appeared. They had actually been searching for Kaori together, but Shizuku had dashed off when her built-in Kaori sensor had started tingling.

Their arrival finally got Shizuku to stop her lecture. She took a proper look at Kaori and saw that she was tottering on the edge of unconsciousness. Grumbling to herself, Shizuku took out a mana potion and dumped its contents down Kaori's half-open mouth.

Kaori gagged in surprise, but Shizuku mercilessly ordered her to gulp it all down. Shizuku gently propped Kaori up as she drank, and when she was finished she wiped away the drops of liquid that had spilled from her lips.

"Shizuku, you look just like her mo—"

"Suzu, if you don't want her to kill you, I think you should just stop." Eri hurriedly stopped her friend from signing her own death sentence.

Around the time Kaori was regaining the ability to think clearly, the four girls heard someone calling out to them. It appeared Kouki and the others had arrived.

"Kaori, thank goodness you're safe."

"Man, it's not like you to be this crazy. I know we came back here to rest, but you could've still asked us to help you out with your training. We won't get mad, you know?"

Kouki sat down next to Kaori and smiled reassuringly as he placed a hand on her shoulder. Ryutarou said his piece and scoffed. In their own way, they'd both been worried about her, too.

"I'm sorry for making you all worry about me. I thought I'd be able to handle the monsters around the town on my own at least... but I guess I went on for too long. I'm really sorry." She bowed her head, feeling guilty about making everyone worry because of her recklessness. Shizuku finally stopped fretting over Kaori like a mother hen, and a pleasant mood settled over the students.

Kouki proposed they all return to town, to which everyone else nodded in agreement. But when Kaori tried to stand up, she stumbled unsteadily. While she was no longer mana-less and groggy, her physical exhaustion remained.

Kouki hurriedly extended a hand to support her, but...

"You okay, Kaori?"

"Shizuku-chan... Thanks. Sorry, looks like I can't walk very well." Shizuku quickly materialized at Kaori's side, and Kouki's helping hand had nowhere to go. His eyebrows drooped sadly, but like a true hero, he refused to let that deter him. Undaunted, he tried to offer to carry Kaori, since she couldn't walk. Naturally, he was going to take her back princess-carry style. However...

"Sheesh, you're hopeless. Learn from your mistakes and stop running off on your own, okay?"

"W-wait, Shizuku-chan. This is embarrassing."

"Heh heh, it's your punishment for leaving me behind."

A girl strong enough to go toe-to-toe with monsters in the lower floors of the abyss could easily carry a single person on her own. And so, it was Shizuku who took on the duty of carrying Kaori back. Kaori blushed in embarrassment as Shizuku carried her like a princess back to town. Shizuku cut a gallant figure, with her cool demeanor and the imposing sword strapped to her waist. She looked just like a prince from a fairytale, complete with a princess to save.

"Oh my god, Shizuku...you're so cool."

"Aha ha... It really feels like you two are a couple."

Suzu was blushing a little, and Eri was smiling awkwardly. Kouki was standing behind them, his hand still outstretched. It was a testament to his fortitude as a hero that his smile never crumbled. His best friend gently patted his shoulder in sympathy.

"Even in another world, Kaori's knight will always be Shizuku... Good luck, Kouki."

"It's fine, Ryutarou, it doesn't bother me at all. Nope, not at all. Really, it doesn't."

"I see. Let's just forget about this and get something to eat."

"...Yeah."

It was rare for the muscle-brained Ryutarou to show compassion.

Some time later, the group met up with Captain Meld, along with Nagayama's and Hiyama's teams, and they set off to explore the uncharted seventieth floor. No one realized that one of their number had brought a bomb along with them. Or that a dangerous shadow had begun creeping up on the group. But that is a tale for another time...

❖❖ ❖❖ ❖❖ ❖❖ ❖❖ ❖❖ ❖❖ ❖❖ ❖❖ ❖❖ ❖❖ ❖❖ ❖❖

Mountains of corpses lay scattered all around. Deep at the bottom of the Reisen Gorge, a hellish spectacle spread out in every direction. Some monsters had their heads caved in, others had their heads blown clean off, and yet others had been charred into shapeless black lumps. They had died in various ways, but they'd all died instantly. There was, of course, only one group that could enter the gorge—the ravine feared by all as a hellish execution ground—and leave such carnage behind.

"There goes another one!" *Boom!*

"Out of the way." *Fwoosh!*

"Piss off." *Bang!*

Hajime, Yue, and Shea.

After Hajime and the others had left Brooke, they'd rode Steiff all the way to the entrance of Reisen Gorge. They had then made steady progress after entering the ravine and were already two days out from the hidden cavern that housed the teleportation circle to Orcus' house.

The monsters of the gorge seemed incapable of learning from their mistakes, as they once again attacked Hajime's party in droves.

Each swing of Shea's war hammer was a literal deathblow, shattering skulls with every strike. None of the monsters could afford to even get close. They were all ground to a pulp.

The few that did manage to get past the mochi-pounding bunny of death were burned to a crisp by Yue's magic. Though it took more mana than usual to activate her spells, her enormous mana pool, combined with the mana she'd stored into her accessories, meant she never ran out. The gorge's mana dispersing abilities lowered her range, but also decreased her cast time, so she was able to throw out blazing fireballs almost instantly.

Hajime's techniques were no joke either. Even while driving Steiff, he never missed a single shot with Donner. Despite powering Steiff and his Lightning Field simultaneously in the gorge, he didn't seem to be running out of mana at all.

The ferocious beasts that prowled this harsh land were nothing but fodder for the group. They slaughtered armies of monsters over the course of their hunt for an entrance to the labyrinth. In the few days they'd spent there, they'd already filled the ravine with corpses.

"Haah. Knowing the entrance is somewhere in Reisen is just too vague a lead." They'd thoroughly examined every cavern they'd passed, but they still hadn't found anything resembling an entrance. Hajime was starting to grow impatient.

"Well, we're just checking this place out on our way to the volcano anyway, so finding something is just a bonus. And who knows, we might find some more clues after we clear the volcano."

"Guess you've got a point."

"Yeah...but these monsters are starting to get on my nerves."

"Same here. I guess you'd really hate this place, Yue-san."

Even as they complained, the trio pressed onward. And so, another three days passed.

They hadn't found anything that day either, and as the moon's light began to illuminate the ravine, Hajime decided to make camp. They set up their tent and began preparing dinner.

Ingredients were brought out, seasonings measured, and dishes set. Everything from the tent to the tableware had been crafted by Hajime, so it was all of artifact quality.

The tent was augmented with heatstone and coldstone, which regulated the temperature inside. Thanks to the properties of coldstone, Hajime had been able to craft a refrigerator and freezer as well. The metal frames of the tent had stones interspersed within them too. These stones had been imbued with the "Hide Presence" skill, making it difficult for monsters to locate their camp.

The pots and pans all heated up in proportion to the mana poured into them, removing any need to start a fire. Even the knives had been enchanted with Gale Claw, making them razor sharp. He'd also made a makeshift steam cleaner. They were all beloved creations that made his travels more comfortable. And because they were only useful to people who could control mana directly, no one would want to steal them.

"Ancient magic from the Age of the Gods sure is handy." Those had been Hajime's exact words when he'd created all these Artifacts. Any present-day practitioner of magic would have fainted upon hearing the relatively pointless things Hajime used his abilities to make.

Tonight's dinner was Kululu meat boiled in tomato soup. Kululus were basically chickens that could fly. Their meat tasted identical to that of regular chicken. Kululu dishes were apparently very popular in Tortus. They'd already marinated and cut the Kululu meat, so they just boiled it together with some vegetables in a tomato-based broth.

The Kululu's flavor was further enhanced by the butter smeared over it and the tangy hint of tomato that had soaked into the meat. The other vegetables, all of which resembled one kind of earth vegetable or another, and the soup itself—they were all exquisite. Even the bread they'd brought to dunk into the soup tasted amazing.

After they finished their dinner, Hajime and the others settled down to chat for a while, as they did every night. Thanks to the stealthstone in the tent, they didn't have to worry about monster attacks. The few that wandered nearby by accident were summarily dealt with by Hajime. He'd just stick his hand out of the window designed for the purpose, then shoot them down. When it was time for bed, the three of them would rotate the watch until morning.

Tonight, it was Hajime's turn to be on first watch. Yue and Shea prepared for bed while he got ready. The tent was furnished with soft futons as well, so they could sleep well even out in the wild. Right before they fell asleep, Shea walked out of the tent.

Hajime gave her a questioning look, and she replied casually.

"Just going to pick some flowers."

"There's no flowers down here."

"Ha-ji-me-san!" Her nonchalant facade crumbled and she glared reproachfully at Hajime.

"My bad," he said without remorse, realizing what she actually meant.

Shea pouted angrily as she stepped out of their camp and trotted off. A few minutes later...

"H-Hajime-san! Yue-san! I found something! Come over here!" She had forgotten that monsters still swarmed the ravine outside of their camp and screamed for help. Hajime and Yue exchanged glances before running out of the tent.

Shea's voice was coming from where one of the boulders had fallen against the ravine wall, creating a small gap. She was waving her arms wildly right in front of it, her face filled with excitement.

"Over here! Look at what I found!"

"All right, all right, stop pulling me. Your body strengthening's on full blast. Just calm down."

"...So annoying."

Shea grabbed both of their hands and pulled them deeper into the crevice. Hajime tried to calm her down, while Yue just showed her frustration on her face. As she led them inside, Hajime saw that the wall had been hollowed out on one side, making for a surprisingly spacious room. Shea puffed out her chest proudly and pointed to a section of the wall that was halfway between the entrance and the back.

Hajime and Yue looked at what she was pointing at and blinked in confusion. A rectangular signboard was carved directly into the stone wall. Written on it, in cute cursive letters, was this:

Welcome everyone~! Welcome to Miledi Reisen's heart-pounding dungeon~!

The exclamation marks and tildes only served to exasperate the reader.

"The hell is this?"

"...What?"

Hajime and Yue spoke simultaneously. It looked as if they couldn't believe their own eyes. That cutesy handwriting was completely out of place in the desolate gorge.

"What's that supposed to mean? This is the entrance, obviously! When I was going to the bath...I mean, when I was looking for flowers, I found it here by accident. To think Reisen Gorge really was the entrance to another one of the labyrinths." Hajime and Yue finally recovered from their shock enough to stare at each other in disbelief.

"Yue. You think this is really it?"

"......Yeah."

"That was a long pause. What makes you think so?"

"...Miledi."

"Makes sense..."

Oscar's notes had informed them that Reisen's first name had indeed been Miledi. The name Reisen was famous, but most people hadn't known her first name. And so, the fact that it was written on the board made it highly likely that it was the entrance to the labyrinth proper. The only reason they were doubtful at all was because...

"What's with this stupidly cutesy writing?" Hajime thought back to the numerous life and death struggles he faced in the Great Orcus Labyrinth. If this labyrinth were anything like it, he'd be in for a tough fight. And yet, the entrance was marked with this utterly incongruous, lighthearted sign. Yue, too, had felt firsthand just how harsh a labyrinth could be, so she couldn't help but wonder if this wasn't just someone's idea of a prank.

"But there's nothing that looks like an entrance here. The cave just leads to a dead end further up..." Oblivious to their inner turmoil, Shea glanced around the cave and tapped the walls, searching for an opening.

"Hey, Shea. Don't..." *Clunk!*

"Fu-whah?!"

"Don't touch things carelessly like that" was what Hajime had been trying to say, but before he could, the wall Shea had tapped suddenly flipped around, dragging Shea toward whatever was on the other side. It was just like one of those trick doors you'd see in a ninja hideout.

"......" As Shea had just found a secret entrance, the words carved in the stone suddenly seemed more believable. *So the entrance to Reisen's labyrinth really is here.* Hajime was already starting to miss the more serious atmosphere of Orcus' labyrinth. This seemed more like an amusement park than a dungeon. He located the revolving door that Shea had disappeared through, exchanged a sigh with Yue, and pushed forward.

Whatever mechanism operated the door activated, pushing Hajime and Yue through as well. Darkness greeted them on the other side. The door finished its revolution, eventually coming to a stop in its original position.

An instant later there was an odd whirling noise, as a bunch of *somethings* flew straight for Hajime. Upon activating Night Vision, Hajime was able to see what was coming at him. Arrows. They were painted jet-black to make sure not even a sliver of light reflected off them.

Hajime pulled out Donner and shot most of them down. The rest he blocked with his prosthetic limb. Clanging noises filled the room as metal impacted on metal.

There had been around twenty arrows. The arrows were made entirely of metal, as if they had been carved into that shape. After the last one hit the ground, silence returned to the room.

Faint light started permeating the room around the same time. They were in a room about ten meters wide on all sides, with a hallway extending out of the far end. There was a stone slab in the center of the room with a message carved into it in the same cutesy handwriting as before.

Hey, did I surprise you? Well, did I? I bet you peed your pants, didn't you? Ha ha ha. Any of you get hurt? Maybe someone in your party died? Hee hee~!

"....." Hajime and Yue were in complete sync as they read the message.

"Annoying bitch."

Only the laughter in the message was carved deeper into the stone to emphasize its presence. She was being purposely irritating. Had someone wandered in and actually lost a member of their party due to that trap, they would surely have been furious.

As it was, Hajime and Yue were still quite angry, but Yue's anger suddenly faded away as she realized something.

"...Where's Shea?"

"Ah."

Remembering the remaining member of their party, Hajime quickly turned back to the revolving door. Since the door did a half-revolution with each activation, it was possible Shea had been sent back outside when they'd come in. What worried Hajime was that she hadn't tried to come back in even though a good minute or two must have passed. And so, he hurriedly activated the door again.

As the door turned around once more he saw... Shea. Stuck to the door.

"Uuuu... Hic... Hajime-saaan...don't look at meeee. But please take these off. Let me down, but don't look at me. Pleaseee." The poor little bunny girl. Shea must have been greeted by the hail of arrows too. Though she couldn't see in the dark, her sharp senses must have allowed her to dodge. But it had been a near miss, so the arrows had skewered her clothes, pinning her to the wall in a comedic pose reminiscent of those emergency exit signs.

Her rabbit ears were twisted in a weird zig-zag pattern, so it was clear that it had taken everything she'd had to dodge. The reason she was crying wasn't because she'd nearly died, though. The puddle at her feet was the cause of her distress.

"Oh yeah, you were in the middle of your 'flower picking,' weren't you...? Well, whatever. Happens all the time."

"No it doesn't! Ooof, why didn't I just finish my business before calling you guys over!" Shea wept uncontrollably. Not only had she wet herself, but she'd done it in front of the man she loved. Her rabbit ears twitched again. Though, considering how pathetic she'd looked when she'd first met Hajime, this was basically a drop in the bucket. That was why Hajime was more annoyed than disgusted as he gazed up at Shea. However, his look only served to hurt her feelings more.

"Don't move." As a fellow girl, Yue did feel a little sympathy for her, so she quickly removed the arrows pinning Shea to the door.

"You should be able to handle threats of this level...amateur."

"I'm sorry, I'll work harder from now on... Hic..."

"Hajime, we need a change of clothes."

"You got it." He pulled a spare set of Shea's clothes from the Treasure Trove and handed them over. Red faced with embarrassment, Shea quickly changed.

Once she was ready, Shea spiritedly ran forward, only to stop when she saw the stone tablet in the center of the room.

Her bangs covered her expression as she read the inscription. After a few seconds of silence, she suddenly drew Drucken and swung it down with all her might. With a thunderous roar, the tablet shattered into a thousand pieces. That tablet must have been the last straw, as Shea continued to slam down her hammer on the already shattered stone over and over.

But once it was pulverized, new words carved themselves into the pieces of stone. Now it read:

Too bad~! After a little while the stone regenerates~! Eeheeheehee~!

"Graaaaaah!" Overcome with rage, Shea mindlessly swung Drucken down again. The entire room shook as if it were in an earthquake, and a massive shock wave spread out from the point of impact.

Ignoring Shea, Hajime started talking to Yue.

"Miledi Reisen might have been the only Liberator that really was an enemy of humanity."

"Agreed."

The Great Reisen Labyrinth was surely not going to be anything like the Great Orcus Labyrinth, but not quite for the reasons they were expecting.

•/• •/• •/• •/• •/• •/• •/• •/• •/• •/• •/• •/• •/• •/•

A few hours after Shea's crazed outburst, Hajime had discovered that the dungeon had far outstripped even his pessimistic estimations of how it would turn out.

First, they couldn't use magic properly inside. Whatever it was that dissipated the mana in the gorge was far more powerful down in the depths. Yue was hit especially hard by that. She couldn't even form her higher-level spells, and her more intermediate ones were extremely limited in range. Five meters was often the upper limit. It was still serviceable enough to use in fights, but she could no longer blow monsters away with a single attack.

Even the reserves she'd stored in her magic stone accessories were drained at an alarming rate, so she had to be careful. That was how much mana it took to do anything. A normal person wouldn't have been able to cast anything at all in this dungeon.

Hajime was adversely affected as well. Both Aerodynamic and Gale Claw required maintaining magical energy outside of one's body, so he couldn't use them very effectively, and even his Lightning Field was crippled. Donner and Schlag operated at less than half of their usual power, and even Schlagen could only fire with as much force as Donner normally did.

Hence, body strengthening was essential to clearing this dungeon. Shea's area of expertise. As such, the reliable rabbit of Hajime's party was...

"I'm gonna murder you... Once I find your hideout, I'm going to tear you limb from screaming limb!" Shea was screaming as she hunted her prey, a dangerous gleam in her eyes. She'd completely, utterly, totally, lost it. Even the way she talked sounded more feral. Miledi Reisen's love of teasing others seemed to have gotten to Shea.

Hajime and Yue completely understood the feeling, so they didn't say anything. And as long as Shea stayed comically enraged, they'd be able to maintain some semblance of composure by looking at her. It said something about how much their mental states had deteriorated that they needed Shea to keep them sane. They'd made decent progress since entering, but they'd already run into a number of frustrating traps and annoying inscriptions. Without Shea's anger to calm them, Hajime and Yue would probably have lost it long ago.

Shea had already devolved into a madly cackling mess, but everyone still kept a sharp eye out for traps as they valiantly pressed forward.

Finally, they found themselves in a strange room. The stairs, connecting passageways, and even the layout of the room was completely haphazard. It looked like a three-year-old had just randomly assembled a bunch of Lego blocks. The staircase leading up to the third floor then connected to a sloping path that led back down to the passage leading out of the first floor, while the staircase on the second floor seemed to just end at a wall.

"Well, I guess this place *is* a labyrinth."

"...Yeah. Looks easy to get lost in."

"Hmph, I should have expected this from that rotten bitch. This twisted room is a reflection of her terrible personality!"

"Believe me, I understand how you're feeling, but I think you need to calm down."

Shea's rage still hadn't cooled. Hajime gave her a look that was half-exasperation, half-pity and posed a question.

"So, which way do we go now?"

"Hajime. There's no point thinking about it."

"Hmm, guess you're right. We'll just have to mark and map the place ourselves as we explore."

"Yeah..." Yue nodded in agreement. Mapmaking was a fundamental skill needed to explore dungeons. However, with how winding the labyrinth's construction was, Hajime wasn't sure how accurate his maps would be. He frowned, clearly unhappy.

The marking he had been referring to was another one of his special magic skills, Tracking. This spell let Hajime mark certain locations with mana. He could then find those marked locations no matter where he was. If he marked a living creature, he could track its location. He was going to use it in the labyrinth to mark where they'd been, so he could map out their location. He could also make his marks visible so Yue and Shea could see them, too. As the mana was attached to an object, it wasn't dissipated like the other spells they cast.

Hajime decided to start with the passage on the right-hand

side, and marked it before going in.

The passageway was around two meters wide, made out of brick. And like in the Great Orcus Labyrinth, the walls glowed faintly. They weren't illuminated by green glowstone, though. The light in this dungeon was a pale blue.

When he checked what it was with Ore Appraisal, he discovered it was called linrock. It glowed upon coming in contact with air. The first room they'd been in must have been enchanted somehow to not glow until someone stepped inside. The passageway resembled the mine in Laputa, actually. The one where they met the old guy who could talk to rocks. It seemed that linrock never stopped glowing after coming into contact with air even once.

Hajime reminisced about an anime from his homeland as he headed down the long hallway. *Clunk.* One of the tiles on the floor sunk a little as Hajime stepped on it. That was the first time the floor had done that. He looked down at his foot in confusion.

Then, suddenly—*fsssssh!* The sound of something slicing through the air suddenly filled the hallway as two circular saws appeared from either side of the wall. The one on the right was about neck height, while the one on the left was waist height. The two blades sped toward the party.

"Everyone, dodge!" Hajime instantly Matrix-dived backwards, narrowly dodging both blades. With how short Yue was, all she had to do was crouch to avoid both of them. Shea managed to weasel out of danger as well. They could hear Shea crying out in surprise as the blades sped past her. Since her cries didn't sound pained, Hajime assumed she was safe.

Shea had actually only just barely managed to dodge, and some of the fur on her rabbit ears had been shaved off...but it was no big deal.

After the blades had passed Hajime and the others, they vanished into the walls as if they'd never existed. For a while, Hajime just stood there, warily waiting for a second wave. But none came. He let out a relieved sigh, then turned back to the others. As he did so, chills ran down his spine.

Following his instincts, he grabbed Yue and Shea, then threw himself forward. Not even a second later, guillotine blades slammed into the floor where they'd been standing. They vibrated as they came down, slicing through the floor like it was butter.

Sweating profusely, he stared at the blade that had fallen inches from his feet. Yue and Shea stiffened in fear as well.

"They're all physical traps. That's why my Demon Eye can't sense them." He'd been so focused on magical traps that he'd failed to take into account the possibility of physical ones. Because the traps he'd encountered in his labyrinth excursions so far had all been magical, his eye could easily spot those. But relying too much on his eye was what had led to him lowering his guard. He'd put too much faith in his abilities.

"Haah. I-I thought we were done for there. Wait, Hajime-san! Why didn't you just stop them? You've got a metal arm!"

"Those things are pretty sharp, you know? Even if it wouldn't cut right through, I'm pretty sure they'd have damaged it pretty bad. I can't use Diamond Skin here, remember?"

"D-damaged...? What's more important to you, your

equipment or my life?"

"I mean, you got out all right, didn't you? What's the problem?"

"Hey, don't avoid the question! You wouldn't really leave me to die, right? I'm more important, right? Right?" Shea clung to Hajime as she stubbornly pressed him for an answer. But Yue was the one who answered.

"...Runny Rabbit. The only reason you almost died is because you lack training."

"R-Runny—you take that back, Yue-san! That's too much, even for me!" And thus, another moniker was added to the "something something rabbit" series. Despite nearly dying twice in the few hours they'd been exploring, Shea was still quite lively. Her true strength was how sturdy she was. Though she'd probably complain if anyone told her that.

Still, what Shea had said was true. Though he had chosen to dodge, Hajime could just as easily have blocked with his arm and gun. His coat was made of monster leather, so it would have served well in defending him. And if the blades pierced through all of that, he had metal plates protecting his vitals. Traps like this wouldn't kill him easily.

Even so, those blades had clearly been overkill for regular humans. Normal armor would have been cut clean in two with how fast they'd been vibrating. Unless it was something on the level of the armor Hajime had made with the ore he'd found in the abyss, any would-be explorer would have had to dodge.

"Well, if this is as bad as it gets, then I should be all right." Hajime ignored Shea and Yue's usual arguing and muttered that to himself. No matter how strong the traps were, he was fine as long as they weren't augmented by magic. And Yue had her automatic regeneration. So even if she got caught in one, she'd survive. Which meant...Shea was the only one whose life was in any serious danger. Whether she realized that or not, it was clear she was the most stressed out of everyone present.

"Huh? Hajime-san, why are you giving me that pitying look?"

"Hang in there, Shea..."

"U-uh, what? Where'd that come from? And why do I have such a bad feeling about this..." Shea rubbed her arms gingerly, clearly put off by Hajime's uncharacteristic display of kindness. She kept a constant lookout for any more unpleasant surprises as they headed further down the passage.

So far, they hadn't encountered any monsters. It was possible there weren't any in this labyrinth, but unfounded optimism usually led to an early grave. Chances were they'd jump out of nowhere, just like the traps.

After a few more minutes, the path opened up into another room. This one had three different corridors leading out of it. After marking their location, Hajime picked the leftmost path, a staircase leading down.

"Ooof, I've got a bad feeling about this. Something bad always happens when my ears get all twitchy." They were halfway down the staircase when Shea said that. Just as she'd said, her ears were standing on end and twitching slightly.

"Hey, don't jinx it. Someone always ends up stepping on a trap right after someone says that... See, look."

"I-It's not my fault!"

"Jinxer rabbit."

While they were talking, there was an ominous rumbling noise, and the staircase flattened out into a slide. It had been quite a steep staircase, so they wouldn't easily be able to keep their footing. To make matters worse, slippery black liquid started pouring out from tiny holes in the staircase.

"Kuh, damn!" Hajime quickly transmuted the metal plates in his boots into spikes, along with the fingers on his artificial arm. Thanks to that, he was just barely able to keep his balance. Yue had leaped toward Hajime in the split second before she fell, so she was safely supported by him. She had correctly predicted that he would brace himself. The two had spent enough time together to be able to read each other's moves.

Unfortunately, the latest addition to their party wasn't in such perfect sync. Shea had failed to predict Hajime would anchor himself.

"Gyaaaaah?!" Without anything to support her, she tumbled down the slide, hitting the back of her head on the ground. She let out a grunt of pain, and within seconds she was covered in whatever lubricant had sprung up. Gravity did its job, and she slid, crotch first, right into Hajime's face.

"Buh?!" The force of the impact dislodged his left arm from the wall he'd thrust it into, and he fell backward, his right hand still holding onto Yue. His foot spikes came out too, so he slid headfirst down the slide. Shea rode on top of him as they slid down.

"You stupid, clumsy rabbit! Get off already!"

"I'm shorry, but I can't mobe."

They started sliding even faster. Hajime struggled to stop their movement with his spikes, but they were already too fast for them to do any good. Changing tracks, he then tried to transmute the staircase directly, but the mana dissipation was too strong and he couldn't do it.

Shea finally struggled to a sitting position. She was now riding Hajime like a horse.

"Use Drucken's stake to hold us in place somewhere!" Hajime yelled out. One of the tricks he'd added to Shea's Drucken was a stake that could extend out from the hammer. He had wanted to give her a piercing weapon too, in case she needed it. A stake that large could still potentially stop their fall.

"O-okay, leave it to—wait, Hajime-san! Look, the path!" Shea moved to grab Drucken but then suddenly stopped.

That was all she needed to say for Hajime to understand. This slide was trying to spit them out somewhere.

"Yue!"

"Okay!"

Hajime called out to Yue. He didn't need to say anything more as she'd guessed his intentions.

"Hang on tight, Shea!"

"O-okay!" Shea clung to Hajime.

The slide came to an abrupt end, and for a moment they were all suspended in midair, weightless. Yue took advantage of that split second.

"Updraft!" This was one of the most basic wind spells. It was normally used to increase one's jumping power. Skilled practitioners could use it to emulate flight for a short period of time. But in this dungeon, magic was crippled. Even Yue could only keep them afloat for a scant few seconds.

"More than good enough." Hajime said triumphantly. Those few seconds were all he needed to examine his surroundings. Yue had done more than enough.

With both girls still clinging to him, Hajime pointed his artificial arm at the ceiling. He poured a little mana into it, and with a pneumatic hiss, a wire with an anchor attached shot out of his wrist. It embedded itself in the ceiling and held fast.

Hajime let out a sigh of relief when he saw the anchor wasn't coming loose. All three of them dangled there, held by a single thin wire. They risked a glance at what lay below them and instantly regretted it.

Slither... Hiss... Clack... Fwoosh... Slither... There was a pit of scorpions directly underneath them. They were only around ten centimeters long. The scorpion Hajime had faced in Orcus' labyrinth was probably more dangerous, but seeing so many of them crawling around was more mentally damaging. Goosebumps rose on his arms as he realized a single wire was all that separated him from scorpion hell.

"......" Everyone fell silent. No one wanted to think about what awaited below, so they all pointedly looked at the ceiling. As they did so, they realized letters were forming on it. They already knew what to expect, but they read the message anyway.

—Those scorpion's stings aren't poisonous, but
they will paralyze you. I hope you enjoy sleeping
with my cute little babies for a while, Bwhaha—

She must have made the linrock that held the message especially dense, as it glowed brighter than its surroundings. Anyone who fell in would be doomed to lie there, paralyzed, as scorpions scuttled across their prone bodies. They'd desperately try to stretch their hand out to the ceiling only to find those words.

"......" The silence continued, but for a different reason this time. Everyone was desperately trying not to snap at Miledi's taunting.

"Hajime, over there."

"Hm?"

Noticing something, Yue pointed to a spot below her. There was a little tunnel there.

"A tunnel... What do you think we should do? We can climb back up, or we can see what's down there."

"I-I'm fine with whatever you decide, Hajime-san. All I ever do is make things worse for us, so..."

"Don't worry, we'll punish you properly for that when we get out of here."

"Now I am worried! Couldn't you have just left it at 'don't worry?!'"

"How impudent. Your punishment's been doubled."

"You too, Yue-san?! Man, I won't be able to catch a break even after we finish with this place."

Hajime and Yue were as merciless as always.

"Haah, if only you could use your future sight to show us where to go."

"Umm, I'm still not that good with it yet. I *have* been practicing, but..."

Future sight was the only special magic Shea could use. It allowed her to see one of the potential futures that might unfold. But because of how much mana it took, she could only use it once a day. And because her strength was dependent on her body strengthening, without any mana she was just a worthless rabbit. She had been practicing when they had time, lowering the amount of mana it took little by little, but...she still had a long way to go before she mastered the technique.

"Well, no point in complaining about what we don't have. I'd rather keep pressing forward, so let's check the tunnel."

"Okay."

"Works for me."

Hajime fired another anchor from his arm and tarzaned his way over to the tunnel.

The tunnel, like the rest of the labyrinth, was illuminated by linrock. It didn't seem to branch off as far as they could tell and continued straight forward. The fact that there wasn't even a single turn was suspicious. Or perhaps Miledi's constant harassment had just made them all paranoid.

Warily, the group made their way down the passage. They went on for a few hundred meters without incident. The utter uniformity of the tunnel made it hard to gauge distance accurately. Everything was so eerily unchanging that they started to wonder if they were just walking in place.

Just as they were starting to grow suspicious, there was a change in the monotony, as if the cavern had anticipated their worries. There was a spacious room up ahead. The group relaxed a little, hurriedly rushing into the room...only to hear the familiar sound of another trap activating.

"What is it this time... Oh, the ceiling."

"Shea."

"Y-you got it!"

Everyone looked up at the ceiling and saw that it was slowly coming down on them. It was cliche, as far as traps went, but as their magic was practically sealed, it was quite an effective one.

From the hallway, it would have looked like the room had suddenly vanished and been replaced with a wall. That was how fast the ceiling had fallen. The hallway they had come from was now a dead end.

Silence filled the room.

It seemed impossible that Hajime and the others had managed to avoid being crushed to death. The silence made it seem even more likely they were gone.

However, something happened a few minutes later. Red sparks began flying off the wall opposite the one Hajime and the others had come in from. And after that, a hole large enough for a person to crawl through appeared. From within, Hajime, Yue, and Shea all clambered out.

"Haah... Haah... Th-that was close."

"Yeah. Would've been annoying if we got crushed back there."

"It would've been a lot more than just 'annoying.' Normally, you'd die if you got crushed by that, you know?"

There'd been nowhere to run to, and they wouldn't have made it to the hallway on the far side in time, so Hajime and Shea had held up the ceiling for just a few seconds while Hajime transmuted a hole directly above them.

Because of the unique properties of the labyrinth, he'd been forced to work four times slower, with his range reduced to only one meter around him. Worst of all, the whole ordeal had taken far more mana than it should have. They'd all huddled together in the small space he'd crafted for them while he slowly transmuted a path out. *To think I'd have to dig through the walls again like this... I haven't felt such humiliation since I first fell into the abyss.* He expressed his displeasure with a string of curses.

"God dammit. I can't believe I've been reduced to this again. Worse, my high-speed mana regeneration isn't even working. Hell, my mana's not recovering at all." Next to him, Yue took out a small vial from her pocket, then offered it to Hajime with a smile.

"How about a mana potion, then?"

"Don't mind if I do."

"Does anything ever faze you two?"

Hajime loosened up a little, then leaned tiredly against the wall. He could replenish some of his mana with the reserves he'd stored in in his magic stones, but he wanted to keep them for when he really needed them. A mana potion was probably the better option.

Smiling at their little skit, Hajime took the vial and downed it in one gulp. It tasted like an energy drink. While the potion only restored a fraction of the mana one of his stones could, and at a much slower pace, it had the added benefit of curing his fatigue. Revitalized, Hajime stood back up, ready to beat this stupid dungeon.

However, before they'd taken even a few steps, more vexatious words popped up on the ceiling.

Doohoohoo! You're starting to panic, how lame!

Miledi Reisen had spared no effort in making sure she annoyed her visitors at every turn.

"W-we are not panicking! Not at all! And we're not lame!" Shea followed Hajime's line of sight up to the annoying letters floating on the ceiling and snarled back at them. Her hatred for Miledi had already begun to consume her. She couldn't help but react to every single sentence they found floating around the labyrinth. Had Miledi still been alive, she would surely be chortling with glee at having found such easy prey.

"Whatever, let's just go. Don't let every little word get you riled up."

"That's just playing into her hands."

"Ugh, fine."

The passageways and rooms they discovered from that point on were all booby trapped. One room fired poison arrows at them from every direction, another had a pitfall filled with acid, and yet another had turned into a whirlpool of sand with a worm-like monster waiting for them at the center. Without fail, each room would have something snarky written on the walls or ceiling after they cleared it. Everyone was stressed beyond belief.

Nevertheless, they cleared trap after trap until they finally found themselves in a passageway larger than any other they'd seen up to that point. It was six to seven meters wide, had quite a steep slant to it, and curved to the right. It was like a spiral slide descending into the depths.

Everyone tensed up. After all, the passageway just screamed "trap."

As they descended, they found their instincts had been right on the mark. The ever-familiar clunk that heralded some hidden switch activating echoed between the walls. Due to his experiences, Hajime was convinced that regardless of whether they tripped the switch in any given room, the trap would activate anyway. *So what's the point of having a damn switch in the first place?!* But he knew yelling that aloud would only invite more ridicule from Miledi, so with herculean effort, he kept his mouth shut.

They watched their surroundings carefully, straining to catch a glimpse of whatever was coming at them next.

Rrrrrrruuuuummmmmbbbbbllllleeeee! Something heavy was rolling toward them.

"......" The three of them exchanged worried glances before looking back. Because of the curved nature of the path, they couldn't see very far above them. The sound gradually continued growing louder, until...a huge boulder the size of the entire passage could be seen hurtling toward them. Naturally, it was spherical. Quite possibly the most clichéd trap of all. And they were certain that wherever their mad dash led them, there'd be another annoying set of letters lying in wait.

Yue and Shea quickly turned around and began running for their lives, but they stopped after going only a few paces. They had noticed Hajime wasn't following them.

"...Hm? Hajime?"

"Hajime-san?! You'll be crushed if you don't hurry!"

Instead of answering, Hajime simply bent his knees and thrust his right hand forward, as if he were trying to take aim with his fingers. He then squeezed his left arm as hard as he could, making it let out a metallic screech. Smiling fearlessly, he stared down the boulder thundering toward him.

"It's just not my style to let you keep one upping me over and over!" The noise from his prosthetic arm grew louder. And then... *Boom!* With an explosive bang, his left arm hit the boulder. The force of the impact pushed him back, but he transmuted spikes out of his boots and dug his heels in. Cracks spread out of the boulder from the point of impact, and its speed slowed considerably.

"Raaaaaaaah!" With a spirited shout, Hajime dug his fist deeper into the boulder. The fierce struggle between his fist and the boulder came to a conclusion, and his fist emerged the clear victor. With another loud crack, the boulder shattered into a million pieces.

For a few seconds after the boulder was gone, he didn't move, alert for any extra surprises. After he was sure nothing more was coming, however, he let out a relieved sigh and brought his fist back. The screeching from his arm had stopped. He experimentally clenched and unclenched his left fist a few times, then turned back to Shea and Yue after making sure it was in working condition.

The stress from earlier was no longer present on his face. Instead, there was an exultant smile there. Though he had tried to not let it show, he had been getting worn down by the traps he couldn't sense or prevent from activating.

Hajime had combined his Steel Arms skill, the same one he had used to defeat Jin back in Verbergen, with a high frequency vibration he'd achieved by pouring mana into his prosthetic arm. That was what had allowed him to destroy the boulder. Though, because of the strain it put on his arm, he had to perform maintenance after only one use. Originally, it had been one of his trump cards but...he'd been so annoyed he'd used it on a simple trap.

Shea and Yue were in a celebratory mood as they ran up to Hajime.

"Hajime-san! You're amazing! That was so cool! I feel alive again!"

"...Yeah, same."

"Ha ha ha, I know, right? Now we can finally relax a little and—" Hajime's elated reply was suddenly cut off by a new noise.

Rrrruuuuummmmbbbllllleeeee! A very familiar noise. His smile stiffened. As did Shea's, and it appeared as if Yue's blank expression grew a shade darker as well. Like a broken doll, Hajime jerkily turned around. Behind him, he saw...a shiny black metal boulder.

"No way." He let out an involuntary gasp.

"U-umm, Hajime-san... Is it just me, or is there some weird liquid flying off that thing as it rolls down?"

"...It's melting the walls."

There were countless small holes dotting the surface of the boulder, from which an unknown liquid was being sprayed out. Anything the liquid came in contact with let out an ominous hiss as it melted.

Hajime took a look for himself, let out a tired sigh, and turned back to Yue and Shea, stiff smile still stuck to his face. Finally, it vanished and he yelled "Damn it, run!" before dashing off at an inhuman speed down the passageway. Yue and Shea exchanged glances before sprinting off after Hajime.

The boulder was slowly gaining speed as it sped down the passage.

"Noooooooooooooo! I don't want to be squish-melted to death!"

"...Same. Let's keep running."

Shea's wails echoed throughout the corridor.

"And Hajime-san, I can't believe you ran off without us! How cruel! You demon!" She protested loudly.

"Oh, shut up, it wasn't on purpose! Just keep running!"

"I can't believe you're taking that attitude with me when you left us behind! Do you not care at all about what happens to me?! Waaaah, I'm coming back to haunt you if I die!"

"Sounds like you're doing fine, Shea." Judging by the fact that she still had time to complain, Yue assumed she wasn't in any real trouble.

A few seconds later, they saw the end of the passageway. Using his Farsight, Hajime was able to ascertain that the room it opened up into was quite spacious. Still, there was something strange about its layout. The floor was the furthest thing from them, distance-wise. It appeared the corridor ended somewhere close to the room's ceiling.

"We're going down, guys!"

"Okay."

"Got it!"

They slid the last few feet of the corridor, fell to the room below, and—

"Guh?!"

"Hm?!"

"Eep?!"

Three simultaneous screams of surprise rang out. Below them, the floor was submerged in a pool of dangerous-looking liquid.

"Dammit!" Hajime shot out a barrage of knives from his left arm along with an anchor to fasten himself to the wall, then grabbed Yue with his right. The giant metal boulder flew past them and fell into the pool below. Smoke billowed as the boulder slowly sunk into its depths.

"Wind Wall." Yue's spell blew away any stray splashes of acid that got close. Hajime vigilantly watched his surroundings for a few minutes longer, but when nothing more happened he relaxed.

"Oof... Hic... I'm just... I'm just... Waaa..." Turning around, he saw Shea pinned to the wall by the knives that pierced through her clothes. She was sobbing as always.

"What're you crying for this time?"

"Are you on your period?"

"Isn't it obvious? You pinned me to the wall, but you're carrying Yue-san? Hajime-saaaaaan, can't you be at least a little nice to me?"

"I saved your life, didn't I?"

"That's not what I mean! Can't you save me in a more, like, gallant way? You know what I mean, right?! I want to be carried tenderly like that too!"

"Shea."

"Hic... What is it, Yue-san?"

"You have to face reality."

"What's that supposed to mean?!"

"Look here, Shea. I do think of you as a comrade, and it's not like I don't care about you, but...the girl I'm in love with is Yue, so you can't blame me for thinking of her first."

"Waaah."

In spite of the fact that what Hajime said was absolutely correct, or perhaps because of it, tears started falling from Shea's eyes. On the other hand, Yue blushed and snuggled even closer to Hajime.

"Just you wait, I'm going to make you fall for me so hard that you'll be begging to save me!"

"You never give up, do you?"

"Yeah. She has guts. I need to watch out."

Even when they were hanging for dear life above a pool of burning acid, they still had time to act out their romantic comedy skits. It really didn't feel like their lives were in danger.

Using his anchor like a pendulum, Hajime was able to swing himself across the pool of acid and land safely on the floor. The room they'd found themselves in was long and rectangular. Along the wall were numerous alcoves, and ensconced within each was a statue in a full suit of armor, complete with sword and shield. In the deepest part of the room was a flight of stairs, beyond which stood an altar. Past the altar was a majestic door. Placed atop the altar was a diamond-shaped yellow crystal. Hajime frowned as he took in his surroundings.

"What a door. Does it lead to Miledi's secret base? If so, that's great news, but...am I the only one that's got a bad feeling about those suits of armor?"

"Don't worry, I know her by now."

"Doesn't that mean these things are going to jump out and attack us? Shouldn't we be worrying a lot right now?"

As predicted, when the three of them reached the center of the room, something happened. A very familiar noise reverberated across the chamber.

Clunk! They all came to a halt. *I knew it,* the three of them thought simultaneously. The statues' eyes began to glow ominously. And with the sound of metal scraping against metal, the knights stepped out of their alcoves. There were roughly fifty of them.

As one, they all lowered their stance and raised their shields. The army of inhuman knights shuffled forward and encircled Hajime's party.

"Ha ha, I knew it. We should have destroyed them before walking up. Well, no point crying over spilled milk... Yue, Shea, you ready?"

"Yeah."

"A-aren't there a bit too many? I mean, I'll still do it, but..."

Hajime unholstered Donner and Schlag. Normally, Metzelei would be more suited to these numbers, but he was worried the Gatling gun might set off more traps. He could more than believe if he let loose a hailstorm of bullets that at least a few would trigger more switches. So, he decided to stick with his twin pistols for the time being.

A fierce fighting spirit dwelled in Yue's eyes. She knew full well that she was most disadvantaged by the dungeon's unique properties, but she would die before letting herself become a burden to Hajime. She was Hajime's partner. There was no way she'd let something as trivial as this slow her down. Especially not when a potential romantic rival had appeared, regardless of how slim Shea's chances actually were at seducing Hajime.

Shea, however, was beginning to get cold feet. Even if she was the least affected by the mana dispersion, she was also the one with the least amount of practical combat experience. The five days she'd spent fighting monsters at the bottom of the gorge hadn't been nearly enough. And even if she included Yue's training, she still had barely two weeks of experience under her belt. Combine that with the fact that she was one of the gentle Haulia, and it was hardly surprising that she was a little worried. The fact that she hefted Drucken and dug her heels in anyway was a testament to her outstanding courage.

"Shea."

"Y-yes?! Wh-what is it, Hajime-san?" Her voice quavered a little. *Is it just my imagination, or did Hajime sound a little...kinder just then?*

"You're strong. I can guarantee you that. These scrap golems have nothing on you. Don't worry too much and just beat them to a pulp. And if things do get hairy, we'll save you."

"...Yeah. You're my disciple—I won't let you die."

Shea began tearing up. But this time, they were tears of happiness. Because of how roughly they'd treated her, Shea had started worrying that they might have thought of her as a bother...but she finally realized that couldn't possibly be true.

They trusted her, so even if she was still a novice at fighting, she'd do everything she could. She let the mana flow throughout her body, strengthening her limbs, and stepped forward.

"Oohoo, you finally said something nice, Hajime-san. Now I'm really pumped! Yue-san, the day your disciple beats you isn't far off!"

"Don't get ahead of yourself." Hajime and Yue said simultaneously, but Shea was too energized to care. She looked straight ahead at the closest enemy.

"Bring it! You scrap metal robot!"

"Seriously, where do you keep picking all this stuff up from...? Ah crap, I should've just kept my mouth shut."

"Scrap metal robot!"

"I'm not gonna say anything. Nope, not gonna say anything."

Hajime sighed tiredly, and not because of the fifty golems bearing down on him. Whether they noticed his feelings or not, the golems all charged as one. Despite their massive frames, they were quite agile. Their armor clanged as they ran, and they cut quite an imposing figure with their glowing eyes and raised swords. It was like a wall of metal was closing in on them from all sides.

Hajime was the first to strike. Even if his pistols were reduced to half their effectiveness, they were still a little more powerful than the average anti-materiel rifle back on Earth.

Two streaks of light headed unerringly toward two golems' heads. They both got stuck in an eye, and the golems arced their heads back in recoil. As they fell, two new knights ran in to take their place. Hajime began firing as fast as he could, throwing their ranks in disarray and keeping them from finishing their encirclement.

Some of the knights were able to weather the hail of bullets by using their shields, swords, and even fallen comrades as protection, and made it all the way to Hajime. But those that made it that far were met with the wrath of Shea Haulia's war hammer. She had strengthened her body to the limit, and she mercilessly pummeled anything that got close.

"Deyaaaaaaah!" With a spirited shout, she swung Drucken down, pulverizing a knight into a thousand tiny pieces. It had tried to raise a shield in an attempt to ward off the attack, but Shea had simply crushed that along with the rest of its body. In fact, the impact had been so powerful that there were cracks running through the ground.

Seeing an opening, one of the knights that had been standing nearby lowered the shield it had used to withstand the shock wave and bore down on Shea with a sword in hand.

But Shea was aware of the plan. She twisted Drucken's handle, then pulled the trigger once its transformation was complete.

With an explosive roar, Drucken leaped off the ground. A barrage of shotgun shells fired out of its barrel. Using the momentum of the recoil, Shea spun around and slammed her hammer into the flank of the knight that had been about to cut her in two.

"Raaaaaaah!" The armor crunched as the hammer dug into it. The force of the impact made the knight double over as it was sent flying. It looked like it'd just been rammed by a truck. The limp body slammed into another one, and they both tumbled to the ground in a tangle of limbs. The entire torso had been caved in, so it didn't look like it'd be moving any time soon.

Shea's ears perked up as she heard the sound of wind whistling in the distance. She looked up and saw the knight she'd sent flying earlier had let go of its sword, which was now whirling through the air. She leaped into the air, grabbed it by the hilt, and flung it at another one of the approaching knights.

It flew down at inhuman speed and glanced against the knight's raised shield. Taking advantage of the momentary distraction, she swung her hammer up at the enemy. It hit directly into the stomach and sent the knight flying through the air.

In a final act of desperation, the knight tried to swing its sword down on her, but Shea utilized the force of her swing to dodge aside. Then, before the knight could hit the ground, she smashed Drucken down again.

A golem cannonball was created, and it knocked down a few comrades before crumpling against the wall in a shattered heap.

Shea's lips curled up into a smile. She wasn't enjoying the fight itself, but she was glad that she could hold her own alongside Hajime. It was only then that she truly felt she'd earned the right to travel alongside him and Yue... But that happiness lead to her lowering her guard.

In battle, even a moment's distraction could prove fatal. And before she knew it, there was a shield in front of her face. One of the knights had thrown it at her. These golems weren't bad at all. Since she was strengthening herself, it wouldn't be able to kill Shea, but it certainly had enough force to give her a concussion. Still, it would be easy to imagine what would happen to her if she let herself get disoriented.

She just hadn't expected a knight of all people, even a golem knight, to throw their shield. That was the kind of underhanded tactic reserved for thieves. There was not even enough time to yell out "Crap!" anymore.

The most she could do was brace herself for impact. But just before it hit her, a jet of water slammed into it, diverting the shield from its intended path. It flew past Shea's side and smacked into a golem behind her instead.

"Never let your guard down. Now your punishment's been tripled."

"Fweh?! That was your doing, Yue-san? S-sorry, and thanks! Hey wait, tripled?!"

"Yeah... Stay focused."

"O-okay! I'll do my best!" Shea curtailed her earlier excitement after getting scolded by Yue. Reflecting on her mistake, she refocused her attention. As she engaged the knight coming at her from the front, a jet of water bisected the one sneaking up on her from behind. A warm feeling spread through her chest when Shea realized Yue had her back. She made sure to keep her attention on the fight at hand though so as not to disgrace her master any further.

Any other knight that tried to get into Shea's blind spots was also cut down by a jet of water sharper than any sword. Yue was using the intermediate level water spell, "Rupture." It gathered the water in the atmosphere, compressed it, and shot it out as a high-speed cleaver.

There were two large metal water canteens dangling from Yue's waist. Another two were dangling from her shoulders. She'd taken them out of Hajime's Treasure Trove. Every time she muttered the spell's name, more water flowed out of the canteen and turned into a deadly blade.

Yue hoped using water already present instead of taking the extra step to compress it from the atmosphere would lower the amount of mana required for each cast. And since she was manipulating water already present rather than forming it with magic, the spell itself couldn't be dissolved once it was fired. There was a mechanism attached to the canteens that accelerated the water as it exited, too, so even the force of the water blade couldn't be negated by the magic-draining air.

Yue augmented Shea's explosive close combat power by guarding all of her blind spots. Unable to penetrate that ultimate combination, the knights' numbers continued to dwindle.

Hajime smiled as he watched their seamless teamwork out of the corner of his eye.

"Sheesh, they sure know how to fight. I better step up my game or they'll lose faith in me." Hajime mumbled that to himself, then continued to fire Donner and Schlag incessantly.

He blocked a knight's sword with Schlag's barrel, and then blew its helmet off along with its head using a point-blank shot from Donner. He didn't even watch as his opponent slumped to the floor. Without even looking, he fired Schlag behind him and shot down a second knight. He then ducked, avoiding a horizontal swing, and crossed his arms before firing, shooting down the knights to either side of him.

However, without Lightning Field, his bullet didn't have enough power to penetrate the knight's shield, so it ricocheted off, slamming into a nearby knight's knee instead. Without a leg to stand on, its balance crumbled, and Hajime leaped over it, shooting both it and a nearby knight down from overhead.

Another one of the knights tried to swing down at him the moment he landed, but he kicked off the sword and danced through the air once more. He fired a single bullet in all four directions, and each one took the head of a different knight. As he landed again, he pulled a round of bullets out of his Treasure Trove and spun both his cylinders to reload instantly. He then turned in place and began firing indiscriminately. The knights surrounding him were blown away one by one.

He continued cutting a swathe of destruction through the golems' ranks, making sure not to accidentally let any of his bullets hit any part of the room. However...

"What the...?" As he continued dodging the golem's attacks, he furrowed his brows suspiciously. Despite having destroyed a fair number of them now, it felt like their ranks hadn't thinned in the least.

Yue and Shea had noticed this as well. When they took a closer look at the battlefield, they realized the golems they'd destroyed were nowhere in sight.

"Are they regenerating?"

"So it seems."

"No way! How are we supposed to stop them, then?!"

Indeed, every time a golem was destroyed, the same light that glowed from their eye sockets enveloped their entire body for an instant, and then the golem was made whole again.

An edge of panic crept into Shea's voice as she mowed down another wave of knights. It was hardly surprising. At this rate, no matter how many they destroyed, it was pointless.

However, Yue and Hajime both remained calm, their minds working furiously as they kept the knights at bay. This was where the difference in experience came into play. Obstacles of such difficulty had been commonplace in the abyss. In fact, since they were stronger than they'd been back then, this was nothing.

"...Hajime, if they are golems, then they should have a core." Just as Yue had said, the golems must have had a core hidden somewhere inside them that was the source of their power. Most cores were created with mana crystals harvested from monsters. That was what had been written in Oscar's diary regarding his cleaning golems at least. Yue was thinking that if they could destroy those cores they'd stop the golems. Unexpectedly though, Hajime frowned unhappily.

"About that. I don't think these guys have any."

"You sure?"

"Yeah, I'm checking with my Demon Eye even, but I can't see anything. There's faint traces of mana coming from all over each golem's body, but..."

"Th-then, what are we going to do?! At this rate we're just going to lose eventually!" Shea was completely panicking now. Hajime ignored her and used Ore Appraisal on a golem. *Maybe it doesn't need a core because the golems themselves are made of some kind of special ore?*

Bullseye.

◊ SPIRIT STONE

A stone capable of absorbing large quantities of mana. Two or more spirit stones filled with the same type of mana attached to a different kind of ore can be controlled remotely.

So that means there's someone out there controlling these spirit stone golems? They weren't actually regenerating, the operator was simply rearranging the stones of the broken golems to fix them, taking extra from the room if there wasn't enough. It was more reconstruction than regeneration.

Upon closer inspection, Hajime saw that parts of the floor were made of spirit stone too, and that it had been gouged out in places. That was probably used to supplement any missing stone in the golems. Unless they took out the operator, there'd be no end to them.

"Yue, Shea. Someone's controlling these guys. There'll be no end to them if we keep fighting, so we're busting through!"

"Okay."

"B-breaking through? Roger!"

At Hajime's signal, they both turned around and made a run for the altar. Hajime fired Donner and Schlag as fast as he could, opening up a path before him, while throwing two grenades behind to stave off pursuit. There was a loud explosion, and the shock waves sent rows of knights tumbling to the ground.

Shea leaped into the opening Hajime had created and swung Drucken around, mowing down everything in her path. The golems threw their shields and swords at her, aiming for the brief window of time Shea needed to recover her stance, but Yue used Rupture to cut them all down.

Hajime brought up the rearguard and continued shooting down any of the knights that got too close. Shea was the first to reach the altar, and she quickly set herself up in a position to assist Yue and Hajime. Yue followed seconds later, leaping over the altar and heading for the door.

"Yue-san, is it opening?!"

"Nope... It's sealed."

"Ah, I knew it!"

Even at a glance, it was obvious the altar and door were important. It made sense for them to be sealed, after all. That was why they'd tried to finish off the golems first, so that they could take their time figuring out the seal. Shea grumbled in annoyance as she beat down the knights that made it up the stairs.

"Let's let Yue handle the seal. It'll probably take me too long to break through that with Transmutation."

Hajime fought his way over to where Shea was standing. It was probably possible for Hajime to break through with Transmutation, but in this dungeon it would take a vast amount of his mana. In which case, figuring out the riddle of the altar and the yellow crystal was probably the smarter route. That was why Hajime decided to let Yue, who was currently the most disadvantaged in the fight, worry about the seal.

"Okay...leave it to me." Yue replied instantly, and shifted her attention to the yellow crystal. It looked like two pyramids had been joined together at the base, and upon closer inspection Yue realized the whole thing was actually made of interlocking three-dimensional pieces.

She took the crystal in her hands and turned back to the door. There were three depressions on its face. After thinking for a moment, she started dismantling the crystal. She was hoping to rearrange the pieces into three cubes so they'd fit in the depressions.

While she worked, she examined each depression in greater detail. When she looked closely, she noticed each of them had writing so faint it could easily be overlooked. Written within was...

Can you solve it? Well, can you? If you don't finish up quick, everyone's gonna diiiie! Don't worry if you can't, though! It's okay, you guys aren't geniuses like me! So just relax! Even stupid people can live... Well, I guess they can't, huh?! Too baaaaad! Pwah ha ha ha!

The same annoying insults as always. Even Yue couldn't help but be irritated. She frowned ever so slightly, resisted the impulse to punch the door, and continued working on the puzzle.

Hajime and Shea sensed her shift in mood, but they decided not to say anything and continued beating down the undying army of golems.

"Hajime-saaan. Can't you blow them away with that other thing you used before?" The knights swarmed up the staircases like cockroaches, annoying and hard to kill. Tired of hitting them back, Shea begged Hajime to use his grenades again.

"Moron. What if it triggers a trap? I can't throw them out just like that. There's no telling what'll happen."

"That army of golems has already trampled every inch of the staircase!"

"This is Miledi Reisen we're talking about here. What's to say there isn't some kind of switch that doesn't react to golems?"

"Ugh, the scary thing is that you might be right..."

They conversed with surprising nonchalance as they blew through wave after wave of golems. Though Shea had been panicking at first, after seeing how calmly Hajime and Yue had handled the situation, she'd regained her composure.

"You know, I'm actually kind of happy."

"Huh?"

Shea whacked another golem off the staircase before continuing.

"For so long, all I was good at was just running away. But now here I am, fighting shoulder to shoulder with you, Hajime-san... That's why I'm happy."

"...You're a real weirdo, you know that?"

"Ehehe. I'm going to flirt with you so much once we're out of here!"

"Whoa, slow down there. Don't just go putting up death flags for no reason. The tragic heroine role doesn't suit you, so just stop."

"This is where you're supposed to say 'I definitely won't let you die, honey!' Come on!"

"Now that deviates from the script way too much. I'm actually a little scared by how optimistic you've gotten recently, but...I guess I can't say anything."

They continued chatting idly like that for a few more minutes. One could say they were flirting, even. Suddenly, a dark shadow loomed behind them. Yue.

"No flirting."

"We weren't flirting."

"Oohoohoo, is that what it looked like? Aww, you're making me blush."

"Shut up, you." Yue glared angrily at Hajime and Shea. The latter of the two was starting to grow a little tiresome. But she knew it wasn't the time to discuss this, so instead she puffed out her chest a little and reported her success.

"It's open."

"Wow, that was fast! You're amazing, Yue. Come on, Shea, we're going!"

"Okay!"

Hajime glanced back and saw that the door was indeed now open. There didn't seem to be anything too special about the room beyond. Regardless, he turned around and started heading for the door. If they could reseal that door, they'd be able to halt the golems' advance. Yue ran through first, followed by Shea. They stood on either side of the double doors, ready to close them the minute Hajime got through.

Hajime threw some grenades at the golems as a parting gift before sprinting through the doors. The golems surged forward, determined to stop the intruders. And yet, the grenades exploded before they could. Those that weren't blown apart lost their balance and fell. And in that moment, Yue and Shea slammed the doors shut.

Just as he'd checked with Farsight earlier, the room was completely empty. Even if it hadn't been Miledi's room itself, Hajime had at least been expecting a clue, so the whole situation was rather anticlimactic.

"Is this another one of her tricks? Have this big old fancy door and seal but put nothing behind it?"

"It's possible."

"Stupid Miledi! How long are you going to keep making fun of us?!"

As the three of them all hung their heads in disappointment, they suddenly heard the noise they'd come to hate.

Clunk!

"Wha—?!" The room suddenly started trembling. Suddenly, Hajime could feel G-forces hitting him from the side.

"Ugh—wait, is this whole room moving?"

"Looks like i—?!"

"Gawhaah?!"

Just as he said that, they found themselves being assailed by G-forces from above. The unexpected shift made Yue bite her tongue, and she held her mouth shut with tears in her eyes. Meanwhile, Shea was sprawled across the ground like an upside-down frog.

The room kept going in all different directions for a good forty seconds before it came to a sudden stop, ignoring all laws of inertia.

Hajime had managed to use his spiked shoes to keep himself in place, and even brace himself against the impact of the sudden stop, but Shea wasn't so lucky. When the room came to a halt she slammed into the wall headfirst. All the rolling around from before had already been bad for her, but this was the last straw. She tottered to her feet like a drunk, pale-faced and completely frazzled. She would be out of commission for a few minutes. Yue had clung on to Hajime the moment she'd realized what was going on, so she'd been fine.

"It's finally over... Yue, you all right?"

"Yeah, I'm fine."

Hajime untransmuted his spikes and stood up. He examined his surroundings, but nothing in particular stood out. Considering how much they'd moved, chances were if he opened the door they'd come through they'd be in a different room.

"H-Hajime-san, aren't you going to say something to me, too?" Shea covered her mouth to keep herself from puking as she glared at Hajime. She didn't look too happy about being ignored.

"I'm pretty sure if I said anything you'd get so excited that you really would throw up...and we don't need to add 'vomiting rabbit' to your list of nicknames, right?"

"That might be true, but a girl still wants to be cared about, you—*blaaaargh*!"

"See, what'd I tell you? Look, just get some rest."

"Ulp... Bleh..." Ignoring Shea, who was retching on all fours, Hajime and Yue looked around again. There still wasn't anything new, so they decided to head for the door.

"Now then, what's she going to throw at us next?"

"The guy who was controlling the golems?"

"Possible. Miledi's supposed to be long dead...so who was controlling those things?"

"It doesn't matter what pops out. I'll protect you, Hajime... And you too, I guess, Shea."

"I can hear you, you know?

Hajime relaxed a little when he heard the confidence in Yue's voice. He softly ran his fingers through her hair. She closed her eyes happily and snuggled up to Hajime.

"I've been meaning to ask you this for a while, but could you two stop going off into your own little world all the time like that? I start to feel really left out and lonely, y—*ulp*...”

Shea quickly cupped her mouth in an attempt to keep whatever lunch she had left down.

“I've been meaning to ask you this for a while, but could you stop doing that thing you do sometimes where it looks like you came straight out of a horror flick? I start to feel chills run down my spine.”

“H-how dare you? I'm just a maiden in love that wants to— *ulp*... That wants to be pampered like Yue-san. So hug me and pamper me already! *U-urgh*...”

“Please don't say that when it looks like you're about to throw up...and stop adding to your requests like that.”

“You're one hundred years too early to be hugged by Hajime, Shea.”

Shea somehow managed to drag herself over to Hajime and looked up at him with pleading eyes, her hands still covering her mouth. He ignored her and turned back to the door. Behind him Shea was going “Hey—*bweeeeh!*” but he pretended not to hear.

So what's behind the mystery door? Miledi's hideout? The golem master? More traps? With a fearless smile, he pushed open the door. Beyond it was...

“Doesn't this room look familiar?”

“Very familiar. Especially that stone tablet.”

There was another room past the door. A stone tablet in the middle and a passageway heading off to the left were all that was visible. The reason it looked so familiar was because...

"This looks just like...the room we started in?" Shea said what they were all thinking, but no one wanted to say. However, it did indeed look just like the room they'd first started in. In fact, it didn't just look like it—it was that exact room. The proof was in the letters that appeared on the tablet.

Hey, how does it feel? All that hard work just to end up at the start again. What'd you feel when you first realized it? Come on, tell me. How're you holding up? Well?

"......" Hajime and the others were all shocked speechless. Their expressions were bloodcurdling. None of them so much as twitched as they read what was written on the tablet. A few seconds later, more words appeared.

Oh yeah, I almost forgot. This labyrinth morphs after a set amount of time. Miledi-chan wanted to make sure you guys wouldn't get bored by running through the same paths over and over. Are you happy? Well? You better say thanks! She did this all out of the goodness of her heart! It should have finished changing by now, so whatever maps you made are useless. Feel free to thank me! You didn't make any, did you? Oh, did you poor souls work hard on mapping everything you could?

"Ha...ha ha ha."

"Aheheh."

"Eeheeheehee."

All three of them devolved into hysterical fits of laughter. The screams of "Milediiiiiiiiiiiii!" that followed were surely heard by all the creatures in the labyrinth. Those screams only grew louder when, upon exiting the passageway, they'd found she'd been true to her word. The entire layout of the dungeon had changed.

It took some time, but they finally managed to regain their composure and continued their expedition. Naturally, things did not go smoothly. Shea especially even fell for the most basic of traps, like metal basins falling from the sky, getting caught in birdlime, being sprayed with some sticky white liquid that smelled disgusting, and more. Eventually, she became a very agile rabbit.

CHAPTER IV
Miledi Reisen

IN A CORNER OF HEILIGH PALACE was a salon that had been opened up for the exclusive use of the summoned students. Each of them had been assigned their own butler as well, and the moment it looked as if they needed anything at all in that salon, their butler was by their side. Whether it was food they wanted, or drink, they merely had to ask and their servant would be off with a flourish.

They each had their own personal servant to take care of them in their rooms as well, but as they grew lonely cooped up alone, most students spent their free time hanging out in the salon.

Of course, they hadn't been summoned here to lounge around. They were the human side's main force in their battle against their sworn enemy, the demons.

So why was it that most of them spent their days idling around in the salon just killing time? Well, simply put, most of them had been traumatized. They had come face to face with death just a few months ago, after all. Down in the depths of the Great Orcus Labyrinth, where the light of the sun never reached, they'd stared down monsters that would have killed them without mercy. Many of them had been convinced they would die there, and one member of their group had actually been defeated, vanishing into the gaping maw of that ravine.

...A fantasy adventure with swords and magic. They'd had that kind of lighthearted idea about what they were in for, but harsh reality had crushed those hopes and dreams rather quickly. On the battlefield, people died. It was obvious when stated, but the incident in the labyrinth had carved that fact into their souls.

At first, they had happily practiced honing their skills, improving the talents their jobs had given them, and looked forward to mowing down waves of monsters. But now, there wasn't an iota of that positive attitude anywhere. "People die if they are killed," after all. When that reality had been thrust into their faces, many of the students had lost their nerve. Not only could they no longer fight, they feared even stepping out of the capital.

The king and high-ranking members of the Holy Church naturally tried to convince the students to fight again, but they didn't go so far as to force them. In the end, it was all just attempts at persuasion. But the students, who had been weighed down by their fear, only felt more cornered at their words. They were worried that if they didn't comply, maybe they would be chased out of the castle. Then, they'd have no one to protect them as they were thrown out into this harsh world where people died at the drop of a hat.

It was then that the one who possessed a rare and invaluable job, the only adult to have been summoned, the teacher Aiko Hatayama, returned from her expedition to solve the kingdom's food problems.

When she heard about the boy who'd failed to make it back alive, she'd been visibly shaken. But when she saw how much worse it had affected the other students, she quickly pulled herself together. With renewed determination, she headed to the king and other nobles to convince them to stop pestering the students to return to the war front. She even used herself and her rare job as a bargaining chip.

As a result, she succeeded, and the students were all put under Aiko's protection. It was for that reason that they could spend their days idly chattering away in the salon.

"Hey, did you hear? Amanogawa's party made it all the way to the seventieth floor."

"Seriously? Weren't they just setting foot in the sixty-sixth floor a few days ago?"

"I guess that's just how good the hero's party is. He's on a completely different level from average kids like us." The male student who said that, Atsushi Tamai, shrugged his shoulders, an odd expression on his face. He was jealous of them. He was jealous of Kouki and the others, who continued challenging the unknown even after their close brush with death. At the same time, however, he was embarrassed at how pathetic he was and at the fact that he averted his eyes from the truth. But every time he thought back to that day, he started trembling in fear.

It was not just Atsushi either; most of the students who chose to stay behind felt the same. All they wanted was to go home, back to Japan. But in order to do that, they would need to win the war against the demons and ask the Holy Church's god, Ehit, to send them back. Still, they couldn't bring themselves to fight. Fear, dark as the abyss they had witnessed, snuffed out their wills.

"Yeah. You'd have to be as amazing as Kaori-chan or Shizuku-chan to keep up with that guy."

"I know, right? Shizuku's so cool, isn't she? I'm totally falling for her."

"Aha ha, seriously? But I thought you liked Suzu, Yuri!"

"Wait, Suzu-chan's like *that,* really?!"

"Nah, she's just a perverted old man inside, so she doesn't count."

Like the boys, the girls also acted cheerful and joked around, but on the inside they felt jealous and guilty for not being there for their friends. They talked for a while, exchanging hollow, empty words, as if they were afraid of letting silence settle in.

While the servants posted to the salon never looked directly at any of the students, they still stole furtive glances at them. Not only had they been chosen by Ehit, their comrades were still out there fighting. And yet, they wasted their time chattering pointlessly in this luxurious room. However, at the same time, the servants saw the fear that lived in the students' hearts, and sympathized with their plight. They were stuck here, unable to go home, and it was the people of this world that had driven them to such actions. Thus, they gazed on expressionlessly. The nobles and clergymen who knew the situation held similar feelings as well, as they'd seen the students' dilemma firsthand. Naturally, it varied from person to person.

The students had realized how those around them looked at them, too. To avoid dwelling on it, the students turned once more to hollow conversation in an attempt to lick their own wounds.

One of the students mumbled something.

"...Even Shizuku's just a normal girl..." It had been barely a whisper, not something meant to be heard by others. But there had happened to be a lull in the conversation just then, and so those whispered words reached everyone in the salon.

They all turned to look at the person who'd muttered that. It was Nia, Shizuku's personal maid. She realized she'd misspoken and quickly bowed her head to apologize, but—

"What? Got a problem with us?" Atsushi furrowed his brows and growled at Nia. Despite his tone, he couldn't bring himself to look her in the eyes. He knew his anger was misdirected.

"No. Not at all. I'm truly sorry for my poor choice of words." Nia bowed to everyone again. But her honest attitude only aggravated Atsushi further, so he continued pestering her.

"No one asked you to apologize! Do you think we're all idiots?! You trying to say that because Yaegashi-san didn't change... because she's still going anyway, we're all pathetic for calling it quits here?! Why not just say it to our faces then, huh?!"

"H-hey Atsushi...give it a rest."

"What good's hitting a maid going to do?"

Atsushi's friends, Noboru Aikawa and Akito Nimura, tried to calm him down. He was throwing a tantrum like a child.

"Shut up! I just... I just... Dammit..."

"Atsushi..."

"Tamai-kun..."

Gloomy feelings whirled around him, and Atsushi let out a frustrated yell. Akito and Aikawa looked away, unable to say anything else. Some of the girls opened their mouths, thinking of saying something to him. After all, everyone understood those feelings he couldn't explain that wrapped around him like an inescapable spider's web.

Atsushi hung his head, and Nia took a step toward him.

"Atsushi-sama, I'm terribly sorry I offended you. But I did not mean to imply that any of you are cowards. Please try and believe me..."

"Nia-san... No, umm, I'm the one who... Sorry..."

In the face of her sincerity, Atsushi could only look away awkwardly. He apologized as well, having calmed down a little. Not only had he thrown a temper tantrum, he was the one being apologized to. There could be nothing more humiliating.

Nia smiled gently, then went on to explain the true meaning behind her words.

"Allow me to apologize to the rest of you as well. I did not mean to cause offense. But as Shizuku-sama's maid, and as her friend, this is what I think. That she, too, deserves to be protected, to rely on someone else, to let herself be spoiled, just like any other girl."

"...But she's so strong. Everyone goes to her for help... I can't imagine her ever needing to rely on someone else."

"Yeah..." The girl who spoke was Nana Miyazaki. There was a bitter smile on her face as she said that. Her friend Taeko Sugawara voiced her agreement.

"It's true that in my time serving Shizuku-sama, she has never once shown any such weakness before me. However, I do not believe a perfect person like that exists. Shizuku-sama is also just a teenage girl who was a student only months ago. She may still look fine for now, but...I'm sure not being able to rest even when she returns to the palace and having everyone around her say things like 'It's obvious that Shizuku-sama can do something like that' must be a huge burden on her."

"Nia-san..."

It was obvious Nia spent a lot of time thinking about Shizuku, so her words shook the students.

Nia was actually from a family of knights. From a young age, she'd learned swordplay from her father and brothers. She must have felt a kinship with Shizuku, who had been born and raised in similar circumstances. At first, she had been nervous serving someone the priests had called Ehit's messenger, but she'd eventually come to see her as a friend. She was worried for Shizuku, who was bravely challenging uncharted floors. That was why it had bothered her when everyone had treated Shizuku like some kind of special being. She was worried their exaggerated expectations would wear her down.

One of the girls who had so far remained silent in a corner of the salon opened her mouth.

"Everyone's...still the same, huh?"

"Yuka? What's wrong? Are you all right?"

"W-wow, I haven't heard Yukacchi speak in ages... You okay?"

Nana and Taeko looked over in surprise and worry at their friend, Yuka Sonobe. Their reaction was warranted. Ever since their brush with death, it had looked like Yuka's soul had been sucked out of her. She acted completely lifeless. Originally, she had been a very spirited girl, one that stood out in her class, for better or worse. But after their excursion into the labyrinth, she barely ever spoke, and unless her friends dragged her out she'd spend the whole day just sitting in her room, staring blankly out the window. She was the one who had been most traumatized by that experience, so it was only natural everyone was surprised to hear her speak without being asked a question.

Still, she ignored her two friends and kept talking, empty eyes staring off into the distance.

"That's right. It's not just Shizuku. Kaori-chan and Sakagami-kun and Nagayama-kun and Hiyama-kun, and even Amanogawa-kun...haven't changed. At the very least, he was normal... No, he was even weaker than normal. But...more than anyone... And yet, I... Even though we're all... If I..."

Her words had ceased making sense. She was no longer trying to convey a message but simply letting her mouth speak whatever came to mind. Something had begun stirring within Yuka's heart.

Her two friends looked at her worriedly, but as she continued spouting nonsense, Yuka's empty eyes began to glow with a faint light once more. Taeko and Nana looked at each other. The other students all exchanged confused glances as well.

"Nia-san, when is Ai-chan-sensei leaving again?"

"Aiko-sama? I believe she's scheduled to depart tomorrow morning. They're heading to the lake town of Ur, so she won't return for at least two to three weeks."

"Whoa, tomorrow, huh...? No, actually, that's good. It'll only get worse if we wait too long."

Yuka smiled wryly at that and stood up vigorously. Taeko and Nana's jaws dropped in surprise when they saw that. Their friend had never been so lively before. Nana timidly opened her mouth.

"U-umm, Yukacchi? What's wrong? I have no idea what you're saying."

"I'm fine. I just can't stand sitting still any longer. Guys, I'm going to join Ai-chan on her expedition tomorrow."

The rest of the students looked on in awe. Their shock was expected. Yuka had been hit hardest by that experience. All she'd done since returning from the labyrinth was gaze blankly at nothing, sometimes tremble in terror... But now she'd suddenly recovered in the span of a few seconds.

"W-wait, Sonobe. Seriously, what's going on? You're not acting normal. Calm down." Having finally returned to his senses, Atsushi tried to talk her out of it. However...

"I am calm, Tamai-kun. And this isn't sudden. I've been thinking for a long time now that I can't keep living like this. Ever since he died, I've been scared and confused...but I need to do something. Aren't you all thinking the same thing, deep down?"

"......" Atsushi held his breath. He then closed his mouth, like he'd thought better of what he was about to say. The other students looked away awkwardly.

Yuka didn't say anything. Instead, she simply shrugged her shoulders and headed for the salon's door. She understood their feelings very well.

"W-wait, Sonobe! You're really going to go?! You might die for real this time, you know?! This isn't a manga or a movie! There won't be any convenient act of God to save your life! That's why... That's why *he* died! Even though he was weak, he still tried to act like a hero, and then he died—just like that! I-I don't want to end up like that loser... Sonobe, don't be stupid." Though he started off shouting, his voice gradually petered off, until finally he was hanging his head sadly. Yuka didn't even turn around.

"But that worthless, weak boy saved my life. No, he saved all our lives."

"But—"

"I'm not asking you to come with me, Tamai-kun. I just don't want to let his death be in vain. That's all. Of course, if you want to come with me, I'd be glad to have you." She finally looked back at that moment. She looked nervous, but she still smiled resolutely at the others. Atsushi could only flop his mouth like a dying fish before collapsing into his chair. Yuka left the room.

Taeko and Nana were still in shock, but they left the other despairing students and hurriedly followed after Yuka. When they finally caught up to her in the hallway, they couldn't hide their confusion.

"Hey, Yuka. Are you really going to go with Ai-chan-sensei? He was right, you might die."

"I know. Still, I can't just sit around any longer. I don't have the courage to follow Amanogawa-kun and the others, but I can at least be Ai-chan's guard." When they saw the determination in her eyes, Nana and Taeko exchanged worried glances. Timidly, Nana opened her mouth.

"Yukacchi...did you, umm, maybe *like* Nagumo...?"

"Don't be silly. There's no way I'd be doing this for such a simple reason."

"Really?"

"Obviously. Besides, after seeing the hellish training Kaori-chan's putting herself through just because she still believes he's alive, you'd have to be braver than a hero to try and take him from her. If I had that kind of guts I wouldn't have stayed behind in the first place."

"Well, I guess..." Yuka Sonobe was none other than the girl Hajime Nagumo had saved from Traum Soldiers back in the Great Orcus Labyrinth. That was why Nana had come to that conclusion, but one look at Yuka's face told her she obviously didn't think of Hajime in any sort of romantic sense. Though, she *did* appear to have some other complicated feelings regarding him. Even Nana, who was usually bursting with curiosity, fell silent.

There hadn't been any lie in what Yuka had said. She really just didn't want his sacrifice to go to waste. She didn't want to spend the life he'd risked his own to save rotting in a castle. When she'd said everyone was still the same, that had included Hajime as well. He'd saved her despite being the same weak person as before, and she felt it would be betraying his memory to just sit around and wallow in misery while others continued to fight.

Her friends realized this, and after exchanging an awkward glance, nodded to each other. Then they both told Yuka that they were going with her.

"Are you sure? You don't have to force yourself, you know?"

"Just like how you don't want let the life he saved go to waste, I don't want to let the life *you* saved go to waste either. I'm coming with you, Yukacchi."

"Same. There's no way I'm letting you go out on your own, Yuka. You saved my life too, remember?"

After Hajime had saved her life, Yuka had pulled herself together and rallied some of the other students. Taeko and Nana had been part of that group. Both of them knew that it was thanks to her that they'd survived long enough to escape. And so, they decided if Yuka was going to get back up, they were bound to follow.

"I see. Well, all right, then I guess we'll protect Ai-chan from both the monsters and the really hot knights the Holy Church sent to escort her." Yuka had hoped her two friends would join her, so she broke out into a beaming smile when they offered. Nana and Taeko gave a spirited "Yeah!" in response.

The shadow of fear disappeared from the three smiling girls' eyes, replaced instead by the faint glow of hope.

❖ ❖ ❖ ❖ ❖ ❖ ❖ ❖ ❖ ❖ ❖ ❖ ❖

Mist swirled about the castle grounds on the dawn of their departure. The sun was just beginning to poke its head over the horizon, and the crisp morning air kept everyone awake and alert. Despite the pristine weather, one of the travelers had a glum expression on her face. Aiko Hatayama. The leader of the expedition.

"Girls... Are you sure you want to do this? I already have the Holy Church's knights to protect me."

"We're not leaving, Ai-chan-sensei. And besides, those knights are more dangerous than helpful. It's obvious they're agents sent to try and seduce you into their faction."

"That's right, Ai-chan-sensei. Don't fall for their charms just because they're all hotties, okay?"

"Though, if you ask me, it looks like their plan backfired. But still, you're our Ai-chan-sensei, so we just want to be extra careful."

Aiko shrugged her shoulders helplessly at their insistence. She'd already tried to dissuade them when they'd talked to her last night about joining her expedition, but no matter how much she stressed the dangers of the journey, they never faltered. As such, she knew nothing she said now would change their minds.

Furthermore, Yuka's claim that the Holy Church was trying to seduce her into its camp was more than just a baseless accusation. On every single trip Aiko had gone on, they had, without fail, assembled a team of good-looking knights to accompany her. And without fail, each and every one of them had tried to make a move on her. All in order to control the one person in the world with the ability to completely revolutionize agriculture. But as Taeko had said, all of the knights had instead become her loyal followers. The same charm that had led all of her students to love her had toppled the army of hot guys as well. Aiko herself was as dense as a dating sim protagonist though, so she hadn't realized that little tidbit as of yet.

She was glad her students were worried about her, and that they'd recovered enough to want to try again, but at the same time, she was worried about the dangers they would face on the road. Unable to resolve the conflicting feelings inside of her, she just cradled her head. A few seconds later, she could hear a huge commotion coming from across the courtyard.

Aiko and the girls turned around and saw the knights bringing over their carriages. However, there was an unexpected group of guys facing off against them, so they were seemingly in the middle of a heated argument. Aiko's eyes went round in surprise, while Yuka and the others looked taken aback.

"T-Tamai-kun? Aikawa-kun and Nimura-kun, you're here too? Why are you all..."

"Oh, Ai-chan-sensei. How's it going? We're coming too."

Atsushi and the others greeted Aiko casually, a complete turnaround from the stern glares they'd been sending the knights mere moments ago. Aiko opened her mouth to argue, but Yuka cut her off before she could.

"You're coming? That's a surprise."

"Shut it... You're not the only one. We wanted a chance to stop being losers, too. Though I think the rest of the guys are still too scared."

"I see. Well, welcome aboard. Let's do what we can with what we've got." Yuka shrugged her shoulders nonchalantly. Despite their nervous expressions, the boys still let out a spirited cheer.

One last student showed up to join a few minutes later. After multiple altercations with the knights, Aiko's agricultural reform expedition was finally formed. Everyone burned with the resolve to stand up on their own two feet once more.

"I can't believe I let it happen again... I couldn't even hold back a single one of them... I'm such a bad teacher... *Waaa...!*" Aiko cried by herself in a corner of the carriage. The knights all felt moved by her plight and tried to offer a helping hand, or words of condolence. However, Yuka and the other girls snarled angrily at them to keep them at bay. No one noticed that their constant bickering was giving Aiko, the person they were supposed to be protecting, a headache. And it seemed their journey would continue along those lines for quite some time...

In a certain room far underground, three people huddled together close to a wall that was glowing with a faint blue light. Hajime, Yue, and Shea.

They were sitting with their backs to it: Hajime in the middle, Yue to his right, and Shea to his left. The room was silent, but if you listened closely you would hear the sound of soft breathing. Yue and Shea were sleeping. They each had their arms wrapped around one of Hajime's, using his shoulders as pillows.

A week had passed since they'd entered the winding Reisen Labyrinth. The never-ending barrage of traps and annoying insults had been more exhausting mentally than physically. They'd been sent back to the start seven times, triggered lethal traps forty-eight times, and suffered minor pranks like getting stuck in birdlime, being covered with smelly white liquid, and being hit on the head by falling tubs one hundred and sixty-nine times.

At first they'd been furious with Miledi Reisen, but around the fourth day or so, staying constantly angry had become too tiring, so they'd just become apathetic.

Their overwhelming stats kept them from dying, and they'd brought plenty of food, but those were the only silver linings in the godforsaken maze. They slept intermittently, like they were now, as they continued exploring. After a week of searching, they'd noticed that there was a pattern to how the maze rearranged itself. By using his Tracking skill, Hajime had been able to figure out where each block was moved.

They were finally making progress. Pleased, Hajime looked down at the two girls sleeping on his shoulders.

"I can't believe you guys are sleeping so peacefully... We're in the middle of one of the Seven Great Labyrinths, you know?" He whispered softly with a smile on his face. It was his turn to be on watch. He somehow managed to extricate one of his arms and started gently running his fingers through Yue's hair. Her lips curled up in a faint smile. Hajime, too, smiled as he gazed down at her.

On his other shoulder, Shea had her mouth open and was drooling all over his shirt. Such a soundly sleeping face didn't fit the harsh environment of this labyrinth at all. Hajime suddenly remembered that she'd always wanted to have her head patted too, so he softly placed his hand over her pale blue hair.

He ran his fingers over her fuzzy rabbit ears as well. Her normally relaxed expression loosened even further. She was completely and totally at ease. Perhaps she felt secure knowing Hajime was keeping watch. Or perhaps she was simply happy to sleep next to him. He twisted his mouth into a wry expression as he ran his fingers through her pale hair.

"Seriously, what do you even see in a guy like me that you're willing to follow me all the way out here?" He looked down at her with surprising tenderness as he said that. While he doubted he could ever fall in love with her like Shea wanted, he was still amazed by her overly positive attitude and her stubborn streak that kept her going even when her face was a mess of tears. That was why he'd grown a little kinder toward her.

And in that moment, Shea decided to mutter something in her sleep.

"Mmm... Oh, Hajime-san, you're so bold. Doing this outside, where everyone's...watching."

"......" The kind light suddenly vanished from his eyes. He stopped stroking her hair and instead pinched her nose, while also covering her mouth. Her peaceful expression quickly transformed into one of extreme discomfort.

"Mmm... Mm? Mmmm?! Mmmmmmm!!! Pwah! Haah... Haah... Wh-what was that for?! I know I told you to attack me in my sleep, but I didn't mean like that!" Hajime just looked at her coldly while she drew in deep ragged gasps.

"And? Just what kind of pervert do you take me for in your dreams? What was I doing with you outside, hmm?"

"Huh...? Wait, that was a dream?! Nooo...! I finally got to see you be nice for once, Hajime-san. And then, because you were unable to control your burning emotions, you said all these embarrassing things to me and took me in broad—bweh?!"

Unable to listen any longer, Hajime strengthened his fingers and flicked her on the forehead. The force of the blow made Shea smack her head against the wall behind her, and she crouched down in pain. *In the end, she's still the same worthless rabbit.*

Gingerly rubbing the back of her head, Shea muttered her complaints.

"Feels like I was having this really great dream...but I can't remember it now." She must have unconsciously noticed Hajime stroking her hair in her sleep. But if he told her that she'd get carried away again, so he kept quiet. Since Shea had already been awoken, albeit rather forcefully, Hajime decided to wake Yue up too.

"Mmm... Hwah?" Yue slowly opened her eyes as Hajime gently shook her. She looked up at him and nuzzled her head against his shoulder for a moment longer before getting up and straightening her clothes.

"Man, Yue-san looks so cute... That's how a girl's supposed to wake up! Compared to her, I'm just..." Yue gave Shea a confused stare, but then came to the conclusion that "that's just how she always is" and decided not to say anything.

"Come on, you always knew there was a huge gap between you two. Now pull yourself together. We've got more exploring to do."

"Is it just me, or are you even meaner than before?"

"Huh...? Hajime's always nice."

"...Hic... Only to you, Yue-san. Hmph."

After pouting for a bit, Shea finally stood up. Yue and Hajime were already ready to go. Praying they wouldn't be sent back to the start again, the three resumed their search.

They had spent so much time in the labyrinth that they had reached a kind of enlightenment. Annoying traps and insulting messages had ceased to affect them.

And today, they finally found themselves in a room they hadn't seen since the first time they'd run into it a week before. It was the golem room that had taken them back to the start for the first time. However, this time the sealed door was already open, and instead of a room, it lead down a passage.

"Here again... It'd be a pain if we let them surround us. The door's already open, so let's make a run for it!" Hajime barked his orders.

"Yeah!" Yue quickly agreed, clearly favoring the option.

"You got it!"

They dashed forward as one. Like before, the golems started moving once they reached the halfway mark. But this time, Hajime shot down the ones ahead of him before they could even make it off their plinths.

They sped up and were at the altar before the golems had a chance to catch up to them. The golems were chasing after them as fast as they could, but they wouldn't make it before Hajime and the others slipped through the door. Sure that they were in the clear, Hajime smiled triumphantly.

But that smile was wiped off his face mere moments later.

Because the golems hadn't stopped at the door. They were still chasing them. And worse—

"Wha—?! They can run on the ceiling?!" Hajime screamed, clearly surprised.

"...That's new."

"Gravity, please start doing your job!"

Indeed, the golems were running across the walls and ceiling as they chased after the trio. The sight was made even more surreal because of how heavily their armor clanked as they did so. Even after all they'd seen, Hajime and the others hadn't expected that. Hajime cast Ore Appraisal on the walls and floor as he sped by, but they were all made of materials he'd already examined. Nothing about the hallway suggested it was made of stone that reversed gravity or had suction powers.

"How the hell are they doing that?" Hajime muttered to himself. When he risked a glance back, he saw something even more surprising. The lead golem jumped off the ceiling, flying like a cannonball at Hajime.

"What the—?! Damn you!" Recovering from his shock, Hajime pulled out Donner and fired a barrage of bullets at it. The hail of bullets destroyed the golem's helmet and most of its shoulder. Its head and torso fell off, and it let go of its sword and shield. But instead of falling to the ground, its weapons and body parts kept flying at them.

"Dodge!"

"Okay."

"Waah!"

Hajime and the others ducked and weaved through the golem's head, torso, sword, and shield. The disparate golem parts kept flying past them and crashed into the walls, ceiling, and floor ahead of them, then kept rolling forward after that.

"Hold up, either I'm seeing things, or they just..."

"Yeah...it's like they're 'falling' forward."

"Okay gravity, seems like you're only planning on working sometimes."

Yue and Shea both tossed quips after Hajime's words. It seemed these golems also had the power to manipulate gravity. *But then, why didn't they bother using it last time? Unless it's something they can only do in this passageway, maybe?*

Hajime's thoughts were interrupted as the rest of the golems began "falling" forward toward them. One of them was spinning its sword like a windmill as it fell. Hajime and Yue used gunfire and the Rupture spell respectively to shoot down the golems from a distance, while Shea mopped up any they missed. They kept running as they did, and soon Hajime felt a presence ahead of them.

"Hmm... Hajime."

"Yeah, I know. We knew they could regenerate, so I kind of expected this."

"Th-they've got us surrounded."

The golems that had fallen past them had finished rebuilding themselves. An entire row of them was waiting for the trio. With their shields out, they made for a formidable wall, and there was a second row behind them supporting the first. They'd already realized Hajime and the others could power through a single row.

"Tch, what a pain." Hajime clicked his tongue and holstered Donner and Schlag. From his Treasure Trove, he pulled out another weapon.

Orkan, a rectangular twelve-shot missile launcher. Each of the missiles it fired was thirty centimeters long and packed more explosive power than his hand grenades. With his creation magic, he had imbued Lightning Field directly into the ore the missiles were composed of. As such, they were constantly charged with static electricity, and that electricity ignited the explosives in the warhead on impact. Hajime smiled wickedly as he took aim with Orkan.

"Yue, Shea! Cover your ears! I'm blowing them out of the way!"

"Okay."

"Wait, what on earth is that?!" Shea's eyes widened in surprise. This was her first time seeing Orkan. Yue stuck her fingers in her ears. Shea's rabbit ears were still standing straight up, but Hajime didn't have any more time, so he pulled the trigger. The missiles launched with a whooshing noise, leaving a trail of sparks in their wake. Each and every one of them found their mark.

There was a huge explosion as they hit. The entire passage shook from the force of the shock waves. The golem knights were blasted to either side, blown up beyond recognition as they slammed into the walls. It would take a while to rebuild from that kind of damage.

Hajime and the others sped past the wreckage.

"My rabbit ears! My rabbit ears are—" Shea's ears were lying flat against her head, with her hands covering them. There were tears in her eyes, but she still kept pace with the others. Rabbitmen had the best sense of hearing out of all the beastmen.

"That's why I told you to cover your ears."

"Huh? What'd you say? I can't hear anything!"

"You really are a worthless rabbit..."

They both gave her exasperated looks, but Shea was too busy worrying about her ears to notice. After another five minutes of fending off golems falling at them, they saw the end of the hallway. It opened up into a massive chamber. The chamber had no floor, and there was a square platform standing ten meters out from where the hallway stopped.

"Yue, Shea—jump!"

They both nodded curtly. From behind, golems were still shooting down at them. They continued dodging or intercepting them up until they jumped. With their body strengthening, all three of them could leap far further than any Olympic athlete. A jump that would easily have broken world records back on Hajime's world carried them easily over the gap and directly toward the square platform.

Still, unexpected surprises were this dungeon's specialty, so while they were still in the middle of their jump, the platform started moving.

"What?!" Hajime had lost count of how many times he'd yelled that down here. At this rate, they were just going to fall down. And a quick glance below showed that the hole was quite deep. Hajime thrust out his left hand, ready to fire an anchor, but Yue acted first.

"Updraft!" A surge of air lifted them up, carrying them a few feet higher. It wasn't much, but it was enough. Hajime just managed to grab on to the ledge as he fell. He transmuted spikes into his left arm to keep him fastened there while Yue and Shea clung to him for dear life.

"N-nice one, Yue."

"That was amazing, Yue-san."

"Mhmm. Praise me more."

Hajime and Shea smiled, praising Yue for saving them from whatever hellish pit awaited below. Yue was exhausted from burning so much mana, but she still managed to puff out her chest proudly.

However, their celebration was cut short by an army of golems flying at them. This time they were just floating through the sky. It must have been their gravity controlling powers at work. They headed toward Hajime and the others at frightening speed.

"Yue, Shea, get up there!" Donner was already in his hand before he'd finished talking, and he fired a barrage of bullets at the incoming golem knights. Yue and Shea clambered up over him and onto the platform. Once they were over, Hajime vaulted up himself.

One of the golems' swords thrust into the platform's side a second later. Had Hajime taken a second longer, it would have speared him. Taking advantage of the golem's brief opening, Hajime bombarded it with bullets.

"Dammit. I don't know if it's gravity control or what, but these guys are getting more and more precise with their movements."

"...It's probably this place."

"Aha ha, I don't even know what common sense is anymore. Everything's floating." As Shea had so aptly stated, everything in the room they were in was floating.

The platform had taken them into a massive spherical room. In fact, "massive" didn't do it justice. The room must have been two kilometers in diameter. There were numerous stone platforms floating around, moving every which way. Gravity may as well have not have existed in this space. Despite that, Hajime and the others were still affected by it normally. It seemed only objects made out of a certain material could ignore gravity.

The golem knights were able to fly in whatever direction they pleased. But it definitely felt like they were reorienting which direction gravity applied to them in, as their movements were jerky and sudden. Living creatures would have probably died from the G-forces exerted on their frames. However, their movements had continued to get steadily more precise the further they went in, which meant...

"The golem's controller should be around here, right?" Yue and Shea nodded in agreement with his statement and tensed up, ready for a fight. For whatever reason, the golems were just circling them without attacking. Hajime looked around, scouting for any possible exits. There was no telling if this was their final destination, or if there was still more to come. *Either way, this must be near the end of the labyrinth.* The increased precision of the golems and the strange nature of the room supported his hypothesis.

Hajime activated his Farsight to scout out the room. But before he could get a good look, Shea yelled out a warning to him.

"Run!"

"Wha—?!" Hajime and Yue unquestioningly heeded Shea's warning and leaped to the side as fast as possible. Fortunately, there was another block floating a few meters away for them to jump to.

A second later, something crashed into the block they'd been standing on with the force of a meteorite. The impact shattered the block completely. Meteorite was an apt description for what had just landed, as whatever it was shot straight through the block and kept falling, a nimbus of friction-induced heat surrounding it.

Cold sweat ran down Hajime's back. Had it not been for Shea's warning, they would have taken that head on. And since he couldn't use Diamond Skin here, it might actually have killed him. It wasn't that he hadn't been able to sense the attack. In fact, he'd felt the presence bearing down on them an instant after Shea's warning. However, it had been traveling so fast that he wouldn't have been able to dodge in time after sensing it that late.

"Thanks, Shea. You saved our lives."

"Yeah...good job."

"Ehehe, thank goodness my Future Sight activated back there. Though I'm completely out of mana now..."

So the reason she sensed it before me was because of her Future

Sight ability? Shea could use her ability voluntarily, but there were also times it activated on its own. When something posed a threat to her life, it would almost always activate. That meant the meteorite had at least enough power to instantly kill Shea. Hajime shivered a little before looking down at where the meteor had fallen. He cautiously poked his head over the edge of the platform. When he peered down, he could faintly make out something ascending at high speed. In the blink of an eye, it was floating above Hajime and the others. Its eyes glowed with a cold light as it stared at them.

"Man, are you serious?"

"It's...so big..."

"S-so this is their boss."

They all gazed up in amazement. Yue's outburst could probably have been interpreted in a not-so-wholesome way, but that wasn't really important.

Floating in front of them was a massive golem knight. It was fully armored like the others, but this one was twenty meters tall. In its right hand was a glowing red heat knuckle. That was what it had used to destroy the platform earlier. In its left was a flail, its fingers wrapped around the chain.

As Hajime and the others prepared for battle, the other golems all started flying in as well, encircling the trio. They stood, or rather floated at attention, with their swords held upright in front of their chests, as if they were saluting their emperor.

Hajime and the others looked around nervously. Silence filled the room, and the tension was almost palpable. The moment one side moved, a fight to the death would break out. Or at the very least, that was the sense the atmosphere gave off until...

"Heyooo! Nice to seeee youuu! It's me, everyone's favorite idol, Miledi Reisen-chaaan!" The huge golem's greeting didn't match its look at all.

"......" Their jaws all dropped open in shock. The cutesy voice coming out of the heavily armed and armored golem was so utterly incongruous that they couldn't help it.

The giant golem frowned in displeasure as it looked down. Judging from its voice, Hajime guessed it was a she.

"Hello? Aren't you going to say anything? It's proper manners to return a greeting, you know? Sheesh, kids these days...no respect, I tell you." That annoying manner of talking was very familiar to them.

"Unbelievable." The golem with a burning knuckle in one hand and a flail in the other shrugged her shoulders in a very human-like fashion. Irritated expressions flitted across the trio's faces. She talked just like the messages they'd seen. Since she'd called herself Miledi Reisen, it was possible it was the Liberator herself, but she was supposedly long dead and a human. Hajime decided to try that angle of questioning first.

"My bad. But wasn't Miledi Reisen a human? And isn't she dead? Anyway, we've never seen a sentient golem before, so we were a bit surprised... Sorry about that. Also, tell us what exactly you are. As concisely as possible, please."

"Oh my, you're quite forward despite being surrounded and outnumbered."

There was no subtlety to Hajime's questions. He just laid his questions flat out. Unsurprisingly, the golem called Miledi was taken aback by his bluntness. But she recovered quickly, and if he didn't know golems couldn't show expression, Hajime would have sworn she grinned.

"Hmm? Miledi was always a golem, you know. Whatever gave you the idea she was human?"

"There were a few things written about you in Oscar's notebook. And don't give me bullshit like 'Oh, but I look just like a human, don't I?' Just keep it short. It looks like you're trying to get in our way, so we'll be turning you into scrap soon enough. That's why there's no need for any annoying banter. Just tell us what we want to know."

"O-oh my! I finally get a chance to talk to someone, and this is how you treat me? And did you just say Oscar? Did you three perhaps clear O-chan's labyrinth?"

"Yeah, we've already beat Oscar Orcus' dungeon. But I'm the one asking the questions here. If you don't want to answer, that's fine, too. We'll just move straight to the part where we crush you to pieces. It's not like I'm dying to know any of this information. All we're here for is the ancient magic." Hajime pointed Donner at the massive golem to accentuate his words. Yue looked on impassively, but Shea, half-impressed and half-nonplussed, let her thoughts leak out.

"Wow. Nothing fazes you, does it?"

"If you want the ancient magic, does that mean you're going to kill the gods? Are you going to take out those conniving little bastards for us? If you got to the end of O-chan's labyrinth, then you must know what's going on, right?"

"I told you, I'm the one asking the questions here. If you want me to tell you anything, you answer first."

"You really are a cocky little brat. Well, whatever. Umm, where to begin...? Ah, guess we'll start with my real identity. Umm..."

"Like I said, keep it short. I don't need an entire novel's worth like when I saw Oscar."

"Aha ha. I guess O-chan can be a little long-winded. He always did like to talk." The massive golem looked up at the sky, quietly reminiscing. She really felt more like a human than a lump of rock. Yue was as expressionless as always, but Shea was glancing nervously at the golems surrounding them.

"All right, so put simply...I am indeed Miledi Reisen. And the secrets of these golems lie in the ancient magic I can use! If you want to know more, then you'll have to beat me first!"

"That's not an explanation..."

"Ha ha ha. I mean, what'd be the point in making this labyrinth if you got all the answers before clearing it?" The Miledi golem wagged her finger like she was lecturing a small child. *If only it wasn't Miledi Reisen doing that, it'd almost look cute.*

"It's who's inside that's the problem," Yue muttered quietly. It appeared she agreed.

Though in the end, they hadn't figured anything out about who was inside either. Hajime's best guess was that if she claimed to be Miledi herself, then she was probably the lingering remnants of her spirit or something. He vaguely recalled that one of his old classmates, Eri Nakamura, had the job of necromancer, which dealt with manipulating such spirits. Though nothing she'd resurrected with her necromancy had the kind of independent will this golem seemed to possess. *So does that mean it's the ancient magic she had that let her spirit have such a strong will even after she passed on?*

Regardless, it seemed that whatever magic Miledi possessed, it wasn't going to help him teleport across worlds. Somewhat put out, Hajime asked his next question.

"Does your ancient magic have something to do with controlling spirits?"

"Hm? Sounds like you're looking for a certain spell. Well, just so you know, my ancient magic has nothing to do with any of this. I had La-kun help me affix souls into these guys."

Hajime's only goal was to return home. It didn't matter if this spell controlled souls or spirits or whatnot, it was of no use to him. But Miledi's response wasn't what he had been expecting. He didn't know who this "La-kun" was, but he guessed they were another one of the Liberators. Whoever they were, they were the ones that had put the spirit of Miledi, who was supposedly dead, into this golem.

"Then what does your ancient magic do?"

"Oh, interested, are we? Do you really wanna know that bad?" Her expression couldn't change, but her tone made it obvious that she was grinning inside. Annoyed, Hajime waited for her to answer.

"If you wanna know...you'll have to answer one of my questions first." Her tone suddenly shifted drastically at the end of her sentence. Her playful, cutesy voice was replaced by a dead serious one. Hajime and the others were slightly taken aback. Still, he didn't let it show on his face.

"What?"

"What are you after? Why do you want to collect ancient spells so badly?" Her tone made it clear that she wouldn't forgive him for lying. It was possible this was her real personality. After all, she was a member of the group that had risen up against the gods for the sake of the people. She had plenty of reason to want to know what the person she entrusted her power to would do with it.

Unlike Oscar, who'd passed away and left only a video recording of himself, Miledi had spent centuries here waiting for a challenger to come and lay claim to her power. In a way, it must have been torture. Her frivolous attitude might only have been a front, while the real her was someone with an immense amount of patience and a strong sense of responsibility.

Yue had picked up on that as well, so her expression shifted ever so slightly. Having spent centuries trapped in a prison of her own, Yue must have understood the suffering Miledi had gone through. And there was more than just sympathy in her eyes. After all, unlike Yue, Miledi had chosen to remain down here in the darkness for centuries of her own volition.

Hajime's gaze met Miledi's, and he told her the truth.

"My only goal is to return home. One of your stupid mad gods summoned me to this world by force. I'm just trying to find a spell that can teleport me back... I have no interest in carrying on your crusade against the gods. I'm not going to risk my life for this world."

"......" She stared at Hajime for a few seconds before turning to look at Yue, then Shea. Seemingly coming to some sort of understanding, she nodded curtly.

"I see," was all she said. Then, her serious tone of voice vanished and was replaced by the cutesy one she had been using before.

"Hmm... I seeee, I seeee! I understand now, you're not from this world. Yeah, that must have been *tough* for you. All right, let's duel! Beat me and get your hands on the power you seek!"

"I can't follow your logic at all, but...in the end, what is your ancient magic? Is it a teleportation spell?"

Miledi only laughed gleefully and said, "Well..." suggestively. She would have made a great host for *Who Wants to Be a Millionaire*

Tired of her games, Hajime pulled out Orkan. If she wasn't going to say anything, then he would just beat her and get his own answers. And yet, before he could fire, she opened her mouth and taunted him.

"Not telling!"

"Then die." Hajime let loose a barrage of missiles. They left a trail of sparks as they slammed into the Miledi Golem and exploded. The explosion echoed loudly across the massive room. Smoke enveloped the space Miledi had been occupying.

"Did you get her?!"

"Shea, anytime anyone says that, the enemy's alive."

Shea was ready to start celebrating, but Yue shot her down. And in the end, Yue's warning proved correct. A burning fist punched its way through the smoke. Miledi swept her hand across, blowing away the smoke.

As the smoke cleared, they saw that while Miledi's forearms were crumbling here and there, she hadn't taken any serious damage. She grabbed one of the nearby floating blocks and crushed it, using the particles to restore her own body.

"Hoohoo, congratulations on landing the first strike. But I'm sure you can do better than that. Come on, I might have the spell you're looking fooor... I'm pretty strong though, so try not to die." Accompanied by joyous laughter, Miledi fired the flail attached to her left arm at Hajime. Not swung—*fired*. There was no windup, so the flail attached to the end of an arm was just suddenly hurtling toward them. She must have been able to control the direction of her gravity like the other golems, so she made the flail "fall" at them.

Hajime and the others jumped to a nearby platform to avoid it. It shattered the block they had just jumped off of, and, like it was swimming through the air, turned around and returned to Miledi's hand.

"Let's do this. Yue, Shea, we're taking Miledi down!"

"Okay!"

"Roger!"

At Hajime's shout, the final battle of the Reisen Labyrinth, one of the Seven Great Labyrinths, began in earnest.

The golem knights that had been on standby until then suddenly sprang into action. Like they had in the hallway, they pointed themselves like bullets at Hajime and the others, then fell straight at them.

Yue lithely dodged out of the way, thrust one of her canteens forward, and swung it from side to side. The highly compressed water shot out with considerable force and cut through the golems like a laser.

"Aha ha, pretty good. But there's fifty of these infinitely regenerating golems, and me. Will you really be able to get them all at once?" With a wicked cackle, Miledi fired her flail again. Shea leaped out of the way and onto a pyramid-shaped block above her. Instead of dodging, Hajime emptied Donner's chamber on it.

There was only one gunshot, but all six bullets were fired. The six bullets hit the flail almost simultaneously. Even a giant mass of metal like the flail couldn't ignore six railgun enhanced bullets. And so, it was flung off at an angle, away from Hajime.

Meanwhile, Shea leaped off her platform and swung Drucken down at Miledi's head.

"I can see *right through* your tricks." Miledi suddenly shot sideways through the sky. She had reoriented her gravity.

"Kuh, damn you!" Gritting her teeth, Shea pulled Drucken's trigger. There was a concentrated explosion along the face of the hammer. The recoil of the blast allowed her to correct her trajectory. She spun around thrice before delivering a blow backed by the power of centrifugal force squarely into Miledi.

Miledi raised her left arm up to guard herself, but Shea's strike was so powerful that it crushed her arm entirely. However, Miledi seemed unconcerned and swatted away Shea with her crushed arm.

"Kyaaa!"

"Shea!"

The force of the blow sent her flying. She somehow managed to stabilize herself by firing Drucken multiple times, then made an emergency landing on one of the floating platforms.

"Heh, looks like you're just fine. Hey, Yue, just what kind of training did you give this girl?"

"...I just cornered her a little."

"I see. No wonder she's so good at surviving." Hajime nodded approvingly as he watched Shea make her way back, jumping from block to block. The amount of golems swarming them was more than Yue could handle alone.

Hajime pulled Metzelei, his Gatling gun, from out of his Treasure Trove. Then, back to back with Yue, he started firing 12,000 rounds of death a minute.

The six-barrel Gatling gun rotated at ridiculous speeds as it fired. Gunshots echoed throughout the room and streaks of red light filled the air as a hailstorm of bullets ripped the golems apart, sending them all hurtling to the depths below. The knights that attempted to circle around and take him from behind were cut down by Yue's water jets.

Within seconds, over forty golems had been turned into hunks of fractured rock. They fell unceremoniously down to whatever was below. They'd return fully rebuilt, of course, but at least they wouldn't bother them for a while. And that meant they had enough time to take out the Miledi Golem.

"Hey, what the heck was that?! I've never seen or heard of

anything like it!"

Hajime ignored her question and put Metzelei back into his Treasure Trove. Then, he took Donner out of his holster and yelled in a voice loud enough for Shea to hear:

"Miledi's core is where a human's heart would be! Destroy that!"

"Wha—how do you know that?!" she asked, clearly surprised. It hadn't even occurred to her that Hajime might have a demon eye that could see the flow of mana. Now that they knew the Miledi Golem's weak point, Yue and Shea's eyes glinted with a predatory light.

There weren't even ten regular golems left to protect Miledi. *As long as we coordinate our attacks, we should be able to take out her heart.*

Hajime leaped from platform to platform, looking to close in on Miledi. With his weakened railgun, it would be difficult to shoot down Miledi's core. And so, he'd have to rely on a point-blank shot to blow off her armor, then finish her core off with a grenade.

But no matter how frivolous her attitude, Miledi was still a Liberator capable of using ancient magic. He doubted it would be so easy. Miledi's eyes flashed bright, and one of the platforms floating overhead shot down toward Hajime.

"Huh?!"

"I never said the knights were the *ooonly* things I could control."

Hajime ignored her and activated another one of his left arm's features. With a resounding bang, a shock wave fired out of his elbow. More specifically, he fired a shotgun blast. It couldn't be accelerated with his Lightning Field, but the burst contained far more blastrock than Donner's bullets. Though, the recoil was also that much stronger in turn. Hajime flew through the air, narrowly avoiding the falling platform. He somehow managed to land on the block he was aiming for too.

Naturally, Miledi tried to drop the block he'd landed on as well, but before she could, Shea jumped up behind her, aiming for her head. Since she needed to flash her eyes before controlling the platforms, Shea had decided to crush them along with the rest of her face.

Unfortunately, Miledi noticed Shea in time, so she sent her remaining golems after her while she was still mid-jump. In the sky, Shea was defenseless. But just before a knight's sword sliced her in two—

"...I won't let you." Yue suddenly popped up behind her and diced the golems into little pieces with her Rupture.

"Thanks, Yue-san!" Her obstacles now removed, Shea swung down her hammer with all the might of her body strengthening behind it.

"Do you really think you can beat a golem in a contest of strength?" As if to prove her point, Miledi turned around and swung her burning right fist up at Shea.

There was a thunderous crash as Miledi's heat knuckle and Shea's Drucken collided. The shock waves were powerful enough to send all the nearby platforms spinning away.

"You liiiiiittle!" Shea let out a bestial roar as she struggled to push through Miledi's fist. However, she was unable to match the golem's strength, so she was blown away.

"Kyaaa!" Shea screamed loudly as she flew through the air. Her body had been temporarily stunned by Miledi's fist, and there were no floating platforms in the direction she was headed. At this rate she would fall, but Yue suddenly jumped next to her, grabbed her mid-flight, and used Updraft to correct their trajectory to a nearby platform.

"You've got quite the coordinated little team there." Miledi looked down at Yue and Shea, her voice smug. But just then, another voice rang out from right beside her.

"I know, right?"

"Wha—?!"

As Miledi turned around in surprise, she saw Hajime. He had fired an anchor into the gap between her armor and found himself a foothold. In his hands was the railgun-accelerated anti-materiel rifle Schlagen, pointed directly at her heart. Sparks were flying down the length of Schlagen's barrel.

"Wh-when did you—" Miledi was interrupted by the sound of a bullet being fired. The point-blank rifle shot sent Miledi flying backward, obliterating the armor around her chest. With his Lightning Field weakened, Schlagen was only as powerful as Donner normally was. Still, that was more than enough to destroy metal armor. Even in this dungeon, Donner was powerful enough to blow away the normal golem knights' armor, and since Miledi seemed to be made of the same material, the most she could have done to her armor was make it thicker.

Smoke billowed from her chest as she flew backward, and the recoil sent Hajime flying in the opposite direction. He fired another anchor off at a nearby platform and swung himself up onto it. Then, he took a closer look at what had become of Miledi. Yue and Shea jumped onto nearby blocks as well.

"...Did you get her?"

"I definitely felt it hit, but..."

"I really hope this is the end." Yue looked cautious, while Shea seemed hopeful. Hajime's expression, on the other hand, was unreadable. As he expected, Miledi started drawing nearby platforms to her as if nothing had happened and spoke to Hajime with a voice full of admiration.

"Maaan, that was close. I actually thought I was done for. If this dungeon didn't dissipate mana, and that artifact had been able to fire at full power, I really would have bit the dust. Yep, I'm a genius for spending so much time making my labyrinth like this!" All he heard from the Miledi Golem were words of admiration for herself, which Hajime paid no heed to. His expression was grim. Behind her regular armor plating had been another set of jet black armor. Schlagen hadn't even been able to scratch that. He remembered seeing that armor before.

"Hmm. So you're interested in this, huh?" Miledi noticed where Hajime's gaze was directed and pointed to her jet black armor as she spoke gleefully.

"Well..." she continued suggestively, but before she could continue, Hajime spat out a curse and answered her question.

"Shit. It's Azantium."

Azantium was the hardest metal in this world. Plenty of Hajime's own equipment was forged out of it as well. Even a light coat of it would be tough enough to withstand a full power shot from Donner. *No wonder Schlagen didn't do anything.* Breaking through Azantium was next to impossible, which made Hajime furrow his brows.

"Oh? You already knew about it? Well, I guess that makes sense. You beat O-chan's dungeon, after all. There's no way someone capable of using creation magic wouldn't know of it. Now, since you're finally starting to despair a little, how about we get started with round two?!" Miledi finished repairing her outer armor with materials stolen from the platforms and fired her flail while rushing forward at the same time.

"Wh-what do we do now, Hajime-san?!"

"We're not out of options yet, but we have to seal her movements first somehow."

"Okay, leave it to me." Shea was on the verge of panicking when she realized they lacked sufficient firepower. But Hajime still had a trump card up his sleeve. He'd need to stop the Miledi Golem from moving to use it, though. When he mentioned as much to Shea, she regained her composure for the most part, and together with Yue she prepared to jump out of the way of the flail. However—

"Not thiiis tiiime," Miledi said in a singsong voice, as she started rotating the block they were standing on.

Hajime and the others all lost their balance. The flail smashed into their platform with overwhelming force. The trio was flung away from their now pulverized foothold. Before Miledi could reel her flail back in, Hajime grabbed onto its chains. Yue used the crumbled remains of their old platform as a foothold while she used Updraft to carry her to safety. Meanwhile, Shea maneuvered to a nearby platform using Drucken's explosive bursts to propel her.

Next, Miledi followed up by swinging her heat knuckle down on them.

"Kuh!"

"Mmm!"

They managed to avoid a direct hit, but the heat of the explosion generated by the impact still scorched them. Even while they were crying out in pain, they didn't stop fighting. Yue used Rupture to hack away at Miledi's arm, while Shea activated Drucken's spike and drove it into Miledi's armor.

While Yue's Rupture managed to cut partway through Miledi's arm, it couldn't sever it. She jumped back to safety with a frustrated expression.

On the other side, Shea had managed to climb up Miledi's left shoulder and aimed a swing right at her head. However, Miledi changed the direction of her gravity again, making Shea lose her balance and fall.

"Kyaaa!" Shea screamed as she fell. Hajime swung himself off the flail's chain and caught Shea in midair.

"Hajime-san!" Shea cried out joyfully. She was finally being carried by Hajime like she'd always wanted. Even though she knew this wasn't the time, she couldn't help but be happy. But of course, Hajime had to ruin the moment. He held her up with one hand, like he had the time he'd thrown her into a mob of monsters.

"H-Hajime-san?!"

"Do it again!" With a metallic whoosh, Hajime reloaded his arm shotgun and fired it again. He started rotating in place and used the centrifugal force to aid his throw.

"Hajime-san, you bastaaaard!" Shea let out a scream of enraged desperation as she readied Drucken. Just when she thought her wish had finally been granted, he'd thrown her to the wolves again.

Even Miledi was taken aback by the heartlessness of Hajime's actions. However, she still moved to intercept, and made a fist with her right hand. But before she could fire her heat knuckle, the chain that had returned to her along with her flail exploded.

"Wh-wh-wha?! What was that?!" Miledi cried out in surprise. When he had still been hanging on to the chain, Hajime had attached a large number of grenades to it. The force of the explosion blew half of the chain away and ruined Miledi's left arm. The shock waves were powerful enough to throw her off balance. And it was at that very moment that Shea appeared with Drucken in hand.

"Hiyaaaaaaaaaah!" With a spirited yell, Shea pulled Drucken's trigger, firing off a barrage of shotgun shells. The recoil accelerated her hammer to mach speeds.

Miledi reflexively raised up her damaged left arm to guard, but Drucken slammed into it with tremendous force, pulverizing whatever remained of Miledi's arm, shattering it from the shoulder down.

The force of her swing sent Shea spiraling through the air. Trying to get revenge for her destroyed left arm, Miledi swung her heat knuckle down on the defenseless Shea. But before she could reach, a jet of water surged up from below and struck the area that had been cut earlier. The second wave of water was enough to cut through it completely, so Miledi lost her right arm as well.

"Eehee, you let your guard down." Yue smiled triumphantly as she said that.

"You! How dare you!" Miledi's facade finally cracked, and anger spilled into her voice. Meanwhile, Hajime had used his anchor as a pendulum, swinging around on it to catch Shea. But he wasn't doing a princess-carry this time. Instead, he held her beneath his arm like a sack of potatoes.

"Hajime-saaan, that was the perfect opportunity to carry me like an actual girl. Don't I deserve a reward? Read the mood a little."

"Please don't talk about me like I'm dense or something. In fact, why don't you learn to read the mood instead? You're always trying to twist every situation into an opportunity to satisfy yourself."

Shea started complaining the moment they landed, but Hajime shut her up with a tired rebuttal. For some reason, Miledi wasn't drawing nearby platforms to her in order to repair her arms. Instead, she was looking up at the sky, her eyes glowing brightly.

Hajime stiffened. *I've got a bad feeling about this.* Shea, who was standing right next to him, paled as well.

"Hajime-san, Yue-san! Run! She's making them all fall!"

Hajime assumed Shea's Future Sight must have activated again. That could only have meant that something life-threatening was about to head their way. Hajime spared a quick glance at Yue, who was standing nearby, before readying himself.

A second later, it happened. The entire room rumbled. Rocks started raining from the sky. No, they weren't rocks. Miledi was bringing the entire ceiling down on them.

"Huh?! No way!"

"Oohoohoo, here's my revenge. Aside from the knights, I can't give multiple objects orders at once, but I can make everything fall. Try dodging *this*!" Miledi's words irked Hajime, but there wasn't any time to worry about her. There were a few platforms making up part of the room's wall, but its ceiling was made almost entirely of platforms. Each of those platforms was easily ten tons, and they were falling as thickly as raindrops. Cold sweat poured down Hajime's forehead.

"H-Hajime-san!"

"We've gotta regroup with Yue!"

Hajime hugged Shea close and swung down from his anchor toward Yue. Yue too, was jumping from block to block to try and reach Hajime.

Meanwhile, Miledi continued staring up at the ceiling. She'd mentioned it before too, but the way she controlled the platforms was different from how she controlled the golems. Judging by how quickly they adapted to their situation, the golems must have had some level of autonomy to them. That was why she could coordinate with them and give them sophisticated orders.

However, giving precise commands to things without autonomy was difficult, which was why she could only control one or two objects at once. Even giving orders as simple as "fall" to numerous objects took up all her concentration.

The time it took for her to focus also bought Hajime and Yue enough time to regroup. The moment the three of them met up, the sky started falling.

Rrrrrrrrrrrrrrrummmmmbbllle! When the shaking finally stopped, it was replaced by a series of loud booms as the platforms started falling. Worse, because Miledi could control their trajectories to some extent, the platforms were heavily concentrated where Hajime and the others were standing. Considering the fact that Miledi probably didn't intend to kill herself, too, Hajime guessed the space around her must have been safe. However, the falling rocks were nearly upon them, and they only had time to huddle near a wall. It was too late to try and make a break for her.

"Yue, Shea, grab hold of me! Don't let go, no matter what!"

"Okay."

"You got it!"

The moment they grabbed on, Hajime took Orkan out of his Treasure Trove. Then, he started firing missiles at the rocks coming down from the ceiling. Each missile found a mark, and Hajime pulverized stone after stone.

The sky, which had been covered in gray stone, finally started to show some cracks due to Orkan's barrage. Slivers of sky could finally be seen through the blanket of stone. Hajime returned Orkan to his Treasure Trove and instead pulled out Donner and

Schlag, firing both of them repeatedly. In order to increase their chances of survival by even one percent, Hajime accurately calculated where he needed to shoot to break apart the right fragments, then he shot them down with precision.

But even he could only do so much. The rocks were finally upon them. After making sure Yue and Shea were still hanging on tight, Hajime activated one of his special magic skills, Riftwalk. The world suddenly slowed down around him, and Hajime could make out each piece of death falling toward him.

Using the minimum amount of movement possible, Hajime nimbly weaved his way through the falling barrage. At the same time, he reloaded his pistols and shot aside the rocks he couldn't evade. He couldn't afford to make even a fraction of a mistake. Even the level of perception he'd had when he'd first learned Riftwalk in the fight against the Great Orcus Labyrinth's guardian wouldn't be enough. He would need to surpass all his limits to survive. Hajime activated another one of his skills, Limit Break.

Crimson light enveloped his body, then dissipated seconds later. Normally, Limit Break would triple his base stats, but because mana was dispersed upon being released from the body, it was rendered ineffective. That was because Limit Break achieved its effects by wrapping its user in an aura of mana. But it also wrapped the inside of its user's body with another layer of mana. Which meant that even if the strengthening were rendered ineffective, his heightened senses from using the skill remained.

He was breaking his limits in the very literal sense of the phrase. Naturally, this placed a huge burden on his body—especially because he'd already enhanced his senses to the limit earlier with Riftwalk. Had his body not been transformed by monster meat, it would have broken apart from the strain of his own abilities. As it was, Hajime was still bleeding from his eye and nose because of the burden.

With fluid motions, he dodged death by a hair's breadth time and time again. This was all the more impressive because Yue and Shea were still clinging to him. He jumped from crumbling platform to crumbling platform with a godlike level of balance, sometimes even using the falling rocks as footholds.

Now that time was moving in slow motion, Hajime was able to see the cracks in each stone as it fell past. Having long since surpassed the limits of any human, Hajime continually found the one thread of life in a sea of death. To Miledi, who was watching from across the room near the far wall, it looked as if Hajime had been swallowed by the barrage of rocks. *They fought hard, but I guess they just couldn't handle that kind of barrage.* Slightly disappointed, Miledi released her hold on the rocks.

The few platforms that hadn't been totally destroyed floated aimlessly among the remnants of the fallen sky.

"Well, I guess it was too much for them after all. But if they can't even survive this, they'd never have been able to take on those bastards." Sighing, Miledi started searching for Hajime's corpse. But at that moment—

"I thought I already told you that I don't care about fighting those bastards."

"Huh?"

She heard a familiar voice. It was the voice of that arrogant white-haired boy that wore an eyepatch and used artifacts she'd never seen before. It was Hajime's voice. Miledi turned around, her voice a mixture of surprise and joy. He looked down at Miledi from his perch on one of the few intact platforms. He was bleeding from his eye and nose, but otherwise looked unharmed.

"H-how did you...?" She was sure she'd seen him get swallowed up by the barrage of rocks, yet here he was, standing before her. Hajime smiled victoriously.

"I don't mind telling you...but don't you think you should be worrying about something else?"

"Huh?" she said again. But her confusion vanished an instant later when a magical attack slammed into her.

"Rupture!" Yue's cool voice rang out through the crumbling chamber, and multiple jets of water cut through Miledi's back, legs, head, and shoulders. Entire chunks of her armor were cut off.

"No matter how many times you try, the result won't change. I'll just fix it all up when I fix my arms!"

"You won't get the chance to." Hajime fired an anchor at Miledi and reeled himself close to her. He was holding Schlagen in his right hand.

"Aha ha, this again? You know that can't pierce my Azantium armor." Miledi was still confident they couldn't win. She even let Hajime swing up to her and point Schlagen at her chest again. She didn't bother trying to block with any of her remaining platforms.

From her perspective, it made sense. The fact that Hajime's weapons couldn't penetrate her Azantium armor had already been proven. She assumed that because they were trying the same thing again, they'd exhausted all other options... But that negligence proved to be fatal.

"I know!" Hajime fired, and Schlagen's enhanced full metal jacket bullet slammed into Miledi's body. Like before, Miledi was blown away by the force of it. But this time, Hajime didn't fly back after firing. He kept the anchor firmly embedded to stay close to Miledi, then fired all of his prosthetic arm's shotgun shells into her chest. She was sent flying even further back and crashed into one of the floating platforms behind her.

"N-no matter what you do, you still..."

"Yue!" Hajime ignored Miledi's words and shouted out to Yue. Yue jumped up and fired another spell.

"Freeze—Crystal Coffin!" She chanted the name of a spell meant to encase its target in a tomb of ice, but it was an advanced level water spell. In this labyrinth, Yue shouldn't have been able to use anything stronger than an intermediate spell. However, in order to restrain Miledi, they needed it.

The part of Miledi's back that was resting on the floating blocks froze, keeping her stuck to the platform.

"Wha—?! How can you use advanced level spells?!" Miledi shouted out in surprise. The reason Yue had been able to use the spell was simple. Like with Rupture, if she used water that was already present, then the amount of mana required to cast the spell went down. Yue had coated the block Miledi had landed on with water ahead of time. And when Miledi had shown an opening, Yue had doused her back with water as well. That was what her initial Rupture had been for.

Even then, it had taken up a huge amount of mana, and Yue had depleted all of her accessories' stored mana to cast it. Panting, Yue retreated to a platform further away.

"Nice job, Yue!" Hajime stood on top of Miledi's chest and pulled his trump card out of his Treasure Trove. The object he pulled out was a two-and-a-half-meter-long cannon. The outside was covered in all manner of odd knobs and switches, while the inside was loaded with a twenty-centimeter-wide jet-black spike. There were four sturdy stands attached to the lower part of the cannon, while the middle part connected to his prosthetic arm, allowing him to operate it.

Hajime used the arms to hold it in place over Miledi, who couldn't move, and fired two anchors for good measure. All told, there were six stands firmly holding the cannon in place. Then, Hajime started pouring mana into it. Red sparks started flying off the cannon, and the jet-black spike inside it started to rotate.

Whiiiiiiir! The spinning spike let out a high-pitched whirring noise. Hajime's smile was so ghastly that had Miledi not been a golem, she surely would have stiffened in fear.

This was one of the auxiliary weapons for his left arm, a pile bunker. With his compression synthesis, he had managed to fit a four-ton mass into a spike twenty centimeters wide and one meter long. The entire thing was coated in a thick layer of Azantium, making it the densest, hardest object on the planet. He ignited the massive amount of compressed blastrock inside the pile bunker and accelerated it with Lightning Field for good measure.

"Eat this." He drove the spike straight through Miledi's heart, as if he were staking a vampire.

With a resounding crash, his pile bunker pierced through Miledi's Azantium armor. Cracks spread around the point of impact, the damage spreading throughout the plating. The platform Miledi was stuck to had nearly shattered, the force of the impact pushed it down a good distance, and the friction of the spinning pile bunker created enough heat to make plumes of smoke rise from her chest.

...However, the light in Miledi's eyes was still burning bright.

"Ha...ha ha. Looks like even that wasn't enough. But well, props to you guys. You pierced through a good three-fourths of my armor, you know?" Her voice was shaky, but she tried to feign confidence. Internally, she was panicking. The pile bunker she'd just experienced had been one not fully accelerated by Hajime's max power Lightning Field. That was the only reason it hadn't penetrated all the way to her core. And yet, despair still didn't color Hajime's eyes. It was almost as if he'd expected it to not be enough.

"Now, Shea! Finish it!" Hajime put everything but the spike back into his Treasure Trove and leaped out of the way.

From above came Shea, falling from a great height. Her rabbit ears were flopping in the wind as she held Drucken high over her head.

"Wha—?!" Miledi instantly guessed what was about to happen. There was real panic in her eyes now, and she desperately tried to break free. Realizing that wouldn't work, she tried to move the platform she was stuck to instead, but she quickly realized it was too late. At the last moment she stopped struggling, accepting her inevitable fate.

Shea fired off multiple shotgun blasts to accelerate her even further, then slammed down her war hammer with all the power of gravity behind it.

With a thunderous roar, the spike sank deeper into Miledi. But even then, it didn't pierce all the way through. Shea squeezed Drucken's trigger relentlessly, blowing all of her ammunition.

Bang! Bang! Bang! Bang! Bang! Bang!

"Aaaaaaaaaaaaaaaaaaaaaaaaaaaaaaaaaaaaaaah!" Shea's scream echoed across the room. She poured every last ounce of her strength into her war hammer. Every. Last. Ounce.

The platform fell even further from the force of her blow. It crashed into the floor below at breakneck speed. Finally, the spike pierced through Miledi's last layer of Azantium armor. There was a satisfying crack as her core broke.

The moment the platform hit the ground, Shea somersaulted over Drucken and leaped into the air. Then, with her body strengthening focused on her legs, she kicked Drucken's handle, making doubly sure that Miledi was done for.

The spike drove even further into Miledi's chest, breaking the core apart, shattering it completely.

The light faded from Miledi's eyes. Shea let out a sigh of relief, then let the tension drain from her body.

☘ ☘ ☘ ☘ ☘ ☘ ☘ ☘ ☘ ☘ ☘ ☘ ☘ ☘

She heard two objects land behind her and turned around. As she expected, it was Hajime and Yue. Shea broke out into an ecstatic grin and gave them a thumbs-up. Both of them smiled back and returned her gesture.

They were certain of it now. They'd cleared the final trial Reisen's labyrinth had to offer.

"Nice one, Shea. That last smash of yours was perfect. I might even respect you a little now."

"...Yeah, you did good." Dust as thick as smoke swirled about them as they talked.

A spiderweb of cracks radiated out from the crater that had formed when the Miledi Golem had crashed into the ground. Shea was exhausted enough that she had to lean on Drucken just to stay on her feet.

She would have gladly just slumped to the ground, but she wanted to look cool in front of Hajime and Yue. And as a reward for her efforts, the two of them gave her looks of admiration.

"Ehehe, thanks guys. But Hajime-san, shouldn't you be saying you might have fallen in love with me a little instead?"

"Not happening. Not even a little." Though his words seemed curt, his expression was nowhere near as stern as it usually was when it came to Shea's pathetic jokes. In fact, he was even willing to admit to himself that Shea might have just looked a *little* sexy when pounding the finishing blow into Miledi.

The fact that she'd been able to fight so well despite never even holding a weapon until a few weeks ago was because of how strongly she'd wanted to stand on the same stage as Hajime and

Yue. It was that strong determination, combined with Shea's own latent abilities, that had allowed her to overcome the trials of one of the Seven Great Labyrinths and deal the finishing blow to its guardian.

In truth, Hajime hadn't necessarily needed Shea's help to finish off Miledi. He had expected the pile bunker would fall short, so he had a backup plan for powering it all the way in. But he'd seen how such a gentle and peace-loving bunny girl had resolutely stood by his side through all of their trials. Despite having no combat skill to speak of until just recently, she had never once cried that she wanted to go back, and despite all of her fear and uncertainty, she'd pushed valiantly forward. That was why he'd decided to entrust the final blow to her. A choice he was glad he'd made now.

That last strike of hers had actually been cool enough that Hajime would have fallen for her under normal circumstances. The depth of her feelings had been conveyed to him together with the shock waves generated by her attack. However, Hajime still couldn't give her the kind of affection she sought. In any case, the strength of her determination and guts had moved him. As a result, he definitely looked at her with kinder eyes than he used to.

"Fweh? I-Is it just me...or are you actually being nice to me for once, Hajime-san...? I-Is this a dream?"

"Now look here... Err, actually, I guess it makes sense that you'd think that considering how I've been treating you..."

Shea pinched her cheeks to make sure she really wasn't dreaming. Hajime wanted to protest, but he realized that he really didn't have any right to say anything.

Yue walked up to Shea, who was still busy pinching her cheeks. She grabbed Shea's arm, pulled her down into a crouch, and gently patted her head. Then, she started to straighten out Shea's disheveled hair.

"U-umm, Yue-san?"

"It's a shame we can't get Hajime to pat your head. You'll just have to make do with me for now."

"Y-Yue-saaaan. Huh? Why am I crying? Fweeeeeeeh."

"...There there."

Shea waffled about in confusion for a moment, but burst into tears and hugged Yue tight when she realized she was being praised. *Taking on one of the Seven Great Labyrinths for her first trip outside the forest must have been pretty tough.* Only the resolve to stay together with Yue and Hajime had kept her going. Finally being accepted as someone capable of fighting together with them after overcoming such a difficult trial was more than enough to move her to tears.

As an aside, even Yue's comment didn't persuade Hajime to pat her head. Since Shea was the kind of girl that got carried away easily, Hajime didn't want to give her the wrong idea by being too nice to her. Dealing with her misunderstandings was too much of a hassle for him. With all that they'd been through, Shea was definitely a member of his family. Still, the kind of love Hajime felt for Yue wasn't something that he could really share between multiple people. After all, that was what having a "special someone" meant. Besides, Hajime couldn't imagine ever doing anything that would make Yue sad.

And most of all, when he saw Shea crying tears of happiness and relief into Yue's bosom while Yue gently patted her head... Well, he could guess where things were probably headed.

Hajime watched on with a strange expression on his face. Suddenly, a voice called out to the three of them.

"Ummm... Sorry to interrupt your little party, but things aren't looking so hot for me, so I'd like to get this out of the way before it's too late." They knew that voice. The three of them all turned back in surprise. The light from Miledi's eyes, which had gone out moments ago, had returned. Instantly, they all jumped back. They all eyed Miledi warily, as they were certain they'd destroyed her core.

"Hey, hey, no need to be so tense. You did it! You won! I'm just using what little power's left in my core to talk to you guys for a bit! I'll be gone for good in a few minutes." The fact that the light in her eyes was flickering and fainter than before, combined with the fact that she didn't move, seemed to support her statement. She was on the verge of disappearing for good. *Really does look like she's gonna die in a few minutes...*

Relaxing slightly, Hajime cautiously responded to her.

"So? What'd you want to talk to us about, you half-dead golem? Seeing as you're about to die and still can't read the mood...I guess I'll posthumously award you the title of most insensitive Liberator."

"Heeey, there's no need to be so mean. I was just starting to like you, too."

"Whatever. Anyway, I thought I told you I have no interest in fighting your world's shitty gods." It almost felt like Miledi sighed before she responded.

"Don't worry, that's not what I wanted to talk about. There's no need to. I'm just...here to give you a piece of advice. Even if the spell you're looking for isn't in the labyrinths you explore, you'll need to acquire all of the ancient magic the Liberators left behind...in order to achieve your goal..." It certainly did seem like Miledi was on the verge of disappearing. Her voice was growing fainter and there were long pauses between sentences. Unconcerned, Hajime continued pressing her for answers.

"All of it, huh...? Well, why don't you tell us where all the other labyrinths are, then. The records have been lost and no one knows where most of them are anymore."

"Ah, I see... So it's already been so long...that people have forgotten where the labyrinths are... Okay, well...they're..." Miledi's voice grew weaker and weaker. It looked like she was reminiscing about the past. Yue and Shea looked down at her silently. They respected her determination. For the sake of her goal, for the sake of her dream, she'd abandoned human form and transferred her spirit into this inanimate object.

Miledi mumbled out the location of the remaining Great Labyrinths. Among them was one that came as a surprise to everyone.

"That's all of them... Good luck."

"You sure are acting nice now. What happened to all the harassment and traps you sprang on us?" Like Hajime had said, the annoying, cutesy speech and insulting tone were nowhere to be heard. Instead, she was speaking with a sincerity he could hardly believe, coming from her. She had shown hints of this personality before their fight, so Hajime was beginning to suspect this really was her true nature. And now that she was moments from death, she had no need to keep up the facade.

"Aha ha, sorry about that, really. But you know...those bastards...are real scum... They do these kinds of underhanded, annoying things all the time... So I just...wanted to help you get used to it before..."

"Hey... How many times do I have to say it? I have no interest in fighting your mad gods. Quit assuming I will."

The reply that came back had such an earnest tone to it that Hajime couldn't doubt her words. "You will. As long as you stay the same...you'll...definitely kill them."

"...I don't get what you're trying to say. I mean, sure, I guess I'll blow them to kingdom come if they get in my way, but..." Hajime replied hesitatingly. Miledi only laughed cryptically in reply.

"Haah haah... That's fine...live your life however you wish... I know...your choices...will definitely...help this world..." Glowing blue light enveloped the Miledi Golem. It flickered faintly, like the pale light of a firefly as it floated up to heaven, like a soul finally being freed. It was a wondrous, mystical sight.

Yue suddenly walked up to Miledi. There was almost no light left in her eyes.

"What is it?" Miledi's voice was barely a whisper. Yue replied in the same hushed whisper, giving her last parting words to the great Liberator.

"...You did well. You can rest now."

"......"

Words of praise. It was all one of the living could give to her, an almost legendary hero that had waited all alone in the darkness for centuries, never giving up hope that her dream would one day be realized. It might have been odd hearing those words from someone far younger than her. Still, Yue could think of nothing else to say.

Miledi hadn't been expecting that either. She just stared in surprise for a while. Finally, she spoke. Her muttered words were far gentler than anything they'd heard her say thus far.

"...Thank you."

"Mhmm."

Just get on with it already! Behind them, Hajime was nearing the end of his patience. The way Miledi had sounded so sure about what he was going to do had pissed him off. And yet, Shea pinned his arms behind his back and covered his mouth with her hand before he could do anything.

"Who's the one who can't read the mood now, huh?! Just stay quiet until they're done!" Shea whispered furiously into his ear. Fortunately, neither Yue nor Miledi noticed them, so the solemn atmosphere between the two of them remained.

"Now then...it's finally time... I pray that...the blessings of the gods...never reach you..."

Hold on, those were the same words Oscar told us back in his house... With that parting remark, Miledi Reisen, one of this world's Liberators, vanished. Entranced, Yue and Shea watched as the light of her soul rose up to the sky.

"...At first I thought she was just a rotten, twisted little woman, but she really gave it her all, didn't she?"

"Yeah..."

Their words were somber. However, one member of their party didn't seem to care about Miledi's passing at all, and hurried the two of them up.

"All right, done yet? Let's get out of here. Also, I know for a fact that that annoying part of her personality wasn't faked. There's no actor that good; she had to have been a bitch from the start."

"Come on, Hajime-san. There's no need to speak ill of the dead. That's just cruel. See, I knew you were the one who was worst at reading the mood."

"...Hajime, are you dense?"

"Not you too, Yue... Bah, whatever. Also, it's not that I can't read the mood. I'm just choosing not to."

In the midst of their conversation, they noticed a section of the wall had begun to glow. Cutting their discussion short, they started heading toward it. It was relatively high up, so they'd have to hop across a few floating blocks to reach it. But the moment they jumped onto the first one, it started moving and took them right to it.

"....."

"Whoa whoa whoa, it just started moving on its own. Well, at least it saved us some trouble."

"Is this a reward for winning?" Shea yelled out in surprise, while Yue tilted her head. Only Hajime looked unhappy. After ten seconds of travel, it stopped about five meters before the glowing part of the wall. At the same time, the light began to fade and the part of the wall that had been glowing fell away. Behind it was a passageway made of polished white stone that shone with a brilliant radiance.

The floating block they were standing on began taking them through the passage. *I guess this is what's going to take us to Miledi's house?* A short while later, they found themselves staring at a wall engraved with the seven Liberators' crests. It was the same wall that had led to Oscar's house in his labyrinth. As they approached, the wall slid to the side. The block didn't slow at all and took them through that opening as well. On the other side, they found…

"Hey there! Not-so-long time no see! It's me, Miledi-chan!" A miniature version of the Miledi Golem.

"……"

"What'd I tell you? I knew she'd pull something like this."

Shea and Yue were stunned speechless. Hajime just looked annoyed. He had been hoping his guess was incorrect.

He'd already guessed that both the serious Miledi and the prankster Miledi were just two facets of the person that was Miledi Reisen. The intricacy and annoyance factor of her traps was too great to have come from someone who was just putting on a facade. Furthermore, she'd purposely chosen to leave her spirit behind to judge potential challengers. In which case, it didn't make sense for her to set things up so that she'd just vanish once she was defeated. After all, that would mean subsequent challengers would no longer have any trials to overcome.

That was why Hajime had predicted that even if they destroyed her golem, Miledi herself wouldn't vanish. His assumption was confirmed when the block they jumped on started guiding them on its own. Only Miledi could freely control those blocks.

In stark contrast to Shea and Yue's glum expressions, Miledi seemed sickeningly cheerful.

"Huh? What's this? Why's everyone all quiet? Come on, shouldn't you be more surprised? Or are you just so surprised you don't know what to say? I guess my surprise was a huge hit!" The miniature Miledi Golem looked a lot more human than her giant counterpart. She had a white mask over her face and her slender body was clad in a white robe. Though it was rather off-putting that her mask was in the shape of a smiley face... Speaking in the same cutesy manner she had when they'd first met, Mini Miledi walked up to them. Yue and Shea's bangs were covering their faces, hiding their expressions. Hajime could see where this was headed and quickly took a step back.

Yue and Shea whispered quietly.

"...Then what was that back there?"

"Hm? Back there? Oh, did you think I died? Nah, no way! I'd never leave!"

"But we saw light leaving your body."

"Hoohoo, pretty good performance, right? I'm such a good actor! I really am a genius at everything I do!" Miledi got louder and louder as she spoke. She became proportionally more annoying as well. Yue stuck her hand out while Shea pulled out Drucken.

"Uh oh, did I go too far?" Miledi muttered worriedly.

"U-umm…" She looked apprehensively from Yue to Shea, momentarily at a loss for words, but then she seemed to resign herself to her fate as she spoke.

"Ehehe, juuust kidding!"

"Die."

"I'm going to kill you!"

"W-wait! Please wait! This body's really weak! I really will die if you smash it! Calm down, please! I'll apologize, I promise!"

That marked the start of a scuffle in which a great deal of the surrounding area was destroyed, but Hajime paid it all no mind and explored the room they were in instead. The floors and walls were all white, and aside from the magic circle engraved into its center, the room was empty. There was a single door set into the far wall, which Hajime assumed led to Miledi's house.

Hajime walked over to the magic circle and started examining it. Miledi hurried over to him when she saw what he was doing. A bloodthirsty vampire and a murderous rabbit chased after her.

"Heeey, don't touch that. Also, they're your comrades, right?! Don't just ignore me, do something about them!" Miledi cowered behind Hajime's back, hoping he would provide some protection against the two demonic girls chasing her.

"Hajime, move. I have to kill her."

"Please move, Hajime-san. We need to kill her. Soon, preferably."

"Didn't think I'd be hearing that from you guys. Anyway, quit playing around, we've got work to do." Hajime reprimanded Yue and Shea in a tired voice. Behind him, the Mini Miledi jeered.

"Yeah, that's right, take this seriously!" But then she was cut short by Hajime's metal arm grabbing her face. He tightened his hold on her until her smiley face mask was twisted in a grotesque expression of pain. There was an ominous creaking noise coming out of her head.

"If you don't want to end up like your bigger self, hand over the ancient magic."

"Heeey, you do know you totally sound like a villain—" *Creaak!* "Okay, okay, fine, I'll give it to you! I promise, so please stop! I'm really going to break if you keep going!" Seeing Miledi finally humbled, Yue and Shea calmed down a little as well. Realizing any more fooling around might really get her destroyed, Miledi quickly started up the magic circle.

The three of them stepped inside it. Since Miledi herself had been the one to test them here, there was no spell that searched their memories like the one in Orcus' home. Instead, the knowledge of how to use the ancient magic she protected was transferred directly to their brains. Hajime and Yue had gone through this once before, so they didn't show any reaction, but Shea jumped in surprise when it happened.

In just a few seconds, all three of them had the knowledge of how to use Miledi's ancient spell.

"This is... I knew it! A spell that lets you manipulate gravity."

"That's riiight! My specialty was gravity magic. Make sure you use it well... Or so I'd like to say, but it looks like you and that bunny girl over there don't have any affinity for it. Like none at all—holy cow!"

"Oh, shut up. I figured that would happen anyway." Just as Miledi had said, though Hajime and Shea now had the knowledge of how to manipulate gravity, they wouldn't easily be able to use it. It was like how Yue didn't have any aptitude for the creation magic Hajime used.

"Well, that bunny girl over there can at least use it well enough to make herself heavier. And you... you've got your creation magic, so think of something. At least Blondie over here is fit to use it. Train hard until you master it, okay?" Hajime shrugged his shoulders, Yue nodded seriously, and Shea looked stricken. She'd finally gotten her hands on god-level magic, only to be told the most she'd be able to do with it was make herself heavier. The shock must have been pretty great. Obviously, she had no intention of making herself heavier, but even learning how to make herself lighter wouldn't be of much help. Becoming lighter could mess up her body proportions just as badly. Either way, it was of no use to her... Shea sunk to the ground, clearly depressed. Hajime ignored her and continued mercilessly making more demands.

"Hey, Miledi. Hand over the proof that we conquered this dungeon. Oh, and give us all the useful artifacts you have hidden here and all the high-quality spirit stone you've got stored up."

"You do realize that you sound like a mugger right now, right?" It felt to Hajime that the eyes behind the now warped smiley face mask were glaring at him angrily, but he ignored them. Mini Miledi ruffled through her pockets before pulling out a ring and throwing it to Hajime. He caught it in midair. Reisen's crest was two ellipses connected by a single stake piercing through both of them.

She then brought out a large quantity of ore, seemingly from nowhere, then rifled through it, picking out the same ore the dungeon was made from. She must have had a Treasure Trove of her own. *Considering how easily she agreed, maybe she planned on giving all this to us anyway.* For whatever reason, Miledi seemed convinced that Hajime would indeed end up fighting the gods, so it made sense for her to offer all this assistance.

Though, leave it to Hajime to not be satisfied with all that. He started packing the ore into his own Treasure Trove while he looked coldly at Miledi.

"That's a Treasure Trove, isn't it? Hand it over. You've got some good artifacts in there too, right?"

"N-now look here, that's everything I have to give you. I need the Treasure Trove and all the other artifacts I have left to repair and maintain this labyrinth."

"Like I care. Hand it over."

"Hey, I said no!" Miledi hurriedly stepped back, away from Hajime's grabbing hands. *Besides, these things wouldn't be of any use to them anyway.* She explained as much to Hajime, but it seemed to be of no use.

"Hmm, I see... All right, hand it over." At this point, he really was acting like a villain.

"I told you already, I can't! Now go home!" Miledi fled from Hajime's groping clutches and jumped up onto the block that had led them here. She manipulated it so that she was floating somewhere near the ceiling.

"Don't run. I just want everything you own as part of my

reward for clearing your dungeon. I'd say that's a fair thing to ask."

"There's something wrong with you if you think that counts as fair! Ugh, can't believe I ended up saying the same line O-chan always used to give me..."

"Just so you know, it's O-chan who taught us this is fair."

"O-chaaaaaaan!"

Hajime eventually managed to corner Miledi with the help of Yue and Shea, who still held a grudge toward her for all the teasing she'd done and wanted payback. She knew half of this was her own fault, but the part that really stung was that half of it was the fault of the guy who'd made the other labyrinth.

"Haaah, to think the first people to conquer my dungeon would be this crazy... Whatever, I give up. I'm sending you three out of here! You better not come back!" Just before Hajime could leap at her, a rope suddenly appeared from the ceiling, which Miledi promptly pulled.

"Huh?" Hajime looked up in confusion, but then he heard that same terrible noise he'd grown to hate.

Clunk!

"Wha—?!" She'd activated another trap.

A second later, water started rushing into the room from all four walls. Because of the angle it came out at, the room they were in was soon a raging whirlpool of water. At the same time, the magic circle in the center of the room sunk, creating a neat little hole in the floor. The whirlpool started draining into it.

"Hey! You little—" Hajime stiffened as he realized the humiliation they were about to be subjected to. A circular white room, a hole in its center, and water whirlpooling its way down said hole... Miledi had led them to a massive toilet.

"How about we let this water wash away our animosity too?" Mini Miledi's mask winked at them.

Annoyed, Yue quickly tried to cast her usual flight spell. Mana in this room didn't get dispersed, possibly because the magic circle was in this room, which was why Yue could easily have lifted them all up despite her depleted mana reserves.

"Up—"

"Nooope!" Before she could finish, however, Miledi stuck out her hand, and Hajime and the others felt an enormous weight press down on them. It felt like there was an invisible object trying to crush them. Miledi had increased the weight of the air pressing down on them.

"Bye byyye! Good luck with the other labyrinths!"

"Ugh... Damn you! We're not shit to be flushed down! I swear I'll come back and destroy you!"

"Urgh... I'll never forgive you."

"You're dead, you hear me?! Dead! Graahh!"

With those parting remarks, Hajime and the others were sucked down the massive toilet bowl. Just before he vanished from sight, Hajime chucked something at Miledi in a last desperate act of revenge. Once Hajime and the others had disappeared, the water drained away as fast as it came, leaving the room looking the same as it had before.

"Haah, what a bunch. Still, to think he'd be a Synergist like O-chan... Hoohoo, it almost feels like fate. Keep struggling for the sake of your dream... Now then, looks like I'll be busy fixing the golems for quite some time... Hm? What's this?"

Miledi wiped nonexistent sweat off her artificial golem brow as she mused to herself. A second later, she noticed something strange at the corner of her sight. There was a knife stuck to the wall with a black object dangling from it. *What on earth is that?* As she got closer, she realized she recognized that shape.

"Huh?! Wait, isn't this—"

The black object was one of Hajime's hand grenades. Just before he'd disappeared down the drain, Hajime had thrown it as his last act of revenge. Since he'd used it so many times in the dungeon, Miledi recognized what it was instantly. Panicking, she quickly tried to get away. However, manipulating gravity took up large amounts of mana, and Miledi had used all of it up in that last chase, which meant she had no means of softening the explosion.

She tried to make a break for it on foot, but it was already too late. The moment Mini Miledi turned around was when the grenade went off. The entire room was enveloped in light, followed by a massive shock wave.

Miledi's screams echoed throughout the labyrinth. Some time after, there might have been a very depressed golem going around crying as she had to spend even more time repairing her dungeon. Meanwhile, the trio that had been flushed out of the room was currently being carried down a long tunnel by a powerful current. There were no breaks for them to take a breath, so they just got swept along. It took all of their concentration just to stay conscious and avoid crashing into the walls.

They caught sight of a number of shadows passing them by as they were being swept away. Fish. The tunnel they were being funneled through must have connected to a river or lake somewhere. Unlike Hajime and the others, the fish were able to swim against the current, and many of them passed the trio.

One of them even came up to Shea's face as it swam by, keeping pace with her. She looked over at it. Their eyes met. Hers and the fish's. Or rather, what she'd thought was a fish. Though it had the body of one, its face looked like that of an old man. It was a difficult impression to convey, but that was the best way to describe it. Shea had run into a fish with a person's face. Its apathetic expression was oddly reminiscent of the fish in the old game Seaman.

Shea opened her eyes wide in surprise. She almost let out the breath she'd been holding in, but she managed to clamp down on her mouth in time. Still, she couldn't take her eyes off it. The two of them stared each other down as they were swept away by the current. They might have spent all eternity gazing into each other's eyes, but Shea was abruptly interrupted by a voice that popped up in her head.

What the heck are you staring at?

It was even accompanied by a mental clicking of the tongue. This time Shea couldn't contain her surprise. She opened her mouth with a garbled scream, letting out the air she'd been holding in. *Wait, is this fish a monster of some kind?! One that can use the telepathy skill?* But Shea's question would remain forever unanswered as the torrent of water swept them away, while the fish continued swimming in a different direction.

All that was left behind was a white-eyed bunny girl suspended limply in the water as their party continued to flow down the water for quite a while...

❖ ❖ ❖ ❖ ❖ ❖ ❖ ❖ ❖ ❖ ❖ ❖ ❖ ❖

A single carriage escorted by a team of horses plodded down a beaten highway. The horses' hoofbeats punctured the silence at regular intervals. They naturally had people riding them. Three men and one woman, all of them dressed like adventurers. The carriage was being driven by a fifteen-year-old girl and a...cross-dresser that resembled a monster.

"Sona-chaaan, there's a spring coming up ahead, so let's take a break there."

"All right, Crystabel-san."

This Crystabel was the same Crystabel that had helped outfit Yue and Shea back in the town of Brooke. The girl sitting next to him was the receptionist of the Masaka Inn that they'd stayed at, Sona Masaka. Despite her strange-sounding name, she was an ordinary girl with maybe just a little more curiosity in the more adult side of things than was normal for her age.

The two of them were on their way back to Brooke after an excursion to the next town over with a hired escort of guards. As his giant frame would suggest, Crystabel was insanely strong, so he often went out to collect his own supplies to craft his clothes. This trip, in fact, had been one such instance. Sona had come along because one of her relatives in the next town over had gotten pretty badly hurt and her parents were too busy to go, so she'd delivered get well gifts in their place. The adventurers had been on the way back from a quest, so they decided to tag along as well.

They were around a day's ride out from Brooke. The party decided to rest at a nearby spring for the afternoon.

They let the horses drink from the spring while they made preparations for lunch. Sona headed to the spring to get water for the group. The moment she put her canteen into the spring, it started frothing. Gouts of water flew up from its center, splashing the nearby area.

"Kyaaa!"

"Sona-chan!"

Sona let out a surprised shriek and fell back. Crystabel instantly rushed over to protect her, with the other adventurers not far behind. The fountain's spray increased in intensity, creating a column of water rising ten meters high.

This spring was a well-known resting place for travelers, and never once had anyone reported something like this happening. Hence why Crystabel, Sona, and the other adventurers gazed on in shock, heedless of the spray that was soaking them. A few seconds later...

"Gaaaaaah!"

"Aaaaaaah!"

"......"

Three people were spat out of the fountain...two of which screamed as they flew out. Crystabel and the others cried out in surprise. The people flew a good ten feet through the air before crashing spectacularly to the ground on the opposite shore.

"......"

"Wh-what on earth was that...?" Crystabel and the adventurers were shocked speechless, while Sona muttered what they were all thinking.

"Ack... Ugh... God, that was terrible. I'm gonna crush that little bitch into pieces, mark my words. Yue, Shea, you all right?"

"Ack, urgh... Yeah, somehow."

Hajime spat out a string of curses while making sure Yue and Shea were fine. However, only Yue responded to him.

"Shea? Hey, Shea! Where are you?"

"Shea...where'd you go?"

There was no response. Hajime quickly jumped back into the water and started looking for her. As he'd expected, Shea was laying at the bottom of the spring. She'd lost consciousness and didn't float because of Drucken's weight.

Hajime pulled a really dense ore out of his Treasure Trove, making him quickly sink to the bottom. Once he'd grabbed Shea, he kicked off the ground and leaped back out.

He dragged her with him to the shore. Then, he laid her on her back and took a closer look at her. She was pale-faced, her eyes had rolled back into her head, and her heart wasn't beating. She must have seen something quite terrifying as her expression was still frozen in one of disgust.

"Yue, you've got to give her CPR!"

"CPwhat?"

"Gah, I mean you need to clear her airway of water and..."

"Huh?" He tried to get Yue to give Shea CPR, but she just

looked at Hajime blankly. *Does the concept of CPR not exist in this world?* She wasn't exactly injured, and feeding her more liquid when she was already drowning seemed like a bad idea, so the Ambrosia probably wouldn't be of any help. Yue wasn't very well versed in healing magic, so he doubted she could cast something specific enough to make Shea spit out all the water and get her heart pumping again.

He didn't know when it was she'd lost consciousness, but at this point time was of the essence. Hajime steeled his resolve and started performing CPR.

Naturally, that meant he would have to do mouth-to-mouth as well... Yue watched on unhappily. But she realized Hajime was doing this because it would somehow save Shea, so she kept quiet. Instead, she just stared.

Hajime tried to ignore that cold stare as best he could while he worked to get Shea's heart pumping again. *Unbelievable. I'd just started to think you might not be that worthless after all, but then you go and nearly kill yourself after we've already won... You really are just a worthless rabbit.* Hajime grimaced, and after a few rounds of CPR, Shea finally started coughing up water. He turned her head to the side so she wouldn't choke on it again. From an outside perspective, it looked like he was kissing her passionately.

"Hic, ack... Hajime-san?"

"Yep, that's me. Unbelievable. I can't believe you almost got yourself killed—mmf?!"

Despite his harsh words, Hajime looked thoroughly relieved.

Suddenly, Shea interrupted him by throwing her arms around him and giving him a deep kiss. It was so unexpected that Hajime didn't have any time to move out of the way.

"Mmmf?! Mmmmm!!!"

"Mmmph... Mmm..." Shea wrapped her arms and legs around Hajime, locking him in place while she mercilessly ravaged his mouth with her tongue. Her inhuman strength and the leverage her position gave her made it impossible for Hajime to break away.

Somehow, Shea had been aware of all the "kisses" Hajime had given her while he was performing CPR. Perhaps it was a special condition brought on by the fact that Shea had activated her body strengthening right before she'd lost consciousness.

Regardless, Hajime's repeated kisses had flung her into full overdrive mode. She kept Hajime firmly pinned in place while she returned his kisses a hundredfold.

Off to the side, Yue looked...very unhappy, to say the least. Still, she did nothing to stop them. In a small voice, she muttered, "As a reward, just this once..." It appeared she was willing to forgive this transgression.

Though it was obvious from her expression and the dangerous look in her eyes that she was quite conflicted. Tonight, she was going to make sure Hajime spent the whole night with her... She wouldn't let him rest for even a second.

"Wh-wh-wha! What's going on?! A-amazing...they're completely soaked, but they're wrapping around each other so passionately... A-and... they're doing it all outside! These people aren't normal!" That exclamation came from none other than the easily excitable girl, Sona. Next to her, Crystabel muttered "Oh? Aren't you two..." It seemed he remembered them. Off to the side, the three male adventurers were burning up with jealousy, and it was with great effort that they managed to keep their swords in their sheaths. The single female adventurer gave them a withering glare.

Shea was still half-delirious from passion and near-death euphoria. She panted heavily as she kissed Hajime, until finally he got so fed up that he lifted himself to his feet, taking Shea with him. He then grabbed Shea's plump butt, giving it a firm squeeze.

"Aahn!" She let out a garbled moan. In that second, her iron-clad grip loosened. Hajime peeled her off and flung her into the spring.

"Eyaaaaah!" He watched as she fell into the spring with a tremendous splash. Then, he took a few seconds to catch his breath and comb his hair back.

"I-I was careless. I didn't think she'd come at me like that...just after regaining consciousness." Hajime watched as she lumbered out of the spring like a banshee, her bangs covering her face, and shivered.

"Ooof... How cruel. Hajime-san, you're the one that started it."

"Excuse me? I'll have you know that that is just a lifesaving technique, nothing more...and wait, you were conscious that whole time?"

"Well, I'm not exactly sure...but I could kind of tell what was going on. Just that you were kissing me over and over, Hajime-san! Ahehehe."

"Please stop laughing creepily like that. Look, I only did that to save your life, nothing more. Don't get any weird ideas, okay?"

"Really? But a kiss is still a kiss. At this rate, you might really fall for me!"

"Like hell I will. And Yue, you could have stopped her, you know?"

"Just this once... I mean, Shea worked so hard...but still..."

"Yue? Earth to Yue?"

Yue stared back with blank eyes, muttering incoherently. Hajime sighed as he realized she was done for, too. Finally, he turned to Crystabel and the others. They'd been staring at them this whole time.

His gaze passed over the four adventurers, stopped for a second at Sona, and returned to her after he took one look at Crystabel. He'd like to pretend he never saw Crystabel at all.

Sona jumped with a start when she realized Hajime was looking at her, then blushed bright red.

"S-sorry for interrupting you two! D-don't mind us. By all means, please continue!" She turned around to run, but Crystabel grabbed her by the scruff of the neck before she could. She then walked up to Hajime and the others. Hajime nervously stepped backwards, but Shea greeted her with a cheerful "Oh, hey, you're the shop owner." It appeared she knew her.

After they sorted everything out, Hajime discovered they'd been spat out a day's ride from Brooke, so they decided to head back there with Crystabel and the others. Crystabel offered to let them ride in their carriage, which they happily accepted. They changed out of their soaked clothes and chatted amicably with the others as they rode back. The sound of hoofbeats became the soundtrack of their travels as the warm rays of the sun smiled down upon them.

Together with their newfound comrade, Hajime and his party had cleared their second labyrinth. Hajime let the feeling of victory settle in as he lay down in the back of the carriage. Warmed by the sun, he smiled faintly as he thought of all the travels that still yet awaited them.

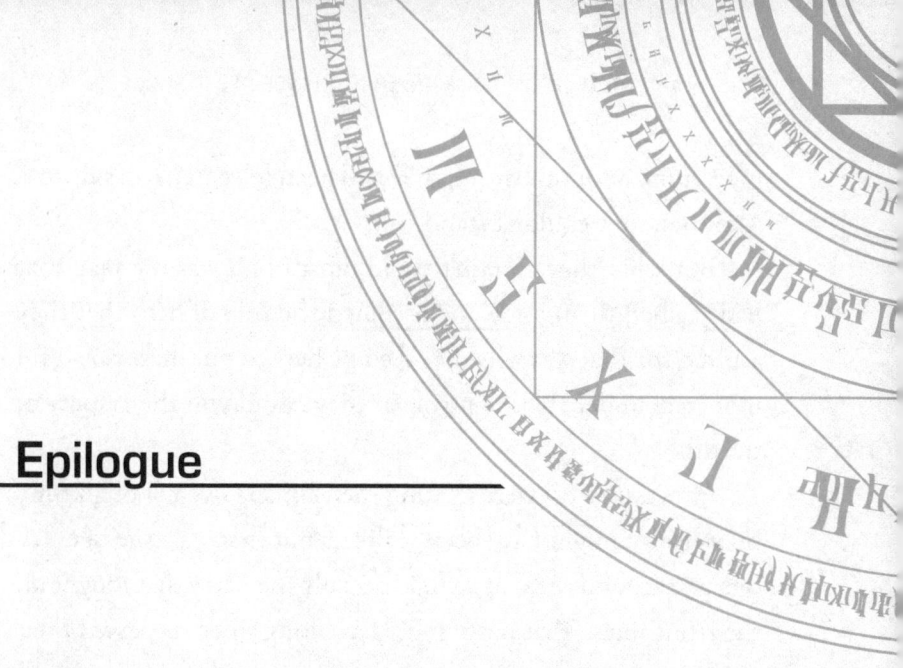

Epilogue

"**You are truly fit to be a hero.**" A clear voice rang out through a mountain valley illuminated by the half moon and bedecked in everlasting autumn leaves. The man who had spoken narrowed his eyes and extended a hand in front of him.

"B-but I..." The person he was addressing gulped audibly as they stammered. They realized they were standing on the edge of a decision that would change their life irrevocably, and the temptation and dangers of each choice led them to hesitate.

As they looked around, they saw the legion of monsters that had bent to their will. The Mountain Range that sprawled north of the lake town of Ur rested near the top of Heiligh's territory. They had left the safety of their comrades behind and come here alone to do something about their tenuous position. Despite the fact that they had been summoned among the chosen heroes, despite the fact that they had a talent that surpassed most humans of this world, they had been relegated to a side role. And that, they couldn't stand.

But what they couldn't stand most of all was the man that had pushed them aside and assumed the role of hero that they aspired to. That was why they'd come here to put these powerful monsters under their control, so they could win the respect of the others.

However, they were nearing their limit. Given enough time, their dream might have been realized, but that was true of everyone else around them as well. Especially the party that fought on the front lines. That party must have long since surpassed their skills. Even though they wanted to be admired and loved by all, they'd been too scared to go back to the labyrinth. At this point, there was little chance they could catch up to the best. They'd told themselves over and over that with the right methods, it could be done. Despite that, they'd never been sure, and oftentimes they'd been on the verge of giving up, believing that they just weren't born with the kind of talent real heroes had. And yet, they persevered.

That was why the sudden appearance of the man that had told them "You are indeed special" had been so moving and why his invitation sounded so appealing. Even if in exchange for accepting his offer, they would have to give up something irreplaceable.

"W-will you really turn me into a hero? You won't turn around and betray me?"

"Of course. As long as you're truly willing to throw everything away and come to our master's side, that is. You'll have to prove yourself by fighting that agricultural goddess of yours and her bodyguards, but if you do, we'll treat you as our hero. I promise we won't betray you. There's no one else we can rely on. It's precisely because you're special that we want to invite you to our camp."

"Me...a hero. I'll finally become the protagonist of my own story..." They gulped again at the man's seductive words. The black flames of ambition burned fiercely within their eyes. Their desire and desperation spilled forth like a burst dam, staining their silhouette black. Without even bothering to hide their excitement, they nodded vigorously and licked their lips.

"I'll do it. I'll become your hero." Their expression couldn't be called heroic by any stretch of the imagination.

"A wise choice. I look forward to working with you...hero." The man smiled gently, while internally cackling to himself. Not only was a wonderful slaughter about to occur, it would be brought about by one of their own. The irony was simply delicious.

In a quiet corner of the Northern Mountain Range, two sets of laughter overlapped each other. The only ones present to bear witness were the forlorn half moon and a legion of unthinking monsters.

ARIFURETA:
ARIFURETA SHOKUGYOU DE SEKAISAIKYOU

**FROM COMMONPLACE
TO WORLD'S STRONGEST**

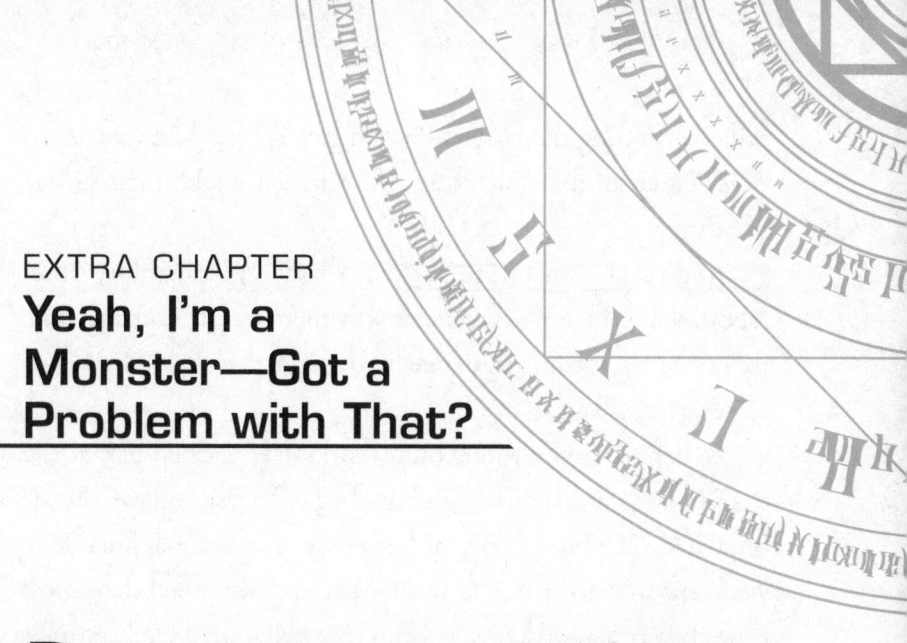

Yeah, I'm a Monster—Got a Problem with That?

DEEP WITHIN THE MISTY FOREST, a single figure was running with all its might. Her pale blue hair blended in with the mist, but the speed at which she moved sent ripples through the fog. Despite how lightly her hair was fluttering through the wind, her expression was anything but light. In fact, she was crying as she ran.

It was quite easy for a young girl of five or six to get lost and eaten within the Haltina Woods, a place considered by most men to be a den of monsters. Still, there was no worry of this particular girl getting eaten. It was hard to tell because she was crouching, but the girl running through the fog had a splendid pair of rabbit ears growing out of her head. She was a member of the beastman race that inhabited these woods—a rabbit girl.

The rabbitmen were considered the weakest of the beastmen races, but in return they had the best sense of hearing and were skilled at hiding themselves. Even a girl like her had very sharp ears. Few creatures could escape the notice of a rabbitman's sense of hearing.

And this bunny girl in particular had a special ability other rabbitmen didn't possess. Hence why there was little chance this particular girl was in any danger of dying, especially as she was so close to her village.

As expected, the young bunny girl safely reached her village, despite her loud wailing. The fog began to thin out as she approached. The boundaries of her hometown were defined by a well-kept wooden fence. It was far better maintained than most other beastmen settlements, even those that belonged to other rabbitmen tribes. The fence posts were close enough together that one wouldn't easily be able to peek inside, and each of them were three meters high.

Normally, most rabbitmen's only options when it came to a confrontation were to run or to hide. Both in regards to themselves, and in regards to their villages, they rarely focused on heavy defense. As long as it could buy them enough time to run away, and was spaced out enough to give them a good view of the situation outside, it was a good enough fence for them.

At first glance, the fence surrounding this village appeared quite strong, but a closer inspection showed that the planks used to hold the fence posts together were surprisingly fragile. It seemed almost as if this village was focused more on making sure their fence couldn't be seen through than creating an adequate defensive barrier.

The young bunny girl circled around the unusual fence and went inside. The rabbitman guarding the gate said something to her as she passed by, but she ignored him.

Many other rabbitmen called out to her as she ran past, but she ignored them all and headed straight for her house.

"Oh my... What's wrong, Shea? Your bunny ears are drooping." The five-year-old bunny girl, Shea, looked up to see an older rabbit woman come out from inside a room. She had the dark blue hair that was characteristic of her race and gentle eyes that belied a powerful will. The latter was a rarity among rabbitmen.

"Mom!" Still crying, Shea leaped into the arms of her mother, Mona Haulia, with a speed that seemed unthinkable for a five-year-old girl.

Mona let out a very unseemly grunt as Shea barreled into her. But Shea didn't notice, as she was too busy wiping her eyes and nose on her mother's chest.

The rabbitmen's traditional clothing was surprisingly revealing. Women wore what was basically nothing more than a bikini and miniskirt. For rabbitmen, heavy clothing would only get in their way when they were trying to run. The sound of rustling clothes would alert their more perceptive enemies to their presence. Because of the perpetual fog, the temperature didn't vary much year round, and there was little point in keeping clothes that would have to be discarded if they ever had to run.

And so, Mona's cleavage was soon smeared in tears, snot, and drool. But she didn't seem bothered by that at all. In fact, she was currently busy coping with the pain in her stomach and making sure she didn't throw up all over her daughter.

With tears still in her eyes, Mona gently patted Shea's back, and once she'd calmed down a little, she asked her what was wrong.

Shea sniffled and looked up at her mother. Instead of an answer, she replied with a question of her own.

"Mom... Am I...a monster? Am I evil?"

"...Shea."

It was rare for a girl so young to think about such terrible things, but Mona knew about her daughter's peculiar abilities, so she could guess what must have happened.

Shea's light blue hair wasn't the only thing special about her. She also had the ability to store and manipulate mana, something no beastman should have been able to do. Furthermore, she was even able to use special magic of her own.

Not even humans or demons could do the last two things, which were abilities unique to monsters. And monsters were hated by all, regardless of race or nationality.

This was why the Haulia village's fence had been made to prevent anyone from seeing inside. Her family had done their best to try and raise her inside the village so that no one could find out about her existence. If anyone discovered who she was, even just among the beastmen of Verbergen, she would surely be executed.

Had Shea not been born to a tribe of rabbitmen, who were known for valuing familial love over all else, she would surely have been executed the moment she was born. Only the Haulia would be willing to take such risks to protect her like they had.

But no matter how much the adults tried to protect her, there was no way a curious young child would be satisfied living in the confines of her small village. It was only natural for her to want to explore the outside world.

"Shea...you went out again, didn't you?"

"Oof... I'm sorry, mom. But... But..."

Shea hung her head apologetically, and Mona smiled gently. Someone must have spotted Shea on one of her excursions.

While beastmen didn't lose their sense of direction in the fog, their vision was hampered just like every other race. And while Shea was curious about the outside world, she knew how much trouble it would cause her family if anyone spotted her. Which was why she had used her innate stealth abilities, which far surpassed many adult rabbitmen's, to stay out of sight when she left the village.

So even if anyone had spotted her, Mona doubted they'd gotten a good look at her. Meaning there could be only one reason Shea was crying.

"A white silhouette running through the trees. No matter how quickly you chase after it, it vanishes like an illusion before you can catch up. It must be some kind of new monster, or perhaps an evil spirit that has haunted the forest for centuries... Is that what you've been hearing people say about you, with those sharp little ears of yours?"

"Mom... You knew?"

Mona nodded as she softly ruffled Shea's bunny ears. She had heard the rumors her fellow rabbitmen had been whispering about. For now, it was still nothing more than an urban legend of sorts, the kind of thing people talked about just to have something to talk about. There were more legends about this forest than there were trees, so it wasn't anything to be concerned about yet.

Though of course, Shea must have been quite shocked upon hearing them for the first time. She'd already known that she was different from the rest of her family. And she knew she could do the same thing monsters could. She'd avoided thinking about it as much as possible, but it was hard not to when she heard people talking about it.

Maybe I really am something different. Maybe I really am some kind of freak that isn't monster or beastman.

Fresh tears welled up in the corners of Shea's eyes, and she sniffled. Mona gave her daughter a look that was equal parts kind and equal parts stern, but all of it filled with love.

"Shea, do you hate monsters?"

"Huh? O-of course I do!"

"Why?"

"B-because..."

Shea couldn't understand why her mom was asking this. *Does Mom think I'm a monster, too?* she thought sadly, her bunny ears twitching. Mona gently cupped her daughter's cheek, and looked gently into her eyes. There was a surprising amount of weight to her gaze.

"You're afraid because you're different from everyone else. It's scary, and lonely, and sad. I know. But you know, Shea. Mom's jealous of you. She's jealous, and she's happy to have such a wonderful daughter."

"Why?"

"Because if you're different from everyone else, that means you can do things no one else can. Don't you think that's amazing?"

Mona's words made no sense to Shea, and she looked around restlessly while sky blue tears dripped from her eyes.

"Amazing? What would you do if you were like me, mom?"

"Fufu. Weeell, your mom's always wanted to be a hero, ever since she was little."

"A-a hero?"

Mona had a surprisingly weak constitution and was usually sick in bed for half of each month. Shea blinked in surprise as she looked up at her mother. It was an odd thing to say, for someone as weak as her, but then Shea nodded, thinking it was very like her to have such a wish.

"That's right, a hero. You know, I've always wanted to be someone who could protect their family. And not just spend all my time running away or hiding. I wanted to be the kind of person that could stand up to anything that tried to hurt the people I love." The rabbitmen were gentle, peace-loving people. It was rare for one to be as assertive as Mona. However, she had too weak a constitution to become the kind of person she wanted to be. Though she had a stronger will than any of her brethren, and a stronger heart than any of her family, fate had dealt her a body that was frail even by the low standards of her already-weak race. Could anything be more ironic?

But that was precisely why she had prayed.

"I had always prayed my child would be stronger than I... And Shea, you were everything I could have hoped for. You can't imagine how happy I am to have you as a daughter."

"Mom..."

Mona hugged her daughter fiercely, trying to convey the depth of her happiness and pride.

"Shea. It doesn't matter if you're a beastman, or a monster, or even a freak. They're all just words. Only you can decide what kind of person you want to become. And all that matters is you become that person. It's precisely because you're different from a normal rabbitman that you can become anything your heart desires."

"......"

Shea could see from up close just how much her mother loved her. Captivated by her gaze, Shea stared back.

Then, like a prophet, Mona started predicting the future.

"Shea. I'm sure you'll face many hardships in the future. Far more than any normal person would. Growing up will be hard. That's what happens when you're different from others."

"Mom..."

Shea's rabbit ears drooped, and she looked around uneasily. But that wasn't the end of Mona's prophecy.

"But I know you have the power to overcome all of them. That's why, Shea—never hate yourself. Stay bright, stay cheerful. Blow away all those nasty things with a smile. Puff out your chest with pride: 'I'm Shea Haulia, got a problem with that?!' As long as you still love yourself, everything will turn out okay."

"Everything?"

"Yep, everything."

"Okay. I'll try."

"Hee hee, what a good girl you are."

Her unnaturally bright hair bobbed up and down as she nodded. She decided first she'd start by trying to love the color of her hair.

Mona's serious gaze vanished, and she smiled playfully.

"Oh, yes, Mom has one more prediction for you."

"?"

"One day, I'm sure you'll meet some wonderful people. It's possible they won't be rabbitmen, or even beastmen. They might not even be from this forest...but they'll be different, just like you, Shea."

"Just like me?"

"Yep. I'm sure you'll meet them eventually." *She can't see the future like me, so why is she so sure?* Shea tilted her rabbit ears to the side quizzically.

"After all, it'd be too sad...if you were the only one of your kind in the world. The world can be a cruel place, but it can also be a kind one. That's why, I'm sure you'll meet them one day, Shea. People you can trust to have your back and who will trust you to have theirs."

"Are there really people like that outside the forest?"

"There are, I'm sure of it. Fufu. Who knows, maybe one of them will end up being your husband."

"Fweh?! M-m-m-m-my husband?!"

"Yep, and there'll be a girl you'll fight with over who gets him that'll come to be your best friend!"

"Fight with?!"

Mona looked like she was really enjoying herself now. The young and impressionable Shea drunk in every word of her mother's prophecy.

She had long since forgotten her sadness at being called a monster and talked happily with her mom. Then Cam, who'd just returned from gathering food, and all the other Haulia who'd seen her run past came into the house and started teasing her about her future husband.

Cam looked a little disappointed upon hearing that Shea was already going to be married, but both Mona and Shea ignored him. No one could have foreseen that her supposed future husband would go on to turn the Haulia into a race of bloodthirsty raiders. Not even Mona could see the future that accurately.

"Mmmmm..." A single girl's yawn vanished into the general tumult of the busy inn. She stretched and opened her eyes.

"Mmm, it's morning already?"

"More like it's past noon already. Just how much longer were you planning on sleeping, you airheaded rabbit?"

Those words instantly brought Shea to alertness, and her bunny ears perked up sharply.

She looked around and saw Hajime sitting by the window, polishing his revolver and staring at Shea with a look of disdain.

"Huh? What are you doing here, Hajime-san? Wait, don't tell me you snuck in here to—abwha?!"

"I just said it's past noon. Yue left to go shopping ages ago. We promised to go together, but you wouldn't wake up even after I tried shocking you, so she left by herself."

"I-I see. Sorry. I'll get ready and then we can go catch up to her... Wait, so then why did you stay behind in my room?"

Her bunny ears tilted quizzically. Shea had thought Hajime would have gone with Yue. Hajime grimaced and muttered "I'm... not good at dealing with that monster of a clothing store owner."

The clothing store owner that Hajime and the others had traveled back to Brooke with seemed to put him on edge. He was so unwilling to meet with him that he'd even turned down a date with Yue.

Shea smiled awkwardly and replied, "He's a nice guy once you get to know him, though." The way Hajime had said "monster" bothered her a little. Probably because of the dream she'd just had.

"What's wrong, Shea?"

"Huh?"

Before she knew it, Hajime was staring intently at her. He must have somehow sensed her discomfort. Though she was happy he'd noticed, she wasn't sure how to respond. Before she could think of what to say, Hajime answered for her.

"Is it something to do with your mom?"

"Huh?!"

"Do you have a mind-reading skill too or something?!" Shea asked, amazed. Her bunny ears flattened in shock, and she brought her hands up to the voluptuous chest she'd inherited from her mother.

"Nope. You were just muttering 'mom' a lot in your sleep."

"Oh… I see. Aha ha, how embarrassing. I can't believe I'm still doing stuff like that even at this age."

Shea scratched her head in embarrassment, but Hajime didn't buy it and kept staring at her with the same intensity. Finally, it seemed he'd realized something, and he shrugged his shoulders dismissively.

"Well, it didn't look like you were having a nightmare, at least." Shea's heart skipped a beat as she realized he must have been worried about her in his own classic way. She hadn't told either Hajime or Yue about Mona. It wasn't like she was trying to hide it; there just had never been a chance to bring it up. Hajime himself had guessed what must have happened to her considering that she hadn't been anywhere among the Haulia, and that Shea never talked about her. He thought it was a topic she preferred to avoid.

He was far more considerate of her now that they'd cleared a labyrinth together. Shea's ears and tail flapped about happily.

"Yes, it was a very nostalgic dream. My mother died ten years ago from an illness. Her constitution had always been weak, and after she gave birth to me the doctors said it would be a miracle if she lasted another ten years, even."

"Really?"

"Yes. Don't worry, she didn't die when we were being chased by the empire, and I was at least able to say my farewells to her, so it's not like you need to take any extra care not to mention her or anything."

"Who said I was?"

Hajime turned around sulkily. Shea followed up with a "Someone's not being honest with themselves—hee hee," to which Hajime responded with a flick to the forehead. Shea rubbed at the red mark that had appeared on her forehead before continuing cheerfully.

"I was actually thinking of telling you and Yue about my mom sometime soon. Would you like to hear about her?"

She wore the same expression she had when she'd told Hajime there were some futures you couldn't change no matter how hard you tried. Perhaps she had been thinking about what had happened to her mom when she said that. Though this time, there was a hint of pride mixed into her voice as well. Hajime could tell just how much pride Shea must have had in her mother.

"Go ahead. I'm tired enough to sleep through a whole barrage of electric shocks. So since we'll be staying in here a while longer, I might as well hear some stories about your mom to pass the time."

"Ehehe, okay."

Her ears flopped about happily. Hajime found them rather charming and stretched out his hand to scratch them. Obviously there was no deeper meaning behind that action, he just wanted to know what they felt like. But at that moment...

"No flirting."

"Oh, Yue. What're you doing there?"

"Wh-wh-wha?! You scared me for a second, Yue-san."

Yue's emotionless face was glaring at them through the open window. The bags in her hand indicated that she'd finished shopping, and had returned to invite Hajime and Shea to go out with her.

Hajime leaped out the window. Shea quickly got dressed herself and followed after the two.

The warm rays of the sun, something she'd seen little of in the sea of trees, shone down on her as she watched crowds of adventurers and merchants and craftsmen go about their business. Shea closed her eyes happily and skipped lightly through the street.

Many sad things had happened in her life. Most of them had been things she couldn't change. She'd lost many things important to her. But just like her mom had said, Shea had met them. And that meeting had saved her family. That meeting had led her out into the sunlight. And now, all of Mona's family had become the kind of determined fighters she'd wanted to be herself.

"You can become anything your heart desires." Mona's words echoed through Shea's mind. "Do you hate monsters?" *Nope, definitely not.* Shea could say that with certainty now.

"Hajime-san, Yue-san."

Because next to her were her two favorite people in the world.

Hajime and Yue turned around and exclaimed "Yeah?" and "... Hm?" simultaneously. Shea smiled, then said the following.

"I'm glad I was born a monster."

She smiled, content with who she was.

Hajime and Yue looked at her blankly for a moment. They exchanged a brief glance before smiling back at her. She couldn't tell if it was an exasperated smile or a happy one. Regardless, this is what they said to her:

"Stop talking nonsense and get over here, you troublesome rabbit. If you lag too far behind, you'll get a crowd of people begging you to be their slave again."

"...Yeah. Come closer. I don't want to have to go looking for you if you get lost."

Not exactly words of encouragement. But their expressions were gentle. Shea knew that even if they didn't say it out loud, they treated her like a member of their family now.

Her rabbit ears twitched merrily.

"I'm coming, I'm coming!"

"Oi, you—who said you could get between me and Yue?"

"You've got guts, Shea. If you want a duel, I'll gladly take you on."

Shea purposely butted in between Hajime and Yue while taking both of their hands. Their empty threats were always just that, empty. As the sun neared its zenith, the town grew even livelier. The trio's banter became just another part of the hustle and bustle of the busy main street. *Mom, I've found the husband and best friend you said I would. Well, he's not exactly my husband just yet, but... I'll do my best to change that!* Shea resolved to herself, praying that her words would reach the soul of her departed mother.

FROM COMMONPLACE
TO WORLD'S STRONGEST

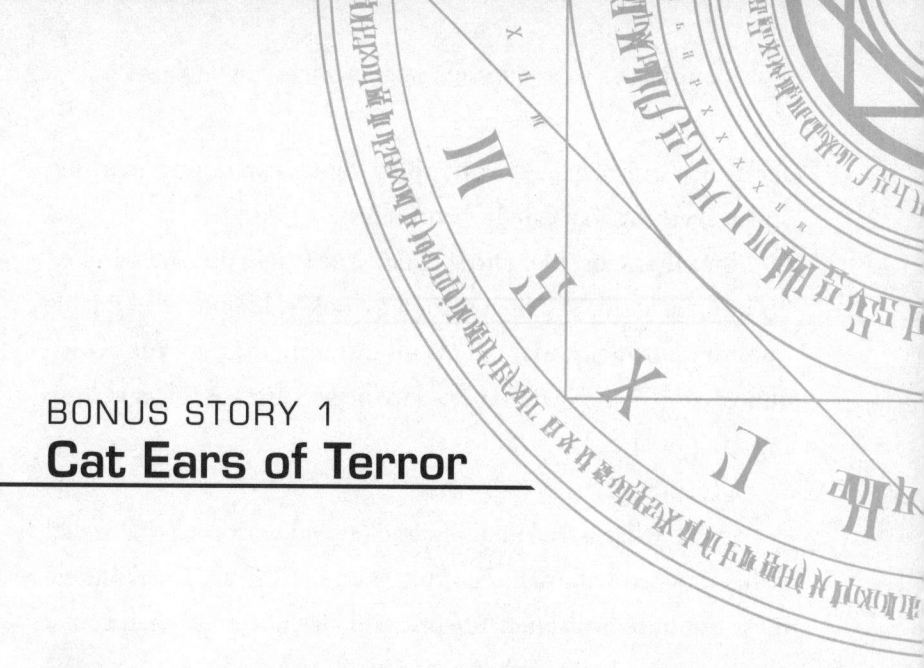

BONUS STORY 1
Cat Ears of Terror

ONE AFTERNOON, Hajime, Shea, and Yue were strolling down the town's main street, looking to stock up on supplies for their upcoming journey. It was a rare moment of respite in between their constant labyrinth-conquering excursions. The street was filled with the sounds of people haggling over wares, the smells of a hundred different spices mingling together as food stall owners began preparing meals, and the sight of a thousand different stores each with their own unique goods for sale.

One couldn't help but get excited in such a lively atmosphere—especially Shea, who hadn't ever stepped foot outside her small village in the sea of trees until recently. Her rabbit ears were twitching happily as she looked around, the excitement evident on her face. Every few seconds she'd come back to her senses and quickly look around to make sure she hadn't been separated from Hajime and Yue. After making sure they were still there, she'd then once again start hopping about, examining anything and everything that caught her interest.

"Shea looks just like a little child." Yue laughed as she watched Shea run around. She then turned to look at Hajime, seeking his opinion. Normally, Hajime would instantly react to Yue's voice, almost as if on instinct, but for once he was just spacing out, looking straight ahead.

"...Hajime?"

"O-oh, what is it, Yue?" Hajime replied with a start. Puzzled at his unusual behavior, Yue furrowed her brows. Realizing he must not have heard her, Yue just said "It's nothing," then kept a closer eye on him after that.

A second later, she noticed Hajime's gaze was fixated on a certain individual. When she followed his gaze to that individual, she felt a wave of jealousy wash over her. But upon closer inspection, she saw that his gaze wasn't fixated on the individual, but rather a certain part of their body.

"I see," she mused to herself. It appeared Hajime had quite a soft spot for "those." Her jealousy vanished somewhat, but she still lamented the fact that she did not possess "those." And she still couldn't forgive another girl for stealing Hajime's attention, even if it was only one part of her that had done so. Also, the words "give up" and "back down" didn't exist in her dictionary, so steeling her resolve, Yue tugged on Hajime's sleeve.

"Hajime, let's split up for a bit. Take care of Shea, okay?"

"Split up? If there's something you want to see or somewhere you want to go, I don't mind taking a detour. We can go together."

"No. I don't want you to know about it yet." Yue pouted and turned away from him. Hajime was shocked; this was the first time she'd ever taken that kind of attitude with him. However, Yue simply gave him one last sidelong glance.

"Don't follow me. I'll get mad at you if you do."

"O-okay, I won't..." Hajime tried to hide how shaken he was but failed miserably. Then, without even a backward glance, Yue trotted off into the crowd.

"What on earth is up with her?" Hajime just stood there, dumbfounded, not realizing that he was the cause of her strange attitude.

That evening, Hajime and Shea had returned to the inn and started discussing Yue's odd behavior earlier.

"Yue-san sure is late."

"Yeah. W-well, I-I'm sure she just wants some alone time."

"Hajime-san, you look pretty flustered..."

"What are you talking about? I'm perfectly fine. Besides, what could possibly have flustered me, anyway? See, nothing's, uh, wrong. Yeah, nothing's wrong at all."

"You're answering your own questions... That sounds like a problem to me." Shea was starting to get annoyed by Hajime's attitude. She'd never seen him like this before, and while it seemed obvious to her that Yue would never leave him, it looked like Hajime didn't trust Yue enough to even be sure of that. She was annoyed that he couldn't believe in Yue the way she believed in him, and her displeasure spread into her voice.

"I can't believe you, Hajime-san. Yue would never leave you, so why are you acting so worried? Can't you just calm down?"

"Huh? You must be misunderstanding something. I know that she won't leave me. I'd be more willing to believe you if you told me the sky was falling tomorrow than if you said Yue would leave me."

Realizing she'd misjudged what had gotten Hajime so flustered, she followed up with, "Then what is it?" Hajime watched her bunny ears as they tilted to the side in confusion. Finally, he spoke in a trembling voice.

"Look, Yue would normally never leave my side. For her to want to split up, I must have done something pretty bad, something she's really unhappy about."

"O-okay, and?"

"And that means she's going to assault me tonight." Hajime's answer only served to further confuse Shea. He then started nervously glancing about the room.

"Yue's definitely going to come to my bed tonight. Any time she's unhappy with me, that's what she always does. She's a monster at night, so I'm not even sure I'll be fit to travel tomorrow."

"I see." Shea's reproachful gaze was more intense than ever. It was only natural; Hajime had just told her he was going to have sex with Yue tonight. From Shea's perspective, it just looked like he was praising her sex game. As someone competing for his affection, all the more so because she'd so far been unsuccessful, it only made sense for Shea to be unhappy with him. Even her rabbit ears were twitching in accusation.

Hajime fidgeted nervously and grumbled, "It's only because you haven't seen what she's like in bed that you can say that.

"Here, let me give you an example. One time, I asked Yue if she was really a virgin."

"Whoa, seriously? That's like the number one thing you should never, ever do."

"Yeah, I know that now. I don't know what came over me, honestly. Maybe I was just too close to breaking under all the constant night raids. Well, it's because she was so good at it in the first place that I began to doubt whether or not she'd really been a virgin."

"Yeah, I bet she got mad."

"'Mad' is an understatement. I honestly thought she'd kill me. Mentally, anyway. I was prepared to end up as Yue's sex slave for life... Those were dark days. Hell, I got down on my knees and begged for forgiveness, even. Can you believe it? Me, begging for forgiveness?"

"Y-you got on your knees? No way..." Shea shuddered in horror. Even if Hajime had called it a night raid, she had assumed the reality was just that they were having some slightly rough sex. She was going to chide Hajime for exaggerating, but when she heard what he had done, she began to wonder just what kind of crazy antics Yue got up to.

An awkward silence spread throughout the room while Hajime nervously looked around, worried his lover might attack him at any second. Shea just watched on, not knowing what to say. With a soft click, the door to their room opened. Shea and Hajime both looked up at once. Yue was standing in the doorway, a pair of rabbit ears on her head.

"I'm back." Her expression was as deadpan as always. She seemed to not mind the fact that there were rabbit ears growing out of her head. Ignoring Hajime and Shea's shock, she sat down on the bed. Both of them finally returned to their senses, and before Hajime could say anything, Shea was screaming.

"Hwha-hwhat the heck is thaaaaat?!"

"...What a strange question. They're obviously rabbit ears."

"I get that! But why do you have them, Yue-san? Are you trying to steal my strong points or something?!" Shea pointed accusingly at Yue, screaming as if Yue had just copied her most important trait. Yue simply turned away and responded in a sulky voice.

"It's all Hajime and the rabbit ears' fault."

"Wh-why does that mean you have to copy my ears? And if they're at fault, why are you wearing them at all?" Shea shook her head. Her bunny ears flopped around as she did so. Hajime looked over at them and Yue mumbled, "I guess in the end fake ones are just..."

Those words finally clued Hajime in on what was going on. Yue had discovered Hajime's secret desire to rub Shea's fluffy bunny ears. And so, in order to compete, Yue had found herself a pair of bunny ears. Most likely at that one store.

"W-well, I guess I can understand your burning desire to have a pair of your own rabbit ears after seeing how amazing mine are. Eheheh, but let me tell you something. Before the real thing, your faux bunny ears are but a pale imitation!" Shea gazed perhaps a bit too triumphantly down at Yue and continued.

"Yue-san, it was a strategic mistake to try and fight me on my home turf! This is your defeat!" Shea was getting a little full of herself, but it was also obvious at a glance that Yue's ears were fake and not nearly as soft or fluffy as the real thing.

However, Yue had done this for Hajime's sake. He already found her cute beyond belief, but knowing that she was willing to go that far just to please him made it clear which pair of ears he considered more important. There was no comparison between the bunny girl, who was busy getting full of herself, and the vampire who had done everything she could to grant him his desire. Naturally, Yue didn't falter in the face of Shea's provocations either. In fact, she exceeded all expectations.

"I never thought my rabbit ears would be able to beat yours. This is just the beginning. The real battle starts here!" Yue whipped off the bunny ears and replaced them with something else. That something looked like a pair of fluffy black triangles resting atop her head. Even more amazing, when she poured mana into them they moved like a real pair of ears would.

"Wh-what on...earth?" A jolt of electricity shot through Hajime's spine. An indescribable sense of awe washed over him. But Yue wasn't done yet. As Hajime's trembling hand touched Yue's cat ears, he let out a shocked exclamation. Before their eyes, Yue pulled out another long and fluffy object, and somehow attached it to an area right above her butt. Upon pouring mana into it, it too moved, just like a real tail. Hajime gulped audibly. Yue got on all fours and crawled over to where Hajime was. She looked unbearably cute. When she finally reached Hajime, she said a single word.

"Meow." What Yue had replaced her bunny ears with was the pinnacle of all animal ears, cat ears. She'd even procured a cat tail to match. She arched her back and playfully pawed at Hajime. In this instant, Myue was born.

"Yue, just how far are you going to test my self-control?" Hajime was cradling his head in his hands, desperately trying to hold himself back. His primal instincts were already on the verge of conquering his reason. But even when he was on his last legs, Yue showed him no mercy.

"Meow." She rolled over onto her back, like a dog showing submission to her master. Her pleading gaze met Hajime. That was enough to push Hajime over the edge. The light in his eyes was replaced by a feral gleam. But just before what might have been the greatest copulation session in history could begin, Shea bravely interrupted them.

"How sly! Yue-san, you really are a cunning woman! It's clear that you thought ahead! Still...! Don't forget that those ears and tail are fake! And my real ears and tail will never lose to fake ones! Look, Hajime-san, these are a real pair of bunny ears. Feel free to touch them all you want!" Betting her very soul, Shea challenged Yue. Her ears and tails twitched excitedly as she leaned into Hajime. But it would seem Yue had predicted even this development. When it came to fighting over Hajime, Yue made sure to prepare for every eventuality.

"You fool. Shea, what makes you think...that my ears are fake at all?"

"What...did you say?"

"I knew you would bring that up, Shea. That's why I got real cat ears. These are no replica. That's why I can move them using mana. Mana also helps keep them from rotting." Yue sat down, then looked up at Shea victoriously. Shivers ran down Hajime and Shea's spines, but for a different reason this time. Given a cold hard dose of reality, Hajime suddenly started sweating. Shea slowly backed away, her entire body trembling. Yue tilted her head in confusion, as Hajime took a moment to gather his wits before asking a question.

"Y-Yue, where'd you find those?"

"Hm? From a general goods store on the main street." Hajime and Shea breathed a sigh of relief. It seemed these were commonly sold in the area—

"...But they weren't the ones selling the real thing." Hajime and Shea stiffened again. So that meant Yue only got her fake rabbit ears from there. Then where did her very real cat ears and cat tail come from? They both looked back at Yue, who puffed out her chest with pride and answered casually.

"I tore them off myself." Those twitching cat ears and cat tail. Were they really moving because of the mana Yue poured into them, or because they were still so fresh that...

Suddenly, those cat ears didn't look at all cute to Hajime. Shea was cowering in a corner, her ears pressed flat against her head.

"She's a psycho. Yue-san's a psychopath," she muttered. Tears were spilling from her eyes and her whole body was shivering.

Yue suddenly shifted her gaze to Shea. Shea jumped with a start as Yue stared at her ears with cold, emotionless eyes.

"Can I...tear those off, too?"

"Noooooooooooooooooooooooooooooooooooo, Yue-san, you're insane!!! You monsterrrrrrrrrrr!!!" Shea leaped out of the room with the speed of a fleeing rabbit. Grimacing, Hajime called out to Yue.

"Umm, Yue?"

"Yeah? Sorry, that was a joke. I feel bad for Shea, but I wanted to have some time alone with you... Also, these are fake ears made with real monster fur, that's all, so you can pet them as much as you want, okay?"

"I-I see. Umm, well, you're really cute, Yue. But uhh, it's not because of the cat ears, it's just because you're you, you know that, right?"

"Yeah. Thanks." Yue smiled warmly. Hajime gently removed the cat ears and cat tail from Yue and hugged her tight. Yue entrusted herself to Hajime and let the strength flow out of her limbs. Marveling at how lovely she looked, Hajime started stroking her hair.

...He decided not to ask why the ears and tail he'd taken off of Yue had been warm.

BONUS STORY 2
Legends of Japan

LONG, LONG AGO, there was a princess known as Princess Kaguya. While her personality may have been questionable, she was an undeniable beauty. She possessed a stunning figure, pale blue hair, and dazzling sapphire eyes. But most importantly, she had something no other person did. Namely, a pair of fluffy blue bunny ears growing out of her head.

In the ancient capital Kyoto, anyone discovered with such strange growths would normally have been considered a target for execution...but as this was a parallel world, such considerations were of no concern.

At any rate, the beautiful Princess Kaguya, who was loved by everyone, was currently saying...

"Haaah. Marriage sounds like such a pain. I'd much rather just spend my time eating snacks forever."

Lazing about, stuffing her face full of meat buns, and

complaining about marriage. Difficult as it was to believe, the capital's number one beauty always acted like this.

Today was the day princes from all across the realm had come to seek her hand in marriage. But as Princess Kaguya had no interest in getting married, she assigned each of the princes an impossible task. Even as they reeled at the difficulty at the tasks set before them, these princes of noble birth continued to fight for Princess Kaguya's favor.

"I am the one most suited to be Princess Kaguya's husband!"

"No, it is I!"

"No, I!"

"C-come on, guys, stop fighting over me. Besides, this is all my fault for being too cute. Man, being popular sure is hard. Eheheh!"

Princess Kaguya was rather full of herself. More so right now than she had ever been before. It was a shame a beauty like her had such a worthless personality. In the midst of this clamor, a small pebble rolled across the room. It kept on rolling until it reached Princess Kaguya. Suddenly, a cold voice rang out across the room. It belonged to the only prince that had not joined in the commotion. A young man who had sat in the corner of the room until now.

"Oi, worthless rabbit. I'll give you that precious treasure of mine, so pick me." Not only did he act haughty, he had the gall to command Princess Kaguya. Furthermore, that pebble of his looked worthless. The room was silent for a moment before the guards drew their swords on him for his insolence.

"Hajime-dono, how dare you take such a tone with—" There was a loud bang, and the guard fell silent mid-tirade. Or rather, he was made to fall silent as he backflipped spectacularly four times through the air, at a speed that would have made even an Olympic gymnast hurl. The other guards all looked dumbfounded at Hajime and saw him holding an unfamiliar weapon with a smoking barrel.

"Oh, shut up. I brought the princess what she asked for, so I win the contest. That's all there is to it." Hajime tapped his shoulder with his revolver, then glared threateningly at the rest of the guards. He looked more like a yakuza...or a bandit, than a prince.

"H-huh? I never asked for a stupid rock like that! I mean, look, it's just a regular old—" *Bang!*

"Hey now, worthless rabbit. Don't be so stingy. That there is my treasure. If you try and get ahead of yourself, I'll rip 'em off."

"Rip what off?" Princess Kaguya trembled in fear as she protectively pressed her rabbit ears to her head.

"Come on, this pebble is the treasure you were looking for, right?" Hajime said, waving his revolver around ominously. Princess Kaguya looked around desperately, searching for help, but...

"Oh heavens, look at the time. I have somewhere I urgently need to be. Do excuse me."

"Oh my, what a coincidence. I too have pressing matters that require my immediate attention." The princes all beat a hasty retreat. They sure were zealous about work. Surely the fact there was a gun waving in front of their faces had nothing to do with their decision. In tears now, Princess Kaguya looked over at the kindly old couple that had raised her for salvation.

"Oh, when did it become so late? My dear wife, I must be off to gather firewood before it gets dark."

"Oh my. Well, I too must away to get the laundry in before it's too late."

Princess Kaguya's parents sure were diligent. Even on this momentous day, they didn't forget to do their chores. Even if their daughter complained, they put their work first. Soon enough, the room was cleared of everyone but Princess Kaguya and Hajime. Princess Kaguya was sobbing because of how unpopular she had suddenly become. Then tearfully, but with a hint of excitement, she said the following.

"D-do you really want me that badly?" Hajime's response was...

"Not really? When I was examining this weapon of mine, I discovered it had come from the moon. What I'm interested in is your hometown. I haven't been able to get in yet, but this is perfect. If I become your husband, then I can obtain their weapons without having to force my way in."

Princess Kaguya collapsed into choked sobs when she heard Hajime's absurd reason. She'd been captured by a demon. But there was still one ray of hope left. Princess Kaguya had in fact been thinking of returning home for a while and had just recently contacted her hometown. The moon had the most advanced technology in the world, so if her family came, they'd surely be able to deal with this brute of a man. That was why even when he consoled her with words like "Sorry about that. I won't threaten you anymore, so please stop crying," her heart wasn't moved at all. Princess Kaguya wasn't that easy.

A few days later. A messenger from the moon came to get Princess Kaguya. Hajime had expected them to come down from the moon riding floating gold nimbus clouds, but instead they came down in oval-shaped UFOs. Truly a close encounter of the third kind. The citizens stared up in awe, while Hajime's eyes glittered with a hungry light as he gazed upon the technology of the moon. Because of his occasional bouts of kindness, the worthless rabbit, Princess Kaguya, had started to think, *This guy might not be able to handle himself without me.* The classic pitfall trap every shoujo manga heroine falls into.

A ramp extended down from the UFO, and down the ramp descended a procession of old rabbitmen... It seemed the myth that the moon was inhabited by beautiful young girls was just that, a myth. But at the very end of the procession of old men was a single young girl. She had beautiful golden-blonde hair and bewitching crimson eyes. Her cheeks had just the faintest blush of rose to them, and her thin pink lips enchanted all who saw her. She looked just like a perfectly sculpted doll. Her impressive outfit made it clear that she was someone of high standing. She was, in fact, a vampire princess that had just hitched a ride with the rabbitmen because she was curious about what Earth was like. Halfway down the ramp, she stopped and stared fixedly at a certain something.

The people began to converse amongst themselves. The incarnation of Venus herself had descended to Earth, and not only that, she was looking at one of the people standing in the crowd.

"Wait, is she looking at me?"

"Don't be stupid, she's obviously looking at me." The guys all started arguing with each other. One youth began walking forward. His gait was brisk and confident. The youth was none other than Hajime. Behind him, Princess Kaguya called out to him.

"W-wait, don't just go off on your own like that. I still need to mentally prepare myself for when I introduce you to my family." Hajime ignored her and kept going. He stopped right before the blonde-haired, red-eyed beauty.

"My name is Hajime, Hajime of the Nagumo clan. May I have the honor of hearing your name?" Behind him, someone mumbled some annoyed words.

"Huh, he wasn't like that when he was talking to me..." However, no one paid her any mind. The vampire princess blushed slightly at his well-mannered request.

"Yue." That was the only word she said as she fidgeted nervously.

"Yue? In our language, that means the moon. A truly splendid name. It suits you perfectly." Yue's face grew even redder. The onlookers all simultaneously breathed out a passionate sigh. Only Princess Kaguya objected.

"Excuse me, what's with that attitude? Lest you forget, you are MY husband." Everyone ignored her. Hajime took in a deep breath, then spoke plainly his thoughts.

"I've fallen for you at first sight. I'll give you even the world if you ask for it, so please be mine."

"Okay. With pleasure."

"Huh? What did I just hear? Aren't I supposed to be the heroine of this story?"

Yue accepted his somewhat ominous-sounding confession without any questions and leaped into Hajime's arms. And so, the boy from Earth, Hajime, and the vampire princess, Yue, were wed. They then went on to conquer the world, after which they lived happily ever after. For some reason, they were also accompanied by a worthless rabbit wherever they went.

ARIFURETA:

ARIFURETA SHOKUGYOU DE SEKAISAIKYOU

**FROM COMMONPLACE
TO WORLD'S STRONGEST**

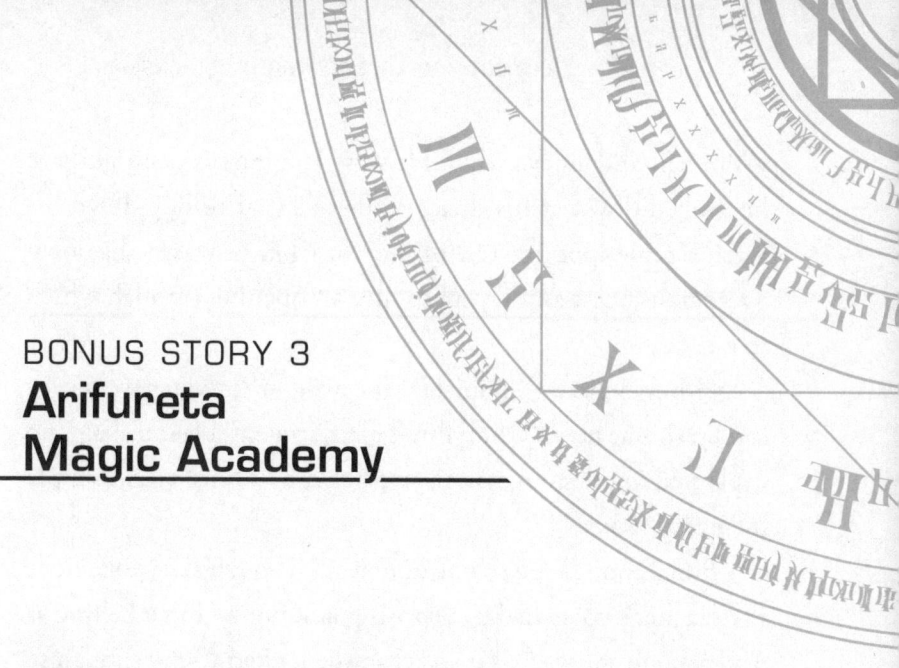

BONUS STORY 3
Arifureta
Magic Academy

A BLAZING SUNSET shone its orange rays into a hallway. The dying light of the sun cast long shadows everywhere it touched. In this dim twilight that brought about feelings of sorrow, security, and just a hint of mystery, the inside of the school was quiet, devoid of people. Only the faint sounds of sports club members practicing outside could still be heard.

All of the classroom doors lining the hallway were closed. This peaceful school was actually a magic academy, located in a certain country of a certain parallel world. Unlike most, it wasn't restricted to only nobles, and opened its doors to commoners, and even beastmen. So long as someone could pass the entrance exam, they would be accepted. Thus, this school had become this world's largest magic academy.

Inside what should have been an empty classroom in this massive school were two figures. One was a young boy with white hair and an eyepatch. He was gripping his pen tightly as he looked down at his desk, beads of sweat rolling down his forehead. He appeared terribly nervous, like he was facing down a ferocious beast and trying to find an opening through which to escape.

"H-hey, Sensei. I've finished the assignment you gave me, so can I go home now?" The white-haired student, Hajime Nagumo, explained to the source of his stress that he'd finished his supplementary lessons.

"Hmm, nope. You're not done yet." Though she spoke little, the teacher's voice had a surprising amount of force behind it. And though she was his instructor, she looked young enough to be a student. Everything about her, from her appearance to her actions, had a subtle layer of seductiveness to it.

In truth, she was a three-hundred-year-old vampire who was older than most adults. Her blouse had a very low cut, and her eyes seemed to look out in invitation from behind the wire-thin glasses she was wearing. To make matters worse, the way she kept crossing and uncrossing her stocking-clad legs was just too alluring. The effect was further multiplied by her perfect figure, golden-blonde hair, and ruby-red eyes.

"Wait, why not? I finished my assignment, even though it made no sense, so hurry up and let me go home." Hajime thrust his finished assignment paper in front of Yue. Every single question was filled out. However, it was the questions themselves that were rather questionable. For example:

1.) What kind of girl is your type?

2.) What do you think of older women?

3.) Do you believe forbidden love can ever work out?

The questions went on along those lines. None of them seemed in any way related to a magic curriculum. It was obvious this teacher was only interested in seducing the poor male student sitting before her.

"No. I need to check your answers first."

"Aren't I the only one that'd be able to tell if they're right or not? I mean, it's not like I lied about my answers."

"I'm just going to make sure...by examining your body."

"Whoa, whoa, whoa, wait just a minute! Control yourself, you sex-starved teacher."

Yue straddled Hajime and began licking him all over. Her lust was truly insatiable. She lifted her skirt up just a little, so Hajime could catch a glimpse of what lay beneath. That, combined with the soft sensation of her body resting on his knees, her slender arms caressing the back of his neck, and her sweet scent...all started to overwhelm his rationality.

Seconds before Hajime resigned himself to entering an illicit relationship with his teacher, they were interrupted.

"The hero arrives! Stop right there, Yue-sensei! I won't allow you to break the Hajime Nagumo anti-monopoly law!" With a thunderous bang, Shea Haulia, another student, flung open the poor classroom door with enough force to break it. Hajime was about to protest this law he'd never even heard of, but Yue pushed his head into her breasts and responded to Shea's words instead.

"Laws were made to be broken." And so, Hajime's protest died in his throat. Instead, he just enjoyed the sensation of being smothered between Yue's breasts.

"Nnngh, stubborn as always, I see! Then I suppose I'll have to do things the hard way! Body strengthening, full power! I'll take Hajime back by force if I have to!"

"Hmph. Bad kids need to be punished. Prepare to be banished to the counselor's realm."

"As if you're one to talk! I'll get you fired for daring to lay a hand on one of your students!"

A moment of tense silence passed between them. The school's scholarship student and the strongest body strengthener on campus were about to face off against the most renowned magic teacher in the entire academy. The pressure exerted by both of them was enough to make the peaceful classroom feel like hell.

Realizing he had to do something soon or there would be a bloodbath, Hajime disentangled himself from Yue's boobs. However, despite his effort, Yue simply squeezed her thighs around him and pushed her chest back into his face. Hajime felt his mind go blank. He was useless in this state. Yue stuck one hand out, while Shea settled into a martial arts stance. It seemed like a clash between these two was inevitable. And yet, just before they started fighting—

Whoosh. Countless crosses made of light assaulted the two of them. Yue and Shea instantly switched their focus, ready to beat this surprise attack off with magic and fists, but the moment they switched their attention, chains of light wound their way up Hajime's and Yue's legs. The chains forcefully separated the two from each other. Yue was flung carelessly to the side, while Hajime was carefully carried over to the classroom door.

"Hajime-kun, are you all right?" Released from Yue's enticing embrace, Hajime once again found himself enveloped in something soft the moment he was released from the chains.

A different kind of of sweet scent entered his nostrils, and when he looked up he found a familiar student smiling kindly down at him. Kaori Shirasaki. Hajime opened his mouth to say something, but he was once again interrupted.

"Aahn. H-Hajime-kun, that tickles." Kaori blushed and tried to squirm into a more comfortable position.

Then let me go, Hajime thought, but then chains of light wrapped around them both and he realized Kaori had no intention of ever letting him go. She hadn't come here to save him, just to steal him away from the others.

"I see. You've got guts, Kaori. I'll send you to the counselor's realm too, so you'd better be ready to make friends with Shea."

"Don't you think a teacher who would assault her own students needs more counseling than us?"

"Let's cut the pointless chatter. I'll defeat the both of you and then claim my prize."

Vast amounts of mana started swirling around the three most beautiful girls in school as they stared each other down. Pillars of golden, sapphire, and white light rose up so high that they passed through the school's ceiling and ascended to the heavens.

Then, with a thunderous noise, a section of the school building was destroyed. The sounds of battle rang out across the grounds. The few students still at school stopped what they were doing for an instant, but when they saw what colors the pillars of light were they just said, "At it again, huh?" and resumed whatever club activities they were indulging in.

A few minutes and many explosions later, the young boy managed to stop the trio from fighting. There was a bright crimson spark, and the school building was restored to the way it had been before. Those who attended this academy were already used to this happening. Among the many magic academies that existed in this world, this was just another normal day.

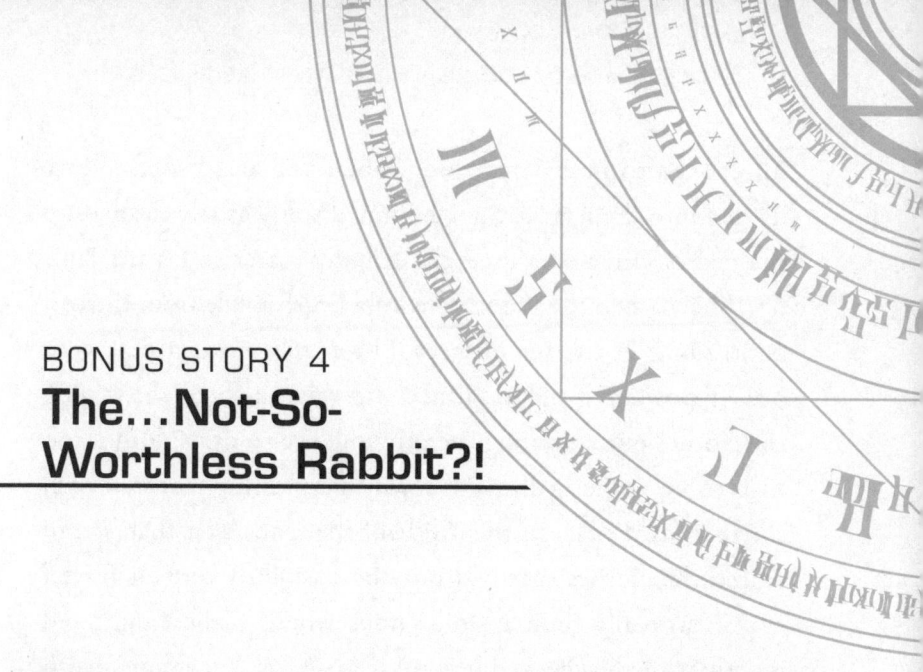

BONUS STORY 4
The...Not-So-Worthless Rabbit?!

"ALL RIGHT, Hajime-san, Yue-san, food's ready." The appetizing scent of cooked food reached their nostrils as Shea took the pot of food off the campfire and called Hajime and Yue over. They had made camp a short while back, and Shea had just finished cooking.

"So it looks like we're having *pot-au-feu* today."

"Yeah. It looks delicious."

Hajime and Yue crawled out of their tent. The stew was filled with delicious-looking vegetables, and there was a freshly baked loaf of bread to go with it. Though it was simple dish, the taste and texture were outstanding. True, it lacked the polish a five star restaurant's food might have, but it had the warmth of a home-cooked meal to it. True home-style cooking, one might say.

Yesterday's meal had been Hamburg steak, and the day before deep fried vegetables, and the day before that, meatbuns.

All cooked to near perfection. When Yue and Hajime heartily dug into their meal, Shea hummed softly as she cleaned up the dishes. Then, she used the leftover water to do the laundry. She washed their clothes with a brush made from the soft bark found in the sea of trees. She'd even made a detergent out of powdered plants. Once she was finished, she wrung the clothes out and hung them by the fire to dry. Clothes too torn to be worn again were sewn into dusting cloths, which she then used to clean the inside of the tent. After that, she repaired the clothes that had only been slightly torn or frayed.

"Shea's really good at doing housework." Hajime muttered quietly while he checked up on his weapons. Yue jumped with a start. She wanted to say that she could do it too, but she held her tongue. She had, in fact, tried to help out with the chores before, using her water magic to clean clothes, or her wind magic to sweep the tent, but all it had earned her was a scolding from Shea, of all people. Naturally, her cooking was subpar as well. Yue could sew, but not nearly as well as Shea. A sudden shiver ran down her spine.

"Wait...doesn't that mean Shea's better than me at housework?"

"Huh? Yue-san, is something wrong?" Unaware of Yue's plight, Shea simply tilted her head in confusion. Her hands continued sewing the whole time, fixing the battle scars the party's clothes had suffered. There was no way Yue could compete with that. For a few hours after, Yue could be found inside one corner of their tent, hugging her knees and sobbing softly to herself...

HALLOWEEN?

"U MM, UHH... how do I look, Nagumo-kun?" The classroom was quite noisy, even though classes had ended for the day. In one corner of the room, Hajime stiffened up. As if a cute ghost had just cast a curse on him.

"Y-you l-look really cute. That's a nekomata costume, right, Shirasaki-san? That cat apparition thing?" Hajime somehow managed to regain enough of his composure to answer Kaori's question.

Her nekomata costume consisted of a yukata and a pair of cat ears and a cat tail. She blushed happily at Hajime's words, making her already adorable countenance reach levels of cuteness that should be classified as a weapon of mass destruction. Half the boys in the class were already bleeding fountains from their noses, while the girls looked on coldly.

Kaori wasn't wearing this because it was a hobby of hers or anything, but because today was Halloween. After many meetings, in which the guys kept on pushing their agenda so that they could see Shizuku and Kaori in cute costumes, the student council had decided to hold a Halloween tea event. A short ways away, Shizuku was putting the finishing touches on her Dracula costume. Many of the girls came up to admire her, and Shizuku was laughing happily with them about their costumes.

As Kaori had made a beeline for Hajime the moment she'd finished changing, many of the other guys in the class were glaring angrily at him. Their monster outfits and monstrous gazes made Hajime wonder if he would be stuck in an actual Halloween nightmare tonight.

"Oh yeah, Nagumo-kun—Shizuku-chan and I were thinking of doing an after-party at her place once this is over. Would you like to come, too?" The guys' gazes grew even more hateful. The stares said it all: *Only Shizuku, Kaori, Ryutarou, and Kouki are going to be at that after-party. How come you get to go even though you're not her childhood friend like they are? You better not say yes.*

It looked like tonight's Halloween party wouldn't end peacefully. And it was all the cat-eared Kaori's fault.

"Oh, Sorry, but I've got something I need to do after this."

"I see. That's a shame, but I guess there's nothing to be done if you're busy. So, can we at least hang out during the party, then? Halloween only comes once a year after all." The way she'd phrased that so casually while putting her hands together like she was pleading belied how crafty Kaori actually was. Had Hajime not felt the immediate threat to his life surrounding him from all sides he would have agreed instantly.

"S-sorry. I-I already made plans..." Hajime slowly backed away, making sure his retreat path was clear, while refusing as politely as he could. Kaori furrowed her brows, unaware of the army of monsters closing in on Hajime.

"You already have plans? Hey, Nagumo-kun, would those plans happen to be with a girl? Well?"

"Huh? No, of course not. Aha ha..." Hajime felt chills run down his spine and quickly denied the accusation. Kaori let out a sigh of relief but then slumped her shoulders the next second. She was still disappointed that he wasn't going with her. One of the nearby guys dressed like a wolf let out a truly wolfish growl. At this point he might have already transformed into a monster on the inside, too.

Kaori bounced back pretty quickly. After all, it wasn't like her to stay down. Suddenly, her eyes glowed and she took out her smartphone.

"Then we can at least take a picture, right? You know, to commemorate the occasion."

"Yeah, that's fine." In reality it wasn't fine at all, but he couldn't refuse her any further. Kaori smiled happily.

"All right then, say cheese!" She grabbed Hajime's arm and squeezed next to him. Hajime understood it was necessary for taking the picture, but...he was treading on thin ice as it was, and she'd just dumped a space heater on it.

"Shirasaki-san, I'm sorry, but can we do the picture later?!"

"Huh? What? Nagumo-kun! Where are you going?!"

Hajime ran out of the room like his life depended on it,

which it quite well might have, as the horde of monsters chased after him the instant he left the classroom.

"I can't take it anymore! Who does that bastard think he is?!"

"Grrrrr!"

"Nagumoooo! Say your prayers!"

"Awooooooo!"

The boys chasing him all yelled out various battle cries. Some of them didn't even sound human anymore.

"Holy crap, that's scary. Why do your eyes all look so bloodshot? And why are you running on all fours?!" Hajime's screams continued to echo throughout the school for a long time after that.

"So yeah, that's what happened. I swear, some of those guys had to have been possessed or something." Hajime finished telling his story to Shea and Yue in between mouthfuls of pumpkin mash. They were eating dinner in the inn's common room. The reason that story had come back to him was because the pumpkin he'd been served had been carved in the spitting image of a jack-o-lantern. There didn't seem to be any corresponding holiday here in Tortus, though. This particular inn just seemed to have a peculiar way of preparing food. Most of it stemmed from the innkeeper's hobbies.

"Oh, your homeland has some interesting customs, Hajime-san. I can't imagine anyone here would willingly wear a monster costume. They'd probably be branded a heretic by the Holy Church."

"Yeah...it looks like your world has more freedom in it than ours. But the important thing here is that...Hajime, you lusted after other girls."

"Hah?! Oh yeah, that's true! I can't believe you got seduced so easily by cat ears, Hajime-san. That's pathetic! Besides, rabbit ears are the greatest animal ears in this world!"

It looked like he'd brought unnecessary trouble onto himself by reminiscing about the past. Faltering underneath the two girls' accusatory glares, Hajime quickly changed the subject.

"By the way, the tradition is for kids to dress up as monsters and go around to people's houses yelling 'Trick or Treat.' The idea is that adults have to give them candy or they'll get pranked, so kids end up with mountains of it by the end of the night."

"I see." Yue muttered. She then whispered something into Shea's ear. Curious, Hajime tried to ask what they were discussing, but they cut him off with questions about the kinds of monsters that inhabited Earth, and once they'd finished barraging him with inquiries they both headed off somewhere. All they said was that they'd be back later and that Hajime should head on up first. Reluctantly, he took their advice and returned to his room. He began maintaining his weapons while keeping a lookout for Yue and Shea's return.

A while later, he saw them coming down the hallway through the open door.

"Okay. Trick or Treat, Hajime."

"Awawa, this outfit is so embarrassing. T-Trick or Treat."

"...Seriously?"

Seriously indeed. Shea and Yue both looked rather stunning,

in more ways than one. Yue was dressed in a short white miniskirt with a matching yukata, showing off a liberal amount of leg. The getup was accented by a crimson sash and crimson sandals, which highlighted her white skin. Despite her short skirt, the sleeves of her yukata were quite long, and only her fingers peeked out as she walked forward with her hands held out like a zombie. Judging by the frost crystals she was making hover around her, Yue was probably meant to be a snow woman.

Next to her, Shea was wrapped completely in bandages and moaning in a somewhat convincing mummy impersonation. The wrapping around her tail was a bit loose, and as she was wearing nothing else, her ass was exposed for the world to see. Whoever had wrapped the area around her chest had clearly held some kind of grudge, as her breasts were so tightly bound that it looked painful.

Though she was slender, Shea had curves in all the right places, and the outfit made only of bandages served to emphasize those curves. Hajime calmed his beating heart and smiled awkwardly.

"I see there's two fearsome monsters who've come to get candy from me. Unfortunately, I don't have any to give out. Had I known, I would have gotten some, but..."

Right around the time Hajime had said "unfortunately," Yue and Shea had happily exchanged glances and blushed slightly. Then, they both broke out into mischievous grins. For some reason, Hajime had felt chills run down his spine just then, and trailed off. Yue licked her lips suggestively and responded to him.

"Well, whether you had treats or not, we were always planning on tricking you. Sexually, that is."

Hajime's smile stiffened. He started looking for an escape route, but Shea beat him to the punch. With her body strengthening up to full, she quickly wrestled Hajime into submission. In order to free himself, Hajime began gathering mana to use Lightning Field, but he was a second too late.

"Candy secured."

"Moron! That's not candy, that's—aaah, stop, stop—"

Shea woke up the next morning after she'd been knocked out by Hajime's lightning to find him staring off into the distance with dead eyes. Yue was next to him, looking rather satisfied. Hajime's next words rang out rather clearly in the predawn gloom.

"Halloween is scary..."

ARIFURETA:
ARIFURETA SHOKUGYOU DE SEKAISAIKYOU

**FROM COMMONPLACE
TO WORLD'S STRONGEST**

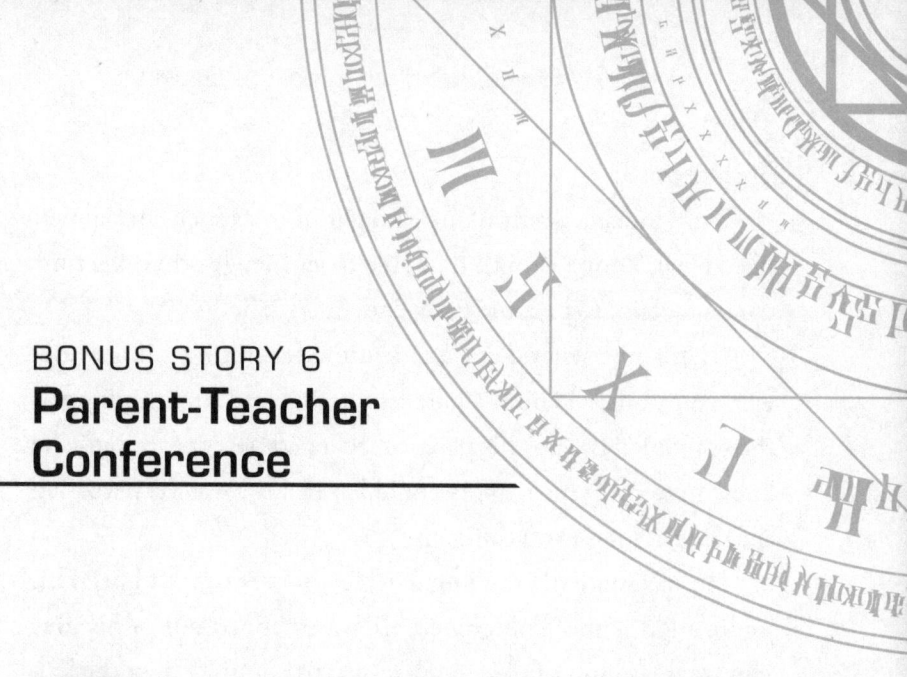

Parent-Teacher Conference

"**M**OM, DAD, please, PLEASE don't say anything embarrassing." Those words echoed through an evening-lit corridor of the school.

"Come on, Hajime, what are you so worried about? It's just a parent-teacher conference. We're just going to talk about how you're doing at school and stuff."

"Seriously, what a worrisome child. Just because your homeroom teacher's a legal loli doesn't mean we're going to mess with her or anything."

"That's EXACTLY the problem! Please don't use words like legal loli in front of my teacher. Seriously, no one else's parents are like that. Please, I'm begging you, just hold it in, okay?" Hajime looked surprisingly serious. But his mom, Sumire, and dad, Shuu, were just grinning like little children.

"Did you hear that, Sumire? He said no one else's parents

are like this."

"I did indeed. To think he thought of us as such special people... Dear, I don't think I'll be able to let him go when the time comes for him to become independent. Hee hee."

"That's not what I meant! Quit interpreting things however you want!" Hajime's parents just ignored him. Today was the scheduled day for his parent-teacher conference. Because he knew how crazy his parents could be, Hajime was very worried they might mess everything up.

He was suddenly reminded of the disaster that had been his junior high school conference. He was snapped out of his musings by the sound of someone's footsteps coming down the hallway. The teacher who came out to greet them was none other than Aiko Hatayama. Standing only 140 centimeters tall, baby-faced Aiko resembled a baby squirrel more than a teacher with the way she always ran around doing her best to help, but ultimately making things worse.

The interview started innocuously, with Aiko talking about Hajime's grades. Shuu and Sumire nodded exaggeratedly as she went over his test scores and the like. They were clearly just acting the part, so Hajime grew increasingly more concerned.

"Umm, so basically, Nagumo-kun is doing fine academically. Though me and some of the other teachers are concerned about his chronic habit of sleeping during class..." Aiko smiled awkwardly, and Hajime smiled back much the same. Then, reluctantly, she opened her mouth and tried to deliver her next lines as tactfully as possible.

"Also, well, Nagumo-kun's interpersonal relationships are a bit..."

An image of Hajime sitting alone during lunch flitted through Aiko's mind. Though his isolation worried Aiko, Hajime himself seemed to not be bothered by it at all. He had even told Aiko not to worry about him, so she wasn't sure how to address it. However, Shuu dismissed her concerns offhandedly.

"Both my wife and I are aware of his lack of friends, Sensei. And neither of us particularly mind."

"B-but..."

"It's fine, Sensei. Our son may be a little passive, but if the time comes when he needs to step up, he will. My husband and I have discussed this at length already...and if the time ever comes that our son needs to run away, we've already prepared several options for him!"

"U-umm, I'm not sure running away is..." Aiko was amazed at how unconcerned Hajime's parents were with his school situation and that they were even willing to help him run away if he felt like it.

Sumire suddenly turned serious. Thinking her previous comments must therefore have been a joke, Aiko too grew serious. She was prepared for Hajime's mom to ask her what she as a teacher was doing to rectify the situation, but what Sumire asked was completely unexpected.

"By the way, Hatayama-sensei, are you dating anyone right now?"

"...Come again?" Aiko opened her eyes wide, metaphorical

question marks floating above her head. An interrobang was floating above Hajime's head, though.

"I asked if there's a guy you're dating."

"N-no, there isn't, but..."

"Then is there a girl you're dating?"

"Of course not! What on earth are you saying?!" Aiko cried out in alarm. Hajime's expression underwent a rapid transformation.

"I see. I've heard that teaching is quite a demanding profession. Also, my son says you even give up a lot of your free time to help the students... Frankly speaking, we're worried about your marriage prospects."

"Th-thanks for your concern! So, why exactly did you bring this up?"

"Well, I was just thinking...why not marry our son?"

"Seriously, what on earth are you saying?!" Aiko exclaimed.

"What the hell! Mom, Dad!" Chaos engulfed the classroom. Shuu and Sumire continued to fluster Aiko even further, while Hajime desperately tried to stop his parents' rampage. However, it only got worse from there.

"Huh? But isn't Hatayama-sensei totally your type?" Shuu asked.

Flustered, Aiko couldn't muster much more than a "Hawawa."

To which, Sumire commented, "Wow, I finally heard someone go 'hawawa' in real life," while nodding in satisfaction.

"U-umm, that's everything I wanted to discuss..." Aiko slumped tiredly over the desk she was sitting on.

A few seconds later, she got up and tottered unsteadily back toward the teacher's office. Dealing with Shuu and Sumire together drained a great deal of mental stamina. Hajime was in the middle of thinking up an appropriate apology when Aiko suddenly stopped in the middle of the hallway and turned back to them. There was a faint blush spreading on her cheeks.

"N-Nagumo-kun! I'm your teacher, so we can't be in a relationship, okay?" She then turned back and vanished into the teacher's office.

"Mom, Dad, how am I even supposed to face my teacher tomorrow?"

Hajime's parents just gave him a thumbs-up.

"With a smile, right?" They both said that simultaneously. For the first time in his life, Hajime felt like he wanted to kill someone.

FROM COMMONPLACE
TO WORLD'S STRONGEST

AFTERWORD

HELLO TO ALL you chuuni lovers out there who picked up this book. It's me, the chuuni lover Ryo Shirakome.

I know it took a bit longer to get this volume of *Arifureta* out, but thankfully the wait is finally over.

The atmosphere of this book's pretty different from Volume 1, and as I'm sure many of you have noticed, Shea's gotten a lot more of the spotlight in the published version compared to the web version.

I'm not sure if you guys liked that more or less, but...as long as you enjoyed that bit with the pile bunker, I'm happy.

Yes, very happy. Man, pile bunkers are awesome... Now then, by the time this novel comes out, I'm sure my readers on Narou will have realized the main story's already over.

So what happens next? Will I keep writing more after-stories for *Arifureta*? Will I return to being just another fan of books?

Will I write an entirely new story? Or will I just think of a hundred sentences and write them all out at random? Unlike Shea, I can't see the future, and I honestly don't know where I'm going to go next, but...well, it'll probably be something new and interesting. I hope.

But first, whether it's a new novel, or a game, or an anime, or even a movie that I work on next, I first need to get down on my knees and beg my publishers for a break. Please support my earnest endeavor to earn a break.

Volume 3, if they let me publish it, will finally be the reunion arc.

I hope you're all looking forward to it as much as I am. I'm hoping I get to add extras into that one, too.

And now, onto the acknowledgments.

I'd like to thank my illustrator Takayaki, my editor, my publisher, my proofreader, and everyone in the editing department. Without you, this book wouldn't be here. Thank you for giving your all to make this book a reality.

And last but not least, I'd like to thank you, dear reader, for choosing to pick up this book.

May we meet again in another volume of *Arifureta*.

—Ryo Shirakome